Two men,
on the

"A HIGHLY READABLE THRILLER ABOUT TWO MEN LINKED THROUGH TIME BY THEIR PIONEER SPIRIT."

United Press International

"The set-up for the adventure is the kind of instantaneous, unconsidered decision that anyone might make. The circumstances are absolutely, chillingly believable."

The Houston Post

"A PROVOCATIVE, FRIGHTENING TALE, TOLD IN THE GENTLE MANNER OF A BEDTIME STORY."

Cleveland Plain Dealer

"Searls blends past and present smoothly and compellingly.... He tells two tales, the modern epic of horror and the 19th-century saga of adventure, with rare skill and insight, employing memorable players on a fascinating backdrop. An enjoyable work."

Louisville Times

Follow their journeys with the map on the next two pages.

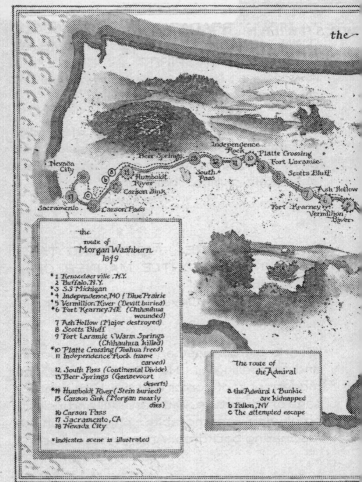

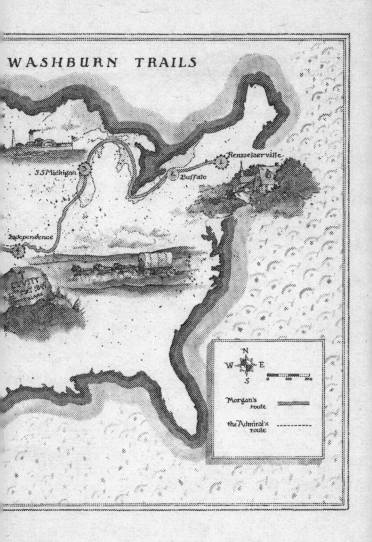

WASHBURN TRAILS

J.S.Michigan

Rensselaerville

Buffalo

Independence

N
W   E
S
0   100   200

Morgan's
route

the Admiral's
route

BLOOD SONG

Hank Searls

BALLANTINE BOOKS • NEW YORK

Library of Congress Catalog Card Number: 83-50866

ISBN 0-345-30663-5

This edition published by arrangement with Villard Books

Endpaper maps by Susan Gaber

Printed in Canada

First Ballantine Books Edition: June 1985

To Niles, for surviving.
And to Bunny, for helping me follow his trail.

HANK SEARLS
NEWPORT BEACH, CALIFORNIA
1984

"The cowards among us never started, and the weaklings died on the road."

NILES SEARLS,
FORTY-NINER AND
CHIEF JUSTICE OF
THE CALIFORNIA SUPREME COURT

SATURDAY

AFTERNOON

MORGAN AND MARY

AN ORANGE SUN PULSED TO THE WEST, PLUMMETING TO-
ward the crest of the Sierras. A gust across Nevada's
Carson Sink sent dust-devils scurrying under the scrub.
A motor home, hurtling after the sun through waves of
heat, swayed and recovered.

Part of everything, knowing all, the essences of Morgan Washburn and his true love Mary enveloped the burning sands. More conscious than when their living cells
had moved toward earthly goals, their presences had been
drawn to this desert place, their attention distracted from
the Spheres of Thought by two living minds which were
seeking to understand their own.

Morgan and Mary were one with all things, but powerless against the winds of time as tumbleweed. Though
they were everywhere and nowhere, in sagebrush and
beyond the daylight stars, they could only watch helplessly as their seed, imperiled, blundered toward a spot
where once Morgan had almost died, an eternity—or a
moment—ago.

The man at the wheel resembled him greatly.

The child was the last of their line.

THE ADMIRAL
AND BUNKIE

THE MOTOR HOME SAILED OVER A RISE, GLIDED DOWN an ebony highway trimmed with gold. The sun had dropped to kiss the crest of a hill on the desert ahead, making the admiral squint. He took a hand from the wheel to yank down the gold-braided visor of the scrambled-egg baseball cap he'd worn on his carrier's flag bridge.

Admiral Stretch Washburn was tall and rangy, with a nose broken forty years ago in football, and deepset eyes of blue. His hair had lately turned to white. His wife Ellen had died of a stroke this year. The trip had been his attempt at therapy, but he knew that loneliness only lay in remission, ready to embrace him the moment he put his granddaughter on an eastbound plane.

He was a proud man, unused to acknowledging errors of judgment, but he would have been the first to acknowledge that such chauvinism as would shortly trap them on the flat Nevada desert was stupid, of another day and age.

The sun was setting on the seventeenth day of his pilgrimage from Independence, Missouri—with his twelve-year-old granddaughter and his dog—across the face of America along the old Emigrant Trail. They had less than five hundred miles to go to their destination, beyond the Sierras near the tail of the Mother Lode.

The motor home had been soaring and dipping across the wasted scrub, evoking a thirty-year-old memory of low-level practice bomb runs which the admiral had flown from Fallon Naval Air Station, not far ahead. His grand-

4

daughter Bunkie, searching for the night's campground in the AAA Campguide, might have been Ellen navigating for him as they'd changed home ports in one of their battered station wagons.

"We have, at Fallon, Nevada," Bunkie announced, "the Hub RV Camp."

The admiral moved to ease his back. "Roger."

"Nine bucks, with sewer hookup."

"OK, Beautiful."

"'Beautiful?'" she snorted. "Don't *say* that! Yuk!"

She'd spent part of almost every summer with Ellen and him, bodysurfing near their high-rise condominium on the Silver Strand at Coronado. When they'd sent her home last fall she'd been tan and sinewy as a boy. But five weeks ago, when he'd picked her up at his daughter's, he'd found her chubby and pale as a caged white rabbit, after a year of imprisonment in her parents' Manhattan apartment. And they had put braces on her teeth, too.

It didn't matter. To him she was still the loveliest child on earth, pudgy, braces, or not. Her shimmering brown hair and her deep-brown eyes—as gentle and perceptive as her mother's or Ellen's—grew more beautiful year by year. He'd been trying to tell her this for weeks.

But the admiral's appearance—still trim at sixty-one— had made her feel like a glutton; she'd had a chocolate-chip feeding frenzy passing through Kansas, and his efforts to bolster her self-image were not going well.

She glanced at the odometer, made one of her lightning calculations. "ETA Fallon, twenty-eight minutes."

"Roger."

She closed the campguide. "Halsey," she ordered, "front and center!"

The admiral's old tan mastiff Halsey yawned and padded forward from beneath the dinette table. She held out the campguide. He took it delicately between his teeth, backed out from between the two, and deposited it in a magazine rack behind her seat. He reappeared so that Bunkie could scratch his ear and returned to his lair.

For almost three weeks the admiral, Bunkie, and Halsey had followed the Emigrant Trail that the admiral's great-grandfather Morgan Washburn had ridden and

5

trudged in '49. The admiral and Bunkie had departed from Independence, Missouri, at the precise ford of the Blue River at which their forebear—a young New York doctor—had crossed. There, their ancestor had begun the journal and series of letters they carried with them, of his five-month march to the Mother Lode.

Their route along highways and county lanes paralleled his trail through country still scarred in places with the ruts of the Great Emigration, past gravestones he must have seen.

In Independence, the young doctor had paid two hundred dollars for a place on a mule-drawn passenger wagon of the Pioneer Line, the ill-conceived commercial venture of a certain Captain Turner. Five months later, having been outdistanced by the whole vast horde of forty-niners, with snows threatening the Sierras ahead, the customers of the Pioneer Line were close to death here on the Forty Mile Desert.

Somewhere near here, at the very end of the antlike procession that had crossed in '49, Morgan had dropped from the wagon train to tend a dying messmate.

The admiral steered to avoid a clump of bouncing tumbleweed. Bunkie shifted in the passenger seat, pulled the typescript of the diary from the map case in her door, and thumbed through it. "Do you think we're near where he got lost?"

"Tingly?" he prodded. They'd had an experience, at Independence Rock, that had brought them very close, and "tingly" was its code.

"Well, kind of."

She squirmed. Maybe she was bored: he was. "Read what he says, why don't you?"

The admiral could remember when she had recited in a schoolroom monotone: now she read like a TV newswoman, and it helped to keep him awake. He listened while she began a passage he knew almost by heart: the nearly fatal trek across the Carson Sink:

"I knew that Mr. Stein would not long evade what Reverend Thistle at home was always impelled to call 'the dread black Angel of Death,' but I was too busy acting as said Angel's instrument to catch sight of him. Our dear

6

departed messmate was a cheerful companion. My heart cries out to hear his laugh. Though life denied him education he was a man of intelligence and a firm companion. He was, I am sure, a competent saddler, and life could not deny his wish to better his lot in the West. Only death itself, after all these weary miles, could stop him in the end. It is sad that he dies here, so far from home and loved ones, but who knows who will join him soon? Two laggard—" She paused. "Lay-guard? Laguard?"

"'Laggard,'" he told her. "Rhymes with 'haggard,' as in 'the old man was haggard, having driven over two million miles since lunch.'"

"Right," she said. *"Two laggard wagons of the Wolverine Company coming into sight, I requested them to lend a hand to bury my departed comrade. They would not tarry—"* She glanced at him. "What's 'tarry'?"

"Would not wait."

"Why *wouldn't* they wait? That sucks!"

He winced. Where the hell had she picked *that* up? And what was the connotation, anyway, today? He really didn't know. "Go on," he said wearily. "Read on, McDuffy."

She glanced at him swiftly, sensing his shock when she said: "That sucks." She didn't know exactly what the expression meant, or why it shocked him: you saw it everywhere, even on TV. "Nukes suck, Reagan sucks...."

She could ask him, but it probably had something to do with sex, and might embarrass him. Her best friend Angela, who'd already had a period, might know, but Angela was in Switzerland, spending the summer with her father.

She read on: *"They would not tarry, their oxen being exhausted, and they doubtless fearing that if they waited the animals would bolt for the Carson River, I know not how far from here across tomorrow's sands. I 'borrowed' a shovel from the second wagon as it passed, and managed to bury him. His persuasion and his race would better have been served had I known the rites of his religion, but feeling that if there is a God there is but one,*

7

and with a few words I remembered from the Book of Common Prayer, I consigned his soul to Whom all profess to look for salvation, though He seems to have absented himself from this place." Her throat grew strangely tight: she swallowed. "*I walked until dawn. It is now near noon. I rest in the shade of a wagon abandoned weeks ago by souls who may be over the Carson Pass . . . or dead. Two oxen lie in harness. Their odor is oppressive, though the bones are nearly clean.*"

She heard her own voice trembling, and the typing blurred. "*There is no one in sight. For the first time in nigh onto four months no other pilgrims on the path to Hell share this dusty track, ahead or behind. No trace of our wagons ahead. . . .*

"*I detect in myself more symptoms yet of scurvy, and am angry to reflect that if Captain Turner had not succumbed to avarice and sold our onions at Beer Springs, I should be playing a better hand.*

"*But I shall not despair. 'Where is life, is hope,' Cicero said. I think it otherwise, and that hope comes first: where is hope, is life. For if I lose hope now, I am certainly dead. . . .*" Furtively, she wiped away a tear.

Her grandfather reached his arm across and began to rub her neck. "OK, honey. That's enough."

She shook her head. This was silly! "*The whole atmosphere glows like an oven! Off to the southwest, as far as the eye can extend, nothing appears but a level desert. This I must cross. The trail branches here. I know not which branch to take. The right branch or the left?*" She took a long, shuddering sigh. "Was he talking about out there?"

"Yes."

The admiral wished he had not asked her to read the passage. It seemed hardly normal for a twelve-year-old girl to dissolve in tears at the story of a great-great-great-grandfather dead for almost eighty years. Like the admiral himself, she'd become too involved.

"It was a long time ago, Lambchop . . ." he muttered, "and don't forget, he made it."

"'Lambchop,'" she murmured. "You called me that in Rensselaerville. I like it. It's what you called—" She broke off, embarrassed.

"Your grandmother," he finished. Well, he thought bitterly, why not? Ellen wasn't using it.

He scanned the shimmering desert. It would be nice to discover more tracks. They had seen plenty of emigrant wagon ruts along the Platte, but the wind and flash floods of the Carson Sink had scoured the sage and tumbleweed outside. Now there was not a trace of the trail in any direction, but near the shimmering highway, over which they sped in their cool cocoon, must lie the bones of Morgan's comrade, baked in an unmarked grave. He pitied the tall young doctor picking his track: right or left? Today, even so late in the afternoon, and so late in the year, the world outside throbbed with heat.

Poor Morgan Washburn: too bright and too restless, born a hundred years too soon, iconoclastic, rebellious, torn by nineteenth-century hypocrisy and a duel that turned his life to hell: finding, finally, shelter in what his tiny family called "the Demon Rum."

But tough he had been, Morgan Washburn, in guarding his hope through all that lay ahead. Thank you for picking the right road, Morgan, and for surviving, or there would have been no Stretch Washburn, or Bunkie either.

Raising his arm to adjust the air-conditioner, he felt a twinge in muscles around the pacemaker under his collarbone.

The rise and fall of the motor home and the drone of its engine were making him drowsy.

"Pops!"

He jerked his head erect and swerved safely from the shoulder of the road. Jesus . . .

Coffee, he needed coffee, before he killed them both. But none was hot. It was cocktail hour, and he wanted a drink. But that could wait until they were settled for the night—*must* wait, damn it.

His attention fell on a gray van parked on the shoulder, a quarter mile ahead. It had overtaken them, speeding, ten minutes before, and he'd glimpsed the driver, alone in the front seat. He was a bearded young man wearing

9

sunglasses. The admiral had eased over to give him room, seen him lift a hand and flash a grin.

Now, as the admiral drew closer, he saw that the young man was standing at the highway edge, holding a red gas can, thumb out expectantly.

The admiral had been born in the mountains ahead and bred in the code of the West. Here on the burning desert, he could sooner have run the stranded motorist down than have passed him by.

"Revise your ETA, Bunkie. We have a traveler in distress."

"*Dad* never stops," she observed, "for anybody!"

He almost said: "That sucks." But he was damned if he was going to be drawn into a comparison between his own mores and those of his son-in-law, who, against all instinct, had managed finally to bestow his blessing on the trip.

"It's different back East," he murmured generously.

He flicked on his hazard light, swung his foot to the brake, and began the Great Mistake.

MORGAN

IN THE WINTER OF 1848, IN THE SNOWBOUND VILLAGE of Rensselaerville, New York, Morgan Washburn, MD, had read and disbelieved the first accounts of California gold. In the parlor of the home in which he boarded, he had smiled with Mary, his betrothed, at the stories of men stumbling over nuggets along footpaths of the great Pacific slope.

Not even President Polk himself, quoted in the New York *Herald*, had entirely convinced him: "There is more gold in the country than will pay the cost of the war with Mexico a hundred times over."

It was simply that Polk—almost a year after the peace had been signed—was still trying to justify the theft of half a continent from a neighbor too feeble to fight.

Five years ago, when he was nineteen, a strange restlessness had drawn Morgan north from the sweeping fields of his father's estate in southern Maryland, to Union College in New York, then to Geneva Medical College, and finally to a medical apprenticeship in this mill-and-tanning town under—thank God—Mary's father, Dr. Cullen.

The California disease had been slow to kindle in the young physician. But when it did begin to burn, in the early spring of '49, he recognized that the malady was his old one—wanderlust—and not gold fever at all.

He had felt the symptoms of claustrophobia—not greed—only last Sunday as he sat crammed, with Sabbath hypocrisy, in a Presbyterian pew, with the village pressing in on every side.

What he really wanted, he had known suddenly in church, was room to move, warm breezes, and a medical practice all his own.

And so today, a full week later at noonday dinner, he had confessed his plans to his father-in-law- and mother-in-law-to-be. The confession had improved his soul but not the meal.

Now he pushed his chair back from the table. He was tall and slim, with thoughtful blue eyes and a full black beard; he wore a gray frock coat and a soft white cravat fixed with a pearl tiepin. He stood up, and slid out Mary's chair as she arose.

She was slender, with red cheeks and an oval face. She had parted her hair into a severe, plaited bun for church; the top of her head came hardly to his chin. She had eyes of amber. Her simple silk gown, with a slim tight bodice, was the color of summer apricots.

She had known for days that he was going to California. But now, for the first time, she agreed: "Yes," she murmured. "Yes, if you come back for me."

11

Helpless with love, he scanned her face. He felt like the lovesick swain in a French romantic painting. She caught his glance, twinkled, and kissed him secretly while her mother covered the roast and her father started for the door.

He looked out. Rain—the heaviest so far in this year of 1849—had been pelting Rensselaerville and—presumably—all of upper New York State for weeks. The sturdy frame house on the main street had almost suffocated under the deluge. But now, during this miserable Sunday dinner, the rain had stopped.

The house—and Morgan—longed to breathe. He had long disagreed with his father-in-law-to-be on the dangers of fresh air for Mary, and now he managed to open a window without alarming him as the older man waddled from the room.

Mary stayed in the dining room to help the hired girl, and her mother moved to the parlor to crochet. Morgan followed the older doctor into the walnut-paneled surgery off the entrance hall. The familiar smell of ether and herbs made him feel drowsy, after the enormous Sunday meal. In the iron-bellied stove, a dismal little blaze struggled with a damp survivor of the winter's stockpile of oak.

Mary's mother's pumpkin pie had not set agreeably, and his stomach was gurgling. He knew that soon his hostess would demand that he play the square piano in the parlor; this he always enjoyed, while Mary sang, but if he waited too long he would have to excuse himself publicly, which would embarrass them all.

He longed to head for the outhouse now, but he saw Mary through the window, escaping in the same direction. Skirts held above the mud, crinoline petticoats flashing white, and rain bonnet bobbing, she was rounding the big maple tree, perhaps a victim of the same malady. Hurry, dearest heart, hurry, hurry, please . . .

Her father reached into the medicine cabinet and extracted a bottle of apple brandy. He poured them both a dram and picked up the Buffalo *Morning Express*. "I have something to show you."

The older doctor was apparently not willing to relinquish the argument that had begun when Morgan broke

12

the news. Dr. Cullen seated himself in his leather chair, adjusted his belly comfortably over his trousers, and began to search the paper. Morgan smoothed his coattails and sat down on the surgical chair, thrusting his long legs out to stretch. He loosened his cravat—though he knew that informality annoyed his father-in-law-to-be. He sipped the brandy, welcoming the fire in his throat and waiting for the glow in his stomach.

Mary's father glanced at him, then, surprisingly, loosened his own collar. "It *is* warm," he admitted. "We must think of Mary, though." He flicked the paper. "Apropos of your proposed venture, Doctor, have you read this latest bunkum?"

Morgan had, of course. It was the talk of the village, a letter dated November 16, 1848, from a Buffalo minister who had gone west as a missionary. It was the last of a series of his missives which had dribbled in since the news of Sutter's Mill.

"Yes sir."

"Do you believe it?"

He certainly wanted to; everyone else thought it gospel, from its source.

"He's a man of the cloth." Morgan smiled.

The older man looked up suspiciously. Morgan's agnosticism had discomfited him since the beginning, though he was too gentlemanly to have pointed it out, even to his daughter.

"God's messengers are not always accurate reporters," he admitted dryly. "So? Do you or not?"

"Well, what *parts* of it?"

The older doctor adjusted his glasses and began to read: "'Gold is found pure in the native soil here, worth more, just as it is taken from the ground, than an equal weight of coined gold from any mint. . . .'" He looked up. "Why would that be, Morgan? You're an educated man."

"Well, obviously it's not." He was getting irritated.

"Not found *pure*, or not worth more than minted coins?" Her father was ragging him, as he often did.

He summoned a smile. *God, if he didn't get his bowels relieved shortly, his sphincteris ani would burst.* "I don't know, sir. I hope to find out."

Her father's eyes were green, and could flare without warning, and they were blazing now. He slammed the paper down.

"But why? Goddamn it, *why*?"

Morgan heard the hired girl in the dining room gasp at the profanity. Blasphemy was unknown here; the old man had held his tongue better last year when Morgan had misrotated a dislocated humerus and the patient had fainted from pain.

"Well, to 'see the elephant,' sir."

A mistake. It was a term on everyone's lips this year but it sounded banal here.

"I hate that phrase," the old man growled. "'To see the elephant.' California is a sham, a disease, a fever of the brain!" He thrashed through the sheets of the newspaper, triumphantly folded them back and thrust them at Morgan. "Read *this*!"

Reluctantly, Morgan stared at the page. Across three full columns was an advertisement, with a drawing of what appeared to be a huge, gas-filled cigar: below it hung a cabin of a similar shape, full of portholes. A windmill-device above the suspended cabin seemed to be issuing out a cloud of steam.

BEST ROUTE TO CALIFORNIA!

R. Porter & Co. (offices room No. 40 in the Sun Buildings—entrance 128 Fulton Street, New York), are making active progress in the construction of an Aerial Transport, for the express purpose of carrying passengers between New York and California. This transport will have the capacity to carry from 50 to 100 passengers, at a speed of 60 to 100 miles per hour. It is expected to put this machine in operation about the 15th of April, 1849. It is proposed to carry a limited number of passengers—not exceeding 300— for $50, including board, and the transport is expected to make a trip to gold regions and back in seven days. (The price of other overland passage to California is fixed at $200, with the exception above mentioned.) Upwards of 200 passage tickets at $50 each have been engaged prior to February 15. Books open for subscribers as above.

Morgan smiled. "A hundred miles an hour! It appears that I've picked the wrong horse."

The older doctor sighed and arose. "Morgan, Morgan ... You're a good doctor. You're a finer *surgeon* than I, already! Those hands! Do you want to use them to *dig*?"

His hands, slim, long-fingered, strong, trained to the keyboard from childhood, became sudden embarrassments. He forced them to lie still. "I want to practice medicine."

"You're practicing here."

"*You* are. I'm not."

"You will! I'm almost fifty!"

And you'll last until eighty, and never let go. "You've many years left, sir, I hope. And you're needed here. I'm not."

"Half the quacks in New York State are heading west! Why does California need *you*?"

"Because I'm *not* a quack, thanks to you."

"You're very kind. And, you're right. So there's room for you in Buffalo, or Albany. Or Manhattan! The charlatans are leaving because they're starving. *You* need not go."

Maybe not to California, but to your outbuildings, and quickly....

He made his final argument. When he had decided last Sunday to go to California he had acted instantly on an advertisement read in the *Herald* for the Turner-Allen Pioneer Stageline. It was to be mule-drawn, and the only commercial transportation—with the apparent exception of the humbug airship and a wind-driven wagon he'd read of last month—that anyone planned to establish along the overland trail. He had deposited fifty dollars against a total of two hundred dollars for passage with Turner-Allen's agent in Troy.

He told his preceptor. "So," he said triumphantly, "I'm enlisted without recourse. They have fifty dollars of my money."

"Damn it, sir, I'll *give* you fifty dollars to back out."

15

He meant it: there was no doubt. Morgan's throat tightened. "Sir?"

"Yes?" The older man stared stiffly into the distance, his lower lip thrust out.

"We must stop this. I'm sorry."

Water dripped from the eaves. The kitchen pump squealed distantly as the hired girl began the dishes. The clock in the dining room ticked impatiently: thousands of young men, it was said, were cramming the riverboats, heading for St. Louis and St. Joe.

A blessed sunbeam, the first in weeks, found the brandy bottle. He wished the old man would pour again.

He did not. To Morgan's astonishment, he saw tears in his eyes. "There's cholera in Independence. It may go with you on the trail."

"There's cholera in Albany, it may come to you here."

"Mary'll die of loneliness."

"I'll write her every week."

"And when do you propose to come to get her?"

"When I've seen the lay of the land."

"Her lungs aren't strong enough for the journey now, and they won't be then."

"I'll take her round the Horn. Or across the Isthmus. They say that California's warm and dry."

A golden place, he did not add, *where she'll gaze at mountains a week away, and ride a thousand unfenced miles, hatless in the wind....*

"Don't go," pled the doctor quietly. "Morgan, please?"

Through the window he glimpsed his love returning, slim, lithe, and apple-cheeked, with a face like the Mona Lisa.

He arose. Shyly, he touched the older man's shoulder. His own father, who still owned slaves, was a dry and taciturn man; Morgan had grown to consider the doctor as a kinder, warmer surrogate. But in the two years since the older man had taken him in as apprentice, boarder, and assistant, neither had expressed his feelings.

I love Mary very much, he wished to say. *And her father and mother, too.*

He simply could not.

"Sir," he said huskily, "I'll allow no harm to come to

16

me. Or to Mary, when I take her there. You know that I hold her in great affection. . . . Hold you *all* so. . . . And am grateful. . . ."

Blushing, embarrassed, the older man managed a smile and gave up. "I'm sure of that, Morgan. And we'll pray for you every night."

With all the dignity he could manage, Morgan left the room and sped for the distant outhouse.

THE ADMIRAL

To pick up his granddaughter for the great adventure, the admiral had driven east.

In air-conditioned comfort in a Manhattan heat wave, he had cheerfully blocked 10 A.M. traffic on East 55th while he backed and filled the motor home into a No Parking zone in front of his daughter's apartment building.

It was like docking a carrier in Hong Kong Harbor, with the honking taxis lined up like sampans behind him. Cool and secure in the motor home's cab, he grinned back through the wing-mirrors at the drivers. He enjoyed it immensely, for he disliked New York's hacks.

He'd rented the vehicle just for this trip, in Nevada City, California, where he lived in the home his great-grandfather Morgan had built in 1851.

The motor home was a new Winnebago, twenty-seven feet long and somewhat less agile than an overloaded Greyhound bus. The interior had a musty smell; the decor was beige; everything was Joe Six-pack San Fernando Valley modern.

17

But it was comfortable, more comfortable than any yacht he'd sailed, more comfortable than some junior-officer quarters he and Ellen had known.

The driver's seat, and the passenger's, were armchairs, deep in imitation-leather comfort. They swiveled: when facing aft, they commanded the whole interior.

In the living-dining area, an easy chair sat beneath a reading lamp at a fold-down table to starboard, forward of the side entrance door. A dinette table to port had couch-seats at either side. A kitchen-counter–bar over-looked the dining area. In the compact galley rode a butane stove, and across the passageway a refrigerator-freezer.

Further aft, to starboard, was his sleeping compart-ment, with a double bed. His granddaughter's bed would be a spacious bunk over the cab: she had a reading lamp in her alcove, and a window that looked ahead.

The toilet and shower were at the rear: there was TV, stereo, and air-conditioning. A CB radio mounted on the instrument panel seldom seemed to work.

He'd slung his yellow Honda Trail-90 onto a rack in front of the hood, and left Nevada City with a toot of his horn, to no one.

The whole enchilada was costing him four hundred and fifty dollars a week and twelve cents a mile, plus the gas he poured into its insatiable tank, but the trip was to be surcease from despair, and he did not regret a penny.

He'd learned the vehicle's strengths and weaknesses as he hurtled east with his bull mastiff Halsey, along In-terstate 80, to pick up Bunkie in New York. He made it in six days, arriving in Manhattan during the hottest day of August.

During the whole three-minute parking maneuver, his chubby, moustached son-in-law Howard, a professor at Columbia, writhed in embarrassment in the entrance of the apartment house. The old black doorman giggled, and the admiral's daughter Kelly blushed. Bunkie cheered when the admiral finally drew the front of the motor home out of the flow of traffic.

As he switched off the engine, Bunkie burst aboard. She hugged Halsey, who turned to a slobbering idiot whenever he saw her, and she squirmed to the cab, brushed her grandfather's cheek with her lips as he held her close.

"I got fat," she announced. "So now you know."

"We'll work it off," he promised. "We'll backpack up the Yuba and pan for gold."

"All *ri . . . ght,*" she beamed. They looked deeply into each other's eyes and began their standard greeting. He grabbed her and began to tickle her. She punched him hard in the gut, pulled away. He slipped from the seat and dropped to his knees to spar with her warily. They ended in a warm hug.

Bunkie surveyed the interior. Excited, she wiggled out of his arms, craning her neck up at her bunk. She flicked on her reading light, tried the TV, the stereo, and the galley stove. She was testing the shower by the time her mother enticed her father into the doorway.

"Jesus, Admiral," said Howard, "what an operation! It's a wonder nobody called the cops!"

Kelly fended off Halsey and hugged her father. "Who'd dare?"

He gave them a grand tour of the motor home. They left Bunkie aboard to play house with Halsey and disembarked into sultry heat.

In the creaking elevator, his daughter squeezed his hand. He had not seen her since Ellen's funeral in Nevada City. The reflection of her mother in her dark brown eyes brought him secret pain.

Their apartment was tiny and always seemed stuffy. It was full now of the smell of food. The admiral strolled to the open window and glanced three stories down at the Winnebago.

In the hazy twilight, it seemed immense, dwarfing the line of parked autos. It was as alien to Manhattan as a cockroach in a hill of ants. He tensed as he saw a wooly-headed black in a crazy yellow shirt, jeans, and sandals, inspect it from bow to stern and kick a rear tire. He relaxed as the man passed on. Two teenagers on the other side of the street dodged through traffic, peeked into a window, and sauntered away. Bunkie, under the eye of the doorman and Halsey, was surely safe.

In the Nevada City home, he'd found a photo album his father had kept of the family. He'd brought it east for Kelly and showed it to her now.

They leafed through the pages: Christmases in the Philippines, at the embassy in Madrid, in San Diego, at Quonset Point; himself pinning the Navy wings of gold on her brother Chris; a Navy chaplain reading Chris's funeral service on a carrier fantail at sea; himself on the porch of the Nevada City home, in an Aloha shirt beneath his great-grandfather's shingle, with Bunkie, age two, on his shoulder; another, Ellen and Bunkie lying on Coronado's Silver Strand; a third, the admiral and Bunkie, with tennis rackets after a junior-senior mixed doubles tournament that they had very nearly won at the North Island Officers' club. There was a shot of Kelly, Bunkie, and himself, taken by Ellen at the last family reunion. It struck him suddenly that the picture showed all of the surviving Washburns in a single snapshot.

And pictures of Ellen, Ellen everywhere.

"Bunkie was worse than me, when Mom died," remarked Kelly.

"I know." Bunkie had wanted to leave school to fly with Kelly to the funeral. Howard had talked her out of it. "I was glad you didn't bring her."

"She thought we should go and *live* with you. She said you might..." Her voice trailed off and she looked away.

"Might *what*?" he asked. He continued to turn the pages, but his fingers began to shake.

She shrugged. "Swim out from the Strand, into the sunset. I guess from *A Star Is Born*."

Bunkie had not been far wrong.

"Yeah, well..." He closed the album. "I'm glad you didn't bring her. Funerals aren't her bag."

Kelly squeezed his knee. "Thanks for bringing the album, Daddy."

There seemed nothing more to say. They were an inarticulate clan: he could find no words to tell her how much he had loved Ellen and how much he loved her, too. Anyway, his throat was too tight.

Dinner was roast beef; her mother would have had the same on the eve of any departure. All through Kelly's childhood, she and her brother had lived like the children of gypsies, shunted from one Naval Air Station to another: from Coronado to Newport, Pensacola to Fallon, Jacksonville to Barber's Point. At each major move, on the eve of departure, their mother would cook a farewell roast. Then they would have cold roast beef sandwiches for days, on the road, and save money on roadside restaurants.

"Let Daddy carve, Howard," Kelly said.

A usurpation that Howard didn't like. But he knew why she'd done it. If her father happened to be ashore, he always did the carving, honing the knife keenly, cutting the meat thick. The admiral stepped to the stove.

Her kitchen was pitifully small, smaller even than those he and Ellen had known during his service years. Standards of living for her generation, he had observed, were going down, not up. He felt cramped and uncomfortable. Despite the doorman below, his daughter seemed backed to the edge of poverty.

At least they had stability. Howard had taught at Columbia for fifteen years: they'd lived in this apartment since before Bunkie was born.

It could have been worse. When he was naval attaché in Madrid, Kelly had fallen in love at eighteen, with a Spanish lawyer as phoney as a three-dollar bill. Later, with her father and her brother supplying endless Navy bodies, it was a miracle that she hadn't married some slit-eyed carrier pilot with the mind of a reckless child. Howard was articulate, witty, lovable, once you sliced through his wary distrust. And devoted to Kelly, and to Bunkie.

But the daughter of Stretch Washburn married to a tubby professor? Of anthropology?

Dreary. Stultifying.

Incredible. . . .

He began to carve the roast.

THE ADMIRAL

THE ADMIRAL CRUNCHED TO A STOP BEHIND THE GRAY van on the shoulder of the desert highway. The young man approached, smiling, carrying his red gas can.

He wore scruffy jeans and moved as if in slow motion. Still smiling, he set the gas can on the pavement, plucked off his dark glasses, and put them into his shirt pocket as the admiral rolled down the window. The air was furnace-hot.

The man beamed up at the admiral. His eyes were sapphire-blue, but bloodshot, glazed with fatigue and some hidden pain. His beard glowed bronze in the golden light.

The scene had a certain timeless quality, like a Remington print.

"Problem?" the admiral asked uncomfortably. "I can take you to Fallon...."

"We *had* a little problem, sir," the young man said, too quickly, then reached up and yanked the door open. The admiral stared into the muzzle of a .45 service automatic, trained straight between his eyes. "But it's all your problem now. Cut your engine!"

"Look, you son of a bitch—"

"The engine!"

He thought of trying to pull away, but the motor home had the acceleration of a garbage scow. He switched off the ignition. His fingers were trembling.

"*Out,* motherfucker!" To Bunkie: "You stay there!"

Halsey began to bark hysterically, filling the motor

22

home with sound. For a crazy instant the admiral's instinct was to jump the man while he held the higher ground, go for the gun and pray for a miss, and wrestle him to the pavement.

No way. The last thing he wanted was a bullet ricocheting through the cab. He stumbled down. The man slammed the door against Halsey and prodded the admiral toward the van.

The magnitude of his mistake had not quite penetrated, but the admiral found that he'd raised his hands.

"Get 'em down. Just move!"

"Take what you want, no sweat! OK?"

His own voice sounded high and frightened: he hated the ring of it. Steady, steady, steady . . .

"Thanks," the young man murmured dryly. He checked for traffic both ways, pushed the admiral between the vehicles, quickly patted him down. He took his wallet, yanked a gold ID tag from his neck, relieved him of his class ring. He jerked his head toward the drainage ditch.

"In the ditch."

"What?"

"I said *getnafuckin ditch!*" the man yelled.

If he murdered him, what would he do to her?

He heard the side door of the van sliding, and a second man—Mexican or Chicano—appeared from around the rear of the van. He was a handsome, curly-haired giant, fully six-four, with massive weight-lifter shoulders and slim hips. He carried a sawed-off shotgun, which he trained on the admiral.

He could hear his motor home's engine croaking as it cooled, and then Halsey, free and barking, and his granddaughter's feet scrunching the gravel. "Stay there!" he yelled, eyes on the men, who were swinging their pieces. He glimpsed Halsey, teeth bared, streaking toward the Mexican. The two men fired simultaneously. The dog spun a foot in the air and slammed into the ditch.

There was a moment of dead silence. Gunpowder soured the desert breeze. "You *bastards!*" he heard himself screaming. "Sons of *bitches!*"

The guns swung back. And then he felt Bunkie's body, between himself and the gunmen, her arms squeezing him tightly, her face buried in his chest. She was sobbing, and he pressed her head close, stroked her damp thick hair. He faced the men. His knees were turning weak, his hands beginning to shake. "Take those guns off her!" he ordered. *"Now!"*

Neither barrel wavered, but the blond man said: "Tell her to get back in. I want her up front!"

Bunkie clung more tightly.

"Get back in the cab," whispered the admiral. He looked down, tilted her face, pled with his eyes. "Go on, I mean it, Bunkie. Now!"

She would not budge. He took her hand, led her back, caught her as she stumbled, lifted her in. He turned to find that the bearded man had followed, automatic leveled. He waved it toward the highway drain. "OK, Dad," he growled. "I told you. The ditch. Move!"

The immensity of their danger continued to sap his strength. He looked into the ditch. Halsey, one massive shoulder torn open and a dark red blotch on his chest, was bleeding from the mouth. A glazed eye stared at the sun.

He was sick with fear. He found himself growing dizzy, leaned against the van. "Look," he begged the men, "the little girl's only twelve..."

"His sister's only nineteen," the blond man said tightly, jerking his head toward the van, "and they already shot her." He prodded the admiral with the muzzle, moving him toward the ditch, then glanced toward the motor home. "How many in there?"

"Just her. Look, *take* the thing! Leave us here!"

"We're *going* to take it. Get your ass in gear or I'll blow it all over the highway." He spoke softly to the Mexican in Spanish. The admiral strained to hear, but heard only the words "...en la zanja."

"...in the ditch."

The admiral hesitated, stalling, hoping for traffic, any traffic at all. A woman's voice called out from the van and the blond man left the Mexican and sprinted to their vehicle. The haste of his captors told the admiral that they feared pursuit.

24

All right, no one could escape for long through country so open; where were the helicopters, where were the cops?

Another jab, in the ribs, hard, this time from the Mexican's shotgun.

If he refused to budge, they would simply kill him between the van and the motor home, in sight of his granddaughter. He stumbled toward the side of the road, looked into the ditch, full of highway trash and weeds.

This, then, was the end of a long, lucky roll. The day after tomorrow would be—would have *been*—his sixty-second birthday. He had survived childhood pneumonia, and had ditched in freezing water near a carrier off Seoul. He had ejected over Sangley Point on Luzon Island, lived through a hurricane on a yacht, and rolled a Jaguar over twice, celebrating an Army-Navy game.

He had beaten a fractured skull from the Jaguar crash, and a recent heart attack.

Over Wonsan Harbor, he had once challenged a MiG with a tired Navy Panther, and won.

The gods owed him nothing, and might be laughing now, to see him killed in a highway drain, with a dog for a companion and beer cans for bouquets, hardly a mile from the trail his great-grandfather had bumbled along and survived.

He could almost laugh with them: the rainy night Ellen had died, with his heart erratic and gray fatigue dogging every move, he'd studied his .38 for half an hour, grappling with suicide. Then he'd poured a drink, and another, and put the gun away.

If he'd chosen differently that night, Bunkie would be safe at home.

If he could only get his captors to free the child, they could blow him to Kingdom Come.

THE ADMIRAL

THE ADMIRAL HAD DINED VERY WELL AT THE TINY TABLE in his daughter's apartment, with the sound of traffic on East 55th Street diminishing as they ate. His son-in-law Howard seemed morose, and a little heavy-handed in the pouring of the wine.

When the dishes had been cleared—Kelly was washing them—and Bunkie and Halsey had gravitated again to the motor home, the admiral spread out the AAA road maps for Howard and put the typed transcript of Morgan Washburn's journal on the dinette table, with the copies of the letters Morgan had written home to Rensselaerville.

He'd found the diary and letters in a steamer trunk more than forty years ago, while looking for a slide rule in the attic of the ancient wooden house in Nevada City that he'd disliked then and so loved now.

The old forty-niner's legend held that Dr. Morgan Washburn was the best doctor of the eight—genuine or fake—in the tiny mining town. This had been bred into Washburn bones for the next two generations. Suddenly, to the youth hunkered under the dusty attic window, the old doctor seemed very close. Reading of his hopes and fears, his great-grandson realized that to Morgan Washburn in 1849 the little upstate New York town of Rensselaerville must have been as much a prison as Nevada

City was to him, and the lure of California nuggets as powerful as his dream of Navy wings of gold.

But he'd read only a few pages then, squinting at the browning script and flowing penmanship. Someday, perhaps, he'd follow the old man's trail. In 1939, there'd been no time to finish reading the journal. He was eighteen years old. He had just graduated from Nevada City High, president of the student body. There were Naval Academy entrance exams coming up; he was washing planes to pay for flight time at the tiny local airstrip; he was summer end-coach for the football team; he'd just rebuilt the engine on his Model A Ford and was trying to seduce the queen of Grass Valley High, four miles down the road.

Time in those days was terrain seen from a high-flying plane. It moved slowly beneath one's wings, and there seemed plenty ahead for anything.

For forty Navy years the Emigrant Trail lay dormant in his mind. Then Ellen died. Retired in Coronado, he had been somehow drawn to the family plot in Nevada City to bury her. Then his heart had gone ape, and when he'd recovered, he knew he could never again live in their Coronado home.

He moved into the comfortable Victorian homestead in which his great-grandfather, grandfather, and father had all practiced medicine. Though still enormous, the house, since his youth, had shrunk miraculously in size. For tax purposes, his father had deeded the place to the County Historical Society, stipulating that after Stretch's death it would become a museum: Stretch would be the last of his line to live in it.

Alone and bored, he stayed with Halsey in the ancient mining town, split tragically now by a freeway built to whisk tourists through the Mother Lode.

By then the terrain below seemed closer, as seen from the cockpit of a strafing fighter. Months were suddenly flashing by like treetops clutching for the belly; if he was going to know more of his legendary ancestor, perhaps he had better start soon.

He began to transcribe the forty-niner's diary, typing out a copy as best he could. The journal and the letters

27

were harder to read at sixty than at eighteen. His eyes suffered. But he gradually mastered nineteenth-century circumlocution, poring over the Spencerian writing, which was often jammed crosswise on the flimsy sheets to save paper in the gold-rush days. He extrapolated what he could not read, like a Pentagon cryptographer. He jabbed away at his portable in the dark old surgery, at a rolltop desk under a lace-curtained window. It had taken him half the winter to decipher the flowing handwriting on the stained and weathered pages.

He'd gathered the transcript and maps from the motor home and brought them upstairs. Now, on the dining table next to Howard's after-dinner brandy—remarkable, for his son-in-law seldom drank—lay all of his lonely labor.

The first, easy, half of Morgan Washburn's journey was traced with a yellow route-marking pen. This civilized portion was traveled by stagecoach, canal barges, and sidewheelers from his medical preceptor's home in Rensselaerville to Independence, Missouri.

Here the route on the map turned red, and the tiny nightly circles were campsites his great-grandfather had described on the Emigrant Trail. Each was labeled with a date in the spring, summer, or fall of 1849. To a seaman they looked like fixes on a navigational chart of a ship fighting headwinds. They were spaced some twenty miles apart, and the distance traveled was determined each night by the "wheelometer," a crude mileage-counter on one of "Captain" Turner's wagonwheels.

The circles, joined by the red line, marched in an arc, plodding westward across the Blue, then northwestward along the Little Blue to the Platte, soaring to what was now Casper, Wyoming, and then southward again along the Sweetwater, St. Mary, and Humboldt. Where the Humboldt River sank beneath the great Nevada desert, almost five months from Independence, the young doctor had almost perished.

Howard hadn't realized the admiral had done so much homework, and said so.

"You ought to have it published," he mumbled, a little boozily. "Publish or perish, Pops."

"*He* wrote the journal," said the admiral. "I just mapped it out."

Howard studied him through great, sad hazel eyes. "I wonder why you did. And why take Bunkie, anyway?"

"She seems interested. Unique migration. Historic."

"Historic? To a twelve-year-old?"

Bunkie was no ordinary twelve-year-old, and Howard knew it. What was bugging him?

"He was her great-great-great-grandfather. *I* want to see the things he saw. Maybe she does too. And it'll give her a handle on Mary."

Her great-great-great-grandmother hadn't traveled the overland trail, but she'd tried to study medicine in 1849. Bunkie was already fascinated with the stories he had told her of Mary's life.

"A handle on Mary," Howard repeated bitterly. "Great! She *already* wants to be a frigging astronaut!"

As a lieutenant commander, the admiral had tried to be one of the first seven astronauts, been an inch too tall, and failed in his fight for a waiver. His story of the battle with NASA had interested Bunkie all her life. "I know she does, and she *will* be, too."

Howard looked as if he were going to throw up. "Stretch, you're crazy! Your whole goddamn family!"

"Maybe she could use a little craziness, around here."

Howard snorted, moved to the window, looked out, glanced at his watch. He called the doorman on the intercom and asked him to tell Bunkie to come up. He wandered to the coffee table, flipped open the album the admiral had brought, and stared at the picture of the admiral pinning on Chris's wings.

"Craziness. . . . Chris. . . . Tell me, Stretch. When Kelly married me, were you losing a daughter? Or gaining a son?"

The admiral glanced at the picture. He thought of his golden, blue-eyed boy, always flying too close to the sun, and his throat grew tight. "You're *you*," he murmured. "Chris was Chris."

"And cannot be replaced." Howard slammed the album shut. "Well, when Kelly married me, did you wonder *why* she did? I'm not exactly Navy. Didn't you ever wonder? Why *me*?"

The admiral came from a line in which such things were felt but not discussed. Why were Jews so goddamn ...*intimate*?

"Why *you*? No," lied the admiral. "I didn't."

"Think about it, Stretch. You really should." Howard lit a cigarette, and put on a Southern accent he sometimes affected: "This trip, now: you-all goin' to lay wreaths on your great-grandaddy's campsites, or what?"

The admiral had had it with this conversation, wanted only to get away. But he kept his temper. "His campsites are all under McDonald hamburger stands, by now."

"So why bother? She'll come back bragging about her great-to-the-third-power grandfather," muttered Howard, "the way everybody did at that goddamn reunion in Nevada City, and bore people all her bloody life."

The reunion—in the Nevada City home when his father was still living—had been a warm time of nostalgia, with childhood friends and distant relatives from Rensselaerville and Maryland.

For Howard, uncomfortable among strangers, it had been a disaster; to top it off, he'd got poison oak climbing Sugarloaf Mountain, with Bunkie on his back in a sling.

"That was nine years ago, so you're not still brooding on *that*," mused the admiral. He hated to risk an argument at so late a date, but could tolerate the strange currents no longer. "What's *really* on your mind, Howard?"

"Nothing, Stretch." Howard rose, moved to the window, looked down at the motor home. "Not a damn thing."

"Come on! You've been fighting this trip for a year! You bitched when she came out to visit me and Ellen, and—"

"She's my daughter, I like her around," Howard said tersely.

"You were always invited!"

"But unfortunately, if I don't teach summer session, we can't pay the rent. Also, this time you want to keep her past school opening—"

She was a straight A student, and could make up two weeks' work in a day. But the admiral decided not to

30

dwell on that. "Jesus, Howard, she needs fresh air! She needs room! So do you and Kelly!" He forced himself to lower his voice; he wanted no shouting, only to be safely gone. "You're going to Maine, aren't you?"

"For a week."

"Stay two. I'll stake you."

That was a mistake. Howard whirled, eyes blazing. "I'm not *that* frigging broke!"

"Sorry."

Howard smiled tensely. "I mean, we always got Bunkie's annuity to fall back on."

Ellen had left twelve thousand dollars in trust for Bunkie. He'd never realized that Howard resented the bequest, or even that they'd had to draw on it.

"What's that supposed to mean?"

"She's practically self-supporting," shrugged Howard. "Ninety dollars a month. Kid's pure gold."

"I'll try not to leave her in a filling station."

Howard suddenly stubbed out his cigarette, plunked down in his leather chair, and glared at the admiral. "You asked what was on my mind, I'll tell you."

"Good." Not really good. Bad. He had no idea what was tearing at his son-in-law, but of all times for a confrontation, this was the worst. Howard was probably capable of refusing to let Bunkie go, even now. His sulks, though short, were very deep, and his tantrums monumental.

"What's on my mind," Howard murmured, "is this: *I* got a nice little Jewish father not ten minutes on the subway from here. Also a widower, *also* lonely. Remember him? From Christmases, now and then? Tubby, white-haired, nice smile? Name of Charlie?"

The admiral liked Charlie very much. "Come *on*, Howard!"

"*His* great-grandfather didn't *have* to look for thrills, they always came to him. He didn't make it to the gold rush: he was hiding from the Cossacks, probably, or baking Christian babies—"

"Howard, you're in fine fettle."

Howard's apple-cheeks were red, and his guardsman moustache quivering. "Anyway, *Charlie's* great-grand-

31

father missed the boat. On the other hand, the old bastard was not exactly a nudnik. Most of his kids got to a university, and most of *their* kids too, and one of them was Niels Bohr's lab assistant, and one of *his*—my Uncle Leo—was a neurosurgeon in Hamburg until the Krauts baked *him*. But you know all that?"

"In general, yes," said the admiral.

"Well, *Bunkie's* heard it all. From me. And from my dad, in detail. We had him to supper last night and she heard it again. Hell, he's proud of our family, *we're* survivors too."

"Why wouldn't he be proud?" The admiral began to see the trend of Howard's tortuous argument. "And what does she *think* about the Zaleskis?"

"Nothing, as far as I know. Zilch. The poor guy's pouring out his heart to a total blank. No comments, no questions. All *she* could talk about was the trip she was taking with *you!*"

At last the fester was open to his gaze. He tried to bandage it. "She's excited because she's going on the Emigrant Trail, not because she's going with me." Not entirely true, but what the hell. "She'd be just as excited if Charlie'd suggested the same thing."

"Sure. A little jaunt to Krakow? How about Auschwitz?"

Howard moved back to the window. He was drunk, had to be. And nervous because it was growing dark. Quietly, the admiral joined him. Together, they looked down at the motor home. Softly, the admiral said: "And you think I'll be touting Bunkie's WASP ancestors from Independence to the sea?"

"Fifty percent WASP. Let's not forget it."

"Whatever. You *are* concerned?"

"Yes, goddamn it!" barked Howard. "Since it takes an act of God to get her to even *visit* her other grandfather, the little Jewish one, yes. She—"

"Daddy, that isn't fair!"

Shocked, they turned from the window. Bunkie was standing in the living-room door. The entrance was open behind her. She had been trying to unsnap Halsey's leash from his collar, and it was fouled around his forelegs; God knew how long she had been there. She abandoned the snap and threw the leash aside. Halsey trailed it to the admiral, who released it. Bunkie bolted the door and turned to face her father, face flaming.

"That isn't fair at all!" she repeated. Her voice was strangled. "I went to see him on Passover!"

Howard's face was burning too. "Well," he grumbled, "like I say, an act of God. Why *are* you so hot for this trip, anyway?"

"Because Maine's . . . well, a cabin. Not any bigger than this. We can't go swimming when the surf's up. You don't even like to climb rocks!" She looked at the admiral. "And Grandma's gone, and he . . ." Her eyes filled with tears and she ran to the kitchen. In a moment Kelly appeared, wiping a dish—Jesus, you'd think he could afford a dishwasher for her—and skewered her husband with flashing eyes.

"Damn it, Howie, I asked you not to bring that up. Not now."

"Sorry, Kelly." He licked his lips. He had paled and did not look well. He moved to the window, gazed out. He turned suddenly and smiled, quickly and radiantly. Typically, he was over it. "Kelly's right, Stretch. Bunk, come here!"

Bunkie approached, scowling thunderously. Howard beckoned her to him, put his hands on her shoulders, and gazed into her eyes. "Now, I don't want you to be a heavy-duty Jewish-American Princess—"

"I'm not. I'm *me!*"

"—but I still think you get too much Washburn and not enough Zaleski."

"Well, *I* don't," she frowned.

He placed a finger on her lips. "Your name's Zaleski, Z-a-l-e-s-k-i! So watch what the old bastard tells you, OK?"

For a long moment she held his eyes, fighting to retain the scowl, but her lips twitched and betrayed her.

"Daddy, you're bombed!" she giggled. "Mom, he's *wasted!*"

Howard sighed. "You're right." He looked at the admiral. "Admiral, suh, profit by my shame: watch your booze on the trip. And have a nice one, Admiral, sir. Hear, y'all?"

He shook the admiral's hand, kissed Bunkie and Kelly moistly, and lurched toward the bathroom.

In a moment, they could hear him retching. Bunkie went into the kitchen, shaking her head.

"Oh, my God," Kelly winced, "he *never* does that!" She looked at her father, embarrassed to the verge of tears. "And he's not giving you the right reasons. He doesn't care about that ethnic crap. He wanted her to go to Maine and she picked you. It shocked him. They're getting so close. They play chess, and backgammon— can you believe she beats him? And she's got him jogging in the Park, and they go to the movies, and they go on these crazy diets together. And he's just . . . *jealous*."

Her eyes filled. There was something else. Suddenly he knew.

He had been at sea during most of her childhood; when he got ashore, there was Navy social life, fine for him and Ellen but hardly meant for kids.

"Did you want to come too?" he asked softly.

She nodded. "I guess."

He hadn't even asked her. "I didn't think you *could*."

"Of *course* I couldn't. He'd starve, he can't boil water. Or he'd fall in the washing machine."

"But you wanted to be asked. . . ."

She shrugged. "Maybe."

He'd neglected her for her brother. Once, as a lieutenant, on the eve of departing for his carrier off Korea, the admiral had backed over her tricycle in the driveway. There was no way for him to fix it, only to promise that she'd get a new one: and *that* he'd had to leave to Ellen.

He had read in her baby-eyes no anger, only resignation. Of course he would leave without fixing it; if tomorrow someone made it right, it would be Mama. At three, she knew the way of the Navy world.

He'd left her to Ellen all her life, while he'd camped with his son, wrestled and run and coached him in boxing, and now his golden boy was gone, and Ellen too, and he hardly knew Kelly at all.

They had never jogged together, once.

"I wish we could do it over," he muttered. "I really do."

"No," smiled Kelly, "I wouldn't change a thing. You were sweet. And you get sweeter every year."

She kissed him lightly. He looked into her eyes, and the pain left him. He had a sudden hope.

"Look . . . We'll be there in three weeks. You and Howard fly out. You pick up Bunkie, and I'll pick up the tab."

She smiled. "He won't do it. He hated Nevada City."

"My birthday's coming up," he pressed. "It's your present to me?"

She shook her head.

"My present to myself?" he begged.

"No way, Daddy: he won't."

He was uncomfortable pleading, so he dropped it, and they left the next morning. Howard blessed the departure, in a way, by uncharacteristically hugging the admiral, though he was too hung over to actually go downstairs to attend the undocking. Kelly stood on the street outside as they squeezed into traffic. In the rearview wing-mirror, he could see her waving.

She had been waving goodbye from airfields and piers for nearly all her life, waiting with Ellen to hear the worst while he risked their happiness flying jets from postage-stamp flight decks.

Which was what Howard was trying to say.

No wonder she'd picked an academic who was destroyed when his daughter left for a month, probably considered a voyage to Staten Island fraught with danger, and had tenure until he died.

The admiral, directed by Bunkie, headed for Rensselaerville, New York.

MORGAN

MORGAN WASHBURN CLASPED THE HAND OF HIS BE-
loved.

The stagecoach for Troy was harnessing at the Rensselaerville depot. The lead horse snuffled impatiently.
Morgan's trunk was atop the coach, his brown wooden
medical kit, with surgical instruments and drugs, on the
empty driver's seat. He drew Mary aside from her parents.

The balm of spring was in the air, and the smoke of
hemlock from the mills by the river. He was late, late,
late; the wagons of the Pioneer Line were due to leave
Independence by April 15, to be first to the new spring
grass.

A thousand miles by stagecoach, canal barge, railcar,
Great Lakes sidewheeler, and riverboat lay ahead before
he joined the muletrain on the Missouri.

He drifted with Mary under the slanting hay shelter
behind the stage depot. Mary looked up into his face. Her
eyes were moist, and she began to cry. In the two years
boarding with her family, he had seen her twice close to
death, but never seen her weep.

He took both her hands and pressed them to his lips.
"Dear Mary," he pled. "Please..."

"I'm *sorry*," she gulped. "Drat! I hardly ever..."

"It's all right. Don't start your cough, that's all."

She blotted at her nose with a tiny lace handkerchief.
"Crying is *stupid*!" Suddenly she was smiling through the

tears. She dabbed at her cheeks. "I put on rouge, comme une française, and now it's running! Is it?"

She must have sent to New York City; there was damn little rouge in Rensselaerville. "No."

"Now," she instructed, "you're to forget this and remember me as cheerful! Else you'll find some señorita, and never *will* come back!"

"I'll come back," he promised softly.

The question he asked himself was whether he could bring himself to climb into the coach. A man who would depart from such an angel for a look beyond the hills must have fever of the brain.

"*I'll* come back," he repeated, "but last night your mother put me a threat: Will *you* wait?"

She looked up into his eyes, face framed in her bonnet, tiny white teeth gleaming. She would be twenty next month, and was the wisest person he had ever met. She kissed his hand.

"We're quite affianced, I thought."

"Yes."

"But there *is* Eliot," she mused.

She was teasing, but he didn't like it. "Sure, if you want to spend the rest of your evenings listening to tales of Harvard College. . . ."

"There's George."

"Same, for the Battle of Vera Cruz."

"Michael Severson?"

"Too fat."

"Lowell Tomkins."

"He drinks. And he's clumsy at dancing."

"Listen to the pot calling the kettle—"

"He drinks *too* much. The mesmerizer at the Lyceum wouldn't touch him: said he was in a trance already."

She shrugged. "It appears, then, that I am trapped?"

"Like a little cub in the snow."

She looked up at him, dead serious. "I am no little cub, as you know. And I do not take to traps. If you wait too long, you may find me at Geneva."

Incredibly, God alone knew why, she dreamed of following the notorious Elizabeth Blackwell to Geneva Medical College, his own alma mater. She already knew Latin,

37

French, and Natural Philosophy, and he had taught her some Physic in the surgery, despite the sulks of her father. She'd instructed at Rensselaerville Academy since she was seventeen. At Geneva, the plain-looking Blackwell woman had been voted into the medical school by the students themselves: if Mary somehow got parental permission, they'd greet *her* with open arms.

The idea, for some reason, frightened him almost as much as it would have scared her father, who knew nothing yet of her ambition. But Morgan could not admit his fears: he was for women's suffrage; why not medical school, as well?

"Nothing's impossible," he equivocated.

"Except my father and my age."

"They'd take *you*, if you were ten," he said ruefully.

"I meant the age I *live* in, sir." She sighed, and shrugged. "Well, we'll see what we shall see. And now, there's something I have for you," she said swiftly. It was to have been a surprise for his birthday, she said; she'd had it made when she went to Troy with her mama. She dug into the little handbag that she dangled from her wrist and produced a tiny Daguerrean portrait in a folding, gilded frame.

Even though she stared unsmiling at the lens, as instructed by the Daguerrean, her sparkle had still, somehow, left its imprint on his plate.

He slid the daguerreotype into his waistcoat pocket. He hugged her closely and kissed the tears away. Behind the full skirts and crinoline, he felt her body pressing him back. God, he was a fool....

He heard the driver bellow: "Stage, ladies and gentlemen: Troy stage, folks, leaving now!"

But they delayed until they heard her father calling out her name. Then he led her to the front of the depot. He grasped the older doctor's hand, looked into his eyes; took her mother's palm and pressed it to his lips. Impulsively, she pulled him close and hugged him, despite the coachstop hangers-on.

He climbed to the driver's box to check the lashing on his mahogany medical kit, then swung down through the door to sink into a black leather seat. The carriage was a Vermont Sanderson of uncertain age: it smelled quite sour and musty. A traveling man opposite him lit a fat cigar, without a by-your-leave from the apothecary's wife, bound for Troy to see her sister. Morgan was too subdued from the parting to ask him, for her sake, to put it out.

As the whipster snapped the reins above and the stage creaked away, he twisted to see Mary from the back window.

She was folded in her mother's arms. Her shoulders were shaking. She was sobbing again. Or coughing...

He drew the curtain and faced forward. He could not bear to look.

By late that night he was floating west, on the broad Erie Canal.

THE ADMIRAL
AND BUNKIE

WHEN THEY WERE HALF A DAY OUT OF MANHATTAN, the admiral swung the motor home along a curving road into Rensselaerville, cradled in the foothills of the Catskills. They passed the site of the Rensselaerville Academy, where his great-grandmother Mary had taught at the age of seventeen.

"Can we find the house she lived in, Pops?" Bunkie asked.

He knew from Morgan Washburn's letters that Mary's father's home had burned before the Civil War; Doctor Cullen—his own maternal great-great-grandfather—had then moved north to Saratoga Springs and lived to ninety. Mary had been his only child.

"Gone. All gone. But your grandma and I found the site." He and Ellen had come here the day after they had married in the Air Corps chapel at Presque Isle, for a quick wartime honeymoon away from the bustle of the nation's biggest ferry base of World War II. They had come because he'd always wanted to see the place, and it was only two days drive away from Presque Isle, and he had less than a week to report to his ship in Boston Navy Yard.

Now the motor home passed the ancient foundry. He parked on Crocker Road and Main Street in front of the white-steepled Presbyterian church that Morgan—reluctantly—had attended for Mary's sake. They roamed the narrow streets, with Halsey panting alongside in the fierce summer heat. The admiral's mind was full of the week with Ellen, and Bunkie sensed his mood.

"I miss her too, Pops," she said, squeezing his hand. "She'd *like* to see us—you know—here together. Where you started out?"

"Yes, Lambchop, she would."

Bunkie was not Ellen, but he hid his loneliness as well as he could. He pointed out to Bunkie how much the gray, green-gabled frame houses and white picket fences resembled the place in Nevada City; Morgan must have had these homes in mind when he'd built his own.

Bunkie walked swinging her grandfather's hand, watching Halsey scout ahead. In the motor home she had been reading a guidebook to Rensselaerville, with an ancient map of the town. She'd read some of her great-great-great-grandfather's letters to Mary, too, laughing with Pops at the way Morgan avoided telling Mary that he loved her, and missed her on the trail.

Being here, where Mary had met Morgan, made her feel strange. Seeing where her great-great-great-grandmother had lived when she was young—how many "greats" was it?—made her feel shivery. So did seeing the church, where—so she'd read—Morgan always dozed. They strolled past the place where the Rensselaerville Academy had stood, where Mary taught.

"And the Lyceum was there," she said, pointing down the street.

He checked the guidebook. "Right you are."

They rounded a corner and moved down a shaded lane. She had a funny feeling. There was a word for it, when you had been someplace before, and knew what would happen around the next corner; she'd had whatever-it-was before, and so had her best friend Angela, but you couldn't talk about it: people thought you were out of your gourd.

They'd turn left in a second, and walk a half block . . .

They turned left, and did. Behind an old picket fence stood a trim modern house, one story, with a garage. Near the garage was a fine old tree, heavy with cherries.

"Pops? What is it when you think you've been some-where before?"

"Déjà vu," he said.

"But what makes it happen?"

He shrugged. "Your noggin slips a cog, and something that's happening *now* gets into a memory bank." He glanced at her swiftly. "You having one now?"

"Well, I had one, coming around the corner."

He looked down at her with his admiral-look. "You wouldn't put me on?"

"Why would I? Anyway, it's gone."

"That's very strange, you know. I've been here too."

She shivered. "When?"

"With your grandma," he said softly. "We figured this was the site of Mary's father's house, from the records in town hall."

"OK," she decided, "I saw it on that guidebook map!"

He shook his head. "It's not *on* that guidebook map, Lambchop. It's not *in* the book at all. . . ."

Their eyes met.

Weird. Angela wouldn't believe it.

Bunkie's feet hurt suddenly; she was hot and tired and restless.

41

"I'm hungry," she reported, feeling like a slob. "Pops, do they have an ice cream shop in Rensselaerville?"

The admiral sat across the booth from Bunkie, and watched her as she finished her ice cream.

Strange, her déjà vu . . . He decided that it was brought on by his own body language. Finding the Cullen site with Ellen had been a triumph; when they found it again today, he probably tensed and telegraphed it to Bunkie.

Now she began to berate herself for having the ice cream. She was right, he had better get her weaned to something less caloric, but what the hell, she'd only be young once.

At dusk they drove west of town to park by a bridge on Ten Mile Creek at the Upper Mill, which had once ground grist for the town. It was getting late. They left Kelly's good roast beef in the refrigerator and instead took a pizza from the freezer for dinner. "In case I start getting thin," mourned Bunkie, reading the package for calories. "Yikes!"

After dinner and TV, she clambered into her alcove above the front seat and pulled the curtains. Above the rush of a nearby waterfall, he could hear her portable radio. He turned into his double bed aft. He lay sleepless, too close to the memory of Ellen to relax.

He saw her as she was the night they met in midtown Manhattan, forty years ago, in the midst of youthfulness and World War II, in the crush at the Waldorf Bar. He had seen her gentle brown eyes locked to his along a swarming bar of glittering, raffish uniforms: khaki, Navy blue, olive green.

The Waldorf lounge was crammed: it was late afternoon, and the place was the best snakepit in New York.

He had graduated from Annapolis a week before. His classmates were proud of their new stripes, but to him the bright class ring on his finger and the new gold braid on his sleeves glittered with shame.

High-school friends—civilians in uniform—had been crawling all week long onto a Normandy beachhead to die. He was a professional naval officer—in name, anyway—and was safe on graduation leave in New York. He'd entered the Academy before Pearl Harbor, under an appointment engineered by the line coach, and had never heard a gun fired in anger.

At long last, he was bound for a destroyer in the North Atlantic, but the ship was in drydock in Boston and the orders which gave him thirty days of unwanted leave seemed to be written in stone.

The frustration of it had sent him on a monumental binge. The other uniformed men in the room were drunk, presumably, because they had been to war or because they were happily avoiding it: he had been drunk for a week because he wanted to be in it and was not.

He was putting off the hangover for as long as he could. He had cloudy memories of spending the night before with a blond Army wife, remembered his empty, tousled bed this morning—though he'd temporarily forgotten the name of his hotel—and beige leg-makeup sullying the sheets.

That woman he remembered not at all. But he knew that the face of the brown-eyed girl farther down the bar would stay with him forever. Chin on fist, she was studying him, past the tall j.g. sitting next to her. The j.g. was a Navy flyboy with buck teeth: an Atabrine-yellow cast to his skin meant that he had left New Guinea not too long ago. He wore faded khakis; a crumpled fifty-mission cap perched on the back of his head. He must have earned some ribbons, but wore only a pair of tarnished gold wings that Stretch would have killed for.

But he seemed, thank God, even drunker than himself, and was pushing the brown-eyed lady much too hard.

Stretch could not take his eyes from hers. She held his gaze with a faint, quizzical smile.

He abandoned his barstool to the crowd and pushed through the crush. He squeezed in beside her, away from the j.g., and ordered a drink from the bartender. "I need your name," he muttered, lips unmoving.

"Ellen," she whispered. "Ellen Russo."

"Roger, I'm Stretch Washburn," he said softly. He paid for the drink, backed off, and returned in a moment.

43

"*Ellen!* Baby, I'm sorry! Couldn't find a cab to save my butt!"

"Stretch!" She dazzled him with a smile.

The j.g. came suddenly alive. "Mister, I'm afraid you're half an hour too late." He had a Texan accent. "I reckon she's got new plans."

"Well, sir, what you don't understand, we're *engaged*."

The j.g. regarded him with heavy-lidded distrust. "Y'all can knock off the 'sir,' you know. Just knock off the bullshit, too."

"Language, sir," smiled Stretch. "Can I buy you a drink? Before you shove off?"

"Who's shoving off?" the j.g. muttered. His eyes glittered. He was getting ready to swing.

She looked up into the j.g.'s face. "Listen, Wayne... It *is* Wayne, isn't it? Wayne, there's an MP and a Shore Patrolman cruising this place. You've been annoying the hell out of *me*. Now you're trying to start a fight with my fiancé. Do I have to go find them?"

The j.g. got up, slammed down his glass, glared at the girl, and shrugged. "No. Y'all have fun, Blackshoe, with the fucking cockteaser."

Stretch had been Regimental light-heavy champ his first-class year. He was no taller than the j.g., but felt as if he were tonight, by a good two feet. Rank? The hell with rank.

He tensed, full of joy. The target was dead-center, a right jab to the solar plexus, eight inches below the wings. He'd dropped his fist to do it when he felt her touch his arm.

He froze. "OK, OK," he muttered. "Get out, you son of a bitch." He turned his back to the j.g. and drowned in Ellen's eyes. "You were saying... Where *were* we, Ellen?"

"Let's see," she said. "That you were a half-hour late."

"Or half a lifetime," said Stretch Washburn. "Let's get out of here."

By midnight, dancing to Benny Goodman on the Starlight Roof, he knew he wanted her near him forever. But by that time there was a problem: he'd been lying a blue streak.

He had played it all quite perfectly, only straying from the truth when he really felt he had to. His ship was the *Kearny*: this, at least, was true, but he hadn't mentioned that she was in the relatively safe Atlantic, not the Pacific, where young men on destroyers were dying every day. He spoke of troubled sleep, from the memory of Kamikazes screaming from the sky, and of smells he'd learned to hate: cordite from guns that blazed at dawn, and the stench of jungle shores; Midway, where they'd turned the tide, and the thing in the Coral Sea.

She listened, quietly, and spoke little of herself. Despite her Italian name, he thought she might be a Hunter girl, or Vassar.

At two the band folded. He was deeply in love, another hangover hovered, and he was sickeningly ashamed.

This was no one-night stand; he'd have to tell her soon.

"Stretch?" she murmured. "That j.g.? I'm glad you didn't hit him. I think he's been through hell."

"He probably has, and I'm glad you're glad." He studied his class ring. He would have traded it this instant for the j.g.'s tarnished wings. "El, I've got to tell you something."

She touched the brand-new braid. "OK, but I think I know. I'm guessing, but—well, you've been at the Academy, I know the ring. How long? Four years?"

"Well," he shrugged miserably, "three."

"Since before Pearl Harbor, anyway. You're just an ensign, and it's June, you must have just got out."

His head began to throb. "I did. Last Saturday."

She smiled. "That damn j.g., he did it, with his fifty-mission hat!"

"I snafued, Ellen, I really did. I guess I don't know why."

"Everybody's doing it: 'My regiment rides at dawn.'" She grinned. "Remember what he called me? I don't want you thinking he's right. So can we go to your place? I can't take you to mine."

"Oh, Christ! You're not *married*, or something?"

She wasn't, she said, but a transient, who had roommates where she stayed. By noon, when he awakened to the crash of New York traffic, she was gone. There was no leg-makeup on the sheets, but he found a note on the bedside table by the Gideon Bible.

It was a military address, APO New York.

That was odd, she'd been in civvies. A nurse? WAAC? WAVE?

He called a WAVE he knew, in the Navy Department mail room. The unit, she said, was Jacqueline Cochran's ferry outfit, the WASPS.

At least, this explained her civilian clothes. WASPS delivered to England the hottest fighters known, but because they were women they were inexplicably denied commissions and served under civil service. The squadron, his WAVE friend said, must be flying from Presque Isle, Maine.

He felt sick. He saw her halfway across the North Atlantic, alone and tiny in the cockpit of an Air Corps Thunderbird.

He took his hangover by train to Presque Isle, a million miles from nowhere. He stayed in the BOQ, drinking the O-Club dry. She was due to return from Shannon Airport in ten days: he reserved the chapel the day after he arrived, and proposed in her Operations Hut, where he was waiting when she climbed from her transport. She almost cried in joy when she found him.

His graduation leave was nearly over. They spent their wedding night in his BOQ room, a week in Rensselaerville, while he tried to talk her out of the WASPS, and then he went to sea.

About the Air Corps Thunderbird, he'd been very nearly right. The girl he'd tried to snow had already soloed the Atlantic seven times.

They'd been married for a year before she told him that once she'd almost ditched at sea.

He got orders to flight training while his ship was on the Murmansk run. When finally he got his wings of gold, the first of his wars was over.

She'd had Chris and was pregnant with Kelly by the time his own flying log caught up with hers.

46

Now, in the motor home, he turned on the light. Ellen was too close: he could not sleep.

He opened the transcript of Morgan's letters to Mary, written from Independence in 1849, which Mary must have read not far from this very spot. It worked, and he soon fell asleep.

He was deep in a strange and vivid dream when he awakened. Halsey was barking. In the gray of dawn, someone was pounding on the motor home door.

"Hey, inside? State trooper! Anybody there?"

He lurched to the door and opened it. A young man in a campaign hat, shaking his head, warned him not to spend the night again on Catskill country roads. It was illegal, and besides, he'd wake up robbed and dead.

"Thank you, son. Sorry."

The sun slashed over a wooded hill. His depression was gone, but the day would be hotter than hell. He started the generator and air-conditioner, and still Bunkie slept. He sat at the table, waiting for coffee to perk, with Halsey dozing at his feet.

He tried to remember the dream. It was sinking fast, leaving only a swirl of impressions, as seen from another's eyes: pumpkin pie, and a vest too tight, water dripping from wooden eaves; an angel face in sepia, framed in gold; black leather seats and a stale cigar.

All oddly alive, he thought, in color and stereo sound.

The coffee gurgled. He turned off the flame and woke Bunkie.

It was time, at last, to begin the great trip west.

MORGAN

THE SIDEWHEELER *MICHIGAN*, LARGEST AND SLOWEST on the Great Lakes, rolled ponderously. Under Morgan Washburn's feet her pistons throbbed like great bass drums. A fiddler roamed the smoky salon, sawing out *Oh Susanna* and *Arrival of the Greenhorn* in honor of the gold seekers crowding the long mahogany bar.

He was nauseated from the motion and very tired. He shifted in his seat at the poker table while his new friend Hollister, a bespectacled young lawyer, dealt the cards.

Morgan had taken passage for the Great Lakes voyage in Buffalo five days before. He'd been weary and foot-sore, having found the canal barge so crowded and noisy with Argonauts that he had walked most of the way along the towpath, keeping pace with the mules.

On the Buffalo waterfront, he had taken a bed at Huff's Hotel. He left his medical kit below, behind the clerk's desk, and struggled up the narrow, creaking stairs with his carpetbags. He had piled them by the window and was checking to see that the chamberpot was clean when a pale young man wearing spectacles knocked and entered.

"Good afternoon, sir," said the young man. He deposited a valise in the corner and advanced, hand outstretched. "I'm Isaiah Hollister, of Troy, New York. The clerk tells me you're heading for Independence and the Pioneer Line. I am too. Apparently we're to share that pallet and that pot."

He had straw-colored hair, neatly cut, and a pleasant smile. Of soft build and diffident manner, he was nevertheless a veteran of the Mexican War and said, over a whiskey in the bar: "Since I am a lawyer, they gave me a commission in the Corps of Engineers and made me blow up bridges." He had left his upstate New York law practice and was heading for the goldfields to get rich.

Morgan had liked him instantly, though he hated sharing a bed with any man. By that evening they were friends. The bed and breakfast cost them each one dollar.

The next day—for a premium of one percent—they changed their New York currency to gold coins, since New York State money would be worthless in the West.

Because most gold seekers had already passed, merchants were becoming nervous and supplies seemed very cheap. So, fearing high prices in Independence, they had begun to shop. At a dockside general store Morgan bought a money belt for thirty cents. Then he toyed with a revolver priced at fifteen dollars and hefted it in his hand. It was made by Samuel Colt, and he had heard of the invention, but never fired or even seen one. He did not like the feel of it, and bought instead a Navy Aston pistol for seven dollars. It had been modified from flintlock to percussion cap for use in the Mexican War, and had a good heft in his hand, like the horse pistols his father had kept on their farm. He bought two paired bullet molds, a powder flask, and five boxes of caps. He added a Hall breech-loading Army rifle for sixteen dollars. He bought a rainsuit of waterproof oilcloth for two twenty-five, and a heavy pilot-cloth overcoat for five dollars, which he could never have found in Rensselaerville and would have cost him sixteen dollars in Troy.

He stuck the pistol in his waistband, feeling quite a buccaneer. It labeled him as California-bound. He had been trained in the pistol and dueling foil, like any Maryland landowner's son, and had hunted all through childhood, but had never worn a weapon on his person in his life. Its presence seemed to cut him from his past, but caused nary a glance on the streets of Buffalo, swarming with would-be Californians even better armed than he.

At a Daguerrean parlor near his hotel, he permitted his

head to be placed in a hidden iron brace to have his likeness taken, scowling fiercely at the lens. He wore a calico shirt, a red neckerchief, a new black wide-brimmed hat, and the pistol jammed into a wide leather belt with a shiny brass buckle.

He held his breath for twenty seconds as the black-bearded Daguerrean artist removed the cap from his "magic mirror's" lens, counted slowly, and finally replaced the cap. When the silvered surface was developed and covered with glass, Morgan wrote on the back: "To Mary, from one who holds her in great affection, and is ready for battle with the untutored savage, or worse." He paid the artist a silver dollar for the portrait and mailed it at the Buffalo Post Office.

He and Hollister bought passage on the sidewheeler *Arrow* from Buffalo to Detroit City, planning to buy tickets on the Michigan Central railroad across the peninsula to the town of Niles. But in Detroit they learned that the railroad fare was six dollars, and that if they went by rail they would have to travel afterward by stage to New Buffalo on Lake Michigan and thence by steamboat to Chicago for six dollars more. It would take three days and the cars did not run on Sunday.

So instead they bought cabin passage all the way from Detroit, up Lake Huron, through the Straits of Mackinac, and down to Chicago, for six dollars on the *Michigan*.

Morgan found her saloon to be a floating poker palace.

After his purchases in Buffalo, he had less than three hundred dollars left in his money belt. But he owed his medical degree to his memory for cards. At Union College and then at Geneva Medical College, he had supplemented a meager parental allowance with poker winnings. So he had checked the saloon for riverboat gamblers, seen none to fear, and for the last three days had played, mostly with his present companions, for good substantial stakes.

Tonight, he'd won almost fifty dollars, most of it from a blond, square-jawed Navy lieutenant dressed in worn civilian clothes. The lieutenant was clearly no man to trifle with: though of only medium height, he had impassive, iron-gray eyes, a broad chest, and a body solid as the bollards the *Michigan* had been tied to on the Detroit City docks. His eyes dwelt more and more on Morgan's: obviously, he did not like to lose.

Morgan decided to quit. Fifty dollars was enough for one night's trouble: besides, he was seasick now, and tired.

"Last hand, for me," warned Morgan. He picked it up.

He saw instantly that he should have quit before: he had only a pair of eights. But many were the uses of adversity: he'd been playing cautiously for days: it was time to bluff. He raised the stakes recklessly: all but the lieutenant folded their hands.

Morgan slid a five-dollar goldpiece across the green felt table. "Raise you again."

He belched quietly. His nausea had begun in a gale at the Straits of Mackinac. Of all the maladies he had envisioned on the overland route—cholera, typhoid, grippe—seasickness had seemed least likely, but here it was. The ship was said now to be abeam of a town they called Milwaukee, and the storm was far astern, but the seas, the cabin steward had said, would plague them all the way to Chicago and the Michigan Canal.

The lieutenant sat studying his cards. He had walked up to Morgan on deck, three days ago, moving with the roll of a seaman, and introduced himself as passed-Lieutenant Guert Vanderveer, on a year's leave of absence from the service and bound, as Morgan was, for the Pioneer Line. Morgan judged that, like other naval officers in this year of peace and financial depression, he was without a ship and gambling on the goldfields to clear his debts forever.

The name Vanderveer had plucked at his memory. It must be upstate Dutch. He had heard it, or seen it in print, somewhere.

Perhaps some minor hero from the late great Mexican War....

In his gray, unblinking eyes there was an emptiness and hint of tragedy that had discomfited Morgan from the start; now he was studying Morgan's face. Morgan read his mind: the lieutenant was considering the possibility that he was bluffing; still, Morgan had won almost every hand, and seemed always to play cautiously.

Morgan allowed himself a tiny smile of triumph. It was enough. The lieutenant decided against risking good money after bad, shook his head and threw in his cards, face up.

Three tens....

"Never trust a doctor's smile," Morgan said, showing his hand to make the lesson stick.

"Shit!" the lieutenant breathed.

Morgan was surprised. Seaman's language, he would have thought, more fit for the fo'c'sle than the wardroom. Morgan raked in the pot and arose, swaying to the roll. The lieutenant's eyes widened. "You aren't abandoning us?"

"Yes."

"Might I ask why?"

He didn't feel like admitting to seasickness, in the presence of so salty a man. And it was none of the Navy's damn business, anyway.

He shrugged. "To walk the deck. To write someone at home, perhaps."

Slowly, the lieutenant gathered the cards and began to shuffle. "That's most convenient."

Morgan's new friend Hollister looked embarrassed and cut in swiftly: "He told us he was going before I dealt the hand. I don't blame him, for there's a fine moon out, and you should see his fiancée's daguerreotype! She's the prettiest thing in New York State, and he's been gone nigh on a week...."

"So," smiled Morgan, "good night, gentlemen. And good night, Lieutenant."

The lieutenant's eyes flashed.

"What's *that* mean?"

"It means good night," murmured Morgan. "Why?"

"Do you not include me as a 'gentleman'?"

Idiot, bully ... But careful, careful: naval officers made their reputations on the field of honor, and everyone knew it. God knew how many hotheads this one had winged or killed.

He chilled, but would not buckle.

"Include you as a gentleman? Certainly," he said softly. "If Congress has said so, who am I to disagree?" He suddenly remembered where he'd heard the name. "'Vanderveer' . . ." he mused. "Were you not Mackenzie's lieutenant on the brig *Somers*?"

Vanderveer squared his shoulders. His gray eyes held Morgan's, steady and unwavering. "*Captain* Mackenzie's lieutenant, yes. Why do you ask?"

Six years ago, the saga of the *Somers* had been the sensation of the Eastern press. Just ten days short of New York, sailing from the Barbary Coast, her officers had assembled for a wardroom court-martial, while her captain waited on the quarterdeck, and sentenced one Midshipman Philip Spencer, son of the Secretary of War, and two other seamen to be hanged for mutiny, the first men ever executed by the United States Navy.

Morgan stared at the naval officer. A sullen anger began to grow in his chest. With increasing disgust, in his first year at Union College, he had read the accounts of the *Somers* court-martial.

Spencer, whom Morgan had never met, had preceded him at Union College, where Spencer had been a Chi Psi, like himself. Philip had purportedly been a clown but no villain. His friends spoke afterwards of some practical joke gone awry at sea, or a young man's fantasy taken seriously; of a list, in Greek, allegedly of mutineers, but thought by the brothers instead to contain fraternal secrets that he had hidden all the way to the yardarm.

He was said to have been a lazy, good-humored young man, with an eye unfortunately crossed, no more capable of inciting a mutiny than of commanding the *Somers* if it had succeeded.

The New York press, and even Washington Irving, who knew the *Somers*'s captain well, considered the hanging as a judicial lynching, instigated by an unbalanced commander who simply disliked the boy, and orchestrated by Vanderveer to retain his skipper's favor.

Ashore, the captain had faced the fury of the Secretary of War, been brought before a Navy court of inquiry, and—to no one's particular surprise—been exonerated by his brothers of the blue.

The lieutenant continued to tap the cards against the table. "Do you have judicial comment on the *Somers*?"

"Such comment," shrugged Morgan, "would seem a little late."

"I see," Vanderveer said quietly. "Well, Doctor, our ship's surgeon sat on the court-martial. In your terms, the *Somers* had a tumor. *He* agreed that it should be cut out." He continued to knock the cards. "Apparently *you* don't."

"Surgery can sometimes be delayed, and consultation sought."

Vanderveer smiled tensely. "Many civilians agree, Doctor."

Hollister cut in: "And some of them are jurists."

Vanderveer swung his eyes to the lawyer. "Do *you* think mutineers should escape unpunished, Mr. Hollister? As a lawyer?"

Hollister paled. "No sir. Only tried."

"Is that a fact? Well, gentlemen, fortunately, *your* opinions matter not one goddamn whit." He squared the cards. "Washington Irving and Mr. Secretary Spencer chose to impugn the *honor* of that court. Do you?"

"No, Lieutenant," Hollister murmured tiredly. "Now, would you deal? Philip Spencer is gone, and his shipmates too."

Vanderveer's eyes rested on Morgan. "The doctor hasn't answered! Would *you* wish to take up the poor lad's cause? At daybreak, perhaps, on the stern?"

A swell rolled the vessel: a stovepipe hat fell from the hatrack at the door and bounced across the room. Someone laughed from the bar. Morgan's palms grew sticky. His knees were beginning to tremble. The lieutenant sat stock-still, cards suspended in his fingers, ready to be dealt.

Morgan's mind fled to his childhood home, in Maryland's southern fields. He was twelve years old, and frightened; the house was astir before dawn, but his mother and sisters, if they knew of the matter, by tradition lay abed.

He had known that there would be no breakfast, not for hours. His father, fully dressed, bolted a brandy in the library, jammed a tiny Derringer into his belt, picked up his pistol case, and strode to a brougham with flickering lanterns which was waiting on the drive. He was seconding Morgan's youngest uncle, glimpsed gray-faced through the oval carriage window. The duel, over some stupid land dispute that bedeviled the family still, would be held on a grassy bluff on the Patuxent's wooded banks.

Jeremy, his uncle's body servant, flicked the reins and they were gone.

His father had returned in an hour, alone, shaken, but resolved. "They told you in school that dueling's finished? If you meet your uncle in heaven or hell, ask *him* if it is."

He'd spared little time for Morgan before that, but that afternoon had loaded and capped his dueling pistols once again, and the lessons had begun. Within a month, a hundred balls placed by Morgan into a twelve-inch diameter mark on a white oak tree attested to his father's sudden patience and his own unshaking hand.

His father had taught him to shoot, but to avoid shooting, too. *Never challenge, but never refuse, for you cannot escape in the end.*

Now there was no escape: to walk away was to dishonor his Maryland roots and name. He took a deep breath. "Well, Lieutenant..."

No! There was Mary. He had never dueled in his life before. This challenge he must not accept, to stand up like a fool and die like a brute for a fraternity brother he had never even seen.

And even suppose he should win?

He shook his head. "My profession bids me not take lives, but save them."

"As you may have just done." Vanderveer smiled again. "A convenient calling, that. Might I see your sweetheart's picture?"

"Why not?" He drew it from his pocket.

Vanderveer looked at it, snapped it shut, and handed it back. His voice was sharp: "You do her a disservice, Doctor."

"In what way?"

"When you risk not seeing her again."

The room had heard; the fiddle had stopped. There was silence save for the clink of the bottles behind the bar, as they shivered with the pounding engine far below.

Morgan slipped the picture back into his waistcoat. He hoped that the trembling of his hand didn't show.

Hollister was polishing his glasses. Now he cleared his throat. "Gentlemen, *please* . . . Will you deal, then, Lieutenant?"

Vanderveer nodded. "There'll be no more talk of the *Somers,* gentlemen. Here or on the trail."

He began to flick out the cards. Morgan slid open the saloon door and stepped into the blessed chill of night.

A pumpkin moon danced behind the clouds. He walked to the varnished rail. Through the window of the saloon he heard the fiddle start again. Below him he could hear the ponderous paddlewheels slam into the water, creak and strain, then lift to shake the water free, like bird dogs quitting the Patuxent in the gentle fields of home.

The fresh air made him feel better. He turned toward his stateroom. It was time to write Mary. But he would say nothing of the incident with Vanderveer, who had very nearly pushed him to a suicidal act. He had not seen the last of him, since the lieutenant also had a ticket on the Pioneer Line.

But not a word to worry her, about a lout like him.

THE ADMIRAL
AND BUNKIE

THE ADMIRAL TUGGED UPWARD ON THE LOWER STRAND of barbed wire while Bunkie, commando-style, slithered under the fence on her back. He tossed her bright red rucksack after her.

The Winnebago sat two barbed-wire fences back, in a

public park ten miles southwest of Independence, Missouri, not far from the fork of the Santa Fe and Oregon trails.

Fat white prairie clouds with ominous gray bottoms ballooned slowly past from the east. A sultry, vibrant river-smell had grown heavier, as they approached the hidden Blue through tangled weeds, trespassing on elm-bordered fields of wheat.

While Bunkie held the wire, the admiral carefully squirmed beneath it. On the other side, he lay on his back for a moment, assessing the clouds and getting his breath.

He got to his feet. Halsey was ranging far ahead, and had probably reached the Blue. Bunkie was brushing the dirt and grass from her jeans. She dug into the rucksack, which held Morgan's journal, sandwiches, chocolate-chip cookies, a thermos of milk for her and beer for him, a collapsible rod, and lures.

They were searching for the precise point at which Morgan had forded the Blue, just one day out on the endless trek that had changed his life and fixed theirs.

"Onward, ever onward," he muttered. He squinted at a dark and tangled wood a hundred yards ahead, across a plowed field. He listened. He could hear the whine of cicadas, and the faint rush of running water. "Listen..."

She cocked her head. Her face was red from trying to match his stride, a smudge of dirt on the end of her nose amused him too much to inform on, and her upper lip glistened in the heat.

"Last one to the Blue—" she began.

"No way, Bunk." Two years ago, before the Big Squeeze—which had clubbed him, writhing and grasping his heart, to the floor at the Officers' Club in Coronado—he would have raced her across the furrows, and beaten her too: now, the sprint would have ended their trip where it was beginning.

Her face scrunched in embarrassment. "I'm sorry, Pops."

"Hey, no sweat. I'm going on sixty-two—it comes with the territory."

She grinned, flashing the silver braces that tore at his heart. "You're beginning to talk just like me."

57

He shrugged. "Clichés are the bon mots of the adolescent mind."

She kicked him in the tail and took off across the field. He followed slowly, admiring the firm, jiggling butt and the easy, filling curves.

Whoever won *his* girl, in not too many years, had better thank the Lord above.

Did lady astronauts have kids? Kelly, he knew, planned no more children. His line was dying out, this seemed clear: a shame, for the stock was good.

To worry about it seemed elitist, and very oriental, but lately he did, and there it was.

If Chris only had lived...

Anyway, he would like to see Bunkie's kids before he died.

Improbable that he would...

They carefully scouted the tangled bank for a towering elm Morgan had mentioned, decided that they had found it, and set the rucksack in the bared roots at its foot. The admiral fished for a while, as Morgan had; he caught nothing.

Bunkie dug into the rucksack and they lunched. He sat back against the tree. A cloud was passing the sun, through the lattice-work branches above, and the cicadas, sensing rain, raised their voices. Halsey returned, found them dull, and departed upstream through the rushes.

The admiral was happy here with Bunkie, but too drowsy to fish any more. She began to pick up sandwich crumbs from between her legs and to flick them into the water below.

A dog yapped distantly, perhaps at Halsey. They were on posted land, and he hoped that if the animal discovered them, he would bear them no ill, or be small.

"Pops?"

His eyes snapped open. "Yes sir, ma'am?"

"Do you think that's—you know—*really* one of their wagons?"

She pointed to a few water-scoured planks projecting

from the middle of the stream. They had discussed the objects earlier.

He studied the planks again.

For twenty feet on either side of them, the cottonwoods were younger, and there were no large trees but the elms: men had obviously cut a road to the ford and crossed here. If indeed he'd found the proper crossing, they'd passed by the tens of thousands, and one hundred and thirty years had not erased their channel through the trees.

But artifacts were unlikely. From midstream jutted the planks, roughly squared like the corner of some sort of wagon, but more likely a part of a crate washed down by last winter's rains. Whatever it was, it had grounded there long after Morgan had passed; nothing could have survived in a stream so swift for more than a year or two.

On the other hand, the trip was barely starting and he didn't want Bunkie to lose hope of finding relics.

"No doubt about it, Lambchop." He reached into her rucksack and found the transcript of Morgan's diary. He leafed to the page he had marked for the day, the first entry Morgan had logged after finally hitting the trail:

"When finally the gale passed and the sun shone and our ridiculous procession began to achieve a semblance of sanity, and sensing that we were only a few hours from the first of many rivers we should ford, cottonwoods being plainly visible across the prairie, and thinking to endear ourselves to our new companions by providing fresh fish or meat for the evening repast, I borrowed a better rifle than mine from Mr. Stein, the little Jewish saddler, and Mr. Hollister and I left our carriage. We mounted our eager horses, and rode forward to try our luck at angling in the 'Blue.' The waters were so swollen by the late rains as to be scarcely fordable, and I was concerned for the passage of the wagons following behind, sure that we should see what stuff 'Captain' Turner is made.

"After vainly casting the tempting bait we obtained from the banks to the finny tribe who would not even gratify us by a nibble, I shouldered my borrowed rifle and

rambled through the thickly wooded bottom bordering on
the stream, with no better success at hunting than fishing
until the arrival of the train.

"The absence of fish in so remote a stream, and of
game on its banks as well, disturbs me. Without fresh
meat in the months ahead, what of scurvy? Are we so
late as to have lost to others such bounty as Nature prom-
ised to bestow?

"Hollister thinks not, that the land is too vast. We shall
see."

Bunkie was yawning: he'd observed that the more educated the nineteenth-century writer, the more soporific
his prose, and Morgan was a man of letters, to be sure.
He skipped the rest of the hunting expedition and moved
to the crossing.

"Here: *'The carriages were crossed over with some*
difficulty, and one of the baggage wagons was for some
time mired midstream as the hapless mules strained at
their burden, but all were eventually hauled up the steep
banks by the assistance of drag ropes, after which we
moved onto a high open Prairie about one mile southwest
of the stream where we camped for the night. We are
now beyond the limits of the States . . .'"

"So they *didn't* lose any," mused Bunkie. "Not here,
anyway."

"No," he admitted. "But other outfits probably did.
That thing could be from another emigrant train."

"And you *want* it to be," Bunkie smiled. "That's
cute. . . ."

Gently, she touched his face, brown eyes steady on
his.

Jesus! She was the image of Ellen, when they'd first
met at the crazy Waldorf Bar. Ellen, but chubby and with
braces! And with Ellen's way of tracking down his secret
thoughts. He turned away to hide the tears.

Rain began to splatter on the leaves above. The cicadas
shrieked in joy. The two moved closer under the elm.
When the sprinkle passed, the admiral stretched out, pil-
lowed his head on the rucksack, and sighed in content-
ment. Bunkie gazed up at the branches that had sheltered
them.

"He could have—you know—stood under this same exact tree," she mused. "Right?"

"Possible," he murmured, closing his eyes.

He shivered. Suddenly it was more than possible; he knew damn well that Morgan Washburn had.

As her grandfather slept, Bunkie sat back, watching a fly driven mad by the last of the chocolate-chip cookies in the plastic package. She knew exactly how the fly felt about it. To remove its temptation to land—her dad said flies carried disease—she popped the cookie into her mouth.

The trouble was, she needed no excuse, she would have eaten it anyway. Her best friend Angela could gobble them by the ton, without gaining a pound or an inch in any direction, but all she herself had to do was look at one, and it was Fat City, every time.

Maybe when she "matured," as everyone leered, she'd thin out, grow breasts like Angela's, and turn into a princess.

First Jewish-American Princess to the planet Mars...

She stretched her arms, feeling the tension in her nipples as they strained against her shirt.

She'd mailed three picture-postcards to Angela in Switzerland already: one was of Rensselaerville, another of the Detroit docks, and the third of the courthouse in Independence, Missouri. Angela needed something to remind her of the good old USA, while she sat stuffing herself with Swiss chocolate on the porch of her father's chalet, growing skinnier and more beautiful by the hour.

Angie hadn't *really* promised to get her invited to Switzerland, and she couldn't have gone if she had. Besides, she'd rather be here than yodeling on some dumb Swiss mountain anyway.

At least, she hadn't got stuck in a stuffy cabin with her folks, for a stupid week in Maine.

She blushed, as if her dad could read her thoughts.

She dug a hole in the soft earth between her legs and buried the empty chocolate-chip cookie wrapper. Ecology...

Pops was snoring lightly. She could hear Halsey crashing through the underbrush on the other side of the river. She should whistle for him, she supposed, but she'd wake Pops, and she didn't want to do that, or he'd want to leave, and it was warm here, and nice. . . .

She studied his face. It was more deeply lined than she remembered. Last summer his hair had been gray, she was sure; now it seemed thinner, and dead white. A stray clump of it trembled in the breeze.

He grieved for Grandma, maybe even in his sleep. Awake, for sure. She felt his grief in sentences unfinished and a bleakness in his smiles.

Sometimes when she looked at him he was gone from behind his eyes.

He'd brought his guitar in the motor home, but he hadn't played it once.

Well, she missed her grandma too. Her throat grew tight.

She lay back on the moist earth, folded her hands over her tummy, placed a mental lily in them, and closed her eyes.

Where *was* Grandma, anyway? With Morgan Washburn, and Mary?

She guessed so. But where?

Everywhere? Or *no*where?

The sun was warm on her face. . . .

She awoke to a distant crashing in the underbrush. She sat up, listening hard.

She'd thought she'd heard men shouting, the creaking of wooden vehicles, and the whinny of a horse. But now there was only the crashing, through the rushes around the bend.

Halsey, probably, chasing a rabbit or a squirrel.

She whistled for him.

It was time to wake up Grandpa, or they'd never get back before dark.

For weeks they followed the thick red line on the maps, sometimes leaving the motor home and mounting the bright

62

yellow Honda to track down circled campsites, finding a few, giving up on many.

Morgan's journal, leaving Independence, spoke of fifteen, seventeen, eighteen weary miles each day, finally twenty miles one long hard stretch which consumed half of a moonlit night. He had fished the Blue on May 14, 1849; it was May 27 before he and his friend Hollister buried an Irish emigrant named Devitt on the banks of the Vermillion, one hundred and forty-four miles northwest.

In the motor home the admiral and Bunkie made it to the Vermillion in two days, ranging widely on the bike, stopping every hour or so to scout. From the Vermillion, skirting the south side of the Platte, the admiral reached Fort Kearny in less than a week: it had taken Morgan more than three.

Bunkie and the admiral climbed the cliffs at Scottsbluff, Nebraska—where Morgan had thought the jagged sandstone formation looked like "an ancient castle of the feudal times"—and cruised on U.S. 26 into Wyoming along the North Fork of the Platte. They were poking among the dusty exhibits in the sutler's shop in Fort Laramie Historical Monument ten days after they had left Independence: to get that far, Morgan and the Pioneer Line had taken six long, plodding weeks.

Since the elm on the Blue, the admiral had felt no other manifestation of Morgan's presence.

And then—eight hundred miles west of Morgan's starting point at Independence, Missouri—rising from a Wyoming plain, they found Independence Rock.

They parked in the lee of the great granite mountain, which lay like a beached whale near the banks of the Sweetwater River. They scrambled up a crack in its flank, with Halsey snuffling and barking up ahead. They were searching for a needle in a haystack. The admiral brought his camera, though he never expected to find what they sought on the vast jumbled ridge above.

But once they had made the crest, a truck-sized sandstone boulder, one of a thousand on the ridge, had drawn

63

him like a magnet. He hiked five hundred yards to reach it, into the teeth of the dry plains wind. Instantly, he found their ancestor's name, scratched in familiar Spencerian script among hundreds of others on its face: *Morgan Washburn, MD, 6 July 1849.*

He called to Bunkie, pointing. She leaped along the ridge from rock to rock. Then she stared, stretching on tiptoe to run her fingers down weathered grooves carved one hundred and thirty years before. She turned and demanded: "How did you *know*?"

Halsey whined. The admiral felt a shiver. "It's in his diary, isn't it?"

She waved her hand at the thousands of names scratched on the rocks around them. "The diary doesn't say *where*!" she insisted.

"Well, what are you trying to say?"

She looked puzzled. She was looking at him as if she'd never seen him before. "I don't know. Hey, I'm cold, you know? Let's split, OK?"

They descended and drove on. That night they parked between two ghost-shacks of the deserted South Pass City, astride the Continental Divide. Snug on the settee fronting the dinette table, they had reread the doctor's journal as wind stuttered through the clapboard relics on either side:

"At about eleven in the morning, we halted and nooned on the Sweetwater west of Independence Rock, on which, having climbed it with Mr. Hollister, I wrote my name, perhaps by way of advertisement, in large letters on a rock near the top, fully three yards high."

"See?" she trumpeted. "See? Just 'a rock near the top.'"

"Also 'three yards high,'" he reminded her uncomfortably. "Look, I just lucked out."

Her eyes were confused. "Pops," she murmured, "were you *really* never on that rock before?"

"No, Lambchop. Of course not."

She seemed frightened. He was uncomfortable himself. To change the subject, he flicked on the tube. But they were halfway between Casper, Wyoming, and Salt Lake City, two hundred miles from each and far from TV signals: he got nothing but a blue-green blur.

If he was going to ease her tension, and his own, he must do it with his own bare hands. He drew his guitar from out of the closet. He hadn't touched it since Ellen died. He tuned it swiftly.

"A little punk rock?" He smiled.

"You're kidding!"

"Yes." Bunkie—and Ellen—had always liked his folk songs: he had a good baritone for Burl Ives tunes. "What *would* you like? *The Fox He Did A-Hunting Go? Jack Was Every Inch a Sailor? Shenandoah?*"

She forced a smile and shrugged. "Whatever..."

He played them all, and discovered that he'd forgotten half the words and more than half the chords. And then he found himself playing *Green Grow the Lilacs*.

She drew close to him on the couch as he sang.

"I don't remember that one, Pops," she murmured.

"Song from the Mexican War, I think.... Morgan probably heard it all the time: *Green grow the lilacs, all sparkling with dew. I'm lonely, my darling, since parting with you....*" He strummed a little, and crooned, "*But by our next meeting I hope to prove true, and change the green lilacs to the red, white and blue.*"

He told her that the Mexicans, hearing "*Green grow...*" on the lips of every drunken invader in their steamy cantinas, had begun to call their visitors "Gringos."

He let the chords trail away, astonished. Where he'd picked up *that* gem of history, or where, in fact, he'd learned the song, he had no idea. Strange.

He felt closer to Bunkie than he had ever felt before.

"It's funny," she mused. "I like it. But it makes me feel, well, like I did on the rock."

"And how was that?" He put the guitar away. Despite his ineptitude, he felt better. He'd play her the guitar more often, now, perhaps.

"Kind of—you know—*tingly*?"

He felt more than tingly: he suddenly felt overwhelmingly closer to his gangling, Lincolnesque ancestor, who had died fifteen years before he was born.

Afterwards, as they swayed along Morgan's track through Utah and Nevada, the closeness remained. For Bunkie, too.

"Tingly," they called it, when they felt the frisson, half-pleasure, half-fear.

Fatigue, they finally decided, and too much imagination, and focusing too long upon a single task.

For he did not believe in ghosts: he wished he could.

If Morgan was somewhere, Ellen was too.

If she was, she would come, if only to his dreams, but she somehow never did.

MORGAN

ON THE SUNLIT CREST OF A PRAIRIE HILL EIGHT MILES southwest of Independence, Missouri, Morgan Washburn reined his new horse to a stop. Fluffy clouds were chasing a passing storm. He glanced down at a carefully painted sign. In red characters on a white board, it read: PIONEER LINE, LTD. TURNER, ALLEN & CO., PROPRIETORS.

Later, he would recall the neatness of the sign. Compared to every other placard he had seen on the first eight miles of the Santa Fe Trail, any of which could have been scrawled by the dunce in Mary's first-grade writing class, the sign was evidence of planning and order, and very comforting.

The camp, too, had been laid with care.

On a fine, grassy elevation to the west was a sturdy corral. In it grazed a few horses and some hundred-fifty head of Missouri mules. Below the enclosure, in two military ranks, thirty pitched tents formed a street.

Lined up at the end of the street were twenty passenger carriages. They were smaller than he had hoped, and though covered, like surreys, lacked the huge hooped canvas tops he had expected. But their wheels and iron tires seemed quite sturdy, like those on Army Dougherty wagons, which they very well might be. They were elliptically sprung, as promised. He hoped, for the sake of those who chose wagons over saddles or shanks' mare, that the springs were sturdy too.

Behind the carriages was a line of twenty-two baggage wagons, with sturdier, higher wheels and unpainted driver's boxes. Unharnessed, with their canvas-hooped tops and red wagon tongues lapping at a muddy rivulet, they seemed like huge white elephants drinking at a trickle from the earth. Months later, he would find that they were white elephants indeed....

Beyond the baggage wagons, order ceased. A larger tent—presumably containing the supplies—blocked the end of the lane of canvas. Outside, a jumble of crates and boxes and bags lay where they had been dumped by bullwhackers from the town. Somewhere in the disorder, he hoped, was his own baggage and medical kit, and Hollister's trunk and law books, drayed out from Independence some two days before.

A horse snorted behind him and Isaiah Hollister drew up alongside him on the spotted mare he had bought. The young lawyer pressed on cantle and horn, rising in the saddle to ease the pressure on his buttocks.

"Praise the Lord!" he groaned.

"That's eight miles done, Isaiah, only two thousand more to go."

He was saddle-sore himself, though born to the trotting ring and hunt. In Rensselaerville he had grown soft driving his mentor's buckboard. He had spent this morning twisting and writhing on his mount as they rode along the beautiful ridge which everyone called—apparently because the first of the three Blue rivers they would cross lay just ahead—the Blue Prairie.

They had disembarked two days before from the last of their steamboats, the sidewheeler *Consignee*, at Westport Landing. As expected, they had found the streets of Independence crammed, and California fever heavy in the air.

It had rained the day before they docked, and the muddy streets were steaming. Huge freight wagons—descendents of the Conestogas which had settled Missouri—swayed through the mire, top-heavy with canvas as ships at sea; drayers and mulesters shouted curses in a Deep South patois as foreign to their ears as Siamese.

Trains were forming up, it seemed, and leaving every hour. One bright red wagon led an endless procession of others; on its side was a banner: THE WASHINGTON CITY AND CALIFORNIA MINING ASSOCIATION; the pale faces of the association's drivers and their frightened demeanor gave them away as government clerks, more familiar with quill pens than with the bullwhips in their hands.

Wagons carried the names of towns they had never heard of before. They saw buckboards that seemed destined to collapse before they reached the River Blue, behind nags that seemed sure to die sooner, and emigrants starting with no beasts of burden at all, only handcarts.

From the Post Office, while waiting in a line of men for mail, they saw the departure of the Boston and Newton Joint Stock Association, the Mutual Protection Company, and the Social Band of Liberty. One wagon bore a banner: PATIENCE AND PERSEVERANCE; another: NEVER SAY DIE. The Dubuque Emigrating Society flew a huge American flag; the Peoria Pioneers and Springfield Rangers bore the colors of their states.

They saw a notice on the Post Office board announcing that the Western Enterprise Company was no longer taking recruits: it already comprised forty wagons, with one hundred and forty men and four women. The Granite State Company from Maine, some seventy men in gray military uniforms on horseback, on half-Spanish saddles with holstered Hawken percussion rifles and double-barreled shotguns, rode through the streets behind a blaring brass band, followed by the company's supply train, to the delight and mirth of the mule skinners lounging on the wooden sidewalks.

They watched a company of Frenchmen, formed in Paris, leave at noon, and a German company leave behind them. With each departing outfit, Morgan's impatience increased.

68

On the river they had heard that there was cholera in the town. In Morgan's judgment—though few colleagues would agree—it was likely contagious. Rather than risking contamination in the city, or reporting to camp to sleep under canvas sooner than necessary, they decided to purchase their horses immediately and find a farmhouse to lodge in for the next two days.

They bought two horses from a trader, Hollister leaning heavily on Morgan's experience as a horse breeder's son. They were roundly cheated anyway.

The purchase of Morgan's big bay, Major, had dented his poker winnings from the steamship *Michigan*: in vain had he cajoled and bargained with the spitting Missouri horse trader. The mount had cost him fifty dollars. Hollister's mare, called Jo, though a better bargain, was a smaller animal and—from the effect on Isaiah—just as roughly gaited. They bought stock saddles and tack from a saddler near the County Courthouse, and arranged for their personal baggage to be delivered to the Pioneer Line, eight miles out on the Santa Fe Trail. Through luck, they found lodging for fifty cents a night at a Mr. Caldwell's farm, half a mile from the Independence Post Office, on the outskirts of the city. Here, on Caldwell's kitchen table, while showers pounded the Santa Fe Trail to mud outside, they wrote what they assumed were their last letters from the States.

Their host's crippled mother—a brain stroke, Morgan thought—had naught to do but sit on the porch in a rocker all day long, and she had for weeks amused herself by counting the wagons pressing southwest. She told Morgan that in the last three weeks, since the appearance of spring grass had begun the great race, over two thousand wagons had passed during daylight hours: the Lord only knew how many at night.

Her statistics might not have been accurate—they seemed incredible—and they did not seem to disturb Isaiah at all, but they instilled Morgan with a sense of dread.

Following such a horde, how far from the trail would they have to forage for grass, when once the Pioneer Line began to move?

Morgan finished counting the wagons and tents in the little hollow below. He reined Major up the side of the road, breaking from its muddy bottom just as a train of Ohio men, leading their ox teams on foot, squished past. They were moving, he thought, just a little more slowly than a one-legged man might walk. The leading wagon had on its side, smeared in tar: OHIO MINING COMPANY. SACRAMENTO AND GOLD, OR BUST ON THE OREGON TRAIL.

Morgan waved down at the man guiding the leading team. The Ohioan glanced up and scowled.

It was to be a race, then, with no quarter given. Well, mules were faster than oxen, and for his two-hundred-dollar fare, he had a right to expect that those in the corral had been chosen by experts.

Starting down to the campsite, he felt a twinge of alarm at the number of roughly clad teamsters idling. Recognizable among the passengers in their new Western outfits, the teamsters seemed a robust crowd, but no one seemed in charge.

If the hares didn't move quickly, the tortoises would eat the grass.

They rode up the lane of tents, toward the larger canvas at the end, which seemed to be a sort of headquarters. Morgan saw Lieutenant Vanderveer, whom he'd avoided since the *Michigan* poker table, sitting on a wagon tongue sharpening a broad Bowie knife with a blade a full foot long. Nearby, a slender, handsome young man with chestnut eyes, well-shined boots, curly auburn hair, and a petulant frown was watching a sturdy Darkie sharpen another of similar size. Vanderveer glanced up.

"Well, Doctor! Did you bring your cards?"

"They were the *Michigan*'s cards, Lieutenant. Why?"

"We're to be messmates, I'm told: Carriage Eighteen."

Morgan's spirits plummeted. Well, there was nothing he could do about it.

Vanderveer yawned and rose. "I'll make you acquainted with Mr. Alston Oglethorpe, of Charleston: he's in our wagon, too. Mr. Oglethorpe: Dr. Washburn. And Mr. Hollister, of New York."

"My pleasure, sir," nodded Morgan.

"Mine, sir," drawled Oglethorpe. He evaluated the two with a quick look, apparently decided they were beneath his notice, and took the knife from the Negro. He moistened his thumb and tested it, shook his head and handed it back.

A body servant? On the trail?

"Where can I find Captain Turner?" asked Morgan.

The lieutenant's eyes flashed. "To try to make a change?"

"Only to pay my respects," sighed Morgan, "and to see to my medical kit."

"You'd better, and use it. Our only guide to California is dying on a plank." Vanderveer pointed his blade toward the large tan tent.

Morgan felt a chill. "Cholera?"

"The doctors are trying to decide: join your peers and cast your vote." Vanderveer grinned, but the sea-gray eyes did not lose their ice. "They seem as thick as seagulls in there, pecking at a beached blue whale."

Morgan dismounted, tethered Major to the wagon tongue, and walked into the tent.

The tent was a stuffy caldron, suffused with amber sunlight. It was jammed with crates and boxes, and barrels of salt meat and flour. In a far corner a desk had been made from a crate labeled: "BALL AMMUNITION, GUTHRIE & SON, ST. JOSEPH." Behind it sat a worried, sharp-featured man with a sandy beard, beetle brows, and a red bandana around his neck. He wore a turned-up campaign hat, pushed back; his forehead was beaded with sweat.

Morgan and Isaiah wound their way through the rubble to the desk, avoiding a teamster rolling a barrel of flour. Morgan introduced himself and Hollister to the man behind the desk.

Captain Turner regarded them wearily. "You're just in time, gentlemen. We roll at dawn."

Morgan and Isaiah counted out their remaining fare, in ten-dollar goldpieces. Morgan knew nothing of wagon trains, but the possibility of the outfit's being packed by tomorrow seemed slim. "Dawn *tomorrow*?"

"Tomorrow, yes!" He took their gold and issued vouchers, consulted a passenger manifest, and checked off their names. "Carriage Eighteen, gentlemen. I've manifested you with another New Yorker—a Navy lieutenant."

"We know," blurted Hollister. "But we had a clash with him on the Lakes. We'd like another carriage."

"A clash? Already?" Turner bristled. "Mr. Hollister, our stores from town were two weeks late; I'm told that the Blue is at flood; our accounts are in disorder; my clerk is sick. We are shy six hundredweight of hardtack and a hundredweight of salt. Seven mules are halt; the son of a bitch who sold them to us sent seven more, and *they* are splayed. My only guide is dying. I have one hundred and twenty greenhorn passengers and fifty drunken teamsters to get to California!" He picked up a soggy cigar and jammed it into his mouth. "And now you want to change your carriage!" He glanced at the manifest and shook his head. "The messes are made up; I cannot give you satisfaction. Now, would you sign the articles?"

He skidded a printed contract across the crate. Morgan picked it up. "Articles of Association and Agreement of the Pioneer Line, Ltd...." He skimmed it silently. "Teamsters will only be obliged to drive the baggage wagons.... Six passengers at most shall be assigned to each passenger wagon.... The passengers in each wagon shall form a mess.... Provisions and utensils shall be obtainable at the commissary wagon at no additional expense. ... Firewood to be gathered by the mess.... Each mess to cook its own provisions.... Each to provide from its number a driver for the team.... The mules to be harnessed by a teamster prior to the day's departure and unharnessed by a teamster for grazing at nooning and at night.... Captain Turner to have full authority in regard to choice of route, river fords, campsites, and speed of progress, as well as to assign a nightly watch over the animals."

Clauses dealing with discipline on the trail made Captain Turner a virtual dictator, but that seemed reasonable. Morgan signed the Articles. Isaiah read them and winced.

"*We* must drive? I don't know *gee* from *haw!*"

"I reckon you'll learn, Counselor," drawled Turner. He sat back, removed his cigar, and pointed it at Morgan.

"Doctor, old Black Harris is our guide: he was with Bryant in 'forty-six, you know. He's very sorely fevered. Dr. Marshall—who we're carrying free as camp physician—wants to bleed him. Dr. Cantrell is an older man. He disagrees. Where do you stand?"

"I'd have to see the patient."

Morgan disapproved of letting blood, for bleeding had been discouraged at Geneva Medical College. But good sense demanded that the practitioner take no definite stand, for patients expected to be bled by doctors, and felt cheated when they were not. To refuse to bleed a fevered patient was to risk suspicion of quackery, since only homeopaths and their ilk were reluctant to let blood.

"Will you charge for consultation?"

"Of course not," said Morgan. "He's our guide!"

Turner jabbed the cigar toward the other corner of the tent, where two frock-coated men were regarding Harris, an enormous hulk shivering under a stack of blankets. He lay on an India-rubber mattress, atop a berth made of three long boards supported on each side by steamship trunks.

A lithe, fair-haired man, even younger than Morgan, turned from the patient and introduced himself as Charles Marshall, MD. He had protruding eyes—probably a goiter—and spoke in the slurred accent of Baltimore. It had been years since Morgan had heard the familiar drawl. "And this is Dr. Cantrell," Marshall murmured. "An eclectic physician of—where, sir?"

"Saint Joe," growled the other. "Saint Joe, Missouri." He was a rotund, red-faced man with a veil of alcoholic blood vessels lacing his cheeks. His eyes were bleary; he was pocked; he smelled of tobacco, whiskey, and worse.

He had about him the air of a medicine-show charlatan. As an eclectic, he would be a follower of a school of medicine which ignored two thousand years of medical wisdom and substituted God-knew-what primitive remedies in their stead.

God help the poor wretch on the planks, with a charlatan and a man as young as Marshall meeting to decide his fate.

Still, the quack was right: the victim should not be bled.

Morgan said: "Captain Turner asked me to confer with you." He gazed down at the patient. Harris's eyes were closed and sunken. His nickname spoke of a dark complexion, but now his forehead was pale, though the rest of his skin was cyanotic. Morgan placed a hand on his brow. It was dry and hot. The smell of death was in the air, and vomit, and excrement, too.

"I'm going to bleed him," said Marshall, "when the teamsters find my lancet and cups. Dr. Cantrell can't see fit to lend me his."

"Christ," snorted Cantrell, "he's dehydrated, and he's vomited bile all afternoon, and Marshall's denied him water—"

"You'd give him *liquids*?" asked Marshall, amused. "Are you a *hydropath*, too, Dr. Cantrell?"

"I'm whatever helps my patient: hydropath, allopath, botanic, homeopath, Thomsonian. And I know when a man needs water!" Cantrell spat a stream of tobacco to the muddy ground by the pallet. He glared at Morgan. "Are you another product of some goddamn medical college?"

"Geneva," murmured Morgan, and saw relief in Marshall's eyes: the youth was unsure, and probably felt that help from regular medicine had arrived just in time. "May I examine him? For my own clinical education," he added diplomatically. "We see little of this in the Catskills."

"Now we've got the bug along, you'll see plenty on the trail," growled Cantrell.

The eclectic apparently believed, as Morgan did, in the invisible-animalcula theory of disease. Morgan had seen such tiny creatures under the microscopes of Geneva: logic told him that they might carry the sting of cholera in the very air one breathed. If so, cholera was contagious,

and did not simply issue—as conventional theory had it—
from unhealthy miasma in the earth.

"We'll leave the cholera here," scoffed Marshall, "in
the mud."

Morgan envied him his faith in dogma. There were
advantages in believing that diseases were noncontagious;
perhaps that was why the miasmatic theory anchored
modern medicine to the past. He took a deep breath, held
it, and bent over the pallet.

Harris was a full three hundredweight; the planks sagged
beneath him; the blankets fell short of their task. Morgan
took his wrist: ninety-five pulsations per minute. His thermometer was in his kit, but he knew the man's temperature was above a hundred degrees. "Cramps?" Morgan
asked Marshall.

"Yes, sir," drawled Marshall. "At first he was cold. I
applied a hot poultice of cornmeal, mustard, and cayenne
peppers with good results. I purged him with jalap, sixty
ounces. And ipecac, as well: another sixty. Calomel, thirty
grains." Morgan winced at the enormous dosage, but Marshall didn't notice. "He salivated well. He vomited and
defecated perhaps a pint."

"What was the appearance of the stool?"

"Rice water."

"And his urine?"

"None."

"Cholera," agreed Morgan. Oliguria—cessation of kid-
ney function—was the final sympton. He glanced at Cantrell, who was chewing at his plug.

"Brilliant," the older doctor snorted, jetting another
stream, "since there's a hundred cases in town. It's cholera, all right. But the reason he ain't pissing is he's had
no goddamn water. He's dry as a dead squaw's cunt, and
now you want to take his blood."

Harris began suddenly to writhe, and the steamer trunks
creaked. Marshall pulled a railroad watch from his vest
and took the man's pulse. "Ninety-five pulsations the minute," he announced. "I'm going to *find* that lancet, and
let sixteen ounces."

"You'll find *my* kit just outside, to the right of the

75

entrance," said Morgan. "Black, with the name Washburn. I have cups and a lancet, newly sharpened."

"I thank you, sir, I'll find it." The young man left swiftly.

The older doctor regarded Morgan with disgust. "Lancets and cups. No leaches, Doctor? Why not?"

Morgan held up his hand. "Steady, sir, steady. What do you think of a little placebo? For the attending physician?"

Cantrell's bushy brows creased. "What do you mean?"

"Well, my kit's brown, not black; he'll never find it in the mess out there. Get us some water, but first, *your* lancet, please?"

A smile broke on the doctor's face. He drew a California Bowie knife from a scabbard at his belt, handed it to Morgan, scooped a bandage from his kit. Morgan wiped the knife on the bandage, drew a shallow incision on Harris's forearm which hardly broke the skin, and bandaged it.

"Would you say I'd let sixteen ounces?" he asked.

"I'd say anything, son, but you'll find we're far too late." He found a canteen and handed it to Morgan.

Cradling the dying man's head on one hand, Morgan touched the canteen to his lips. Harris gagged at the water, and Morgan moistened his lips with a finger. He felt the lips moving, trying to talk, but he could not hear what Harris was trying to say. He bent his ear to the old man's mouth, to catch the words.

"You are *late*," he heard. "The snows, the *snows*... Saddle your mules, and ride like *hell*."

A shudder ran down the gross body. Morgan heard the rattle of death, closed the eyelids, and straightened. He found anger, and a touch of agony, in the charlatan's bloodshot eyes.

"Mr. Turner," Cantrell called across the tent. "I'm sorry. Mr. Harris is gone."

Turner and Isaiah hurried over. Turner took his guide's hand in his own. "I knew he'd go."

"Your company physician made sure of it," muttered Cantrell. "Marshall killed him, that popeyed son of a bitch!"

76

"Cholera killed him," Morgan said charitably. "We all lose patients."

"*Mine* die of their disease, not my treatment." Cantrell put his knife back in the holster, turned, and stomped away.

Turner folded the guide's arms across his chest and returned to his desk. He asked Isaiah if the company articles would bind those who had already signed if he simply scratched out Harris's name as guide and substituted his own.

"Certainly: you're a proprietor; anyway, outside the States there'll be no law at all, save articles like these. What will it matter west of the Blue?"

It mattered to Morgan, legalities or not. Substitution of a name hardly qualified a man as a wagon master. Harris had been advertised as a trail scout with the Bryant-Russell party of '46. He wondered what experience "Captain" Turner had: had he been west at all?

But it seemed quite impolite to ask: besides, everyone had a copy of Clayton's *Emigrants' Guide to California*, and Bryant's as well, and with two thousand wagons ahead of them, they could hardly lose their way.

"Tomorrow," said Turner, "we'll not roll. We'll stay for services."

This, Morgan didn't like at all. He had read in the New York *Herald*, three years ago, accounts of the Donner Party, trapped on a Sierra pass by early snow, and turning to cannibalism to survive. "Your guide would have had it otherwise, sir." He repeated Harris's deathbed warning, to saddle and ride like hell.

"We'll stay," snapped Turner, "and bury him properly!"

"Yes, Captain," sighed Morgan.

Turner was probably right. On a journey that might take sixty days, one more could hardly matter.

He left to find his baggage in the jumble by the tent.

THE ADMIRAL

THE ADMIRAL QUAKED AT THE SIDE OF THE HIGHWAY, trying to stiffen his knees. The shotgun prodded him closer to the ditch. Halsey's dulled eye stared up from below. Faintly he could hear Bunkie, still screaming and crying in the cab of the motor home.

He heard a shell slam into the chamber. His vision blurred. He had an absurd impulse to clean his glasses.

He turned from the ditch and summoned a last plea to the big Mexican. "Look, my granddaughter . . . Let her go!"

"Lo siento mucho, abajo, ahora. No comprendo inglés. . . ."

The Mexican spoke no English. The admiral groped for the word for "granddaughter." *Nieta!* Panic engulfed him: when he tried to get the word out, he found his mouth too dry.

"¡Andale! ¡Ahora!" muttered the Mexican. His face was twisted and strained. He jabbed him again with the muzzle.

This was it then.

Bastards, animals! Sorry, Bunkie, Kelly, Howard . . .

"Miguel!" the blond man called from the van. "Ven acá. ¡Ayúdame, ahora mismo!"

"Come here, help me. Quick!"

Braced on the edge of eternity, the admiral managed a glance. The bearded man stood in the open side door.

In his arms he cradled a woman, in a long skirt and a man's white shirt; her shoulder was stained with blood.

The Mexican moved to the van, leaned the weapon against it. Carefully, the bearded man kneeled to hand the woman down. The Mexican handled her tenderly, his face a mask of grief.

"Mi pobre hermanita, chiquita mía..." he groaned. And to the bearded man, in Spanish: "She is worse, man! What are we going to do?"

The answer came in almost perfect Spanish: "We're moving as fast as we can." The bearded one dropped lightly from the van and took her from the Mexican. He looked into her face, touched his lips to her forehead, cradled her head to his chest. The admiral glimpsed his face, worried and distraught. The girl's straight white teeth were bared in a grimace and her dark eyes clouded with pain. For a moment they focused on him.

"Jeff," she moaned, "to kill *another* man? Ees no good!"

"Jesus, Terry, what can I do?"

Through all the admiral's flying life, when he had need, action had somehow preceded thought, as if there were powers beyond himself to draw on, in extremis.

He squinted at the girl, through dust turned golden by the setting sun. From somewhere out of the chaos of anger and fear, a lie came to his lips.

"Look, I can *help* her!" he called.

The bearded man—Jeff?—flashed him a glance. "How are *you* gonna help her?"

His tongue felt thick. "Doctor!" he managed. "I'm a doctor."

There was a long silence. In the distance he could hear the rumble of a jet, and the far blast of its afterburner as the pilot sported over Fallon Naval Air Station, miles ahead.

"¿Cómo? ¿Qué es eso?" asked the Mexican.

"¡Es médico!" cried the girl.

"Horseshit!" Jeff said, starting toward the motor home.

"Un momento," called Miguel. "¿Qué tipo de médico?" *"What kind of doctor?"*

Jeff paused uncertainly. The admiral held his tongue. The less they knew about his Spanish, the better.

"OK, what *kind* of doctor?" growled the bearded man.

"Navy!" His mouth was dry, his tongue felt swollen. "Flight surgeon!"

"¡Cirujano, Miguel!" the girl explained. "¡Un *cirujano*!"

The blond man's eyes were slits against the sun. "You're a *surgeon*?"

"Navy surgeon, rear admiral, retired," he managed. "You got my wallet."

No "medical corps" on his ID, of course, and the Naval Academy ring, already in the bearded man's pocket, was obviously no doctor's. He hoped that they knew nothing of Annapolis or the Navy; anyway, every moment he could stay alive meant a better chance for Bunkie.

He saw hope on the Mexican's face, and the girl's, and the bearded man seemed suddenly thoughtful.

Where is hope, is life...

The bearded young man studied him. The admiral looked into his face. He had spent his life leading younger men, and had thought he knew them well.

Not this one, though: cold sapphire eyes, rimmed with fatigue, and nothing beyond to read.

A crow squawked from a telephone line above. To the west, the jet was pulling an orange contrail across the darkening sky. The girl's eyelids closed, and her breathing became shallow and hurried. The bearded man stood lost in thought.

"Jeff," breathed the Mexican, "¡No comprendo! ¿Hay problema?"

"¡No hay problema, amigo!" And suddenly, to the admiral: "You waiting for fucking sideboys? Climb aboard, you're coming, too."

Dizzy with relief, sick with fear, and under the gun of the Mexican, the admiral led Jeff and the girl inside.

Bunkie sat rigidly in the passenger's seat. He must somehow alert her to back up his lie, but he saw no chance now. He helped Jeff lay the girl down on his double bed in the stateroom aft, made Navy-taut this morning by Bunkie and himself. The Mexican brought aboard a suitcase and the red gas can and took the driver's seat. The admiral swayed as the motor home lurched onto the highway, past the abandoned van.

Under Jeff's eye, he raised the girl's wrist to feel her pulse.

He did not know what else to do.

MORGAN

A HORSE WHINNIED FROM SOMEWHERE ACROSS THE moonlit campground, and the tent flap rustled in the prairie wind.

The Pioneer Line had not moved one foot, and Morgan Washburn was writing in his diary by candlelight.

He had a cold from sleeping on damp ground last night. He coughed and dabbed at his nose with his red kerchief. He lay huddled on his left side, to leave his writing hand free. His writing slab was braced against his medical kit. His inkwell was perched on a prairie clod; the flame of his candle was sheltered against the draft by a row of medicine jars.

He shivered under his blanket, and his left shoulder ached from bracing his upper body, but he persisted at his journal, for tomorrow—"Captain" Turner willing— they would be embarked on the Great Adventure. Because his reasons for the trek were so ephemeral, he felt the need to write about it to give it substance, as he would meticulously keep the medical history of a patient who might die. But unless the writing of it was tackled night by night, he knew that the journal would flicker and go out.

Tonight, he hoped, was the last they would spend in their gathering place; disbeliever in the miasmatic theory of cholera though he was, he was beginning to agree with Dr. Marshall that the campsite was tainted. Who could really know?

They had buried poor Black Harris two days before. Today one "California Bob," a mule skinner, had been laid away with considerably less ceremony. Because California Bob claimed to have traveled the California road with Sublette in '26, Morgan had hoped that he might take Harris's place. Now they would be led by a man who—rumor had it—had no more knowledge of the trail than the greenest of his passengers.

Captain Turner had promised that today they would "roll" after the services, but the promise had come to naught.

He sighed and wrote the reasons why: *The business of "hitching up," as it is termed, commenced at nine o'clock this morning but owing to the difficulties of harnessing one hundred and fifty mules for the first time, it was not completed till late in the evening. Nearly every animal was caught with the lasso and choked down, harnessed by our teamsters—and some of the rest of us—with main strength and placed before the wagons, there to perform sundry feats that would astonish any but a juggler or one accustomed to ground and lofty tumbling. After sundry mishaps such as breaking wagon tongues, harnesses, etc., it being too dark to "roll" by then, and the moon not yet up, we at length unharnessed all and settled to camp for yet another night.*

The decision to wait yet another day was made by Captain Turner. Our first business in this mess thereafter was to satisfy the cravings of appetite, the ration having been packed at the bottom of supply wagons in anticipation of our departure. One would think that with two hundred pounds of flour, three hundred pounds of pilot bread, seventy-five pounds of bacon, ten pounds of rice, five pounds of coffee, two pounds of tea, twenty-five pounds of sugar, half a bushel of dried beans, one bushel of dried fruit, two pounds of saleratus, ten pounds of salt, half a bushel cornmeal and another half bushel parched and ground corn, half a bushel of onions, and a small keg of vinegar being carried for each man jack in our wagon train, we could easily have found sustenance. Such was not the case. All was stowed too neatly to be easily unearthed.

Nevertheless, after an hour's delay we succeeded to the number of four in procuring some coffee, bacon, pilot bread, and sugar. One of our number—Lieutenant V, whom I do not much like—soon levied upon a fence rail with which a fire was kindled and culinary operations commenced. Another hour and we were seated, as on the preceding night, in a circle around our humble supper, eating by a newly risen moon the fruits of our own cooking. No useless table was spread. The Earth is to be our future bed, seat, and table, and we reclined upon her bosom. We partook of our creature comforts with a relish that in our former plentiful hours was wholly unknown.

He closed the journal and took out a flimsy sheet of tissue, to finally write his love her last letter before leaving the States. A teamster returning a wagon to Independence for repairs would mail it. Morgan was already growing short of stationery, for he liked writing letters to Mary as much as he hated keeping the diary.

He began with the happy news that he had received a packet of letters from her, by standing for an hour in one line at the Independence Post Office to find his name on a list tacked to the door, and then in another line for two hours to pick up his mail.

You can imagine with what alacrity I repaired to my lodgings, my precious bundle clutched to my heart, and with what glorious appetite I consumed their contents, and what strange passions entered my heart when I learned that you had miraculously converted your father to the cause of ladies in medicine. So you will leave in autumn? I am not sure that I wish you to be so far from his hearth as Philadelphia, even though you reside with your grandma, but so long as the "Female Medical College" there confines itself to admitting students of the more "delicate" sex, I suppose I have no cause to fear that some young Aesculapian disciple will try to steal you away. Only remember that in a year at the most I shall return to get you, ready or not. Plan your lectures accordingly, for if I have my way, and all goes well, you will not finish.

He followed with a piece of local news: Niles Searls, a balding, bearded young lawyer who had left Rensselaerville to seek a greener pasture than upstate New York, had tried to start a practice in Missouri, and had given up.

He begs me convey to you and your parents his great affection, and asks you to tell all that he kept a law office here in Missouri, but the town he chose was not large enough to hold his shingle, and the law office did not keep him. He has concluded to get rich with the rest of us in California. You must know by now that his cousin Charlie Mulford, too, has joined him here as well. They have been billeted in another carriage.

There seem as many men of the law in this migration as doctors, of whom it is now said, "there are so many that two must ride on one horse." So California will be as well-stocked with legal and medical knowledge as our Rensselaerville river is with fish, and those whom Hollister or Searls do not get hanged, I'll doubtless kill with care.

He yawned and put down the pen. The prairie breeze was worrying the tent flap: a beam of moonlight wandered across the blanketed mounds. It brought to mind the spotlight worked by amateurs in the stage productions at the Lyceum at home. He remembered last season's offering: Mowatt's *Fashion*, starring Mary: he had played the Lyceum Society's portable grand from the orchestra pit between acts.

Mary had been curtsying to tumultuous applause in her second curtain call, only to have her moment of glory snatched away by Lowell Tomkins, tipsy as usual, when he knocked over the reflector he was directing from the footlights at her face.

You should know, Mary, that here on the edge of the States lies one whose admiration for your Thespian talents exceeds what he can express, and who places you on the immortal dais on which trod the Bard and now treads famed Montez; one who believes that had it not

been for our cloddish friend, you might even now be strid-
ing the New York boards instead of longing to follow the
vilified Elizabeth Blackwell into my own profession, so
bleak with tears and heavy with fruitless pain.

You will wonder why our little stage play Fashion *came*
to mind, here on the outermost edge of civilization. Well,
it was an errant moonbeam, searching out the bodies of
my prone comrades, and it recollected not only that stage
play and your part in it, but other moonlit things as well,
on which we shall not dwell.

Moonlit things? Passionate trysts under the cherry tree
while her parents slept, wild kissings on a horse-blanket
spread between the roots—all spiced deliciously with fear.

He assessed the possibility of the letter falling into the
hands of her parents. Of her father, he had no doubts; he
was too honorable to read a single line. But women were
women, curious as rabbits: if Mary's mother suspected
their meetings it would break her grand old heart.

The hell with it. The letter was meant for Mary; he
would speak of what he would.

He heard someone near the tent flap stumble to his
feet. The flap rustled as he left. An interminable stream
of urine began to splatter on the doughy sod outside.

Someone had drunk too much whiskey, or had a bad
prostate; Morgan continued with his writing but changed
the subject, as if the man outside were desecrating their
love.

You will wonder who my companions are. Well, our
mess is made up, with two possible exceptions—one, a
naval officer, the second the handsome scion of an old
Charleston family—of fine men.

Of Mr. Hollister I have already written. Benjamin Stein
is a young Jewish saddler of Manhattan who, though a
member of the "lost tribes," seems a well-spoken, edu-
cated man.

We have in our mess an older doctor from Missouri,
named Cantrell, who may be of the allopathic persuasion,
or perhaps an eclectic or homeopath—I can never keep
those sects straight. I judge him over forty years of age.
He may be a quack, but he appears to have more medical
experience than our "official" camp doctor from Balti-

more, or another doctor I shall not name, who worships an angel in a small Catskillian town.

The young southern prince, Mr. Alston Oglethorpe, is an aristocrat, genus Carolinus. *He is a fop, and the genuine article, as I might myself have been, had I not had the proud fortune to fall into the hands of so beautiful a princess of the North. He has, like the rest of us, purchased a wide hat, flannel shirt, sturdy pantaloons and boots, and goes armed to the teeth, but he brings with him scented kerchiefs and his body servant, Joshua. The latter is a fine-looking Darkie who, since he cannot by his master's edict ride with us, presumably will trudge like an extra mule in our dust for the next two thousand miles. Mr. Oglethorpe intends to hire him out in the mines, but Joshua has been taught to read and write, and will, Hollister and I hope, bid adieu to his servitude the moment his foot touches land beyond the States.*

My messmates seem intelligent, and—with those same maritime and princely exceptions—moral men; enterprising, industrious persons who, if spared to reach California, will turn their time to good account.

So I might have done worse....

The tent flap moved. Silhouetted in the entrance was Cantrell, buttoning his long underwear. One of the mounds near the entrance came to life: Morgan caught the glint of a pistol barrel in the moonlight. Vanderveer's voice cut harshly across the tent.

"Hold!"

The stocky doctor froze. "What the hell—"

"*Hold*, sir! Who is it? Cantrell?"

"Put that down or I'll shove it up your ass!"

Morgan saw the lieutenant tense. "I doubt that. Still, my apologies. I sleep lightly."

"Save your goddamn heroics for the Pawnees," the doctor growled, crawling under his blanket. "We're not yet past the Blue."

Heart thumping, Morgan lay back. What a fine tidbit of news for Mary, to find a character from the infamous *Somers* hanging, haunted by phantoms in the night: the very stuff of a drama for the Rensselaerville Theatrical Arts Society.

Still, he had better not mention it. Such hair-trigger antics, by one he'd travel with so long, would only worry her.

My candle flickers, and I cannot tell if my pen makes a mark. Yours in friendship, love, and truth ... Morgan.

He folded his letter, blew out the candle, and fell into miserable sleep.

He awakened at dawn. His cold was worse. The hitching-up began again, more practiced now. A cold northeast wind was blowing; he feared that if the showers it brought continued through the night, their tent would be inundated.

He was called to the commissary tent. On the same rude wooden bunk which had held poor Harris, their commissary, a Mr. Falkner, lay. Cholera, again, and he had been suffering secretly from it since yesterday morning.

And handling all their food, with the teamsters who assisted him.

He was loaded into the sick-wagon, for today, according to Turner, they would "roll, come Hell or high waters." Morgan returned to the tent to find it struck, and their carriage hitched. Their two mules, one old and experienced, the other young and hysterical, were jostling each other.

The carriage bed was strewn with bedding, and his medical kit took so much space that he decided to ride his horse. Cantrell and Vanderveer were both big men, and Oglethorpe was carrying far too much personal gear. Joshua lounged nearby; he would begin and end afoot.

A pelting shower began. The carriage covers leaked. Books, papers, guns, coats, and baggage were soaked; the Pioneer Line seemed bogged in mud, and had not moved an inch.

"Roll!" shouted a thin voice from far ahead.

Through the mire, a certain marching order began to take form. The baggage wagons led, tall ships of the prairie, formed in column like men-of-war; the passenger carriages followed, their fringe-topped covers flapping in the gale.

No other trains had passed their campground for a full forty-eight hours. There were surely many more to come, the Pioneer Line *could* not be the last. Still, as far as the eye could see, there were none, and Morgan's stomach sank.

They rolled, the passenger carriages bringing up the rear in ludicrous style. At one moment, from his mount, Morgan imagined a funeral procession; the next moment, looking back, he observed that some team, enraged at the task ahead, had plunged ahead and caused a rout.

He saw one of his fellow travelers, terrified at a burst of sudden speed, dive from a carriage and hit the ground, rolling; he arose, shaking himself, and proceeded on foot. Before they even reached the first gentle rise, and were still in sight of the abandoned campground, a baggage wagon, with the gale bellying its great white top like a sail, broke a tongue and limped to the side of the road.

The beginning was laughable and too tragic to bear. But when the last thunderclap sounded and the clouds scudded past, the sky turned deep blue, and the plains came to life.

As far westward as his eyes could see stretched the golden, rolling prairie.

He could see a line of cottonwood on the horizon, and stately elms besides. The Blue, and the end of the States, lay ahead. There were fish, doubtless, in the river and game on the bottomland.

He borrowed Stein's Jennings repeating rifle and found his angling gear in his baggage on the floor of the carriage. He set off at a trot, with Hollister alongside grunting at every jolt.

Morgan kicked Major into a canter and let out a long, warbling whoop of joy.

He was free, and young; his cold had left.

He was California-bound.

THE ADMIRAL
AND BUNKIE

THE ADMIRAL FOUGHT TO KEEP HIS BALANCE IN THE swaying motor home: the Mexican was driving too fast. Good: maybe he'd draw a cop.

Oncoming headlights slashed through the compartment, painting a deathmask on the young woman's face. He lurched as the motor home swerved in the slipstream of a truck, and grabbed the partition between the sleeping compartment and the toilet.

The admiral studied her. In the orange glow of the reading lamp, she was very pretty and very young: Jeff had said nineteen. She was sleeping, now, or comatose: there was an innocence on her lips that moved him deeply, despite all.

Jeff was braced in the toilet. Through the open door, the admiral could see him shaving, hear his own electric razor snarling as it chewed at the golden beard.

His anger flared: *nobody* used his razor. The arrogant son of a bitch....

He assessed his chances of jumping him while he shaved: the .45 lay on the top of the medicine cabinet: if he slugged him from behind, maybe he could reach it in the scuffle.

Ridiculous. He hadn't struck a blow in forty years: God knew how much his reflexes had slowed. If the gun went off, there was Bunkie. Jeff was a good thirty years younger and almost as tall as he, and his chest muscles strained at the blue-denim shirt. Somewhere he'd been pumping iron, and showed it in every move.

My God, he thought, *I'm cracking up: he could bench-press me to the overhead. He's slaughtered Halsey, threatened Bunkie, scared me halfway to another heart attack, and I'm going to jump him for using my razor?*

His judgment had already failed him once today, which is why the man was even here.

Age, pride, and forty years of privilege were his enemies, insidious as germs: if he were to save Bunkie, he must purge them here and now. At sixty-one, it was time to learn caution, or die.

The woman—Terry?—began to whimper, fighting pain. Suddenly she shrieked.

"¿Qué pasa?" yelled Miguel from the front. The Winnebago swayed, and found the road again.

The razor stopped. Jeff yelled in Spanish, ordering Miguel to keep his eyes on the road. Then he loomed in the doorway of the toilet. His face was shadowed.

"What's wrong?"

"Well, pain!" The admiral laid a hand on her forehead. It was clammy and cold. He would have to look at the wound now, and the thought scared him. "When was she shot?" he asked: it sounded professional, and it killed time.

Jeff rubbed his chin. "Around two-thirty."

"This afternoon?"

"Yeah, this afternoon!" The man was very jumpy.

"With what?" The question seemed appropriate, and he kept his voice as calm and reassuring as he could.

"Thirty-eight special, probably. Maybe a magnum."

It sounded as if she'd been shot by a cop. Jesus, why?

"By whom?" His heart began to beat harder.

"NHP."

Nevada Highway Patrol. He took a deep breath. He had to know.

"Why?"

Jeff's face froze. "We ran a light, man. What the fuck do *you* care?"

He shrugged. He could delay no longer.

He had a weak stomach for blood. In his youth, when

his father had done minor operations in the ancient surgery, he had abandoned the house like a place of plague. He had seen plenty of wounded men, at sea, but had always managed to avoid watching their treatment.

He had never seen a seriously injured woman in his life.

She opened her eyes and began to moan. He placed a hand on her forehead again. He recalled from somewhere that the coolness meant that she was in shock.

She looked at him. Her face relaxed. She stopped whimpering. She even smiled, faintly.

"Water, OK?" she pled. "I am thirsty."

An alarm went off in his head, from first aid at the Academy, flight school, or a lecture by a flight surgeon in some forgotten ready room. If she had a stomach wound, no water. But he didn't know where the wound even was, as yet.

"Later, OK?"

He took a deep breath, peeled down the blanket.

Her shirt was stained with blood, but there was little on the sheets. The bleeding might have stopped.

Clumsily, he unbuttoned her shirt, carefully pulling aside the stiffened material. She wore no bra.

He almost groaned aloud.

Below a beautifully sculptured breast, a single crinkled wound oozed blood. Above the entry hole a massive bruise was spreading toward her left shoulder: it seemed to turn darker in color as he looked.

She moved her left arm and screamed.

"Where?" he asked. "Where does it hurt?"

"My shoulder. Ees up there!"

With a shaking finger she pointed to her left shoulder. But the wound was far from there, below the breast. Nerve damage? He had heard of phantom pain, but that was from amputations. The bullet must be lodged above the collarbone.

He was afraid to roll her over to look for an exit wound. He had no bandages, no antibiotics in the motor home; nothing but Bufferin for a hangover.

He pulled the blanket up again.

* * *

Bunkie tried to stop her hands from shaking.

She could not.

She glanced at the big man beside her. He took his eyes from the road, looked at her and shook his head sadly, then gave his attention to the driving once again.

He did not seem as dangerous as the bearded one, but he had been ready to shoot her grandfather, shoot him as they'd shot Halsey....

Was Halsey dead in the ditch? She could not bear the thought. Or wounded, and hurting, and wondering why she'd left?

With his funny pink tongue lolling and the warm, soft spot that he loved to have her rub—just over his ear— perhaps all smeared with blood?

She began to cry. The big man—Mexican, she thought—looked at her swiftly, his brow all wrinkled, as though he were embarrassed.

She hated him. She hated the other man—who seemed to be telling this one what to do—worse. When they had seemed to be ready to shoot her grandfather, she had screamed and screamed at them and neither had even looked.

Halsey, Halsey, Halsey...

She was more frightened than she had ever been, and could not seem to stop sobbing. She turned. She could see the blond man standing in the passageway, and her grandfather leaning over the bed where they had put the lady.

She wanted her grandfather's arms about her, and his soft voice crooning that Halsey would be all right, that *they* would be all right....

She needed her grandfather more than the woman did. Why didn't he come to her?

She lurched out of her seat. The Mexican reached across and gently pushed her back. The motor home swerved. She struggled, and the pressure increased.

"I want to go *back*!" she insisted. "You can't—"

"Lo siento, señorita," he said. "No comprendo inglés."

"I want—"

"No!" he growled, and shoved her back more roughly.

Heart beating, she collapsed, crying angrily in her seat.
If he couldn't even understand her, what was she supposed to do?

The admiral hung to the doorjamb outside the sleeping compartment, steadying himself against the sway, and forced himself to hold Jeff's icy gaze.

"OK, Doc. What do you think?"

He braced himself. "That we have to get her to a hospital, of course."

"No!" cried the girl, eyes snapping open. She reached up with her good arm and grabbed his wrist. Her grip was surprisingly strong. "¡De ninguna manera!"

"Never . . ."

He spread his hands. "I'd need X rays, anesthesia, scalpel, probes, forceps, an assistant."

She struggled to sit up, eyes on Jeff. "¡Tu promesa, Jeff! Hospital, no! You said we will never—" Her eyes flicked to the admiral, and she finished in Spanish: "¡Hospital, no! No más policía. Estás libre. No más cárcel. Viviremos en la meseta en Ipala—"

"Your promise . . . No hospital, no cops, you are free now, no more jail! We'll live on the cliff in Ipala—"

"Cool it," Jeff said sharply.

She shook her head stubbornly. "Ipala, o nada. Ipala, o prefiero morir."

"Ipala, or nothing. Ipala, or I'd rather die."

"I said *cool* it, OK?"

Where the hell was Ipala? The admiral wished she had not mentioned it.

Anyway, now he knew why they were running. Not a robbery, or gang shoot-out, but a prison break. From where? Battle Mountain Jail, or Winnemucca? Elko? Or across the line in Utah?

Jeff was watching him carefully. The admiral kept his face impassive, peeled down the blanket, and began gently to touch—"palpate" was the word, he thought—the flesh around the wound. It was swollen and tight, and he could tell nothing from it, but his action looked professional, and did not seem to hurt her.

He straightened, arching his back. "Hospital," he insisted.

"You heard her."

"I don't speak Spanish."

Jeff flashed him a look. "Well, she says no hospital. She said it, she means it. Get that bullet out if you can. Keep her going to Tijuana, if you can't. But no fucking hospital."

The admiral's mind raced. There was a way, perhaps, to save her life and free Bunkie. The Navy took care of its own. If he could get them on home ground, entice them through the Air Station gates at Fallon, he'd be bound to get a message through to someone, and they would save the woman as well.

Anyway, he could try: "OK. No *civilian* hospital. But there's a Naval Air Station at Fallon, just ahead. No cops, I'll guarantee it. I'll get her into the dispensary."

"Sure you will!" Jeff smiled coldly. The admiral knew instantly that he'd made a mistake. "She's your dependent! Hey, your daughter?" He snapped his fingers. "No, there's that damn *cholo* accent.... Hey! *Wife*, maybe! The peso's down, you bought her in Mexico!"

The admiral felt himself blushing. He had underestimated Jeff, spoken without thinking. Careful, careful...

"OK, OK. Maybe not."

Jeff grabbed his arm. He had a grip like a pro linebacker. "*Why* not? You're an admiral! In the medical corps? Some j.g. doctor going to question you? You got a beano wife, she wasn't cherry, so you shot her. Perfectly normal! They'll call it a hunting accident."

"I told you, I wasn't thinking."

They hit a bump and both men left the floor. "¡Más despacio!" Jeff yelled, trying to slow him down.

"Hay que llevarla al pueblo."

Her brother wanted to get her into town.

"¡Más despacio!" insisted Jeff. "¡La policía!" He turned slowly and grabbed the admiral's shirt. "You son of a bitch," he said softly. "No matter *what* you told them at Fallon, in *ten minutes* that Air Station would be asshole-deep in cops. And Admiral?"

"Yes?" he murmured.

"The problem is, you *know* it." He shoved him forward, hurtling him into a chair, following to tower above him, pistol poised to club him, eyes blazing. "I ought to—"

"El pueblo," Miguel called back. "Fallon!"

"OK, ¡alto!" Jeff yelled forward. The motor home slowed and drew to the side of the highway. "Now Doctor, or Admiral, or whatever the hell they call you, *you* are going to drive through town." He tossed him back his wallet. "We'll be in back. My gun'll be on the kid. If we hit a roadblock, you haven't seen a thing. We get stopped, you talk us through. *No* talking to the kid, but she stays up front."

The admiral stumbled forward and slid into the driver's seat.

Bunkie felt tears of relief come to her eyes. At least her grandfather was where she could see him. "Pops—" she began.

"Shh! Don't talk!" he murmured. He fumbled with his seatbelt, mumbling quickly, between stiff lips: "They think I'm a *surgeon*, Navy flight surgeon, understand?"

She stared at him. "No. Is Halsey—"

"Understand?" he muttered tightly. "I'm a doctor! Bunkie?"

She nodded. "OK. *OK!*" Fear flooded her. Why couldn't he comfort her? Instead of mumbling? "Halsey?" she whispered. "Was he ... dead?"

"Yes, my darling." He had never used the term with her, and it scared her more than anything that had happened. "Yes, he was."

A great sadness grabbed her throat. "Oh, God ... Are they going to kill *us*?"

She felt him squeeze her hand, as sneakily as a boy had once in a science movie when he thought he had the chance. "No, Bunkie. We're going to be OK."

She felt something cold on the back of her neck. She realized suddenly what it was and turned rigid in fear.

It was the muzzle of the blond man's automatic. He was looming in the darkness behind them.

"I said, *no* talking," growled the man. "Now, drive!"

"Put that thing down!" ordered her grandfather, in his sharp Navy voice.

To her shock and amazement, the gun stayed where it was.

Carefully, as if fearing to jar it, her grandfather pulled onto the highway, back to the Emigrant Trail.

Bunkie sat frozen in terror, staring straight ahead.

MORGAN

MORGAN WASHBURN, MD, RODE UP A GENTLE RISE, reined Major to a stop, and shifted his weight. He remained saddle sore; every time the skin between his thighs would heal, it would rain again and his trousers would get soaked and the pommel would chafe his legs. Stein, the swarthy, gentle little Manhattan saddler, had inspected the cheap Missouri saddle and decided that Morgan had been bilked.

This afternoon Morgan had ranged alone a good five miles ahead of the Pioneer train, playing scout and wanting to be first to catch a glimpse of Fort Kearny.

He seldom rode in the carriage anymore. Two days past the Blue, in a rattling hailstorm, the train had stampeded. The wagon overturned when the younger mule bolted and the elder, caught unaware, had been forced to run too. Stein had dropped the reins. Their old mule had finally fallen in the traces; the rig had capsized, spilling gear and bodies into a draw on the side of the road. The wagon top was destroyed.

There seemed no time, skill, or tools to rebuild it, so they had simply righted the vehicle, tossed their bedrolls into the wagonbed, spread the seat cover over it, and lay on top, trying to turn aside the mirth of the other messes by ridiculing them for riding like monkeys in cages.

No one had suffered injury in the accident, except for poor Stein, and that was from being hit in the right hand by a hailstone the size of a musketball; it had actually broken the third metacarpal, which Morgan had set and splinted.

Stein was an uncomplaining, cheerful traveler, but the hand seemed unlikely to heal for weeks, and in the meanwhile, it meant one less passenger to share the cooking and the driving.

The topless wagon, with Oglethorpe's poor slave Joshua limping in its dust, remained a famous shambles in the train: the "Punch & Judy" bunch.

As for Morgan, he was tired of being laughed at, jostled, seared by the sun, caked by the dust, and half-drowned by the rain. Except when it was his turn to drive the wagon, he preferred to ride Major and suffer his saddle sores, or walk and endure blisters.

Now he rose in his stirrups and shaded his eyes against the setting sun. He discerned sod buildings, set on a little rise a mile south of the Platte, five miles away. The settlement slept in the golden haze stirred by another laggard train, which had passed them after dawn. Drawn up beneath the fort were scores of wagons; dimly, he could see the dust cloud hovering over stock being driven to the Platte for water and to forage.

The outpost, by the look of it, was ugly and rude. It was the last "civilization" they were likely to see for months, the only settlement east of Laramie, which, so far as he knew, was not even yet an Army post, but still belonged to the American Fur Company.

Fort Kearny, according to Bryant's bible of the Emigrant Trail, was manned by two hundred soldiers. For a year it had been in the process of erection by Regular Army troops, sent to "protect" the Oregon emigrants from Pawnees farther down the trail.

Rumors from discouraged travelers, heading back

against the stream, had it that the fort's sutler was short of supplies and was overcharging emigrants; that soldiers were deserting en masse for the goldfields; that the Pawnees were stealing horses within sight of the half-finished sentry towers.

He flicked the reins on Major's neck. Major sighed and started down the rise. Even the smell of the Platte, which they'd skirted for weeks, seemed not to inspire him: he had proved a fine and faithful mount, but was as road weary as his master.

Morgan sniffed the wind. A city of bulbous clouds, rotund as Persian mosques, was building in the southeast. Christ! Not rain, again....

The violence of summer storms on the gently rolling plains still surprised him. Over and over during the past weeks, he had awakened to cold northeast winds, seen the thunderheads march down, and endured their onslaught, first with amazement, then with anger, finally with a certain stoicism that he learned upon the trail.

And all the while, the other wagons passed. Nineteen trains had overtaken them this week. The Pioneer Line was full of city men, unused to the rigors of farm and river. Most noncommercial trains were companies of farmland neighbors who had been harnessing stock, plowing with oxen, and harvesting together all their lives. And Captain Turner, a strutting rooster with his passengers, was an object of mirth along the trail and seemed unable to control his teamsters, no matter how hard he blustered. The Pioneers seemed always last to a nooning spot, last to camp at night, and no matter how early rising, last to get under way at dawn.

They had not outraced the cholera quickly. Two more teamsters had died of it, and one passenger—an Irish blacksmith named Devitt. The Irishman had been stricken on the Vermillion a week ago; Morgan, Isaiah, the slave Joshua, and Stein, whose finger had almost healed, were delegated by Captain Turner to bury him on the bank.

Cholera was horrifying, and one did not grow accustomed to the sight of its ravagings. Devitt had been a brawny, smiling athlete, no Paddy at all but an educated, soft-spoken young man with only a trace of a brogue. He was a fine concertina player. He had been healthy, accompanying Morgan's singing at the campfire the night before he sickened: three days later he was dead, a shriveled mummy of twenty-three.

He was an Irish Catholic, and there should have been a priest, but there was none for a hundred miles along the trail. But he had a sense of humor, and might have been amused at his burial detail, symbol of a world turned upside-down for California gold. An agnostic, a Congregationalist, a Jew, and a black Baptist slave dug his grave and laid him to rest by a river not unlike the Shannon that he once fished.

Stein had scratched Devitt's name, with Isaiah's "Arkansas Toothpick" Bowie knife, on a sandstone rock in a glen by the stream, and added the date—27th May, 1849—and Devitt's homeland, County Clare.

Dying in the sick-wagon, with Morgan ministering to him, Devitt had bequeathed Morgan his concertina, a fine English Wheatstone double bass. Morgan, with fingers hungry for piano keys, was learning to play it very well.

There had been no cholera since.

Now, approaching Fort Kearny alone on horseback, with cholera apparently left behind, Morgan allowed himself concern for Isaiah, who was too weary to ride horseback and was back in the carriage with the rest.

The young lawyer had been pudgy when Morgan met him in the Buffalo hotel, and pale of face. Now he was too skinny, and his skin was red beneath his scraggly beard. He seemed overly sensitive to the raw plains wind, and to the sun; his brow and lips were badly blistered. Morgan had been applying lard and, finally, when lard grew scarce, wagon grease to his face, until it was as black as Joshua's own.

Isaiah and Stein were city men; they would never grow accustomed to the overland trail; they should have chosen seasickness, and the Nicaragua Isthmus or Cape Horn.

He put Isaiah from his mind and approached the miserable Fort Kearny: low sod buildings and mired streets, with a half-finished wall on which a squad of blue-trousered, undershirted soldiers worked unhappily; another dozen lounged by a line of rifles, stacked on a muddy parade ground.

Scores of wagons clustered inside. He passed a burly, grimy farmer greasing the hotbox at his wagon's wheels. On the huge hooped canvas cover, in faded, running tar, was written: WISCONSIN VOLUNTEERS! GOING TO SEE THE ELEPHANT!

The man looked up. "Pioneer Line?" he asked.

Morgan nodded. "Yes sir."

The man stood up and stretched. "They say you fellows *bought* passage? Like a railroad, eh? How much?"

Morgan grinned, embarrassed. "Two hundred dollars. Would you care to buy my ticket?"

The burly man shook his head. "Your locomotives seem to have fallen behind you: did they run out of coal again?" The farmer, with the concern for animals of any good husbandman, squatted to check a blemish on Major's fetlock, finally arose, satisfied. "There's a Mormon family said to live t'other side of the fort. Woman sets a good table for you who can pay for it. Ourselves, we're hard pressed to buy flour from the goddamn sutler here."

Morgan thanked him and rode into the fort. At the unfinished wall he turned to study the eastern horizon.

He and Major had left Captain Turner in the lead baggage wagon less than two hours before. Nowhere had Major been inclined to exceed a slow walk. He needed twenty pounds of grass a day, and Morgan had let him range from the road en route, so that he could forage.

Nevertheless, the Pioneer Line was still nowhere in sight.

He rode through the fort. The soldiers ignored him. Past the last of the grimy barracks he spotted a low sod house. A bearded Mormon patriarch was plowing furrows outside, with a sleek fat ox. He called off a yellow yapping dog and sent Morgan inside to meet the lady of the house.

Morgan regarded a haggard woman, the first he had seen—outside of Potawatomi squaws begging at the side of the trail—for nearly a month.

The smell of fresh bread was heavy under dripping ceiling beams; he caught a whiff of roasting pork. He thought for a moment of waiting for Isaiah, abandoned the idea as past the call of friendship.

For a dollar, she yawned, he could eat his fill.

Her yellowing eyes held his. The price for a meal was exorbitant, but the poor soul had jaundice: the old man outside had best profit by her cooking while he could: he'd be a widower soon enough, unless he had other wives.

"I may eat you out of house and home," he said.

The woman smiled wanly, and he sat down at the table to try.

The meal had been truly a pleasure, and the white-bearded Mormon had joined him before he finished, bolting down huge slabs of bread and freshly churned butter while Morgan wolfed pie that his wife had baked from dried apples.

He gave Morgan his reasons for settling here, instead of following the Chosen People to the Great Salt Lake or Oregon.

"Mrs. Kimball was poorly, and I feared to continue. And this is a good place. These plains are fallow now, but some day..." He grinned. He had calm gray eyes, and when he smiled, seemed younger than he was. "Wheat, sir, and corn, as far as the eye can see."

Morgan sat back, stifling a belch, and asked him if the Pawnees would permit the sowing of it.

"They'll see the light, like the Pots. We may school them in God's way. They're not a stupid people. Their enemy is the Sioux, not us, and if they're left alone—"

The family dog began to bark. Major whinnied. The old man got up from the rude table-bench and peered into the dusk.

"Dr. Morgan here?" It was Dr. Cantrell's voice. Morgan went to the door.

There was trouble. Carriage Eighteen stood outside, its mules heaving and panting. In the dusk, Morgan saw that the carriage was driven by Vanderveer, and that Cantrell was alone in the carriage bed with a groaning, cursing teamster named Chihuahua Harry.

Chihuahua, reputedly a hero of the Northern Mexican

101

Campaign, lay on his side. He was a rotund little man with weathered skin and a flattened pugilist's nose. A leg of his trouser had been slashed away, and the other was soaked in blood.

From his right buttock protruded a gleaming, broken wooden shaft. Morgan stared. "An arrow?" he asked incredulously.

Vanderveer seemed elated. "A bit of a muss on the trail." He'd seen some Pawnees stealing a horse from an Ohio company, organized a posse of teamsters, and caught the Indians in a draw. "Chihuahua's our only casualty. We got eight!"

"You *what*?" cried Morgan.

"Got eight of them," grinned Vanderveer. "Their fighting chief, as well."

Morgan moved to the wagon side. Cantrell was shaking his head: "Stupid Navy son of a bitch," he murmured. "Anyway, this man's bad punctured, and I couldn't pull it out. I told him he shouldn't trust Dr. Marshall to do it, and I brought your kit along."

Morgan looked at Chihuahua. He was already drunk enough for the procedure. In the fading prairie light Morgan could see that someone had broken off the shaft of the arrow a good six inches from the wound.

"Clear the table, Mrs. Kimball," ordered Morgan. They began to help Chihuahua to the house.

The teamster's punishment lay ahead, in the sepsis which would follow over the weeks and months to come. Vanderveer had apparently escaped scot-free.

Whatever had happened, the arrow had found the wrong mark.

Inside, the Mormon faced them, furiously. "Eight Pawnees? For a *horse*?"

Chihuahua clung unsteadily to the table, glaring at him. "Fuckin' bigamist! You ain't no better than them!"

"Mind your tongue before Mrs. Kimball!" barked Morgan. "Or I'll pound that arrow *in*!"

They laid the victim face down on the table. Morgan palpated the wound gently. The head had penetrated a good two inches into the right buttock, just missing the gluteal artery.

He had no chloroform or ether; he distrusted them as unstable compounds under the best conditions, and there was no way to keep them on the trail.

Vanderveer gave Chihuahua another drink of whiskey, under the disapproving eye of the Mormon, while Morgan whetted his scalpel. Speed was the weapon of modern surgery, and shock, prolonged, was the killer.

He placed the Mormon, probably the strongest man in the room, on the right leg, and Cantrell on the left.

"You right-handed, Chihuahua?"

The teamster, suddenly sober, nodded.

Morgan's experience had been that a right-handed man would flail with his right arm, so he put the woman on the left and bound the right arm to a table leg. He put Vanderveer, who seemed fascinated, on the right wrist. Surgeons had been virtually emasculated by frantic patients, face down on the table, who had somehow freed a hand.

"All right, Lieutenant," he murmured coldly. "Hang on tight!"

"Aye, aye, sir." Vanderveer nodded, eyes bright.

Chihuahua glanced up at him, his face suddenly wild with fear.

Morgan massaged the back of his neck. "You'll be all right, Chihuahua. Take a deep breath, and be calm, calm, calm..."

He put a hand on the buttock, found it hard as stone, and tense with terror.

Some men, and some women, could relax; then it was nothing. But some could not, even if you waited forever, and then it was hell. You could only pray that the patient fainted.

Chihuahua could not relax. So be it...

Morgan whetted his scalpel on his boot, took a deep breath, squinted in the dim light at the dark blue spot oozing blood from around the shaft, and cut a deep incision paralleling the direction of the shaft into the buttock.

There was a roar of pain from the patient, a tense

103

convulsive jerk of the leg, and Dr. Cantrell went hurtling into the stove. The Mormon and his wife held tight; Vanderveer cursed and hung on; Cantrell came clawing back, and this time held.

Chihuahua screamed and fought, nearly to the end.

But when Morgan began to work the arrowhead loose by prying the haft, Chihuahua fainted.

From then on the operation was simple as the woman's apple pie.

Chihuahua was moaning in the wagon outside, and the shaken woman was clearing the table. Dr. Cantrell stood in the doorway. Morgan showed him the arrow. The head was of rusty iron.

"Bad," said Cantrell, offering Morgan a drink from the bottle. In deference to the Mormon, Morgan refused.

"Very bad," Morgan agreed. He'd observed that, while puncture wounds from clean metal sometimes healed almost without infection, those from rusted iron healed badly. He started with the bloody shaft for the door, to throw it away.

"I want it," said Vanderveer.

"The arrow? Why?"

Vanderveer shrugged. "A memento..."

Morgan stared at him, disbelieving. "Have you a strand of hemp from the *Somers*, too?"

There was dead silence. Gently, Vanderveer reached out, took the arrow, and flung it through the open door. "I'll remember that, Doctor. One day I'll call you to account for it!"

"Why'd you chase them down?" demanded Morgan. "It wasn't your horse! It wasn't even a Pioneer horse! Was it?"

Vanderveer's eyes chilled. "No. It wasn't."

"Then *why*? Did they *ask* us to help?"

"Didn't help *themselves*," shrugged Vanderveer. "Said the hell with it and just kept going! Can you stomach that?"

"Hell yes, Lieutenant! Why didn't *you*?"

"I'm an officer of the United States Navy," said

Vanderveer. "When I see theft against my countrymen, I act."

"This *isn't* the United States," grated the Mormon. "There's no law here but God's!" His jaw worked furiously. "They're not thieves, they know no better, they're only savages! Eight human beings!" he bellowed suddenly. "For an *animal*? That they thought they needed? They're at war with the Sioux, not *us*!"

"They may be now," muttered the woman.

The Mormon stepped to his wife, put his arm around her skinny waist, and held her close. "No, Mrs. Kimball, no," he murmured. "Not with *us*: we have ten-score soldiers within five minutes' ride. Not with us, but with these 'gentlemen.'"

"Let's go," snorted Vanderveer. "I'll not eat here."

"No, sir, you'll not!" Kimball agreed.

Morgan looked into the Mormon's eyes. "I'm sorry, sir." He tried to hand him a silver dollar for the meal.

The Mormon ignored it and blew out the spare candle.

"Tallow I cannot spare, Doctor, but *that* I surely can."

Morgan sighed, thanked the woman for the meal, pressed her to accept a packet of Dover Powder from his kit, which was supposed to help her liver, but probably would not. She finally accepted and he left.

He watched Vanderveer take the reins and snap the mules into motion. The wagon creaked, Chihuahua yelped, Major snuffled and sighed. Morgan mounted.

The woman ran from the house. "Mr. Kimball begs you, Doctor: watch out for Pawnees on the trail."

"Thank you, Mrs. Kimball, that I shall."

That night, in his tent, Morgan heard shouting from the fort, but ascribed it to a drunken Army orgy.

The next morning the man and his wife were dead, and their hut a burned-out shell.

Turner bought flour at five dollars per hundredweight, swearing at the price. He threatened to write the Secretary of the Army, eliciting a chuckle from the sutler's clerk.

The train passed a party of soldiers burying the Kimballs, and then the smoking hut, and plodded to the west. Only Morgan paused on Major to regard the ruin.

Major was very nervous. He pawed at the furrowed ground.

Wheat and corn, the Mormon had promised, *as far as the eye can see....*

Morgan thought not, not in five decades, or ten.

Watch out for Pawnees on the trail...

The horse shook his head and looked after the wagons. Morgan shivered and patted his neck. "Major, I think you're right. Until we reach Fort Laramie, our scouting days are done."

He pressed his heels to the horse's flanks, which had been fat and sleek.

They were bony now, and caked with dust.

They trotted after the train.

THE ADMIRAL

THE ADMIRAL ROLLED SLOWLY ALONG HIGHWAY 50 through Fallon, past the Nugget Casino, the Bonanza, the Waterhole, and Rusty Spur. The neon lights were more garish than he remembered, from thirty years before, and the main street had grown, like everything else, in tackiness and size.

He could hear the woman moaning in the rear. He winced. Whatever she had been accomplice to, she was paying for it now. He could hear her brother begging her to let them take her to a hospital: their voices rose; Jeff seemed to take no part.

"She can't sweat it," called Jeff suddenly from the rear.

106

He came forward. "First RV camp you see, pull in and do something for her."

The admiral's mind swam suddenly in plans. To check into a motor home park, someone would have to register. If they let him do it, a note to the clerk, or a quiet word...

They were all at once through the town. On the outskirts, a white police car turned onto the highway from a sidestreet. It cruised ahead. If he blinked his lights, or sounded his horn... rear-ended him... what then?

"Forget it," muttered Jeff, a foot behind his head. "Just keep driving... There! The Hub!"

On the right side of the highway lay a motor home center, the one Bunkie had picked from the RV guide an hour—or a year—ago. Trailers, campers, and motor homes were clustered near its general store and swimming pool under glaring lights. But the motor home center was almost filled, at this late hour: the farther west they traveled, the harder it became to get a place to spend the night.

He pulled under the portico and parked by the office door. He glanced at his captor. Jeff had finished shaving while he drove. In losing his beard, he'd turned older. The lines at the corners of his eyes seemed deeper, and the jaw narrower than he would have thought.

Thirty-one, thirty-two? It was hard to tell: he was in hard, trim shape, with a flat belly and springy stride.

Anyway, even in the dim light from the dashboard you could see that he'd just shorn himself of a beard. His forehead was tan and his chin was pale. A good cop would notice that.

Perhaps...

"We're going in together," Jeff instructed softly. He pulled a jar of makeup from a suitcase he'd transferred from the van and smoothed it onto his jaw. "You, your granddaughter, and me. I'm your son, she's my daughter, we've been driving all day long. Tell 'em you want a quiet spot, away from the store and the john. Register for three persons; don't try anything with the registration sheet; I'll watch you fill it in. Pay cash, no credit cards. Don't shoot the shit with the clerk. We just sign in and split." He eyed Bunkie, patted her cheek. She flinched. "OK,

107

honey. I'm your daddy, now, so show me how you'll smile."

She watched him impassively.

"I said *smile*, Angel! Smile!" He grabbed her arm.

She tried to pull away. "You killed our dog!"

Jeff's hand flashed, and she recoiled from the first slap of her life. Her hand flew to her cheek. Incredulous, she stared at her captor, then her grandfather, tears coming to her eyes.

The admiral glared at Jeff, fighting to stay cool. *You son of a bitch*, he promised him silently, *I'll have your balls for that....* Aloud, he ordered Bunkie to smile, before she was slapped again.

She summoned a brace-studded grimace. Jeff donned the admiral's leather flight jacket, jammed the .45 into his belt, zipped the jacket over it, and herded them from the motor home. He followed the admiral to the office, holding Bunkie's hand. The admiral stepped to the counter, registered for three, and paid nine dollars in advance for full facilities: electricity, water connection, and dumping site.

All the while Jeff crowded close, pretending interest in a jar of beef jerky at the register, but never taking his eyes from the admiral's hand writing on the registration form. He need not have worried. The clerk was a gum-chewing kid of eighteen, with pimples, probably a moonlighting sailor from NAS Fallon, down the road. He was watching "Family Feud" on a black-and-white TV behind the counter. He made change for a ten, slipped the registration card into a file, and hardly gave them a glance.

The admiral parked at the end of the line of motor homes, hooked the toilet-tank to the sewer-dump connection, and plugged into the electrical post, all under the eye of the Mexican, who kept to the shadows and watched.

He could hear Jeff inside, slamming drawers, searching the Winnebago from bow to stern. In the light from the adjoining trailer's TV, the admiral glanced at his watch.

Eight-seventeen. Over two hours since he'd heard the shell slam into the breech by the roadside ditch. He'd lost

Halsey, his closest companion, but he and Bunkie were still alive.

So far.

His knees began to tremble once again.

He climbed the step of the motor home, to begin his medical career.

He saw that Bunkie had been told to return to her passenger seat, where she could be seen from outside. All the blinds aft had been drawn. Jeff was still going through the motor home's drawers. The admiral's .38 service revolver, which he'd flown with in Korea, lay somewhere in a drawer, unloaded. Jeff would surely find it within seconds. To defuse the matter, he told him where it was.

"I figured, somewhere," Jeff said coldly.

Miguel called from the rear compartment. His sister was in agony.

"Terry's hurting," said Jeff. "Do something, quick."

The admiral moved to the sleeping compartment. Jeff followed him. Terry writhed slowly, fist jammed into her mouth. Miguel backed out to let the admiral in. To look as professional as possible, he tried for a pulse in the carotid artery, failed to find it, and quickly removed his hand.

"Give her something," Jeff breathed. "Now!"

The motor home's entire medical store consisted of a prepackaged snakebite kit, a box of Johnson & Johnson Band-Aids, a pair of tweezers, and an Ace bandage bought in Fort Laramie, Wyoming, when his football knee became inflamed from climbing Chimney Rock.

Outside of the digitalis for his heart, there were no drugs stronger than Bufferin in the medicine cabinet. He took a deep breath and got out the words: "I don't have anything."

"You *what*?" Jeff exploded. He stepped into the toilet. The admiral heard him jerk open the medicine cabinet, fumble through the locker beneath the sink. He reappeared, his eyes narrowed suspiciously. "You're a *doctor*? You got *nothing*?"

"Just digitalis, for my heart." He hoped he wouldn't

need it: his pulse was racing now. "I don't expect to practice on the road."

"T's, Miguel!" called Jeff. "¡Chingada! ¿Dónde tienes los T's?"

"Where are your T's?" The admiral followed the Spanish, but didn't understand the "T's." Or "tease"? Prison slang?

Miguel clawed through the suitcase they had transferred from the van, came up with a knotted condom. He untied it, emptied some half dozen tablets into the admiral's hand. They were peach-colored, with a groove in the middle.

The admiral regarded them blankly.

"Talwins," Jeff said, looking at him strangely. "Talwins, Talwins, you've seen Talwins!"

What the hell were Talwins? But he nodded, poured a glass of water from the faucet in the toilet, and managed to get two of them down Terry's throat.

"Look," muttered Jeff. "They're only fifties! Miguel cooks that many and *mainlines* them. Is two enough?"

"For her body weight," he said, with as much assurance as he could muster. Jeff looked at him dubiously and left. Gently, he raised the woman to a half-sitting position, braced her with pillows, and cut off her shirt with Bunkie's sewing scissors.

This time he inspected her back as well. Nothing. There was only the one wound, and the massive swelling in her shoulder. His heart sank. The slug was still inside.

He covered the wound itself with a large Band-Aid and wound her chest with the Ace bandage. He thought he did rather well.

Carefully, he eased her down. She sighed and slipped away into sleep, or coma: he had no way of knowing. The "T's," thank God, had worked.

The walls of the compartment were closing in. He needed space to think. He moved forward. Jeff sat at the dinette table, relaxed now, opening a can of beer he had found in the refrigerator. The admiral's .38 revolver and ammunition box sat on the table, and he could see from the leaden glints in the cylinder that the weapon was now loaded.

Leaning against his chair was the shotgun. Guns everywhere, and Bunkie sitting rigidly in the passenger seat, exposed to all their dangers.

He smelled gasoline, too. Jeff had picked up the gasoline tank from the highway and stowed it under the table. It had not been empty, after all. Its odor and presence made the admiral as uneasy as the guns. He had no idea what they intended to do with it. If they ran out of gas tomorrow on the desert, pouring a mere two gallons into the Winnebago would be like giving a shotglass of water to a thirsty elephant.

"¿Mi hermanita, está bien?" asked Miguel. He held a can of beer. His eyes were stricken with fear.

The admiral almost answered, then remembered. Jeff was watching him.

"Is she OK, he wants to know?"

The admiral pantomimed sleep for Miguel, his hands to his cheek. The Mexican nodded and smiled, moved to the refrigerator, opened a can of beer, and handed it to him. He longed for a blast of the scotch under the galley, but he didn't want to inform his captors that there was hard liquor aboard, so he settled for the beer instead.

Jeff spun the cylinder of the .38. "This the only piece you got?"

"Yes."

"You sure? I'm going to tear this place apart. I find another one, I'll kill the kid by inches."

"I told you, that's it."

"Let's see that wallet again."

The admiral gave it to him. He spilled its contents onto the table, picked up the Navy ID, inspected it once more.

"This morning I was shitting every time a pig walks by the cell, now I got me an admiral."

With a fucking giant to help you, and three guns, he longed to say. *You're a goddamn living hero, Tiger, all the way.*

Instead, he sipped the beer. They were obviously heading out of the state; the fastest way was west. But past the desert, in the Sierras, were the agricultural inspection stations on the California line. With bulletins doubtless already out, an inspector entering the motor home could hardly miss the fugitives. Even an agricultural inspector might harbor dreams of fame, and the last thing the admiral wanted was a shoot-out. Somehow, before they reached the border, he must signal the outside world that there were innocents aboard.

Jeff flicked the ID card aside. "A real live admiral," he said thoughtfully. "I was a lance corporal. Twice. First Marine Division. In Nam. You too old for that one? Or too smart?"

Careful... "I spent that one in Japan," he said. He had—part of it, anyway—as an Air Group Commander on a carrier operating out of Yokosuka.

"I see. Too smart."

"Naval Hospital, Yokosuka," he fabricated.

"Good old NH Yokosuka," Jeff murmured. He looked up with the startling blue eyes, which had turned icy. "I knew some of your victims." Yokosuka, apparently, would be no bond, but a barrier.

"We did our best." His mouth went dry.

Jeff's face seemed suddenly older. "Two of them are dead, and one's riding a wheelchair. Yeah, there's guys in my squad would love to see me with my own private admiral. " He swished the beer in the beer can and put it down. "We were not big on admirals. Or Navy surgeons, either." He began to roll a joint. "I probably should have wasted you in that ditch."

The admiral could do nothing for the woman, and they'd discover that soon enough. He must try to sell himself as guide and talisman. "You'd have been stupid," the admiral said quietly. He pointed to his identification, the credit cards, the clean legitimacy of the documents spread on the table. "I can get you out of Nevada. Where *was* that cell? Lovelock?"

Jeff smiled thinly. "Come on! We look like city jail?"

His heart dropped. "Carson City? Nevada State *Pen*?"

Jeff nodded. "What you got here is *felons*. We're *bad*, man! I was doing thirty for murder two. He had life, without. She did time two years ago in LA Juvie Hall."

Jesus... *What were they doing on the road to Fallon? They must have feinted north and east, to draw pursuit*

112

toward Utah, then doubled south. Now they were heading for Carson City again, and the mountains to the west.

He took a deep breath. "And you want to get over Carson Pass?"

"Or Mount Rose Grade," Jeff shrugged. "We got no ties left here."

"There'll be roadblocks at the border . . . And the agricultural stations, too."

"No *shit*? Roadblocks? Hey, you must watch 'Chips.'"

The admiral persisted. "I know that country. I was born there. Leave my granddaughter here, stay out of sight in the rear, and I can get you through. I'll do the talking. And I don't panic."

"You looked a little panicky, some earlier."

That he ignored. "You need *me*, with that ID card, but you don't need her. Just let me keep on driving!"

"I think people been letting you drive all your life, Admiral," Jeff said softly. "Am I right?"

The man was studying him with a faint smile. But something seethed behind the eyes that made him uncomfortable. The admiral said, weakly: "I can keep the heat off you better than a twelve-year-old girl!"

"So you're saying, waste her?"

"You know what I'm saying. Let her out. She won't make a peep, as long as you have me."

"No!" cried Bunkie, suddenly. "I'm staying with you!"

The admiral felt tears come to his eyes. "Bunkie," he pled, "pipe down!"

She faced him defiantly. "And if you make them leave me, I will *too* peep! I'll go right to the phone and call the police!"

She'd never disobeyed him in her life. He felt as if someone had kicked him in the gut.

Her tears were flowing now. She put her hands on her hips. "They're going to have to *shoot* me before I leave you! Pops, don't make them—"

"She's right," grinned Jeff. "Leave her in Fallon? All alone? Slots, craps, *prostitution*! Sailors from that NAS! No place for a twelve-year-old!"

The admiral went on: "She doesn't mean it. Let her go!" He was breathing hard; he wondered if he were on

113

the verge of an attack. "Do that," he panted, "and you have my help."

"We got your help right now."

"But you don't need *her!*"

"Yeah, I do. She keeps you interested." Jeff's eyes were steady on his own. "You better hope I think so, anyway. 'Cause when I don't, she's dead."

He refused to give up, though his heart was pounding. "You touch a twelve-year-old girl in Nevada, they'll send you to the chamber!" His voice sounded shaky.

Jeff sat back. "You're behind times, Grandpa: they shoot you now, in this state. With sodium pentothal. Just like a pop at the dentist, and *whammo*, you're home free."

"Well, they'll sure as hell do it if you touch that girl!"

"For *her*? Shit, no!" He chuckled. "Hey, you think your dog's the only KIA? There's a dead state *cop* in Carson!"

The admiral groaned inwardly. He was suddenly as frightened of the police as of his captors. In his youth, half the sheriffs in Nevada had seen themselves as Wyatt Earp and their deputies seemed chosen by lot. Across the California border in his own mining counties, the murder of a lawman was serious enough. But in Nevada, where most of the people seemed related? It would become a hundred-thousand-square-mile minefield for a man who had killed a cop. Or anybody who happened to be near the murderer when they caught him....

"Maybe *two* state cops," continued Jeff. "His partner wasn't looking too swift, either. Plus, one Nevada Department of Corrections pig, name of Kreutzer. You know *that*, Admiral? And the guy that drove that gray van, he's offed too."

"Jesus," whispered the admiral.

"You're getting the picture." Jeff touched his hand to the bulkhead. "Heat? Man, you can feel it through the wall. State Penitentiary Escape Team, Nevada Highway Patrol, Washoe deputies, Reno cops, Nevada Division of Investigation, sheriffs' mounted posses, Civil Air Patrol. *Road*blocks? By now they've called out the Air National Guard!"

The admiral stared at him. Jeff was grinning, his eyes

114

were wild. Psycho? Stoned? Or simply fatigued? Whatever it was, the man, who had seemed so cool at first, was wired. He felt a chill in the pit of his stomach.

Jeff tugged the suitcase open. He groped under a stack of clothes and drew out what looked like a walkie-talkie. A line of red lights at the top showed that it was a scanner. He pulled out its antenna, held it close to the window, and flicked it on. The red lights flickered across the top of the set and suddenly stopped. A woman's voice crackled from the tiny speaker: "—to One Charlie Three Seven. Three David Four Three reported at the junction. You get to Minden yet?

"That's ten-four. I'll report Kingsbury Grade. . . . Traffic on the wounded officer?"

"Stable, at Carson Tahoe."

Jeff slammed the antenna back, turned off the scanner, laid it on the table. He reached up and grabbed the admiral's arm.

"Now, who they going to pop us for? You and your kid? The guy that owned that van, if they ever find his body? Bullshit! They don't care shit about you and your kid! When they get us—which they maybe will—we burn for the cop. And his partner. And that goddamn Kreutzer pig . . ." Jeff sipped his beer, staring into space. Finally he said, softly and slowly: "Admiral—" He looked again at the ID card. "Admiral Washburn, you've been talking too much. And maybe thinking too much, too. You know your best shot? Shut up. You're in boot camp. I'm your DI. Take orders. Hope we don't get made by some badge-heavy asshole that thinks he can shoot. And never, *never* try anything. Understand?"

"Yes."

"Yes, what?"

The sapphire eyes flashed up at him. He was suddenly forty years younger, braced in his room at Bancroft Hall, on his first day as a plebe, with the smell of stencil paint and new uniforms and sweat and his skivvy shirt glued to his ribs with the heat of the Chesapeake. A tiny, sneering upperclassman, the first he had met, was taunting him.

"Yes, *sir*," he managed.

Jeff grinned. "Good." He glanced at the ID card. "Morgan Washburn, IV. Morgan the fourth. You some fucking king, or something? Now, what do your friends call you? What'd your *mother* call you?"

"Stretch," he answered softly.

"Stretch. That's very nice. Muy macho: Stretch Washburn. I bet you played football, Stretch. They play football then? They *fuck* then? I bet you were quite a stud." He saw Bunkie cringing as if struck.

Humiliated, the admiral longed to smash Jeff's smiling face, close the crinkling eyes, batter the lean pale jaw.

"Don't *talk* to him that way!" blurted Bunkie.

The admiral felt his throat go tight. He held out his arms and she came to him. He hugged her closely and whispered: "Quiet, darling, OK?"

"Turn her loose," commanded Jeff, "or I'll hang you out to dry."

The admiral looked deep into Bunkie's eyes, patted her cheek, and pushed her gently away. She whirled, stalked to the passenger seat, and stared moodily out at the night.

Jeff regarded her with amusement, then turned back to the admiral. "OK, Stretchy, we are Tijuana-bound. Now, we probably won't make it, but *none* of us is taking the pop." He reached down, lifted the can of gasoline, swished it back and forth. "This is *our* sodium pentothal, this is *our* gas chamber. If we burn—*blooie*—we burn right here." He looked at Miguel and repeated the last in Spanish. "¿Es verdad, amigo?"

Miguel studied him. Softly, he said: "Para nosotros, sí. Antes que nos tomen. Para Teresita, no, es muy joven."

The admiral let his eyes drift to the window. *"For us, before they take us, yes. Not for Terry, she is too young."*

Jeff chuckled. "Ella será la que me haga encendernos."

"She'll be the one that makes me light the match."

The admiral had seen the look in the woman's dark eyes, and believed him. She meant what she said, every word. They were mad, the three of them, insane....

He dropped all hope of signaling for help. To attract aid would be to trigger disaster. He would be their slave, no matter what the cost, until they set Bunkie free.

Jeff looked at his watch. "We're on, for sure."

He cranked up the TV antenna, and flicked on the set over the dinette table. A heavily jowled TV newsman from KOLO in Reno faced the camera; the prison break and murders led the news.

In forty seconds the admiral knew the story. Jeff Gordon and Miguel Gonzales had killed a guard, broken from the Nevada State Penitentiary at 2:15 P.M., in a laundry truck, had been picked up by a confederate in a Pontiac Pan Am, and had been stopped by two NHP officers in the suburbs of Carson City on a traffic violation. They had killed one officer—father of two—and wounded a thirty-year veteran, Frankie Aguilar.

"Hey, I got a DUI from that fucker, on the way to Reno once," breathed Jeff. "For an empty fucking bottle in the car! If *he's* the one that plugged her, I hope he rots in hell!"

Their abandoned Pontiac had been found west of Reno, on Interstate 80: the newscast implied that the California border was blocked.

There was no description of Terry, or mention of the gray van, or its driver. It might sit undetected on the highway for days.

Jeff's mug shot with his beard, flashed on the screen, hardly resembled the man at the table. Miguel's was better.

Jeff put the can of gasoline back under the table. He was suddenly calm and smiling; the dazzling smile was back. "OK, you say you can get us through. Maybe you can. All the way to T-town? I don't know. But maybe I'll let you try, all that eagle shit on your cute little hat. If we make it..." He shrugged. "Who knows?"

"All right, in *Tijuana*?" the admiral begged. "You'll let us go?"

Jeff gave him a long, cool look. "Suppose I said yes," he asked quietly. "Would you believe me?"

The admiral looked into the sapphire eyes. They were absolutely level. "I don't know," he said slowly.

"OK. We roll tomorrow. Keep us alive, don't pull any shit, take care of Terry, and we'll see."

"About Terry..." The admiral took a deep breath.

"There's no exit wound. That slug's inside. I can't do much."

Jeff leaped to his feet. The cold eyes opened wide.

"She *believed* you! You said you could help!"

His heart was racing, but he got it out: "Without facilities, I can't!"

The beer can crumpled in Jeff's hand. Miguel stared at him, startled. Unheeded, the TV warned of early storms on the Carson Pass. Jeff picked up the gun. His glance flicked to Miguel, then stabbed the admiral. "You fucking *better*, because if she *dies*—"

He tilted his head, listening. A distant siren wailed. A dog joined in, howling, and another dog, and a third.

"If she dies, you'll wish you picked the ditch."

He repeated it in Spanish, to Miguel.

"¿Verdad, Miguel?"

Miguel looked at the admiral sadly. "Es verdad."

SUNDAY

MORNING

MORGAN AND MARY

MORGAN'S PRESENCE—AND MARY'S—SWEPT OVER THE darkening desert with the speeding motor home. When finally the vehicle came to rest on the outskirts of the desert town, they remained.

At first the town throbbed with colored lights, like jewels spilled from the Stillwater Range onto the dark desert floor.

The motor home lay within yards of ruts Morgan had followed one hundred and thirty autumns before. The place had been a deserted campsite when he had first shuffled past it, racing the snows to the Sierras. His stolen mule had smelled moisture and stumbled to a nearby pool. There, where the parched sand swallowed the last trickle of the Carson, he and the animal together had gulped its ruined waters.

Now he and Mary waited as the long night passed.

A thousand miles east of the motor home, daylight began to flood the plains, then washed the Rockies' eastern flank and swamped the Great Divide. But here, where the town had slowly darkened through the night, nothing moved. Deep beneath the pavement lay wagon tracks forgotten by living men.

The man who bore their genes was sleeping at last. He sprawled on the motor home floor, white hair tousled, lanky limbs contorted. The device implanted above his

121

breast seemed to trouble his rest: he clutched at it and stirred.

The girl, youngest and last of their line, slumbered on the settee by the table.

The big Mexican sat by the door, awake; a shotgun leaned on his chair. The other bandit tossed and turned in the bunk over the driver's seat, where once the child had slept. In the bed in the rear compartment, the wounded woman groaned, awakened, and dozed again.

Both Morgan and Mary knew exactly the extent of her injury, but neither knew whether she would survive.

Her fate—and that of their own seed—lay in an ever-learning pool of changing thought, fed by perceptions clutched from living beings. Its unity was gloriously simple to Morgan and Mary, but its future as complex and unknowable to them—and to itself—as to those who breathed below.

As the sun gilded the peaks of the Stillwater Range to the east, their great-grandson shifted, muttered, touched the scar over his breast, fell back into deeper sleep.

He was blind to Morgan's presence: he had had no sense of the Spheres of Thought.

But this was right, and had to be. If living creatures in all the worlds knew the freedom that awaited them, they would cease the struggle to survive. Without living thought, the Spheres would collapse. The mystery and fear were needed; without them the song would die.

Morgan had come close to touching him, but the living seemed deaf to his resonances.

There seemed no way to reach his descendents in their peril, or to guide them if he did.

He sensed suddenly that Mary disagreed. She reminded him that the man following their tracks had lately sensed Morgan's presence and slept for long moments in the person Morgan had been.

And the boulder, with your name on it, on the great gray sleeping rock? And the tune you liked so well?

I did not cause those things, my love. They're random echoes of a song we knew. When his ear is tuned, they come ... or not. I cannot interfere....

Please try?

To what end, love? What good are our echoes to him?

But we touched the child, too, on the banks of the Blue. And on the rock that day. Your echoes may help him save her. He is ready for the Spheres, but she is not.

He and Mary were one, through all eternity, and so he tried again.

But his great-grandson slept on, dreaming of other things, so he knew that he had failed.

The Spheres of Thought drew Mary's vision three thousand miles to the east, where the sun had lately risen, to focus on another of their seed.

The child's mother and her husband were entering a building where men swarmed like frantic ants. Outside the structure rested silver flying machines, in the garish colors of the day. In the mother's hand was a box, wrapped with ribbon as a gift: in the husband's hand another, somewhat smaller.

From the husband's conversation, he would be a reluctant traveler, but the mother seemed determined that the birthday of her father would be a happy time.

They were bound for the home that had been her own.

They would find it empty on the hill.

But there was no way that Mary could warn them, for they too were deaf.

THE ADMIRAL
AND BUNKIE

THE ADMIRAL LAY ON THE COLD FLOOR OF THE MOTOR home, keeping his eyes closed against the morning light: he remembered where he was, and the mortal danger he had brought to Bunkie, and did not want their captors to know he was awake before he had made a plan.

He had had a miserable night, awakened continually by Miguel when Terry cried out in pain, sometimes hearing her himself, before the Mexican acted. Each time he felt more helpless, and more angry at the man, sleeping unconcernedly over the driver's seat, who was keeping her from help.

He fed her Miguel's Talwins, felt her forehead, took her pulse. It seemed to give her comfort in her pain. Once she became delirious as he sat on her bed, his palm against her sweating brow.

"Padre ... Father?"

Priest? Or her own father. He couldn't tell.

"I'm just the doctor, Terry...."

"Yes. I know...."

But later, when he came again—at 3 A.M. this time— she muttered, in Spanish: "Forgive me, Father, I have sinned...."

"I don't speak Spanish, Terry."

She went on, in English: "Father, will I die? I'm shot, you know, they shot me."

"We won't let you die." He felt like a murderer, himself.

"Was it so *bad*, what I did? I love him, I love my brother, too...."

She rambled on in Spanish of a "Mr. D," dope overlord of the prison, a lifer and leader of an "Aryan Brotherhood" prison gang, who had grown to hate her brother.

"Because Miguel would not learn inglés, and I would not bring in enough of those T's to make happy Mr. D..."

Her voice tailed off, and she moved restlessly, then began to ramble again. In a condom in her vagina she had smuggled in their tribute, until Miguel had rebelled.

"Jeff was his compadre.... Mr. D was going to kill them both.... They must escape or they were the same as dead!"

She moved restlessly, touched her arm and moaned. He'd just given her a Talwin, and hoped she'd drift away to sleep, but she tossed and turned and then went on:

"So I brought those pills in, oh, many times, and dropped them in the ladies' room and the trusty would pick them up.... But never, never, never, enough for Mr. D..."

She rambled on in Spanish of a gun she had hidden in a package full of unsuccessful legal writs she'd delivered from Jeff's lawyer when he'd given up on a flawed appeal. No guard, under law, dared inspect them. She had brought two other guns and the scanner radio in the car she drove to wait for them near the Pen.

"I didn't think he'd kill, I swear!" She moaned and tossed her head. "Ipala... Ay, Mamá! Father? *Doctor?* Are we there?"

"Soon," he promised. "Sleep..."

"Ipala," she begged. "I want to be there. I want to be there now!"

She had quieted, finally, and he'd returned forward, adjusted himself on the floor, and tried to sleep again, under her brother's gun.

But the admiral could not sleep. He had visions: Jeff was sighting through his mirrored glasses along his .45 automatic, at the center of his chest: Jeff became his son Chris, with blond tousled hair and flying glasses, and the memory returned of the closest thing to a confrontation that the two had ever had.

Almost fifteen years ago in San Diego, Chris, a Navy fighter pilot with less than a thousand hours, had borrowed a little Cessna lightplane from his fiancée's father. He had invited his mother and father to fly with them to Nevada City. He wanted the girl—the cheerful daughter of a Coronado dentist—to see the family home and meet his grandparents.

Neither the admiral nor Ellen had ever flown with him, but Chris had been flying the dentist's plane for months. On takeoff, the admiral's impression of his son's technique was one of smoothness, marred by overconfidence.

But excess optimism was endemic among new pilots. It struck first at two hundred hours, again at around a thousand. Then, inevitably, some catastrophe would shake it, and, if the pilot survived, he might live to fly forever.

The flight north had been beautiful, over the Valley of San Joaquin, with Mount Whitney and the southern Sierras marching majestically past the window, and the dim and distant outlines of the Coast Ranges off to port.

Over Bakersfield, the admiral flipped the VOR receiver to the Porterville omni range. Chris smiled, shook his head, and flicked it to Visalia instead.

The admiral offered no more assistance. He'd been asked as a guest, not as an instructor: the trip was Chris's show.

They spent a fine, rich weekend with the admiral's father, who had just retired from practice, and his mother, who had always loved Ellen and seemed content with Chris's happy choice of mate. The old man had driven them back to the airport. It had been paved since the days when the admiral had washed the ridiculous little Taylorcraft kites to pay for his flight instruction, at two dollars a quarter hour.

It was just past noon and the weather was hot. The field, originally hacked by a mining company from the forested wilderness, was perched on a ridge at an altitude of thirty-nine hundred feet. Hot weather and high altitude meant a longer takeoff roll.

126

He didn't want to ask, but did: "You check your weight and balance?"

"No sweat, Dad," grinned Chris, but there was a glint of annoyance in his eye.

Careful. This was not the kid he'd taught to box, but a professional pilot, capable of flying modern fighters that he himself had never touched.

They opened up the cabin and let the furnace-air seep out. Then the ladies crammed themselves into the rear while he and Chris unsnapped the tie-down lines and checked the gas. The admiral took the right-hand seat, and waited while Chris walked around the little airplane, checking the control surfaces and linkages to see that all was well.

There was a whisper of wind from the east. The runway sloped downward from east to west. The eastern end was shadowed with towering pines, on a hill which seemed to rise forever, but the western end was clear. Logic dictated a down-hill, downwind takeoff, ignoring the tiny tailwind they might have.

The little engine ticked over quickly, and Chris taxied from the line. He glanced at the wind sock, turned left automatically, and began to taxi toward what, in his father's judgment, was the less preferable end.

The admiral winced. *Ignore the sock, turn the plane around*, he ordered silently. *Taxi to the east, don't let me have to speak.*

Chris continued, testing his mags as he taxied, not bothering to check his flaps at all.

About the flaps the admiral did not care. Some pilots tested them, some did not. But to take off uphill, at this altitude, grossed out with gas and passengers, on a hot day?

The hell with the wind. Take off downhill!

"Chris . . ." he began.

Chris held up his hand for silence, tuned in the Marysville omni, and stopped just off the end of the runway. He ran up his engine, checked his carburetor heat.

"Chris?" he tried again. "I used to fly out of here, all the time . . ."

Chris smiled. "You told me. Your belt fastened?"

127

"Yes. You know, from here this runway slopes up-hill—"

"Belts?" Chris called over his shoulder.

"Fastened," said the girl.

"Mine's fastened," said Ellen. The admiral twisted to look at her. She raised her eyebrows. She knew, though she had not touched the controls of an airplane since long before Chris was born, that he worried about the trees at the end of the runway.

"Those pines down there get pretty high, and there's not much wind today," he observed.

"A little," said Chris tersely, and took the runway.

When you started your takeoff roll almost four thousand feet in the air, it was wise to lean the mixture out on takeoff. Surreptitiously, as Chris added power and the engine howled and the plane began to crawl slowly up the runway, the admiral pulled the red mixture knob a quarter inch out of the panel. Chris caught the motion and pushed it full forward, with a warning glance at his father.

OK, hotshot, thought the admiral, *it's your red wagon now*. His eyes darted between the airspeed indicator and the trees three thousand feet ahead . . . twenty-five hundred . . . Lift-off speed would be sixty knots. Thrashing uphill, it would take forever to achieve it, and the plane, grossed out to begin with, would mush through the air like a pregnant pelican. . . .

Two thousand feet of runway left, thirty knots . . . He smelled heated oil, and warm sweat, and caught a subtle whiff of fear. The trees were growing before his eyes . . . fifteen hundred feet, forty-two knots . . . He could abort the takeoff himself, jam on the brakes, there was still runway left to stop in . . . His feet slid forward, and he felt Ellen's hand on his shoulder . . . She wanted him to wait before he acted . . .

The nose began to come up. He glanced at his son, whose face was impassive, but beaded with sweat. The muscles in his neck were bulging.

You got us into this, buster; get us out.

One thousand feet, forty-eight knots, and the trees had grown. If Chris pulled back on the yoke—which was the instinctive reaction—they would simply lose speed and mush into the branches... The only hope was to keep the nose down, build up airspeed, and zoom at the last moment over the first waving treetops...

Eight hundred feet of runway left... fifty-six knots; six hundred feet of runway... too late to abort... sixty knots, and the nose came up, pointed twenty feet below the highest branches... They were airborne now, five hundred feet short of the beckoning limbs...

He felt Ellen's grip tighten on his shoulder. *If he keeps the nose down and times the zoom right, we can clear...*

His son was tense, muscles rock-hard and straining under his sweat-soaked shirt.

Carefully, so that the ladies could not see him, the admiral sneaked his thumbs to the controls, where he could feel the backward pressure if Chris tried to pull up the nose.

There was no pressure. Good, good... Not yet, we need the speed...

Suddenly his thumbs were bending back. He resisted, as the trees loomed higher.

"Elevator jammed," grunted Chris. "Shit!"

Not yet... Not yet... Now!

He dropped his hands. The nose rose suddenly. The engine throbbed and fought for purchase, the airspeed dropped. He had an urge to fight for the controls and baby the aircraft over the first tall treetops: if Chris didn't catch the first faint shudders of a stall, they would die in the trunks below.

They cleared the tops, Chris eased forward on the yoke, the treetops fell away below, and they were flying.

"Tada!" piped the girl from the rear. "That's my boy!"

The admiral felt Ellen squeeze his shoulder, then caress his neck. "And this is *my* boy," he heard her murmur. "This is mine."

Chris moved the yoke curiously, forward and back. "Damn elevator... It's free now, but..." He stared at his father, suddenly grabbed his left hand, looked at it.

The thumb was flaming red from pressure, the tissue scraped and oozing blood.

Chris looked him in the eyes, nodded slowly, but said nothing.

129

They landed at Montgomery Field in San Diego, just ahead of drifting fog. They taxied to their tie-down spot. Chris had been very quiet all the while.

"Great flight, Skipper," said the girl, as they unsnapped their safety harnesses.

"Thanks," said Chris. He took a deep breath, shook his head, and twisted in his seat. "Before this kaffee-klatsch breaks up, there's something you ladies got to know."

His mother said softly: "What's that, Ace?"

He grinned, and it was the sun coming up. He hugged his father's shoulders. "If we hadn't had the brass along, we'd be smeared against those pines."

Ellen smiled, and the girl giggled: she still didn't comprehend.

"Airspeed," said the admiral, as they walked to their parked car. "Airspeed, airspeed, airspeed. That's all I want you to remember."

"Airspeed," his son echoed, smiling.

He was finishing his first tour off the *Intrepid* when a cold catapult shot flung him, fighting for altitude, into the Gulf of Tonkin. The carrier ran him down.

There was no airspeed to save him then, through no fault of his own, and the news of it had almost killed his dad.

Lying on the motor home floor, the admiral had slipped into a reverie, and the sound of the woman moaning brought him back. He had missed his chance to plan, undisturbed.

He felt a toe prodding him and opened his eyes. Miguel was looking down at him, unshaven, unsmiling. From the floor, the Mexican seemed gigantic. He jerked his head toward the rear. "Ay!"

The admiral rose painfully. His mouth was sour, his tongue was dry, and his shoulders ached. The area around his pacemaker was sore to the touch; he must have slept on it.

The clock next to the TV read 7:28. The desert sun was already heating the roof; the admiral reached up unsteadily and turned on the air-conditioner. Bunkie was in the toilet; Jeff swung down like a gymnast from the bunk over the front seat.

He heard Miguel tell Jeff that Terry had a terrible night but that the Navy doctor had done his best to ease her pain. The admiral had to hide his surprise when he heard Jeff answer that Navy doctors were the best in the world.

Terry began to moan again. "He better give her another T, amigo," said Jeff in Spanish.

"No hay más," said Miguel, his voice full of strain.

No more pills!

The admiral saw Jeff study his cellmate. "Could it be that you have been taking them, Miguel?"

For a long moment Miguel stared into Jeff's eyes. In slow, measured Spanish he said: "When my sister needs them? It is strange that you ask that. No! Tell the doctor he must get more."

The admiral tensed. How was he going to do that?

Jeff turned to him. "He says he's out of the Talwins."

"Well, she needs something!"

"You're going to have to write a prescription at the local drugstore. I'll go along and hold your hand."

Jesus... To stall, he moved aft to examine the girl again. Her brother was explaining to her in machine-gun Spanish that they were going to get better drugs to ease her pain, that Navy doctors were good; that in Tijuana, a certain Dr. Hernandez would take out the bullet if the Navy doctor couldn't; that in Ipala, their Aunt Rosa would take care of her until she healed.

The admiral motioned Miguel out of the way and regarded his patient. She was haggard, drawn, with shadowed eyes. Her shoulder seemed more swollen: when he tried to move her arm she yelped in agony.

He returned to the main compartment. Jeff had put Bunkie to work cooking breakfast: she was breaking eggs to scramble in a frying pan. She had tears in her eyes.

To her grandfather, she murmured: "I was thinking of Halsey all night... I thought it was all a dream... I thought he'd be here, and he isn't...." She was suddenly in his arms, sobbing.

"That's enough," Jeff said. "You hear me, kid?"

The admiral finally had to push her away. He moved to the window, peered out through the Venetian blind. Storm clouds were building to the west. Snow on the passes, so early? October first. It had happened a hundred and thirty years before. . . .

In the next parking slot an old man from an Airstream trailer was hitching it to his pickup. Terry began to scream in pain. The ancient paused, head cocked.

He was hearing her, sure as hell. . . .

The old man started for the office, turned, and wavered indecisively. His wife stepped out of their trailer, looked at the Winnebago. There was a short conference, and she approached.

Too old, slow thinking, he decided. No help there, at all, so he might as well alert his captors to gain favor. "Somebody's coming," he warned.

"Allí viene alguien," Jeff translated for the Mexican. Swiftly, both men scooped up their guns. Jeff grabbed Bunkie and shoved her with them to the rear. "Play it right," he growled at the admiral. "Play it goddamn *right*."

There was a cautious knock. The admiral opened the door. The lady wore a dressing gown and had orange hair piled high: she was pushing seventy, and wearing purple eye makeup. "Is everything OK?"

He told her that he was a doctor, and his granddaughter was jogging yesterday and today she had muscle cramps. "She'll be fine. Sorry she disturbed you."

The woman looked deep into his eyes. He smiled, reassuringly. She seemed impressed with what she saw. "That's all right, sir, we were just worried." She turned away and the admiral shut the door. He had got away with it but his heart was racing.

"You did OK," conceded Jeff, returning to the front of the motor home. "Now sit down." Jeff slid next to the window at the dinette table, where he could watch the trailer-park office through the slits in the Venetian blind. The admiral sat opposite him.

Jeff motioned to Bunkie. "The eggs, Tubby. Quick! 'I have promises to keep, and miles to go before I sleep.'"

"My name isn't Tubby," Bunkie spat. The admiral shot

her a warning glance but she slammed the eggs before Jeff on the table.

Though ordinarily a fine cook, she'd blackened the batch to ruin.

Jeff looked up at her. "You know, kid, you're a hell of a fuckin' waitress?"

"Thank you," she muttered.

"And a hell of a cook, too." He picked up the plate and sailed it over the bar-counter. It crashed against the oven, and the eggs splattered, sizzling, on the galley stove. "Make me a new batch, and one for Miguel, and one for my lady, and then clean that up, and gimme a beer right now."

The admiral moved to get the beer. Jeff clutched at his arm. "Not *you*. *Her!*" When she handed him the can of beer, he opened it, took a drink, and flicked on his radio scanner. The channels were very busy. The radio traffic was staccato police code that eluded the admiral, but Jeff seemed to understand it well. Most of it dealt with the search, and seemed to invigorate Jeff. The admiral heard the dispatcher call a car in Carson: "On the Pontiac Pan Am at Keystone and Interstate Eighty? Those stains on the seat were positive. Frankie hit *somebody*."

"One Mary Eight Seven, ten-four. *Good!*"

"Shit!" exploded Jeff. "They'll have every hospital in the state staked out."

"And every drugstore," warned the admiral. Jesus, he could no more write out a prescription than the Gettysburg Address!

Jeff only grinned. "Well, we can't have Terry hollering all the way to T-town. So a drugstore is a chance we'll have to take."

"I'm not licensed in Nevada." To have a pharmacist question his credentials in front of Jeff would be suicidal.

Jeff shrugged. "You talked that old bat into leaving. And you talked your way out of that ditch. *Now* you're going to talk your way into some dope." His blue eyes gleamed. "You got prescription blanks?"

"Why would I?" muttered the admiral.

"That's true. Why would you?" Jeff seemed amused. "OK, if you try for morphine or codeine without a blank, they'll probably call the cops. So no Class Three drugs, right?"

Class Three? What was that? The admiral nodded wisely. "That's right. No Class Three."

"How about more Talwins?" demanded Jeff. "They Class Four?"

The admiral cleared his throat. "Yeah."

"Then get Talwin Fifties." Jeff thought for a moment. "But even for Talwins you're going to need your Drug Enforcement Agency identification number...."

"That's right," said the admiral bleakly. Whatever the hell *that* was....

Bunkie ladled out another plate of eggs for Jeff, more carefully, and placed her grandfather's Branflakes before him. The admiral found that he had no appetite, but Jeff began to wolf his breakfast down. Chewing vigorously, he regarded the admiral. "Well, your DEA number? You *got* it?"

"At home," the admiral murmured.

"That figures." Jeff smiled. "And you don't *remember* it, I guess?"

"Look, I'm retired! I haven't prescribed a drug for years!" His hands were clammy. "I'll just have to dream a number up!"

Jeff shook his head, watching him with twinkling eyes. "They're computer-generated, Doctor. By the *federal government*. You can't fake it, because any licensed druggist has the formula to authenticate it in his head." He finished sipping his beer and sighed. "You know, I'm kind of surprised you didn't know that."

"I'd forgotten." His voice sounded weak.

"I see." Jeff smiled again. "Well, you better think of something." Jeff finished the last of his scrambled eggs, washed them down with beer, and tossed the beer can into the galley. "Pull the plugs and let's split. There ought to be a drugstore open now."

The admiral started to get up. Jeff grabbed his arm.

"Don't screw it up." The sapphire eyes went hard. "You hear?"

"Yes..."

"Or we'll blow off your fuckin' head."

*   *   *

The admiral cruised the Sunday morning streets of Fallon, and found them bleak as the moon. The first drugstore he spotted was closed. Finally, across the street from the Bonanza Casino and Lounge, he found a smaller one. A customer was entering it, and he could see the druggist working at his counter in the back. The neon sign in the window read STRAUB'S PHARMACY.

The admiral pulled the motor home into the Bonanza parking lot. Jeff stuck his .45 in his belt, put on the admiral's leather flying jacket, and opened the motor home door.

The admiral heard him murmuring in Spanish to Miguel, something about the child. He could not catch the words.

He squeezed Bunkie's hand: they had hardly been apart since they left Independence eighteen days before, and God knew what might happen if the drugstore was staked out.

"Ten minutes, Lambchop," he promised. "Or fifteen. ...Play it cool. And don't make the Mexican mad, no matter what."

There were tears in her eyes. "Pops, be careful?"

He nodded and stepped to the ground. There was no traffic on the street. It was cooler than yesterday: the storm to the west must be a cold front, sending tendrils of chill before it.

"She better *not* make him mad," agreed Jeff. "I just told him to waste her if this thing don't go down."

The admiral whirled on him. "You son of a bitch—"

"So *think* of that, amigo, when you make your pitch in there."

Shaken, the admiral hesitated at the curb. Across the street, in Straub's Pharmacy, he could see the customer leafing through magazines as the druggist stood in silhouette, typing at his counter in the rear.

He felt naked. His heart began to pound. There seemed no way to avoid exposure in the drugstore, and God knew what Jeff and the Mexican would do to him—and Bunkie—when they found out that he wasn't a doctor.

135

From somewhere came a sudden inspiration.

Suppose he *didn't* try to impersonate a doctor? Suppose he just pulled rank?

He grabbed Jeff's arm and stopped him. "Why *should* I tell him I'm a doctor? I don't have my DEA."

"How'll you get the T's?"

"I'm an admiral in the Navy."

"It won't mean a thing in there."

It might mean plenty, if he set it up right. The admiral jerked his thumb at the entrance to the Bonanza. "Let me call him from there first. Hell, if he's going to turn me down, why go in?"

Jeff shrugged. "As long as I hear every word."

They turned and entered the Bonanza. A Modoc Indian woman, wearing pink slacks and blue running shoes, was mopping the fake-marble foyer; otherwise the place was deserted, except for a bartender, a lonely blackjack croupier, a scruffy slot-machine addict, and a yawning waitress swabbing café tables by the windows.

The admiral stepped to a pay phone on the foyer wall. He looked up Straub's Pharmacy. He jabbed the numbers as Jeff watched him with a tiny smile on his lips. Across the street, through the Bonanza's open entrance, the admiral saw the druggist pick up a phone and cradle it against his shoulder as he typed.

"Straub's Pharmacy, Fred Straub speaking." The voice sounded chipper, and efficient.

Good . . . It was owner-operated: the druggist wouldn't be afraid of getting fired.

The admiral pitched his voice a trifle low, and affected a Texan drawl. "Mr. Straub, this is Dr. White at NAS Fallon. I'm duty MO in the Dispensary today. I got a problem."

"Yes sir. Shoot."

He could hear Straub hunting-and-pecking as he talked: presumably typing a label at the counter. Fine: the busier he was, the better.

"There's a retired naval officer on his way to your pharmacy, an Admiral Washburn—"

"An *admiral*? My, my!"

136

"He twisted his knee, on a motor home trip with his son."

"What can I do for him, Doctor?"

The typing stopped. He heard the druggist ripping labels from the typewriter. The pecking began again.

"I wrote him a prescription for Talwin Fifties. But our pharmacy was out of Talwins, so they sent him in to you."

"Fine. I have plenty."

Tap-tap-tap . . . Tap-tap.

He took a deep breath and explained that his pharmacist's mate had forgotten to give the admiral back his prescription and the admiral had left the base without it.

Tap . . . Tap-tap-tap . . .

"Yes?" A note of caution entered the druggist's voice.

The slot-machine player had moved closer. The admiral tried to shield the mouthpiece: he couldn't have the druggist hearing slots. He wiped his brow and continued: "Now, the admiral appears to be in a hurry to get home. I'm afraid he won't look kindly on us if you have to send him back."

Silence. Then: "Well, no *real* problem, I guess," said the druggist slowly, "as long as you mail me the script tomorrow. What dosage, Doctor?"

"Regular."

A pause. "Which is what?"

He took a shot in the dark. "One every four hours."

"As required?" the druggist prompted.

"Right. As required."

"And how many?"

"Fifty."

The typing stopped abruptly. "Did you say *fifty*?"

Shit. He'd overdone it. "No, *sir*! *Talwin* Fifties. A bottle of twenty-five."

Another silence. "All right, he'll get 'em." The typing continued.

"I sure do thank you, Mr. Straub!" The admiral tried to keep the triumph from his voice.

"Not at all," said Straub. "Oh! What's your DEA number?"

Shit! The admiral winced. *Tap. Tap-tap-tap . . .*

"We don't use DEA's much, out here," the admiral

137

said. "It's somewhere in the safe, I reckon." The excuse sounded weak, and the typing stopped again.

"Afraid I *have* to have a DEA number, sir."

If he could just delay . . . He cupped the phone slightly, and called, to no one: "What's that, Chief? Oh, hell! Get her on the table!"

In the foyer, Jeff looked startled, the Indian scrubwoman stared at him curiously, and the slot-machine player glanced up.

The admiral spoke again into the mouthpiece. "They just brought in a kid that fell in the pool! I'll have my duty yeoman call you with my DEA."

He hung up and glanced across the street. The silhouetted figure was slowly hanging up the phone.

Jeff was smiling at him. "So how do you think you did?"

He told Jeff that he'd failed: the druggist was waiting for a call he'd never get.

"We'll try anyway," smiled Jeff.

"Are you crazy?"

"Hell, if he won't give you the Talwins, we'll take his whole damn shop."

His face showed that he meant it, every word.

The admiral had no choice. With his enemy at his side, he crossed the street, remembering to limp.

He braced himself, took a breath, and together they entered the store.

The admiral stood at the drug counter with Jeff at his side. The only other customer had left the shop. It seemed too good to be true, but there had been no mention of waiting for a call from NAS. Through the door of the stockroom beyond the counter, he could see Straub counting out his tablets.

"Been busy, for a Sunday," the druggist called out. He was a bald, potbellied man with rosy cheeks and prissy lips. "But I never thought I'd be stealing business from the air base."

"*I* never thought the Navy could run out of pills," the

admiral said. "I haven't paid for medicine in damn near thirty years."

"This'll be a shock, then, sir. Twelve dollars."

The admiral dug into his wallet for his Visa card, slid it onto the counter. Jeff shook his head. "Cash," he muttered.

The admiral tensed. *He doesn't want an invoice trail, in case they find my body.* But this was not the time to think of that.

"Twelve bucks!" repeated Straub, capping the bottle. "It's ridiculous! Well, he *told* me twenty-five tablets: that must really be some knee!"

"He can hardly sleep, poor guy," Jeff called back compassionately. The admiral stared at him. He was slipping Nytol sleeping tablets into the pocket of the flight jacket, a bottle at a time. Jeff grinned back. "He was thrashing around half the night."

Jesus Christ, insane...

The druggist returned to the counter and put down the bottle of pills. He began to type the label, his tongue between his lips. Two feet from his eyes, Jeff's hand crept toward a digital thermometer on sale. The admiral cleared his throat to warn him, but the hand slid closer and closer until the thermometer disappeared as if by magic into the jacket pocket.

"You're traveling through?" asked the druggist. *Tap-tap ... Tap-tap-tap ...*

The thefts had made the admiral speechless, but Jeff answered: "Got to get him home to Salt Lake City. Got to pack that knee in ice."

"Best thing," agreed Straub. He looked at the flight jacket Jeff was wearing. "You a pilot, son?"

"This is Dad's. I'm a pharmacist. Just graduated."

The admiral's hands turned sweaty, but Straub beamed: "Well, how about that!" He squinted at his typewriter. "*Once every four hours ...* A pharmacist! Good, we need new blood. Nevada?"

Tap ... Tap-tap-tap.

Jeff nodded happily. "School of Pharmacology. Got out yesterday."

"*As required*," the druggist murmured, typing it out.

He rolled the label from the typewriter. "Yesterday?" He raised his eyebrows.

"I wanted to finish early."

The admiral flinched. *What's the bastard trying to test? My sense of humor, or my guts?*

Straub pressed the label on the bottle. The admiral pulled a twenty from his wallet. The pharmacist glanced at his clock. "NAS said they'd call, but I won't keep you, Admiral."

"Thanks." He almost collapsed in relief.

"I'll call *them*," said Straub. He reached for the skinny Fallon phone book and began to turn its pages.

Oh, God...

The admiral met Jeff's eyes. Jeff was grinning.

What was going on inside his head? There was no way to know.

Bunkie saw her grandfather and their captor enter the casino, and later saw them as they walked across the street. She was sitting in the passenger seat, where the Mexican had motioned her. In the mirror on the sun visor, she could see Miguel's reflection as he lounged at the dinette table. He had his scary pistol on the table in front of him. There was a stubble of whiskers on his strong, handsome face.

He had fired at Halsey, and she hated him, but not as much as the other one.

He looked drowsy. If he would take a siesta, she could ease the door to the cab open, quietly, and run to the casino...

Somebody did it on "Starsky and Hutch" once, and got away from a kidnapper. She put her hand on the door handle, gently shoved. It grated loudly. She yanked her hand back as if she'd been burned.

She looked up into the mirror. He was cocking his head, listening. *That* she had better not try again.

Her eye fell on the CB radio. She loved to use it, on the road, though it sometimes didn't work. When they'd started out, Pops had been uptight about it: they didn't have a license, or something. But finally, in Kansas, when

140

she was bored along the Platte, he had let her use it as much as she wanted: she gave herself the call sign "Lambchop," and talked to other motor homes and truckers. She'd convinced a trucker named "Superstud," somewhere ahead on Interstate 80, that she was eighteen, and he'd tried to make a date.

There was an emergency channel: Nine. And an emergency call: "React." Even the highway patrol listened to that, Pops said, in case a driver saw an accident on the highway. If the Mexican fell asleep, and she could raise "React," then they'd be saved.

She looked across the street at the drugstore. Through the store window, she could see her grandfather and Jeff talking to the druggist in the rear.

Pops, be careful, please?

She stirred restlessly, scared but bored. She wished that she could turn on the stereo: she loved music: rock, country, or classical: she and Pops had been awash in country and western, all along the trail.

Well, Mexicans liked music, all Latinos did.

Her eyes widened. *Rock music, turned high, could drown her voice and she could try to use the CB.*

She wouldn't dare.

Or would she?

She turned and somehow forced a smile. "Miguel?"

"¿Sí?"

"Music? You like music?"

He looked blank.

Maybe she should hum a bar of *La Cucaracha*. Somehow she didn't think so. She pointed to the stereo. "Stereo? OK?"

He rose, and backed to the rear, never taking his eyes from her. He asked his sister something.

"Ees OK," the woman called out weakly. "Turn eet on."

Bunkie switched on the ignition and clicked on the stereo. She dialed through three country stations before she found rock. It was the Manhattan Transfer, booming hard and crystal clear. She turned up the volume until the dashboard quivered.

Now, to get hold of the microphone, unclip it from the console, and sneak it to her lips.

Slowly, carefully, she let her hand creep forward, while she planned what she would say.

"React! React! This is Lambchop. Do you copy?"

"Lambchop," they would say. *"This is React, go ahead."*

"Mayday! We've been kidnapped," she would answer, *"Come and get us, we're in Fallon, in a cream-colored motor home ..."*

She looked into the mirror. Miguel's shoulders were moving to Manhattan Transfer's beat. So were hers. She moved her hand further toward the mike, finally clasped it and eased it from its clip on the console, pretending to be working with the stereo.

She clicked on the CB, turned it to Channel Nine. She checked Miguel in the mirror, began slowly to raise the mike to her face. So far, OK ...

She took a deep breath, lifted it the rest of the way to her mouth, pressed the mike button—

"Ay!" shouted Miguel.

She froze, the mike at her lips, eyes on the mirror. Miguel was charging toward the front, with his shotgun in his hands. She heard him slam a shell into it.

But he was looking out the window, not at her. She jerked the microphone from her lips, but was afraid to sneak it across her lap and clip it back into its place, for fear he'd see it. She cringed in her seat, following his gaze.

A police car was pulling up in front of the drugstore. *He would think she'd called the cops, and kill her!*

He squatted between the seats, his gun ready. Absently, without looking, he reached out and turned the stereo off. She could smell his body sweating, and her own.

She must get the mike back to its clip. Slowly, her hand crept toward him and the CB set. His gaze stayed on the police car across the street.

She shivered. *What would happen to Pops, trapped in the store between the blond man and the cop?*

She must not think of that, not yet. It seemed to take

an hour to sneak the microphone back, just inches from the Mexican's arm. Slowly she inserted it into the clip, and flinched as she heard it snap.

Only then did she see wires hanging from the CB set and dangling under the dash.

Sometime last night the blond man must have reached in and torn them loose.

She'd risked it all for nothing. . . .

Stomach churning, she grabbed her mouth, shoved past the Mexican, ran to the toilet, and threw up.

The druggist turned the pages of the phonebook, implacably searching for the number of the Naval Air Station. The admiral's mind was fluttering like a bird trapped in a hangar: there was no escape. When NAS answered, and there was no "Dr. White," Jeff would simply rob the pharmacy and flee, and they'd all go down—Bunkie too— somewhere on the highway in a hail of sheriff's lead.

The druggist found the number. He wrote it down. A chime sounded as someone entered. Straub looked up and smiled. "Hi, Sergeant!" he called, and dialed the NAS.

The admiral turned.

A Nevada highway patrolman, freckled, broad-shouldered, and as tall as himself, in a slate-gray uniform with a star the size of a fist, was threading down the aisle. On his hip swung a pearl-handled .38 magnum.

From the corner of his eye the admiral saw Jeff ease down the zipper of his flight jacket: the bulge underneath seemed enormous.

Outside the drugstore window sat a silver highway patrol car.

The admiral stiffened. He had no thought of trying to signal the cop, only fear for Bunkie.

If Miguel saw the car, and thought they'd blown it, what was he doing to Bunkie now?

The sergeant was carrying a printed poster. "Got something for you, Fred."

The druggist held out his hand, cradling the phone. "What's this?"

"A flier on those fuckers that killed Frankie."

The druggist groaned. "He *died?*"

The sergeant nodded.

The admiral glimpsed Jeff's bearded face on the flier, and caught a flash of Miguel's broad lips. He heard a busy signal from the phone. Slowly, Straub replaced the phone in its cradle while he studied the circular.

"Anyway," the sergeant said, "one of 'em must have got hit."

"Which one?" asked Straub.

"We don't know."

"Well, I hope he bleeds to death."

"We heard about that," Jeff volunteered. He scowled at the pictures, shaking his head. "Bastards! I hope so too."

The admiral's knees began to tremble. He leaned against the counter.

The sergeant looked at Jeff. "You're . . . Who?"

"Philip Washburn." Jeff smiled. He inclined his head toward the admiral. "I'm Admiral Washburn's son."

Jeff stuck out his hand. The sergeant shook it without enthusiasm, then nodded at the admiral. "Morning, sir." He turned to the druggist. "Now, Fred . . . ?"

"Yes?"

"Keep your eyes open. We think they doubled back—"

"Those pills—" began the admiral. He wanted to get back to Bunkie: something awful was sure to happen across the street. "You want to give me those pills?"

The druggist ignored him, and the sergeant continued: "We found a van twenty miles north, out on Ninety-five, and somebody'd shot a dog. The cartridges matched the ones from the shoot-out outside Carson."

"Gentlemen," the admiral interrupted, "we've got a long drive today, OK?"

Straub hesitated, started to pick up the phone again, shrugged and replaced it. He put the bottle on the counter. The admiral took it and turned to go.

"Wait!" called Jeff.

Jesus, what now?

"Don't you get some change, Dad?"

"Right," said Straub. "Sorry, sir."

The druggist scooped eight dollars from the register, handed them to the admiral, and returned to the circulars.

Knees wobbling, with Jeff at his side, the admiral hurried from the store.

"*Limp*, goddamn it," warned Jeff, "or you'll blow the whole damn scene!"

The admiral somehow slowed his pace. They crossed the street and he jerked open the door. Bunkie was emerging from the toilet, looking wan. The Mexican, breathing hard, had seen the police car and still had his shotgun ready in his hands.

Jeff climbed in behind him, and quietly shut the door.

"No problema, amigo," Jeff told Miguel. "Todo fué bien."

Terry was moaning in agony. The admiral carefully spilled two Talwins from the bottle.

Miguel took Jeff aside and whispered to him. Jeff nodded, and told the admiral that Terry's pain was worse, and Miguel didn't think the Talwins would work, by mouth. "He wants to cook some up and mainline her."

The admiral grimaced. "I don't know...."

"Why not?"

The admiral thought it over. He didn't want the woman overdosed. But she was groaning more loudly, and sweat was beading her brother's brow. Miguel demanded to know what the doctor thought.

Jeff pressed him: "He says, goddamn it, will it *work*?"

Under Jeff's cold blue stare he had to answer something. "Well...I guess so."

"Good." There was a flicker of amusement in Jeff's eyes. "Funny you didn't think of it yourself."

"There are contraindications, I'd go easy."

Jeff smiled enigmatically. "'Contraindications?' Think of that." He told Miguel to go ahead. The Mexican melted the two pills in a spoon at the stove, took a needle from the suitcase, and injected his sister tenderly. Soon she drifted into sleep.

In five minutes the motor home, with the admiral at the wheel, was heading toward Carson City, and the Carson Pass beyond.

The admiral was uncomfortable. His disguise was somehow failing: he seemed to be losing Jeff's confidence more with every mile.

Something in the great charade was going wrong.

MORGAN

THE CARRIAGE AHEAD BEGAN TO INCH FORWARD. A HUGE frying pan tied to its rear clanged against an iron washtub, in a head-splitting rhythm Morgan had been hearing for ten miles.

He shifted miserably on the driver's seat and snicked the reins, flicking dust from the haunches of their mules.

The elder, Daedalus, shook his head. Stop and go, stop and go: those who ruled him were insane. The younger, Icarus, responded, too: he raised his tail and defecated.

It was Morgan's day to drive. They were approaching the heights above Ash Hollow, a landmark grove nestling in the bottomlands south of the Platte. In the last six weeks, eight thousand wagons had descended from these bluffs down Windlass Hill, cutting ruts so deeply into the chalky soil that, once the wagon wheels had found them, it was impossible to turn aside.

At least, he thought, no one else could pass them until they had reached the bottom: the grade ahead was said to be so steep that the baggage wagons had to be eased down by winching turns of rope around tree trunks, as sailors lowered anchors around windlasses at sea, and even the light passenger wagons would have to be slowed until their smoking brake shoes shrieked in protest.

All morning long, on the rolling hills behind, they had been passed by trains anxious to beat them to the heights, trying to avoid the Pioneer Line's inevitable congestion before the descent began.

The Line, slowed by its own baggage wagons, was still the laughingstock of the westbound horde. From the first, Turner had decreed that, in order to keep the passengers from outdistancing their belongings and commissary, the carriages must always follow the supply train, eating dust from the paid teamsters ahead.

They were, as Hollister said, a logjam in the river of human progress. Lined up for twenty miles behind them, Morgan knew, were other trains, late themselves, cursing Turner and all who traveled with him.

He should have gone by sea. If he survived the plains and mountains ahead and got to California, when he brought Mary back he would certainly do so: no miseries rounding the Horn or crossing Nicaragua could equal those he was enduring behind the swaying wagons, inching along the Platte. He was caked in dust like an ancient mummy.

Carriage Eighteen was doubly cursed. It was still without a proper top, a full two weeks after the ridiculous capsize east of Fort Kearny. Their plight was no longer funny. They lay atop their gear, unsheltered from sun and rain. When the sun blazed on high—and today it was only three days past its summer solstice—they baked like muffins on an open hearth; when thundershowers swept the plains, they could only burrow under the folded tent in the swaying, creaking vehicle; when the skies hurled lightning bolts, they cringed and cursed the captain.

Captain Turner seemed to think their plight trivial, and blamed the six messmates for abandoning the splintered framework where it lay.

Unless they could find an artisan, they would have to repair the top themselves. Pioneer Line passengers were not used to handling tools. Lawyers, doctors, merchants, surveyors, were no help. Stein, the saddler, had worked with his hands, but knew no more than anyone else of carriage making. Oglethorpe, the gentleman farmer, had palms like a woman's cheeks. Devitt, the laughing Irish blacksmith, could surely have rebuilt it, but *he* slept by the Vermillion in a bed of Kansas sod.

They had surveyed each abandoned wagon they had passed along the trail—they saw more of them every week—but none had framing as light as theirs.

The carriage ahead had stopped. Daedalus sighed and halted; Icarus snorted, farted, and tried to lie down in the traces.

"Shit," breathed Morgan. He looked around guiltily. From contact with the teamsters, his language was deteriorating on the trail. He had not used the word since college.

No one had heard. Stein sat on a pile of blankets, miserable, lost in thought, his arms braced on a broken bonnet frame. Cantrell, who began to sip at his store of whiskey earlier each day, already snored atop the folded tent.

The rest of his messmates were elsewhere. Oglethorpe, the Southern dandy, had good legs, a horror of dust, and preferred to stay at the head of the train; his slave Joshua followed him everywhere. Hollister was on horseback, somewhere up there too. Vanderveer was ranging somewhere far to the south, hunting buffalo alone.

The lieutenant, who seemed able to swallow animosities as quickly as he cooked them up, had borrowed the Jennings repeating rifle from Stein, and asked Morgan to lend him Major.

He was a good rider, for a seaman, and at target practice one nooning, had shown himself to be a deadly shot. Morgan found it easy to lend him the horse, simply for the prospect of fresh meat.

The carriage ahead jerked three feet forward. Icarus stumbled and succeeded in falling. He lay panting in the traces, forcing Daedalus to his knees. Morgan dropped to the ground. He kicked Icarus mightily in the ribs. The mule regarded him reproachfully and began a halfhearted struggle to stand up.

Morgan strolled ahead. The first of their baggage wagons was starting down the bluffs, rear wheels locked with chains, rear axle roped to a worn tree stump, with two teamsters playing out line as the wagon began to move.

He moved to the edge of the bluff and looked down on the plain. In the grove of ash below, a hundred wagons clustered. There was no fodder left *there*, almost certainly.

The spring rains and the summer thunderstorms should have made the bottomlands a sea of grass; instead, overgrazing from the passing trains had turned it to a desert. In the fresh prairie air, one should have been able, from this elevation, to see for fifty miles. But an endless line of wagons was rolling toward the sun, raising a cloud of dust over the brown raped land. The yellow stain ruined the scene from the Platte to the southern hills.

He had read Frémont's journals well, and had Ware's guidebook in his carpetbag. From here, both had viewed Chimney Rock past Courthouse Rock, though it was fifty miles away. Today, one could hardly make out the river through the haze.

He wondered if this prairie land would ever be the same.

He saw Captain Turner, a bantam cock in a saddle, shading his eyes and peering west, like Hannibal astride the Alps.

Morgan wandered over to him. "Good evening, Captain. You see fodder?"

The little man jerked, startled. "No. I'm looking for Scotts Bluff."

Morgan stared up at him. "*Scotts*— You mean Courthouse Rock? Or Chimney Rock, sir?"

Turner glared down. His eyes were bloodshot; he seemed choleric; he had lost weight.

"I *said* Scotts Bluff, I *meant* Scotts Bluff!"

In his eyes Morgan caught a glimpse of fear. Then Turner wheeled his horse and trotted to the men on the tree-stump winch. In a moment he was cursing them for paying out rope too quickly.

Morgan returned slowly to his carriage. Cantrell was awake and sipping meditatively from his bottle, silhouetted against the darkening sky. Icarus had arisen from the dead. Morgan scratched the mule's dusty ear, by way of apology for the kick, and hoisted himself to his seat of pain.

A leaden weight of dread had settled into his stomach.

He was only a passenger. But he knew where Scotts Bluff lay: a full hundred miles from here, across the shrouded plain.

Their leader was either ignorant of the route, or slowly going mad.

Even a fool could get them to Laramie: the ruts were like railroad tracks. But beyond the Great Divide lay mystery, and a score of different trails.

Shit...

The carriage ahead moved ten yards toward the setting sun, the washtub on its rear tolling dismally. The first wagon must have reached the bottom. Morgan jiggled his reins. The carriage creaked forward and stopped again.

Cantrell touched his arm. He turned. The doctor was holding out the bottle. "Unhappy with our progress?" he asked Morgan.

It did no good to grouse. "No. We're moving, bit by bit."

"Well, you seem in low spirits, try mine."

Cantrell's whiskey was terrible, "skull varnish" diluted with molasses. He had bought it at twenty-five cents the quart from an itinerant peddler outside Fort Kearny, when his medicinal whiskey barrel had gone dry. Ordinarily, even Morgan—who had an iron stomach for spirits—avoided it. Now he took a gulp that burned his toes.

As usual, it failed to help.

Mary, darling Mary, I fear evil days ahead.

They finished their descent by moonlight and crowded in among the other camps at Ash Hollow, setting the wagons in their well-practiced pattern. Morgan followed the carriage in front of them into the circular course, reined the vehicle to a stop. Since no teamster deigned to take the trouble, he and Hollister unhitched Daedalus and Icarus, hobbled them, and led them to the herd, which—forage being nil—was feeding on the shrinking stock of hay pitched out from feed wagons.

They returned to lay the wagon tongue of their carriage

on a rear axle of the one preceding, to form a corral for the stock, so that the teamsters could drive them in.

They pitched their tent outside the circle and laid their cooking fires farther out, following a tradition started when Indian raids were thought to be a threat to wagon trains. The theory, never tested by the Line, was that the savages would be silhouetted against the fire, and easy targets for well-armed men.

Vanderveer had not returned by the time their tent was pitched, so they lit a lantern and fastened it to a nearby ash to guide him.

They had pitched their tent within a hundred yards of a Michigan outfit. A rumor swept the Pioneer Line that one of the Michigan company had brought his wife. Stein was trying, for the third time that month, to bake edible bread over their campfire, when they heard the woman's voice, singing, from one of the Michigan fires. Morgan and Isaiah drifted over. A circle of men had gathered for a recital, and the two stood on the outskirts and listened.

The woman's husband played a scratchy fiddle, and the woman had a voice to match. She tackled *I'm Queen of Fairy Land* and *She Wore a Wreath of Roses*, damaging both, but the applause was spirited nonetheless.

Despite her ludicrous voice, Morgan felt his throat tighten in loneliness. He walked back through flickering fires, under a crescent moon. In Mary's home in Rensselaerville, the hired girl would have cleared the table by now, and the doctor and his wife would be sitting in the parlor, she knitting and he scanning the paper. Mary might be singing, in her fine soft lilting way; she would accompany herself on the piano, since her accompanist was a thousand miles away. . . .

Stein's bread was worse than ever, and the salt pork almost rotten. Where were Vanderveer and Major?

They were still missing by the time he and Isaiah, who were assigned to guard the stock from eight to midnight, went to stand their watch.

He felt a chill of apprehension. Lost? Impossible, he would simply have ridden north and intercepted the Great Platte River Road. If Major had thrown a shoe, he'd have led him back afoot by now; if he'd had success in his hunt, he'd have ridden back for help in dressing and butchering his kill.

He disliked Vanderveer thoroughly and loved his horse, but was pleasantly surprised to find that he was more concerned with the absence of the man than the beast. He must be growing in Christian virtue: something in the hardship they were enduring had forged a bond.

No matter how oafish Vanderveer was, he was a strong traveler who did more than his part. He seldom complained about anything but Turner, and in that he was part of a crowd.

Watch out for Pawnees on the trail . . .

Ridiculous. They had seen none at all.

He left Isaiah to guard the stock and moved out of the stench of the animals to the westernmost wagon, near which the captain had pitched his tent.

Morgan ducked in through the flap. He found Turner and his commissary clerk checking lists of supplies, by the light of an oil lamp hung from the tentpole.

He told him Vanderveer had not yet returned.

"Christ!" Turner looked up in annoyance. "I'm low on feed, you've wrecked Eighteen, Nine has a cracked hub, Four's got a busted spring! Chihuahua Harry's poorly—you'd best take a look at his ass—and seventeen mules have the heaves. Now *this*! What do you want *me* to do?"

"Send back a party. He's *your* passenger," Morgan reminded him, annoyed.

"He's on *your* horse," said Turner.

"The hell with my horse! A horse means more to some than others." He was growing very angry. "Eight poor damn Pawnee Indians learned that!"

Turner jumped to his feet. "That was Vanderveer's raid, not mine!"

"You let your teamsters ride with him! You can spare some to look for him now!"

"*You* want to go, Dr. Washburn?"

"No," he said quite honestly, "I don't."

Turner sat down. He shuffled his papers. "I didn't think you would."

"I don't *want* to go, but I will."

The commissary clerk shot his eyes toward the tent flap. Turner glanced up, and Morgan turned.

Vanderveer stood in the entrance. His eyes were blank.

"'Evening, gentlemen," he said coolly. "Doctor, your horse took a ball in the withers. He's with the stock. I never got a shot at the son of a bitch that did it, but you better take a look."

A bolt of terror shot through him. "Shot?" he exclaimed. "By whom?"

Vanderveer said softly: "A Pawnee Indian, Doctor. Who the hell do you think?"

"Pawnee?" exclaimed Turner. "Here?"

"Oh, yes," Vanderveer murmured. "Yes indeed. . . ."

Morgan grabbed a lantern from the camp table, strode into the moonlight, climbing over a wagon tongue to move among the hobbled stock. "Major," he called. *"Major."*

Major whinnied from among the mules, and struggled, limping, to his side.

He lifted the lantern. The ball had entered his right shoulder. He palpated the wound. The bone was shattered.

Major would have to be destroyed.

Vanderveer loomed in the flicker. "I'm sorry, Doctor. When I have the gold, I'll pay you for the horse."

An awful perception was dawning, and he had to know. "I've got a question, Vanderveer."

"'Lieutenant' Vanderveer, please. Or 'Mister.' Fire away."

"*Were* you hunting buffalo," he asked slowly. "Or Pawnee Indians?"

There was a long silence. "Pawnee," murmured Vanderveer. "One Pawnee. *That* one."

"What do you mean, *that* one?"

"There's only one. He's been dogging our wake since Kearny. Chihuahua's seen him too."

Morgan looked into his eyes. "And you didn't tell us?"

"Tell you?" Vanderveer smiled. "Nothing to tell. You wouldn't believe me, and you'd probably never see him. He's like a ghost. I wash in the river, he's in the corner of my eye. I piss at night, he's there. You can't see him, but he's there. The Lower Ford, he was there. The Upper

Ford too, and Green Spring." He shrugged. "I thought he had a bow and arrow, figured I'd draw his fire. I didn't know he had a gun."

"Draw his fire," repeated Morgan. He touched Major's heaving flank. "I have another question."

"Yes?"

"Did you *ride* my horse back, or walk?"

A mule stamped the well-packed soil. Major sighed and nuzzled his shoulder. Distantly, the woman in the Michigan camp trilled of Scotland's bonnie braes.

"I *rode*, Doctor." Vanderveer seemed genuinely puzzled. "Why?"

Morgan put down the lantern carefully. He had boxed at Union College, both bare-knuckled and gloved, for the Chi Psi's in the intramural scraps. He was taller than Vanderveer, but lighter; the fight would be perfectly fair. He shucked out of his jacket and raised his fists.

"You're going to fight. Get up your hands!"

"I'm an officer in the Navy," Vanderveer laughed. "I won't soil them brawling in horseshit!"

Rage was burning inside him. "Perhaps fear is soiling your trousers now!"

"I think not."

"Put up your goddamned fists!"

Vanderveer smiled. "*You're* challenging, *I'll* choose the weapons. Pistols, sir, at fifteen yards. Now, or tomorrow at dawn?"

Major was breathing quickly, fighting to stay afoot. A coyote howled on the prairie; the distant fiddle played.

To strike him, under the Code Duello, meant a duel to the very death. Slowly, Morgan lowered his fists. "I won't risk a life for a horse," he murmured. "Mine, or even yours."

"You're the coward, then, sir, not I!"

Vanderveer spun on his heel and left. Morgan picked up his jacket and donned it again. He felt drained, and strangely weak. Major whinnied, struggled to retain his footing, and went down.

"Major, poor Major." He threw his arms around the silken neck and hugged, drew the Navy Aston from his

154

waistband and cocked it, pressed a cap onto its firing nipple.

Quickly, quickly, while you can . . .

He put the muzzle to the fine long head and fired.

Major jerked, quivered for a long moment, and finally was still.

He reloaded the pistol slowly, jammed it into his belt, and joined Hollister for his watch.

THE ADMIRAL

FOR AN HOUR THE ADMIRAL DROVE SOUTHWEST, WITH Bunkie silent at his side. He heard no more moans from the rear: the injection had worked: the woman must be sleeping. The men behind him were mostly silent: when he heard a voice, it was usually Jeff's, murmuring to Miguel of yesterday's break. He seemed to savor especially the memory of the murdered guard, apparently shot in the face. "Se le rompió la cabeza como un melón . . . ¿no?"

"*. . . head opened up like a busted watermelon.*"

Thank God Bunkie spoke no Spanish. . . .

Skies ahead were darkening. They passed a monument to "Ragtown," on the Emigrant Trail. It had never been a settlement, just a grove of cottonwood by a little spring. The surviving emigrant trains, filthy from the crossing of the Forty Mile Desert, had drunk there, and laundered; then hung their clothes on the cottonwood branches to dry. The waving shirts and trousers had beckoned those who followed in their tracks.

Morgan Washburn, struggling to overtake the Pioneer

Line after burying his comrade Stein, had seen the fluttering laundry and rejoined the Line—or its remnant—within a few short yards of the highway.

Regret weighed in the admiral's chest. If only he had not stopped yesterday, Bunkie and he would have been breakfasting at the spring by now, sipping waters that Morgan had drunk.

Now Bunkie noticed the historical marker. They had stopped at every one, for the last two thousand miles. He reached out and squeezed her hand. He felt Jeff's eyes on the back of his head, and was afraid to speak.

They reached the limits of Carson City, from which the three in back had fled. He expected Jeff to tell him to skirt the town, but he did not. They passed down Carson Street in heavy traffic, past the museum and state capitol. In the inside rear-view mirror he could see Jeff at the table, peering through the slats of the Venetian blind. The admiral chilled. Less than twenty-four hours ago he had murdered a prison guard here; now he was grinning broadly.

Jeff's eyes met his in the mirror. "Just don't run the next stoplight, they shoot you," he called. "Hey, don't sweat it! Didn't you ever read 'The Purloined Letter,' Doc? Safest place for us today in the whole damn State of Nevada!"

He was probably right: no lawman would believe he would ever double back.

Jeff picked up the admiral's Polaroid camera. "This thing work all right?"

"Yes."

"Good. Turn left here, on Fifth."

Puzzled, the admiral turned up a tree-shaded street.

"¿Qué pasa?" cried Miguel, alarmed. "¿Por qué?"

Jeff ignored him. "Drive till you see a bunch of shit-brown buildings, about a mile ahead."

He heard Miguel protesting: "¡Madre de Dios! ¿Estás loco?"

The admiral tensed. He knew Carson: he had schussed down Spooner's Summit when skis were wooden and nine feet long. If they were heading now where he *thought* they were, Miguel was right: the man in back was insane.

156

Or weighing balls? But whose? His own, Miguel's, or mine?

They passed through quiet tree-lined streets, and abruptly back into open desert. The admiral winced. Sure enough, the grim tan walls of the ancient penitentiary loomed ahead.

"Park over there," Jeff said, glancing at the shrouded sun. "So the front end faces away."

The admiral pulled to a graded area off the road, swung in a half-circle, and parked. In his side-view mirrors, he could see the prison gate, a massive porte-cochere towering three hundred yards away.

Uniformed guards seemed everywhere, leaving the place en masse, dressed in well-pressed green uniforms, badges glittering in the feeble sunlight.

"¿Qué pasa?" demanded Miguel again.

Jeff ignored him. "Those fuckers are shined up like an honor guard!" He thought for a moment. "Kreutzer's funeral! ¡Qué fantástico! ¿No?" He jabbed Miguel, handed the Polaroid to the admiral. "Hit the pavement, you old fart, see if you're too scared to shoot a picture." He motioned Miguel to cover them from the cab, and moved in front of the motor home. The admiral hesitated, glancing at Miguel. The Mexican was scowling at his cellmate's back. Jeff turned and motioned the admiral out.

Reluctantly, the admiral opened the driver's door and climbed to the ground.

Jeff, hidden from the front gate by the vehicle, pointed to a spot for the admiral to stand. He opened his shirt, yanked his .45 from his belt, held it across his chest, and smiled dazzlingly into the lens. The admiral peered through the viewfinder: Jesus, the guy looked as if he were posing at a picnic, while his own hands were shaking like leaves.

"Get the gate into the picture! Steady, man, don't drop it!"

The admiral was suddenly angry. Drop it? He'd been through deeper shit in his lifetime than this kid would ever see. He took a deep breath, held it to steady the camera, pressed the shutter, drew out the print.

He forced himself to stand casually as the image came slowly to life. Thank God, it was crystal clear. He wanted

157

to get back to the motor home. God knew what would happen if anyone saw the gun. Bunkie was in a potential line of fire: he wanted to be with her. He cleared his throat; damned if he'd let his voice quaver.

"OK," the admiral called. His hands still trembled. Four guards in a white prison van were pulling from their parking lot, heading toward them on the road.

"Take another one," commanded Jeff. And the .45 stayed out.

Oh, God! The admiral's anger returned: the son of a bitch was trying to get them killed. The admiral composed the picture, shot it, furtively looked at the van.

It passed within twenty feet. The guards inside were laughing and never glanced aside.

The admiral marched stiffly back and climbed into the motor home, wobbly on his feet.

"One for me," Jeff said quietly, "and one to send the warden, when we're out of the goddamn state." He reached out his hand for the pictures and studied them. "Hey, not bad! Not bad at all. I thought you'd fuzz 'em up."

"Yeah?" He smiled, feeling a thrill of pleasure. Annoyed, he wondered why.

Miguel's face was heavy with contempt. He loomed suddenly over Jeff. "¡Qué macho eres! Muy macho, amigo."

"How brave you are! Very brave, my friend."

Jeff flushed. In Spanish he said: "Calm down, amigo. Have a beer, or take a T."

"*They* are for my sister, not for me. Now, understand *this*, compadre! And understand it well! We shall not stop for games again, you hear?" Miguel turned suddenly on the admiral. "¡Y usted! Muy macho también, señor Doctor. Mientras tanto, mi hermana muere."

"Very brave, señor Doctor. Meanwhile, my sister dies."

The admiral, startled, pretended he didn't understand and climbed behind the wheel.

Christ, he'd had no choice. Did the son of a bitch think he'd *wanted* to take the pictures? Or *cared* if Jeff thought he had the guts to do it right?

He knew suddenly that he did care. He'd shown Jeff he could keep his cool. And not just once, but twice.

He glanced at Bunkie.

She was frowning strangely. "Did you *like* that?" she whispered incredulously.

"What could I do?" he murmured.

She only shrugged and looked away.

He pulled back onto the blacktop and headed for Carson Pass.

Bunkie huddled in her seat. She seemed smaller: she'd been frightened half to death. He reached across and squeezed her hand.

He was suddenly ashamed. Nothing mattered, *nothing*, that didn't get her free.

MORGAN

MORGAN WASHBURN BASKED IN A BRANDY-GLOW OF good fellowship on the Army surgeon's crude adobe porch. The sun was dropping behind Laramie Peak, and the sweating soldiers, in dusty blue and gold, were trooping faded colors to a sadly broken drum.

The surgeon's brandy was warm in his glass and his belly, and he felt marvelously free. For weeks Chihuahua Harry, like the Mariner's albatross, had been hanging around his neck: today Morgan had unloaded him at the Laramie Post Hospital.

Chihuahua's arrow wound had not healed properly, as Morgan had feared from the start. The site had turned septic. Morgan had spent the last week with a scalpel, debriding flesh which had scaled and scabbed around the infected area, and trying to treat the wound with poultices on the road. But in the jolting sick-wagon, under Dr. Marshall's stony stare, there was little he could do but endure the man's complaints.

The infection had only worsened. Chihuahua was sometimes delirious, but unwilling to be still. Yesterday Morgan had lured him into the post hospital, on the promise of medicinal Army spirits, dispensed by a generous hand.

The post surgeon was a kindly man, sympathetic to Morgan's problem and Chihuahua Harry's pain. Despite Chihuahua's drunken ramblings, he allowed him a bunk at the end of the dark, low-ceilinged hospital ward in his quarters. But the room was crowded with emigrants already. Many were Easterners, victims of accidental gunshot wounds inflicted by themselves and others; most city men had never handled firearms before the Great Migration began.

"If you'd throw yourselves on the Indians' mercy and toss your guns away," the army surgeon smiled, "there'd be more of you in California at the end."

The surgeon had refused to keep Chihuahua permanently, so Morgan, a half hour ago, had brought in Isaiah to plead his case.

The surgeon sat at his rolltop desk, shaking his head. "Mr. Hollister, I have eight civilian gunshot wounds, three cholera patients, and an emigrant in a coma from half-drowning at the ford." He ran a hand through sandy, wispy hair, glancing at the end of his row of beds. Chihuahua slept in a drunken stupor. "He's a good deal of trouble, you know."

"I know," admitted Morgan. "Still—"

"If you dose him up, he gets too drunk. Saw Indians at our window last night, kept the whole damn ward awake!" He faced Morgan. "The truth is, Doctor, as you know, he doesn't *want* to stay! He wants to go to California with the rest!"

"He'll stay," promised Morgan. "He wants to live, and I've proved that I can't help him on the road."

Isaiah argued that the Army owed him care. "He took Chihuahua City twice: once with Colonel Doniphan, and again with General Price."

160

Morgan had never believed in Chihuahua's military record, but from Isaiah it had the ring of truth.

Isaiah added that if he were kept here and got better, he'd doubtless reenlist. "What else *can* he do?"

The Army paid a bounty for recruitment. The surgeon's eyes grew thoughtful. "All right, I'll keep him here and see."

He stepped to his medicine cabinet, poured them government brandy, ushered them to the front of his quarters to watch retreat, and went to treat his colonel for the ague.

Now Morgan watched the clumsy, shambling ranks parading. The troops had manned the place for less than thirty days, but already their feet and their horses' hooves had pounded the parade ground to the hardness of cement. The outpost had only yesterday formally become Army property, title bought by the United States from the American Fur Company for a thousand dollars. The ceremonies, which no emigrants had taken time to notice, had been lengthy, and the sulky troops were showing it today.

Isaiah Hollister leaned on the railing, gazing at the troops. "I'd forgotten how much I hated it, the Army."

Morgan did not hate the Army; he was grateful to it for taking Chihuahua Harry, for the brandy in his stomach, for the break in the long, long trail.

Now that the sun had dropped below Laramie Peak, there was a chill to the evening air. By the river, a train was hitching up: many companies now, left far behind and frightened of Sierra snows, were traveling by moonlight half the night.

But seldom the Pioneer Line....

The drilling continued: the sergeants' voices yelped; the leather belts creaked; the faltering drum rattled on. A soldier dropped his piece, picked it up, stumbled back to his place as the sergeant cursed him out.

Isaiah was right: the garrison's lot was a brutal one. "It does seem a hell of a life."

"Worse than hell. You saw the guardhouse?" He pointed to a low adobe, with bars across the windows, past the parade ground.

"Yes."

"Their troopers still have to quarter under canvas, but they damn well built *that* first."

"And filled it, too, I'm afraid," mused Morgan.

Deserters from the Oregon Volunteer Battalion, heading for the goldfields and caught by regular cavalry, were crammed into cells too low to stand in, suffering from the heat: Morgan had seen them from a distance this morning, stripped to the waist and squatting like caged apes, when he washed his clothes in the stream behind the jail.

"And they're only volunteers," muttered Isaiah. "What kind of drumhead justice will they get from a bunch of regulars?" He jerked his thumb toward "Old Bedlam," formerly the dwelling of the trading-post factor of the American Fur Company, but recently turned into officers' quarters. Lounging on its shaded porch were a major, a captain, and several lieutenants. Tunics unbuttoned, they ignored their men on the parade ground and chuckled at some story that Lieutenant Vanderveer was telling.

"No justice, I'm sure," said Morgan. "But that we'll never know."

They'd be gone at dawn tomorrow, to overtake their train. The Pioneer Line—except for their own carriage—had pulled away at noon today. Yesterday they had lightened up for the rough country ahead. Each passenger was told to pick the personal gear he most needed, and to abandon the rest. From this point on, by Turner's order, no passenger's luggage could exceed a hundred pounds.

Morgan's Hall rifle weighed twelve, and they were out of Indian country now. He had never fired it, preferring Stein's repeater for hunting. He sold it to a gold seeker heading home to New Hampshire. The man had lost his brother to cholera near South Pass, and his taste for gold as well. Morgan had paid sixteen dollars for the gun in Albany; he got three dollars for it here, so surfeited was Fort Laramie with abandoned emigrant stores. Well, its barrel had rusted from exposure to the rain, the New Hampshireman would be traveling through Pawnee country alone, and to sell it for three dollars was better than to leave it with his books.

Carriage Eighteen's stacks of abandoned baggage lay at the side of the road: clothes and musical instruments, mining tools and bedding, books and boots and wardrobe trunks.

They were waiting for the repair of the carriage roof. Yesterday, Stein had found the Army artificer. The man was busy salvaging abandoned goods, and disinclined to reason, but finally Isaiah had wandered over to plead their case, and the craftsman agreed to build them a carriage top.

In this mecca of the Philistine, where every private was a sutler, and Army officers were selling wagons found scuttled on the road, the roof would be exorbitant. Captain Turner had disclaimed liability, pleading lack of funds: they would have to pay for it themselves, more than five dollars each.

At least, with the easy half of the journey done, now they would begin the rough going under shelter and in shade.

Morgan lounged on the surgeon's porch, sipping brandy with Isaiah, until after dark. Then they returned to their campsite. They inspected their carriage, and found the work fair.

They slept in their tent that night for the last time: it had been decreed that to save weight they would abandon it here, and sleep in the open from now on.

Morgan awoke at dawn, shivering under his blankets. He grabbed his shabby towel and a bar of lye softsoap he had bought from the sutler's wife, and hurried to the stream behind the guardhouse. Passing the door, he heard the clank of cooking gear and saw a trooper, unshaven as his half-naked prisoners, moving from cell to cell, ladling soup from a huge tureen.

It was cool now, but he pitied the torments the deserters would endure under the rising sun.

He stripped, exciting the mosquitoes along the riverbanks, and waded into the cool water, soaping as he went. When he emerged he felt reborn, though he knew that in an hour he would be as grimy as before. He had abandoned his razor when he quit trimming his beard three hundred miles back along the trail.

While he was drying down, Oglethorpe arrived, with Joshua limping in his wake.

"Good morning, Mr. Oglethorpe," said Morgan. He liked Oglethorpe no more now than the day that he had met him on Blue Prairie, at the start.

"Morning, Doctor," the Charlestonian drawled. He began to strip. Joshua waited, his sad dark eyes musing on the guardhouse.

"Joshua," said Oglethorpe, "you know why those prisoners are there?"

"They run off, suh, I hear say. From the Army."

"Well, you 'hear say' right, young Joshua. Please draw off my boots?"

Joshua pulled off his master's boots, and then his own, which from the look of them were hand-me-downs from Oglethorpe. He rolled up his trousers and sloshed into the river to scrub his master's back.

"I wonder," Oglethorpe said casually, "would you object, sir, to another look at my Darkie's foot?"

"Most happy to oblige."

Joshua had been limping from the first, when he'd bruised his heel wading barefoot across the Blue. Morgan diagnosed it as a trauma to the *plantar* ligament, and warned that it would never improve while Joshua trudged on it for twenty miles a day. Oglethorpe, who had paid only a single fare, had not seen fit to pay more to let a slave ride in the sick-wagon.

Now Morgan squatted on the riverbank and prodded the heel, his eyes on Joshua's face.

Joshua's teeth flashed in a grimace and his broad black forehead wrinkled. He grunted as Morgan's fingers found the spot. Morgan could feel swelling under the heel pad, and new scar tissue, too. Every step he took toward California must be hell.

"He has to ride in something," he decided. "Starting now."

Joshua's eyes swung from Morgan to his master, then closed, as if in prayer.

Oglethorpe, toweling off, frowned down at them. "I thought perhaps you'd have some kind of poultice...."

Morgan arose. "The only poultice for that heel is rest."

Oglethorpe studied his Darkie. "He's a mighty lazy nigger, sir. I've found him to malinger, all his life."

"He's not malingering today. He rides."

"But *today*? Now, that's a problem, isn't it?"

"Why?" Morgan pointed out that Oglethorpe had walked half the distance anyway, for exercise; he could walk one more day for Joshua. "When we catch the train tonight, put him in the sick-wagon, if you want."

"I'd gladly walk," smiled Oglethorpe, "but I can't ask my messmates to ride with a Darkie. Can I?"

Morgan sighed. Oglethorpe evoked memories of his own plantation past. "I believe Mr. Hollister drives today, sir. Joshua can join us, on the box."

Oglethorpe looked at him strangely. Then he smiled, shrugged, and began to draw on his trousers. Joshua grabbed Morgan's hand, pressed it, then kneeled to help his master with his boots.

As Morgan passed the guardhouse he looked back. Joshua was still on his knees. In his dark and brooding eyes he caught the glint of tears.

Isaiah tied Jo to the rear of the carriage and mounted the box next to Joshua. He flicked the reins. Icarus balked, Daedalus tugged mightily; the carriage, with its new top, creaked into motion. Morgan set a foot on a front-wheel spoke and let it carry him up, then slid onto the driver's seat beside Joshua.

He felt clean from his river bath.

But as they drove past the post hospital, the surgeon's tubby medical corpsman waved them down. "Doctor, your patient's flown the coop. Sneaked out last night!"

Morgan's heart dropped. "Chihuahua? He *left*?"

"Gone to see the elephant, as they say." He seemed amused. He tapped his forehead. "Moonstruck, I think. Or I may have overdosed him with that brandy. He was crazy half the night. Indians at the window, gold on the Emigrant Trail..."

"He couldn't have ridden!" protested Morgan. "And he can hardly walk!"

"He's walked plumb out of sight, my friend. A picket saw him heading west: you'll catch him on the trail."

Morgan groaned aloud. Chihuahua seemed shackled to his leg, like a prisoner's iron ball.

"Wait!" Vanderveer called from the rear. He scrambled out the back, dropped to the ground, moved forward to look up at Isaiah. He had Stein's repeating rifle in his hand. "Can I borrow Jo?"

Isaiah winced. "Lieutenant, you already owe *one* of our number a horse—"

Vanderveer shrugged: if Chihuahua wandered off the road, it would be on their consciences, not his.

Isaiah rubbed his bearded jaw. "All right," he said reluctantly. "Go easy on her in the heat."

Vanderveer dragged Jo's saddle from the carriage boot, untied her from the rear of the wagon, slung the saddle on her back, and began to cinch it up as Isaiah started the mules again.

In a few minutes the lieutenant passed them without a wave. He was moving at a gallop.

"*Easy*, I said," muttered Hollister. "That son of a bitch!"

Morgan watched the rider cantering down the road. Jo, like all their stock, was growing thin; she should be walked, not galloped.

Morgan hated to see horseflesh abused, but it would almost be worth it if Vanderveer fell off and broke his neck.

He craned past their new carriage top to look back at the fort.

The tiny outpost would be the last they would see of civilization until they reached the end of the world.

They creaked and crawled over rolling ground, hoping to noon at a point called Warm Springs. Here was water, according to Ware's guidebook, which, though warm, was drinkable, and flowed from the base of a great high bluff; here they might find grass for the mules.

They were alone in the vast brown hills. For the first time in weeks, no other wagons passed them, though equipment lay everywhere, and they passed three grave-markers.

"Good God," asked Isaiah, "are we the *last*?"

They detoured around an abandoned, high-bowed Conestoga, ghost of another age. In such wagons, it was said, Missouri had been settled, and parts of Kansas, too. This one, thought Morgan, had sailed out west to die, and lay like a hulk in a channel, rotting in the sun.

As the ruts wound through the rolling hills, they expected at every moment to find Vanderveer, waiting with Chihuahua for the carriage to arrive.

Cantrell dozed in back; Stein sat savoring the shade of the new top; Oglethorpe slept on the floor of the carriage bed; Morgan baked with Hollister and Joshua on the driver's box under the blazing sun.

They sighted the bluff as the sun peaked. Cottonwoods at its bottom told of water, but the entire countryside, so far as Morgan could see, had been grazed out by those who had passed before, and they saw no sign of grass.

At the base of a boulder-strewn canyon splitting the bluff, they pulled up. The mottled shade of cottonwoods crisscrossed a brackish spring. Morgan leaped down and felt the water. It was cool: good. He tasted it: a little alkaline, but potable. With Joshua, he began to unhitch the mules, which were strangely restive, to let them drink and forage for what little they might find. Cantrell awakened and began to pass out pilot bread he had bought at the sutler's store.

"Psst . . ."

Morgan froze. He swung his eyes up the canyon, but saw no one. Imagination, or a trick of the wind. He slipped the bridle from Icarus's head.

"Don't unhitch!" A hoarse whisper, from rocks up the canyon's side.

"Who's that?" he called. "Chihuahua?"

He sensed movement, heard the sound of sliding rock, left the mule and struggled a few feet up the canyon. Behind a boulder, pistol drawn, cringed the teamster.

"Jesus, Doc, get me out of here!"

Thinking he had fallen, Morgan took a step toward him,

sticking out his hand. The teamster recoiled. His flattened nose was quivering; his bloodshot eyes were wild.

"No! That Pawnee's up there!" He motioned toward the crest of the bluff with the pistol barrel. "Fired at me an hour ago, from the edge! He tailed me from the fort!"

Delirium tremens? Morgan grinned. "Come on, Chihuahua, there isn't a Pawnee Indian within two hundred miles!"

"Get back in the goddamn carriage!" Chihuahua grated. "When you're ready to go, I'll break for it. He's *there*!"

Morgan squinted at the ridge. Was there movement on the rim of the bluff? A shiver traveled his spine.

He wished he'd kept the rusty Hall, that he had it loaded in his hand. Vanderveer had Stein's Jennings, the only other rifle in the mess.

He wanted suddenly to be gone. He turned and called to Isaiah to hitch up.

"The mules need grass!"

"Chihuahua's *here*. Hitch *up*, Isaiah. He won't come down till you do!"

He was growing more and more nervous. He felt exposed, but was too proud to take cover in front of his messmates. He searched the edge of the bluff again. Nothing . . .

"We're hitched," shouted Isaiah from below. He sounded amused. "Tell him we're ready to roll!"

Morgan helped Chihuahua from behind the rock. Pistol out, the teamster scrambled crabwise down the canyon side. His breath was heaving, his eyes were wide in fear; when Morgan grabbed his arm to steady him, he found it wet with sweat.

They reached level ground and started for the carriage, Chihuahua hobbling, Morgan supporting him.

Blang . . .

A gunshot roared from the top of the bluff, reverberating down the canyon. Chihuahua's arm was jolted from his grip; the teamster's face went blank with shock; he spun once and crumpled to the ground, flattened nose in the seeping mud.

In the back of his old Army tunic was a fist-sized hole, filling fast with blood.

Morgan whiffed black powder from the ridge. His messmates dropped from the carriage to take cover beneath it. He dove for a cottonwood tree. From its shelter, he peeked at the ridge.

There was movement there now, for certain. A tiny figure against the bright blue sky was frantically trying to ram a new load down the muzzle of a musket as tall as itself. Morgan swung his gaze to the other side of the niche. Vanderveer, rifle in hand, was rising from behind a rock on the bluff across the canyon from the figure. He rested Stein's gun on a boulder, called something to the Indian.

The tiny figure froze. For a moment time stopped. Then a shot from the Jennings rang out, and then another, more sharply than the first. The little Indian doubled, spun, and plummeted over the edge. He held to his weapon, rolling down the shale, hung for a moment from a branch like a rag doll, slipped slowly loose, and slid, clutching his gun, to the foot of the bluff.

Vanderveer waved Stein's rifle. His voice came echoing down: "Haloo..."

Morgan looked up, but said nothing. Vanderveer stood motionless for a moment, then shouldered his rifle and disappeared behind the rim.

The Indian had fallen out of sight, in the midst of a cottonwood patch. Morgan drew his pistol and approached. He stopped for a moment and listened. A cricket chirped, fell silent, chirped again.

There was not a sound from the cottonwood tangle. He crept closer, heard a whimper, which was quickly stilled.

And then he saw the tiny hand, the ancient musket clutched in it. He skirted the clump.

At the head of the spring, half in the muddy stream, lay a child of perhaps ten. He wore a single feather in his shaggy tangled hair; he was lost in a pair of filthy U.S. Army trousers, cut off at the legs by half.

From a wound above his navel he was bleeding far too fast to live: Stein's rifle fired a ball a half-inch through: the little boy was doomed.

The Indian's eyes were glazed with shock, like those

169

of a wounded bird, but his lips drew back in a snarl of defiance as Morgan stepped closer to take the empty piece away. The child cried out and his arm found strength to clutch it to his side.

So Morgan left it where it was, and reached around it to place his hand on the skinny chest.

He sensed Isaiah beside him, and then Cantrell and Stein. Oglethorpe arrived, breathing hard, with Joshua just behind.

"Did he kill the redskin bastard?" drawled Oglethorpe. He drew a scarlet handkerchief and blotted at his brow. "Good Lord, he's just a child!"

Morgan heard Vanderveer dismounting, crashing through the cottonwoods. He joined them, prodding the boy with a toe. The black eyes glittered up at him, full of hate and fear.

"Well, you little heathen bastard! You made my life a hell, and you can't be more than twelve!"

"Ten, I'd say, or nine," Cantrell said acidly. "You going to scalp him now?"

"Dispatch him," said Vanderveer coolly. "With a coup de grâce." He raised Stein's rifle. The child stiffened, eyes widening.

Morgan slammed the rifle barrel up. "You son of a bitch, leave off!"

"He killed your only patient, Doctor. Don't you care?"

"*You* killed my patient, Vanderveer!"

The gray eyes narrowed. "What do you mean by *that*?"

"I didn't cut that arrow out to have him used as bait!"

Vanderveer looked him steadily in the eye. "I heard a shot. I skirted the bluff. I saw Chihuahua below, and this one on the edge. I missed him once at Ash Hollow; I couldn't risk it now; he was bound to get us both. I took time to get set; when he showed himself, I fired."

"You 'took time,' all right. Long enough to get Chihuahua to break cover, so this child would break *his*! An hour? Maybe two?"

Vanderveer studied him carefully. "Doctor, I've challenged you twice already. Both times you've refused. The next time I may challenge you to draw!"

"Then we'd get you hanged for murder," promised Isaiah. "Even here."

The child coughed weakly. Morgan dropped to his knees and felt his pulse. Soon it faltered and died. The glittering eyes went dull. He closed them and rose.

They buried him with Chihuahua, with the musket at his side.

THE ADMIRAL

THE MOTOR HOME, TINY UNDER THE WALL OF MOUNTAINS guarding California, crawled south along the Sierras beneath the growling skies.

The admiral, directed by Jeff, had turned off U.S. 395 to State 206, a narrow road paralleling the ranges. He could hear Jeff's radio scanner crackling on the table: apparently it warned of roadblocks on the better-traveled route.

He craned to look up at the crests.

When he had planned their pilgrimage along his great-grandfather's track, he had deliberately chosen to end their trek in the early fall, when Morgan had. On such a day at the end of September, their forebear had selected what he hoped was the right canyon, turned into it with his stolen mule, and begun his struggle up the mountains to the summit of Carson Pass.

The admiral had hoped for just this weather for the denouement, to let Bunkie savor Morgan's courage at the end.

The first snowfall had been building then, as it was

building now. Today, as with Morgan, blackened clouds were hurtling through the passes; Genoa Peak, his landmark, was entirely lost to sight.

The admiral had his wish, but now he willed the skies to clear, for he wanted no snowbound fiascoes, with the criminals in the rear.

The tiny ghost village of Genoa lay ahead. The gauge was showing empty. "I have to get gas," he called back, "and I'll have to use a credit card: I'm low on cash."

Across from the Mormon Station Historical Monument they found a Shell station. "Use the full-service pump," ordered Jeff. "You stay aboard. Have him check your oil and water. Use that Shell Oil card you got. I'll be watching when you sign it. I want the copy right away."

As the tank was filled, Jeff stayed in the shadows at the table, where he could hear, nervous about a message. Well, there'd be no messages attempted, here or in California. Bunkie and he had survived eighteen hours. If the admiral could get them past the Agricultural Station, Stockton was beyond Carson Pass; Tijuana lay five hundred miles south of Stockton on U.S. 5. He could get them to Mexico by midnight, and—if they didn't murder them—come back with Bunkie, free.

He wasn't going to rock the boat.

The attendant, a ruddy-faced youth with a linebacker's neck, scraped bugs off his windshield as the Winnebago gulped its gas.

"You taking Carson Pass?"

The admiral nodded, afraid to speak.

"Chains required: you got 'em?"

There were chains in the generator compartment. The admiral nodded again. His kidneys were bursting, but apparently he wouldn't be allowed to use the rest room here. He slid out of the seat and headed aft to the motor home's toilet.

He closed the door and lifted the toilet lid. His bladder emptied more slowly every year. He was zipping his fly when he heard Miguel through the flimsy door. He paused, straining to catch the Spanish.

"Jeff, last night Teresa told me she is frightened for our souls in hell."

172

"Hell?" He heard Jeff laugh. *"We just escaped from hell,* amigo. *Heaven is Ipala."*

"Still, she does not want us to kill these two. And she is right, ¿verdad? There is no reason, once el doctor *gets us over the line?"*

Jeff's voice was quiet, but very firm. *"Did she tell you she spoke of Ipala? In* inglés? *And in his presence?"*

The admiral sagged. Fear clutched at his belly. The squeeze on his chest was beginning. He must stay in control. . . . He caught the sink and fought dizziness, dropped the toilet cover and sat down.

"Ipala? This is not possible!"

"¡Sí! When she spoke of Ipala, she killed them herself, surely that is clear!"

"But she was loca!*"* protested Miguel. *"Crazy with her pain!"*

The admiral fought back nausea. He tried to clear his head.

"Nevertheless," he heard Jeff say, *"he knows. Hombre! Be sensible! If we* do *get to Ipala, you want* federales *waiting at your uncle's door?"*

He couldn't stall any longer: he could hear the bull-necked attendant outside yanking the nozzle from the tank. He opened the toilet door and stepped out, adjusting his fly. He looked in on the woman. She still slept. He felt her wrist, for effect, his mind still racing.

Her pulse was weak, and slow. . . . What that might mean, he did not know.

His own pulse was strong, fast, and dangerous. Stockstill, he stood over her, lost in thought.

He must have a plan. There was nothing now to lose.

He had a bad heart, and a pacemaker. He must remind his captors of this. And when they reached the snow line, they'd have to put on chains. Two men outside to lay the links. They wouldn't leave him unguarded inside: they'd have to take him, too. . . .

He reached across the sleeping woman, to a packet of Morgan's letters on the bulkhead shelf. He lay the packet on her chest, hiding it with his own body from the main compartment. He took a letter out and placed it on top. He noticed that it was from Morgan to Mary, in April

173

1850. He pulled out his pen and scribbled a long instruction to Bunkie on the bottom, then put the packet back on the shelf.

Pretending to adjust her bandage, he instead folded the tissue-thin paper, again and again, and palmed it in his hand.

He turned to the main compartment. Miguel had quit arguing. Now he said: "Sí, amigo, *you are right. But you must never tell my sister that she was the reason why*."

Jeff shrugged; his attention was on the admiral.

The admiral reached into a locker above the galley counter. He found the chocolate-chip cookies, offered them around. Jeff took one, Miguel shook his head. The admiral extracted two.

He slid under the wheel, passed a cookie to Bunkie with the folded sheet, and ate the other himself.

Startled, she looked into his eyes, then began impassively to nibble.

At Woodfords, where the Carson trail and the road to Ebetts Pass forked off, they pulled into the Agricultural Inspection Station. A highway patrolman sat in his car near the portal. The inspector was a mousy little woman with a cold in her head. She looked up at the admiral: "Where from, sir?"

"We've been to New York, but I'm from Nevada City."

"Citrus fruit? Vegetables?"

He forced a smile, though his heart was racing. "No. We live on chocolate chips."

"Do you mind if I take a look?"

His heart began to pound. Jeff was in the rear compartment, Miguel in the toilet, gun drawn.

"Ma'am, I'd like to beat the snow." He grinned and flashed his ID card. "I'm an admiral in the U.S. Navy. Just to sneak in an orange, would an admiral lie to you?"

"You're right, would an admiral lie to me?" She smiled, and waved him through.

Soon they were winding up the lower canyons of the Carson River, under the first drifting snowflakes. He leaned forward to start the wipers, and noticed that Bunkie had sneaked the sheet of paper he had given her into the folds of the roadmap. She glanced now and then into the mirror on her sun visor, to see if it was safe to unfold the note and read it.

But apparently she saw no chance, for it remained within the roadmap on her lap.

That's right, my darling, take your time. But see that you do what I say.

She'd be killed if she couldn't or wouldn't, but he had no room on Morgan's letter, or in his heart, to tell her that.

Now that he knew they'd kill them anyway, the whole ballgame had changed.

She—and he—had better play it right.

MORGAN

EARLY IN THE MORNING OF THE FOURTH OF JULY, 1849 —a holiday that would live forever in his memory—Morgan Washburn heard shots and cheers and climbed to the wagon seat to peer along the south bank of the river they had followed since leaving Fort Kearny a month ago.

The celebration was beginning, and the greatest movement of population his nation had ever known was jammed against high water on the Platte.

Like a column of ants frustrated by a trickle, the tide of emigration was spreading frantically, searching for a way across the torrent.

Wagons lined the sandy bluffs as far as he could see. Captain Turner had just ridden past, and estimated that there were a hundred companies—two thousand wagons—crammed along the bank. They had been assigned numbers and were waiting for two scow ferries, operated by Mormons growing richer by the hour, that would take them from the south side to the north.

The situation seemed impossible. But Turner had heard rumors of two rafts for sale, constructed by the Wisconsin Ranger Company. The original builders were long gone, far west across the lofty plains, and the rafts, mythical or real, had been sold and resold a dozen times in the last two weeks. The road ahead was said to be almost denuded of grass by those who had gone before. To buy the rafts, and steal a march on those behind, would more than pay for the extra cost.

For once the Pioneer Line had left its camping place before dawn. Last night, Captain Turner had decreed a further lightening-up, for the river crossing and the Rockies beyond. Now each passenger was allowed only seventy-five pounds of luggage.

Morgan had abandoned his gray frock coat, a dozen white shirts, a three-dollar pair of patent-leather dancing shoes, and his last two books: Velpeau's *New Elements of Operative Surgery* and Melville's latest novel, *Omoo*.

This morning, as he hitched Icarus and Daedalus to the wagon tongue, he had seen a Mexican herdsman, who had gone barefoot since Independence, wearing the dancing shoes.

During this last jettisoning, Turner had not spared his own property: eight carriages were abandoned, and the passengers crowded into the remaining twelve messes. On Morgan's recommendation, Searls and Mulford, from Rensselaerville, had been voted into theirs.

Anvils, spare iron tires for wagon wheels, whiffletrees, horseshoes, sledgehammers, blacksmith tools, a stamp press for a mine, three stoves, a barrel of molasses—all had been piled by the side of the road for Indians or wolves. Turner had capped the pile with a hundredweight keg of gunpowder he had hoped to sell to miners blasting quartz in the Mother Lode.

They had slept the night in the open by their cache, and left before dawn for the river, a half hour away. Now those trains which had camped on its banks, waiting for the ferry, were awakening to celebrate the Fourth.

A few yards down the bluff from Morgan, a grimy, bearded bugler in the uniform of the Granite State Company from Maine—one of the men whom Morgan had seen departing from Independence in such splendor—climbed a rock and sounded reveille. The Granite Staters, reluctant to abandon their trappings, had traveled even more slowly than the Pioneer Line.

Only their pseudo-military ranks and the remnants of their shiny uniforms seemed to be holding them together. They crawled from their bedding now. Most of their steeds were long gone lame; some Downeasters, it was said, had slung their fancy Mexican saddles onto mules.

The Wild Rovers, a St. Joe company camped farther downstream, had found an American flag and lashed it to the top of a willow trunk. Gunfire increased along the riverbank. By the look of the sun, it could hardly have been seven in the morning, but Dr. Cantrell began to scrabble through what remained of his luggage for a bottle of his execrable whiskey.

Captain Turner returned, triumphant. He beamed from his horse at the men of Carriage Eighteen, waiting impatiently at the ford. He announced that he had found and purchased the rafts, for fifty dollars each. The carriages would cross at a point five miles downstream; the baggage wagons, here.

Thank God, thought Morgan. *At last us hares will have our turn. Let the tortoises wait for low water....*

"We cross tomorrow, gentlemen!"

"Tomorrow?" Morgan shouted incredulously, springing to his feet. He strode to the horse and grabbed its bridle. "What in the name of God is this about *tomorrow*?"

Turner flushed and set his lips. "At dawn, we roll!" He kicked at his horse. Morgan jerked its bridle and stilled it. "Leave off, Doctor!" squawked Turner. "What the hell are you about?"

"You'll damn well stay and listen!" Morgan was shaking from head to foot. "It won't *be* at dawn we roll, will it, 'Captain' Turner? It's *never* at dawn we roll. There'll be a whiffletree that's broken, or a goddamn mule to shoe! While fifteen other outfits cross and steal our grass!"

"We stay tonight," insisted Turner. "My stock are tired—"

"Then cross them now! In time to find some fodder!"

"My men are tired too!"

"*Saddle your mules*," Black Harris had warned, a thousand years ago. "*Saddle your mules, and ride like* hell..."

"So we're to freeze on Carson's Pass?" demanded Morgan. "Because your men are tired? It's already the Fourth of *July*! You promised we'd be in California!" He jerked his thumb at the waters rushing by. "Is this the *Sacramento* River, or the Platte? We've yet to cross the Great Divide!"

"We'll make it up. There's a cutoff—"

"Cutoff be damned! We've two full months to go! And it *snows* in the Sierras in October! Have you never heard of the Donner Party? What's this about *tomorrow*?"

The little man cursed and raised his reins again: "Unhand my goddamn horse! Or I'll whip you to a pulp!"

"Steady!" Vanderveer's voice lashed out. Morgan turned. The lieutenant, lounging with his back against the carriage wheel, had his Colt revolver steady on the little captain's head. He was smiling, and the piece was cocked. "Steady, Captain Turner, steady as she goes!"

"Put that away!" called Morgan. He looked up at Turner again.

Astonished, he saw tears come to the captain's eyes, as Turner lowered his hand and stroked his horse's neck. "To be honest, it's none of my doing, Doctor. I'd *like* to cross this morning, but my teamsters will not work."

"What?" demanded Morgan. "Why not?"

"Not on Independence Day."

Morgan sighed. He had known it from the first. Turner was a coward and a fool, no more fit to lead his train than the greenest passenger he'd bilked. It was useless to complain. He shook his head in pity and let the bridle go. Turner rode off slowly, to pass along the word. Morgan looked down at Vanderveer, who still had the Colt in his hand.

"Hardly necessary, Lieutenant. And those damn things *can* go off."

Vanderveer smiled, raised his weapon, and fired into

the air. "So I've heard." He fired again, and once again, until his cylinder was empty. "Three cheers for John Paul Jones," he yelled. "It's Independence Day!"

Morgan's anger passed. It *was*, after all, the Fourth. There was nothing he could do about it but celebrate with the rest. Cantrell passed round a bottle of his miserable stock. On its glow, Isaiah climbed on their wagon box and recited the Declaration of Independence, flawlessly, to a crowd of a hundred men. The bugler from Maine mangled *Hail Columbia* and the assemblage sang *The Star Spangled Banner*.

Morgan, for the honor of the Pioneer Line, squeezed *Green Grow the Lilacs* from his concertina in honor of those present who had served in the Mexican War. He received tumultuous applause.

A squad of the Granite Staters, in perfectly dressed ranks, fired twenty-one salvos from their double-barreled shotguns in less than ten minutes.

As the sun rose higher, Morgan, rocked by too much whiskey, conceived the idea of going fishing with Isaiah; Joshua, finding his master too suffused with good fellowship to object, limped after them.

They dangled their lines in the Platte, shaded under willows from the heat of the blazing sun. Josh's skin gleamed like wet ebony.

"Mr. Hollister, suh, you a man of the law. They's a thing I'd like to know."

"Yes, Josh?"

"Independence Day! I puzzle it since I learn to read. And I hear you talkin' to all them men. But just what do it mean?"

"It means that seventy-three years ago today, we concluded to be free."

Joshua pulled at his line, frowned, let it out again. "We? Who 'we'? You?" he asked Morgan. "You?" He peered into Isaiah's eyes. "Or me?"

Tender ground to tread with a slave, a hundred yards from his master. Morgan cringed inwardly, but Isaiah rushed ahead.

"All of us are free of the British, Josh," answered Isaiah. "But not free of each other, not yet."

Josh fell silent for a moment. Morgan flashed Isaiah a warning glance. His friend met his eye, shook his head stubbornly.

Joshua spoke again, quietly: "*Some* say I free out here, some not." Joshua's brown eyes smouldered. "'Course, I gwine *be* free, Master Oglethorpe say, if I leave the plantation and come. Gwine free me in California!"

"I'm glad," said Isaiah, quietly.

"When I earn the money, he gwine sell me, for a thousand dollars, gold. To me!" His eyes flashed. "Why that? 'Cause *his* granddaddy buy *my* granddaddy, why I have to buy *myself*?"

"You don't," said Isaiah, laying down his pole. He swung to face him. He put his hands on the broad sweating shoulders, looked into Joshua's eyes. "You're free *now*, Joshua. Under the Missouri Compromise, you've been so since we left Missouri and crossed the River Blue."

"Some say so, some say no. What *you* say, Dr. Washburn?" Joshua looked at Morgan. He seemed suddenly frightened. "I hear tell you born in Maryland. What *you* say?"

"The same."

"You own slaves, suh?"

"My father does." Morgan looked into the deep brown eyes. "If he died, I suppose I would."

"Let's say he die, you gwine free them?"

He had never questioned that he would, no matter what the cost. But no Darkie had ever asked him, either, and he paused before he spoke.

He thought of a young fieldhand with a damaged brain, content to sing to horses, and an old cottonhead Darkie, producing nothing, who'd been given a mule and his own field to hoe; of his skinny black nurse from childhood, arthritic and racked with pain. There were others, drugged by a hundred years of bondage to his kind: to free *them*— if they left the farm—would be a sin. "There are some it would be too late to free. Them, I'd have to keep."

"That, I can't believe," exclaimed Isaiah.

Morgan smiled at Joshua. "Can *you*?"

"Yes suh," muttered Joshua. "My daddy: for him it very late." He looked deeply into Morgan's face, and licked his lips and said: "You a Southerner, Doctor. And you been most kind. But say I take my leave with them Granite State boys. They a preacher-man there, say 'come.' Say 'walk with us in freedom, the Good Lord see you through.'" He frowned. "Cain't walk so good, this heel I got. Cain't run. Master ain't goin' track me down? With a dozen other man?"

"Indeed he might," admitted Morgan. "But he'd get no help from us."

Joshua jerked at his line, began to play a fish. "Ain't gwine hook me by the mouth?" he chortled, drawing the wriggling trout to the bank. He grabbed it by the jaws, yanked out the hook. "Master Oglethorpe says I got to earn it. Got to earn it in the mines."

"He's wrong, your 'Master' Oglethorpe," said Isaiah. "Legally, dead wrong."

Josh caught three trout, and Morgan one, and returned to the carriage. They found that Charlie Mulford, from Rensselaerville, was fueled with whiskey and baking a dried-peach pie. They would have a picnic on a canvas, spread on the side of the Platte.

The Granite State Company decided to calk their wagons with tar and oakum and swim their stock across. They were working at it now, as their band played on, and the rifles cracked in salute. Joshua watched them, picking at a fishbone in his teeth.

"Doctor," he murmured, "Master Oglethorpe's dead drunk asleep. It true what you say? I run, you ain't gwine chase me?"

"Not in a thousand years."

"You gwine *help*, though? Tell them I went *that* way?" He pointed east, to the ruts through the cottonwoods, and the road along which they'd come.

Morgan thought for a moment. "It's no good, Joshua. Some would search east, but some would cross and search west."

Joshua smiled faintly. He'd expected nothing more. "Yes suh. Best I stay."

Morgan felt rising rage. Every fiber in his being seemed at war. He remembered his own father, castigating Baltimore abolitionists who had helped a neighbor's slave

181

escape to Pennsylvania. He should not—must not—get involved. Joshua's problems were his own, and Oglethorpe's.

But he could not keep the anger down. "Stay?" he murmured. The dammed-up wrath burst through. "No, goddamn it, no!" He grabbed the black man's arm. "If you cross with those men from Maine, I'll see you're not pursued."

"How you gwine do that?" the black man asked.

"I'll think of something. . . ."

An idea was growing in his mind. It would require Isaiah's aid. But he was damned if he'd see this Darkie hanged for trying to get away.

"Yes suh," Joshua said doubtfully.

"If you'll help yourself, I'll help you. But Joshua?"

The black's eyes were on him, full of fear. "Suh?"

"You must not wait too long."

Under a willow by the side of the trail, Morgan sat with Isaiah Hollister. Between them rested a bottle of Cantrell's whiskey: in Morgan's pocket was a box of sulphur matches, the very last he had.

Isaiah stared at him, shaking his head. "I'm an abolitionist in *theory*, Morgan. Not a mover of events."

"Events? You were quite for liberty this morning, in your speech," Morgan reminded him bitterly. "'When in the course of human events—'"

"I've sobered up."

"Then have another drink," urged Morgan. "'When in the course of human events it becomes necessary...' Isaiah, let's *do* it!"

"No! Our own *company* would lynch us! We'd stampede all our stock!"

"How will they know who set it off?" Morgan sipped the whiskey and chanted: "'We hold these truths to be self-evident—'"

"Have you ever *heard* a hundredweight of gunpowder go off?" The young lawyer waved his hand at the herds along the bank. "It's only a quarter mile from them. Do you know what it would do?"

"'That all men,'" quoted Morgan, "'are created equal...'"

"Let me have a drink of that," Isaiah said. He brought the bottle to his mouth, swallowed, grimaced, and licked his lips.

Morgan moved impatiently. For all he knew, Joshua had fled and Oglethorpe was already awake, looking for him. "*We* set it in his mind to flee, Isaiah. If he does, he'll need someone to throw sand into their eyes."

Isaiah nibbled his lip, removed his spectacles, polished them on the tail of his grimy calico shirt. "I wish I'd held my tongue."

"You didn't." Morgan studied the matches. "Nor did I."

Isaiah replaced his glasses, looked into Morgan's eyes. A tiny smile played on his face.

"Well, I managed it once at Cerro Gordo on Winfield Scott's campaign. We blew up a bridge over the ravine, and I didn't lose a man."

"For a lesser cause than this," Morgan reminded him.

"You are right," Isaiah sighed, and held out his hand for the matches. "I'll see if I've forgotten how to set a charge."

Morgan smiled and squeezed his shoulder. "I'll fire three shots, and wait. And then I'll fire three more."

He watched Isaiah drift back through the trees, toward the powder cache they'd left at dawn, beside the dusty trail.

Morgan sat on the wagon tongue, his eye on the sleeping Oglethorpe. Joshua still wandered the riverbank, undecided, or waiting for the Granite Staters to finish turning their wagons into boats.

Gunfire increased along the riverbank. He treated a Missourian whose pistol had exploded; he had lost an eardrum, probably, but there was no help for that. A Democrat mounted the Maine men's boulder and began to make a speech. A Whig demanded an equal right and fell shouting from the rock. Two wagonmates from the Wisconsin Blues, who had quarreled along the route, began to saw their wagon in half; they would toss a coin to determine who would get the front half, who the rear.

A three-pound cannon from the Granite Company began to speak, once for each wagon that crossed. A fiddler appeared from nowhere, as did three sisters from the Dubuque Emigrating Society train; Morgan fell in love with two of them, and Niles Searls, from Rensselaerville, claimed to love all three, but their father would not let them dance. Morgan took up his concertina and unleashed his fine baritone and sang *Old Virginia Shore* and *The Canadian Boat Song* to impress them. All three smiled with favor, but hung closely by their sire.

By four the brass cannon was hot from firing. It crossed in the last wagon. At last, Morgan spotted a gleaming black head downstream of it, swimming strongly in the lee.

In half an hour, Oglethorpe awakened, hungry. Morgan tensed, but made no move.

The mess had eaten Morgan's trout and Charlie Mulford's pie, on the canvas spread beneath a willow tree. They had toasted home and country, President Taylor, and the Battle of Buena Vista.

Oglethorpe, having missed the feast, was in a foul and vicious mood. He began to call for Joshua, searching everywhere he could.

He returned to Morgan, who was sitting at the deadened campfire. "You seen my nigger lately, Doctor?"

"No," said Morgan. His heart was beating wildly.

"He asked if he could go fishing with you and Hollister."

"He did, and caught some good ones. He's around."

"I wonder, sir, I wonder." Oglethorpe was all at once dead sober. His eyes were narrow slits. He peered across the river, into the failing light.

"He was talking to that preacher from the Granite State Company train," mused Oglethorpe. Suddenly he slammed his fist into his palm. "I do believe he ran away! That black bastard!" He leaped to a boulder, cupped his hands. "Runaway slave!" he shouted. "Get some men! Lieutenant Vanderveer?"

Few Northerners made a move, but drunken teamsters

streamed toward the grazing horses. A Carolina company downstream took up the cry, and horsemen began to congregate at the ford.

The time had come. Morgan grabbed Stein's rifle, fired three rapid shots into the air, waited for a moment, and fired another three. They seemed lost among the others from the revelers.

He waited tensely. Nothing from the powder cache. Had Isaiah drifted off to sleep, or used too long a fuse?

Isaiah! Now, goddamn it, now!

Vanderveer was mounted, on a Carolina horse. Oglethorpe was trying to marshal a posse.

Morgan cocked the rifle once again, and pointed it at the sky.

All at once the heavens split in an earth-shattering roar. From the stockpile down the trail, a horseshoe spun lazily and splashed into the Platte. A canvas top went flying from a Wild Rover wagon, and a tent upstream collapsed on its occupants.

The sisters from Dubuque screamed and oxen bellowed everywhere. Mules began stampeding, from Mormon's Ferry to the bend. A horse reared up and broke his bridle, and departed to the south. From far across the river, they heard a bugle sound, as the Granite Company went to arms. A pyre of smoke appeared to the east; the prairie was afire.

Then there was dead silence. Even the insects along the river stilled; no more pistols or rifles were heard.

The Mormons from the ferry sent a messenger to inquire about the blast. The captains of eight companies convened, and called a meeting of all those emigrants not drunk or chasing stock.

By this time Isaiah had returned, to join in the general outrage. As the teamsters chased their mules, Turner spoke on the subject of malicious pranksters. Vanderveer suggested that when and if their stock were found they start another Indian hunt: Shoshonis had obviously set off the powder to stampede the herds and steal them.

Isaiah mounted the boulder. He suggested, as a veteran of the Vera Cruz campaign, that the explosion was a Mexican plot to disrupt the Great Migration: Manifest Destiny had been threatened. "On our Independence Day!"

A Mexican herdsman who understood English discreetly swam the Platte.

Morgan nominated Isaiah as head of a committee to investigate the matter; Niles Searls seconded. Isaiah was elected by acclaim. He picked Morgan to inspect the site of the explosion, but Cantrell found another bottle and the matter rested there, while they let the hired teamsters hunt for stock.

Oglethorpe, who could not swim, pled in vain half the night with other companies for a horse to chase his slave.

Joshua was never seen again.

They crossed the next day, twenty-four hours behind the Granite Staters, and began the road to hell.

Six weeks later, Morgan Washburn sat on a fallen log at the edge of a dried-up spring. He knew only that it was located on the broken rim of mountains bordering the Great Basin, some one hundred miles north of the Great Salt Lake. Neither Captain Turner nor anyone else in the party knew its name, if it had one.

Turner was secretive, admitting no confusion, but Morgan truly believed that the Pioneer Line was lost.

The train was nooning, allowing the animals to forage and rest while the sun peaked. They would hitch up before three P.M. and travel until well after dark, by moonlight: tomorrow they would rise not long after midnight and, if fortune favored, be under way before dawn. It was Saturday, August 18th. In the dry summer heat of the Rockies it was difficult to realize that snow could block Sierra passes within the next six weeks.

Turner himself seemed oblivious to the threat, insisting on full noonings for the sake of his animals, intolerant of questions. He became more hair-triggered and irascible each day.

The company was fragmenting. Those who trusted Turner were reluctant to rise early and march late; those who did not, with Morgan, grew always more impatient of delay.

Morgan's confrontation with him at the Platte had done no good at all.

Two weeks ago they had crossed the Great Divide at South Pass. The journey from the crossing of the Platte to the Divide had been a blur of hunger, thirst, indecision, and dusty, choking days. A strange lassitude had forced Morgan to quit making daily journal entries; he had started to make them weekly, instead, and sometimes impressions faded before he had them down.

He remembered only a few events and rare hours of joy: conquering Independence Rock with Isaiah, and carving their names in a boulder at the top; a fine day's march of almost thirty miles, shouting to make echoes, from the bluffs on either side, as they tracked along the Sweetwater through the notch of Devil's Gate.

He recalled one afternoon of pure refreshment and delight. They had dug and found *ice* at the side of the road in a slough that Frémont had described, and Morgan had excitedly penned the experience to Mary that very afternoon: *That ice should be found thus imbedded in the earth in midsummer with the thermometer ranging from seventy to eighty, or even higher, is truly strange! Many theories were offered tonight as causing it, but none appeared entirely satisfactory. Isaiah thinks that here the Devil, having found this Valley of the Sweetwater a more satisfactory Purgatory than his own, has simply let the fires of Hell go out.*

Now the letter lay in his folded blanket, with others, waiting for some discouraged emigrant, heading east against the tide, who might post them all at Laramie for a price.

At South Pass he had stood on the backbone of his nation, knowing that all that flowed eastward, toward what he had known, was now behind him; that from this point on, his life ran like the Western rivers to the far Pacific shores.

But the place was hardly equal to a thought so grand. South Pass was not a pass at all, but the easy summit of a gradual slope, not nearly as abrupt as many of the hills behind; certainly nothing so impressive as those which lay ahead. South Pass was simply unworthy of its name.

It was days before he truly comprehended that half the trip was done. By that time he was struggling along a cutoff called Sublette's, across a barren mountain desert toward a river called the Green. Turner—misled by guidebooks—had estimated a one-day forced march of thirty-five miles to grass and water; the wheelometer on Carriage Eighteen's wheel read fifty-two when finally, two days later, the Pioneer Line dragged itself to the stream.

For the past two weeks the fabric of the Line had been tearing. There was a movement afoot—Morgan thought he might well join it—to buy mules from Turner, leave the wagons, and pack on ahead by foot.

Now the miserable passage to the Green was two weeks back, and little had improved. He yawned and pressed his fingers against his scalded eyes, then gazed down at the used-up spring. The trace of a dry riverbed led west, cratered with little wells that some previous train had dug. All the wells were dry.

The Pioneer Line carriages were drawn abreast nearby: baggage wagons rested farther "downstream," though there was no stream, down or up. Teamsters were gathered nearby, grousing in the mountain air: he could hear their voices, but not make out the words. Vanderveer was strolling over to them, curious.

The teamsters—Mexican and white men too—had been sulking for days, some angry because they moved too fast, some because they moved too slowly. Today they had, for some reason, failed again to unhitch Carriage Eighteen's mules: Morgan and Oglethorpe had finally done the job themselves. Now Icarus and Daedalus foraged with the rest, for what sparse grass there was.

The smell of mules and human sweat was heavy in the air: an ox's carcass lay upwind, reeking death across the site.

He rubbed his jaw. His face was tangled with months of growth and caked with a week's trail dust. He had glimpsed himself in Isaiah's mirror a week ago—or two—and would have believed the image to be anyone's but his. He was exhausted, drained of juices; an indescribable dread lurked somewhere deep inside.

For weeks they had eaten no fresh food but onions from the commissary wagon and some trout that Oglethorpe had caught in the Green. He longed for vegetables, or meat, but the passage of some thirty thousand men, this summer, had left the trail bereft of game.

He thought of a venison steak, and his mouth began to water. He poked at his lower gum with a forefinger.

Soft, and sore. He felt a touch of alarm.

Spongy gums?

He glanced at Isaiah, who was sitting on a rock. The young lawyer was young no longer; his eyes were sunken; his face, smeared with axle grease to protect it from the sun, sagged in fatigue. He'd been acting strangely today: now his hat was in his lap, and he was staring into it. His head was exposed to the sun.

"Isaiah," he called. "Put on your hat."

Isaiah looked up. He tried a smile: it was a death's-head grin. "Just remembering," he said softly. "Berries, on Grandfather's farm ... I'd gather them in my hat from the bushes by the barn.... Blueberries, raspberries.... Strawberries, too, in season."

He put on the hat and glanced away, embarrassed.

Morgan looked at Stein, asleep in the shade of the wagon. It seemed to him that the little saddler was pale beneath his tan.

Debility, complexion sallow ...

Cantrell had fainted yesterday, before the evening meal.

Syncope ...

Scurvy? Dear God, no ... Scurvy was a *sailor's* disease, rarely found ashore. He'd seen—on rounds to the almshouse—less than a dozen cases in a full two years of practice.

Surely not scurvy, here on dry land in the Rockies. His gums were simply sore from chewing biscuits, hard as stream-bed rocks; his fatigue had come because he'd walked for days, to save the mules. Stein and Isaiah were drawn and weak because they'd done the same.

Perhaps Cantrell had fainted because his whiskey stock had failed.

He would worry about scurvy in a year or two, when

189

he sailed from San Francisco to bring Mary back by sea. Not now.

A duty loomed in front of him, before they would harness up and roll. He had sworn to write her every week.

Painfully, he got up. He had abandoned his writing case at Laramie with the rest of his luxuries, stuffing only pen and ink and what remained of his paper into his medical kit.

He ached in every bone and joint. They walked now, rather than ride, except Dr. Cantrell, who was over forty years old, and had tacitly taken over the job, to save his legs, of driving the carriage.

Limping on a blistered heel, Morgan shuffled to Carriage Eighteen. He climbed aboard, dug in his kit for pen and ink and paper, sat on one of the two padded benches which ran the length of the carriage.

My dearest Mary...

He stared at the sheet, embarrassed at what his pen had done.

Dearest?

He had never written *that* before.

Better, *My dear Mary*, or simply *Mary, dear*.

He sat, the pen tickling his blistered lips. He regarded the salutation again. Already he had written one letter—of "moonlit things"—which discretion would prevent her from passing around. All Rensselaerville would complain if it were denied another: in such an isolated village, news of the Emigrant Trail would be no little thing. And if she showed this one at the Lyceum, he could see Lowell Tomkins now, grinning like an ape. "'Dearest'? My, our lad grows amorous on the trail...."

Besides, excessive endearments were hardly his style, or hers: his Maryland forebears came from reticent English stock; hers from New York's upstate Tories, dry and taciturn.

Both felt more deeply than they spoke, or wrote; what they said with their eyes need not be expressed. Such hyperbole might come later, with their marriage; he did not know.

Still... he missed her and loved her so much....

He nibbled the pen. He could not cross out the salu-

190

tation, obviously. He hated to discard the sheet and start again, for paper was growing scarce.

The hell with it. She *was* the dearest thing to him on earth: he'd leave it as it was.

My dearest Mary . . .

He had not complained, so far, of the torments of the trail, except to promise her that when he returned to get her, he would never take her overland. Now, his fears and ills welled up and he opened up his heart.

We rest by the side of a spring, nameless and dry. We are in dire straits. . . .

How different is the figure now cut by the redoubtable Pioneer Line from that made at our departure from the abodes of civilized men. Rejoicing at the comforts in store for us while on the "unknown expanse" and with the prospect of a speedy arrival at the goal of our desires, we set out, elated in spirit, only pitying those less fortunate in the choice of their conveyance.

How sadly we have been disappointed. . . .

Icarus poked his head into the carriage, thinking perhaps to graze on the straw which filled the leather seats. The two regarded each other thoughtfully. Icarus farted. Morgan glared at him and slapped his jowl, raising a cloud of dust.

"You stupid ass! Move off!"

The mule snorted and moved reproachfully away.

He dipped the pen: *Weary months have rolled away, bringing with them the conviction that ours, like the journey of life, has its periods of darkness and doubt. . . .*

Unhappily, he regarded his words. He wished he had put it more simply: perhaps he had studied Rhetoric too long at Union College. He longed to write with a master's touch—Hawthorne had been his lifelong guide—but his letters, when he read them back, seemed stilted.

He was suddenly ashamed of his complaints. He'd not asked her opinion before he signed on with the Line, why should he snivel for sympathy on the trail?

Still, we despair not, though present prospects indicate a dissolution of our company before many weeks. Yet with hearts yielding not to despondency, we shall push

191

forward as best we can, fully determined to reach California in the face of every impediment.

He wrote on. Into his consciousness drifted Vanderveer's voice, speaking as if to a crowd. But deep in his task, he paid no attention; there was the voice, the stamping of the mules, a bluejay squawking on a lightning-struck pine, and the scratching of his pen.

And once my practice is established there, you know, my love . . .

His pen stopped. *My love?*

He took her framed daguerreotype from his medical kit, gazed at it for a moment. Her eyes looked levelly into his own. He pressed the picture to his brow; the glass was cool; her touch made his eyes ache less.

He scratched on: *. . . you know, my love, that nothing: not ten thousand miles of ocean, nor Cape Horn's graybeard swell, nor "Roaring Forty" gale at sea, nor Nicaraguan Hell, shall keep me from your side, to bear you triumphant west again, as my Lady and my bride.*

By God, it rhymed! He looked at her picture.

My darling, he thought, *if you read* that *to Lowell Tomkins, I'll be the laughingstock of Rensselaerville! But I mean it all the same.*

He finished the letter and was sealing it when he became aware that Vanderveer was standing by the wagon, staring at him. The lieutenant's crazy gesture in pulling the gun on Turner, though puzzling, had not endeared him to Morgan, who spoke to him only when necessary; he was damned if he'd begin the conversation now.

"Doctor," said Vanderveer, "do you still feel we're moving too slowly?"

Carefully, he put his pen and paper into his kit. "Of course."

"All right. I have something to discuss. It's a matter of life and death. Can we make friends, for that?"

His eyes were cool on Morgan's. Slowly his hand went up to the carriage. Morgan hesitated, finally took it, shook it, and sat back. "What matter of 'life and death'?"

Vanderveer climbed in and sat across from him. "Well, unless the damned fool's got us lost, we'll be at Beer

Springs tomorrow. That's the junction with that cutoff...
'Hudspeth's'? Am I right?"

He nodded cautiously: "According to the *Guide to California*, yes."

Beer—or Soda—Springs, where tartaric acid was said to keep the waters constantly boiling, was a point of decision: one could take the established road north to Fort Hall, or a cutoff named "Hudspeth's," opened only a month ago; rumor along the trail had it that Hudspeth's would save miles and days of travel before it rejoined the Emigrant Trail, far southwest of Fort Hall.

Since no one had yet returned along the trail with first-hand knowledge, Morgan had his doubts: Bryant's descriptions, and Frémont's maps, sometimes bore little relation to the actual terrain.

Captain Turner shared none of his fears, but harbored hopes that the Hudspeth cutoff would provide their salvation, and steal a march on all who'd passed before.

Vanderveer looked at him blandly. "Well, I'm packing by mule, from Beer Springs on. Mr. Oglethorpe's going with me. And *we're* staying on the old Fort Hall road."

Morgan raised his eyebrows. "I think you're probably right."

Vanderveer smiled. "Good. So do eleven teamsters. Three Greasers, eight white. They'll pack too."

This was another matter, from one who'd hanged three men for mutiny. "I find that interesting, Lieutenant. Have you so informed the captain?"

"'Captain,'" snorted Vanderveer. "No. I shall, before Beer Springs. Teamsters are free men, not seamen, not slaves. Their contract doesn't call for them to die for the Pioneer Line. We'll buy some of Turner's mules, and one wagon for supplies. Or *take* them, if we have to. And then ... well, run before the wind. Eleven teamsters, a dozen or so passengers, the strong ones, not the weak. I'm weary of stopping to bury the dead. We're going to move, Doctor, *move*! Sacramento in a month."

Morgan remained silent. Vanderveer noticed Mary's picture on the seat. He smiled. "If you want to see her again, I'd like to have you join."

That explained his pulling the gun on Turner, but not

why he wanted him along. Astonished, he stared at the lieutenant. "Why would *you* ask *me*? I shook your hand, Lieutenant, but we'll never be truly friends."

Vanderveer shrugged. "I got your horse shot. And can't pay you for it, yet. Perhaps I'm making amends."

That was ridiculous. "*That* won't wash."

"All right, because you have strong legs?"

"Because I'm a doctor, I think," said Morgan thoughtfully. "And you don't think Dr. Marshall will violate his contract, and Cantrell's too old." He studied his blackened fingernails. Something had occurred to him. He looked up: "And you think you'll *need* a doctor, am I right?"

Vanderveer was grinning now. "Yes. And I think *you* know why."

He was right: Vanderveer had noticed it also.

"Scurvy?" murmured Morgan. "Well, you've probably seen more of it than I."

"I'm certain that I have," Vanderveer nodded. "How are *your* gums, Doctor?"

Morgan shrugged. "Don't look a gift horse in the mouth."

"Well, mine are bad. We need fresh food, and quickly. I'll die of scurvy for my country, if need be, but to follow a fool along a foolish trail? Not on your goddamned life!"

Morgan thought swiftly. "I'd want to pack my medical kit along."

"Agreed."

"I won't *take* a mule, won't go unless he *sells* me one."

Vanderveer shrugged. "For what you won on the *Michigan,* he'd sell his dying mother."

Morgan glanced out of the carriage at Isaiah. He sat suffering in the noonday sun, apparently too lethargic to seek shade. "And our mess goes too," demanded Morgan. "Isaiah, Stein, Cantrell . . . Searls and Mulford, too, from Rensselaerville: I couldn't face their families if I left them on the trail."

"Searls and Mulford, yes," Vanderveer frowned. "Stein's exhausted, but . . . well, you can't kill a Jew: all right. Cantrell's too old, as you said yourself." He glanced at Isaiah, wilting on his rock, and shook his head. "I think

194

Hollister's had scurvy since the Green River ford. Hollister: no."

Morgan's mind went back to the poker game in the *Michigan* saloon. Vanderveer forgot nothing, ever: in the matter of the *Somers* hanging, Isaiah should have held his tongue.

"Then deal me out," said Morgan. "I stay with him."

The lieutenant gazed at him for a moment, shrugged, climbed from the wagon, and walked away.

The chill of fear returned.

He felt as if he'd refused a lifeboat from a doomed and sinking hulk.

He put Mary's picture into his kit, borrowed Stein's rifle, and went to hunt for game on the barren riverbed.

Beer Springs stood six miles east of the junction of the Fort Hall road and the Hudspeth cutoff, which the Pioneer Line would take.

As Vanderveer, some dozen passengers, and his eleven teamsters cinched the packs on their mules, Morgan stood staring at a strange little crater, hardly three feet high and boiling over with steaming water, like an unwatched pot on a red-hot stove.

A few yards away a spring called "Steamboat" was puffing vapor every few seconds, with a noise that reminded him of the riverboat *Consignee* making the Westport dock.

Next to Steamboat Springs lay a two-foot-wide crevice reaching, it appeared, to the very bowels of the earth: from it issued a sulphurous gas, in a hissing, gasping cloud.

All in all, thought Morgan, a devilish place, appropriate to the departure of a man like Vanderveer.

At least, he reflected, they had found the trail again. As they approached the springs, they had come upon more and more abandoned wagons, carcasses, anvils, guns. A band of Shoshoni Indians was scavenging iron and begging from passing trains: they were fine-looking savages, to his mind, possessing expressions of intellect he had not expected, or seen on other tribes they'd passed. When they pointed ahead he believed them. Turner believed them too and their trust was not misplaced.

It was well known now that Dr. Marshall had chosen not to desert the train. Dr. Cantrell, when finally asked, had refused to leave as well, whether from distrust of Vanderveer or of his own endurance, no one knew. Searls was sick, and Mulford would not leave him. Stein had elected to stay as well.

Oglethorpe had made his farewells to Morgan and Isaiah the night before. "You-all have been good comrades," he conceded. "And you taught me a lesson, too."

"And what is that, sir?" asked Morgan.

"Never let your nigger fish with Yankee abolitionists on Independence Day."

"I don't understand," said Morgan innocently.

Oglethorpe lit a cigar, puffed it, and blew a cloud of smoke. "I do believe, sir, a Maryland copperhead bit that lazy nigger on his big black shiny rump. I reckon you cost me a thousand dollars, that day along the Platte."

Isaiah managed a deathly grin. "An unfounded allegation. Have you proof?"

"You wouldn't be here now to hear it, if I had."

Captain Turner had held a meeting of the company last night to encourage the loyalists. He had seemed angered by the lieutenant's mistrust, but had sold a dozen mules and a wagon without objection, probably hoping that so large a defection would save him from financial ruin. Hay was short in the feed wagons. The scrawny mules, the worn-out wagon, and the skimpy supplies he'd chosen to sell were worth less than the teamsters' wages at the end; he was keeping the departing passengers' fares in full, and would have to feed none of them again.

Around a blazing campfire, the company had sat, while the little bantam addressed them. He had aged on the road, and his voice seemed unsure, but his words were full of hope.

"You've made no mistake, those who stay with the Line. It's simple geometry. *They're* swinging north to Fort Hall, and south again to the Raft. *We* head due west. They'll find themselves in our dust at the Raft, begging to rejoin us." He peered into the crowd, searching for

Vanderveer. "Lieutenant, I'll save you the trouble. Do not even ask!"

Vanderveer stood up in the flickering shadows. "We'll be in California, Captain, by the time your teeth fall out." He smiled at the company. "As for the rest of you? Fair winds, my friends, and following seas: we all die in the end."

He had visited the carriage to see if he had forgotten anything. He said goodbye to his messmates, and looked Morgan in the eye.

"We must meet again, Doctor. We have a debt to settle, and I always settle debts."

"The horse?" said Morgan.

"The horse, of course." The lieutenant smiled. "What did you think I meant?"

Morgan would have gladly forgiven the debt, never again to have set eyes on him. But no doubt, if they lived, Vanderveer was right: somewhere, in the diggings, they were bound to meet again.

Vanderveer left at noon. Afoot, he led the first mule into the sulphurous mist as the springs below belched gas. The animals were packed lightly; their single battered wagon rode easily behind the sturdiest of the beasts that they had got; in three minutes, they had disappeared into the fog around the crater by the trail.

Morgan gathered wood for the cooking fire from far beyond the traveled path; it seemed at every site that they needed to search farther for fuel. With Vanderveer gone, he felt a burden lift. They'd be under way before dawn, on the cutoff; perhaps Turner was right, and they'd win the race; if not, what did he care?

Scurvy was not cholera, lightning swift. The onions helped to ward it off, and they'd find fresh berries somewhere, or game. He'd laugh at his fears in the end.

He was lighting the fire when Cantrell shambled from the supply wagon, in which Turner had set up his office. He was red-faced with anger. He began to hunt for a bottle of port wine.

"Turner! *Damn* Turner! Doctor! You know what that damn fool did?"

"Nothing would surprise me. What?"

"Called a Sabbath break tomorrow, for the teamsters that stayed on."

Tomorrow would be August 19th; summer had nearly fled. The wagons ahead were rolling on, bolting grass, gulping water; the sun swung daily farther north. Sierra snows would be brewing within weeks.

"Oh, no," groaned Morgan. "No!"

"Oh, *yes*! He told me so himself!"

"Then he'd better preach a Sunday sermon. We'll need someone on our side!"

Cantrell found the port bottle empty, held it to the firelight, threw it angrily away. "That's not the worst of it." Cantrell was shaking, with rage or perhaps with fear. He lowered his voice. "I think Hollister has the scurvy—"

"I agree. And maybe all of us."

"So I went to plead for onions for our mess." The yellowed eyes were wide on his. His voice was trembling. "The son of a bitch said he didn't *realize* onions . . . didn't *know* that onions . . ."

A cold dread settled in Morgan's gut. "Prevented scurvy?"

"He sold half of them to Vanderveer—"

The geyser blew, the water swished; he was suddenly on the *Michigan*'s deck, outside the saloon, with the great sidewheel churning below and Vanderveer's first challenge in his ears.

"No!"

"And all the *rest* are rotten at the bottom of the crates!"

Morgan turned and moved blindly away. He found himself flinging rocks into a bottomless crevasse in the black volcanic rock. His eyes were stinging from sulphur gas, and from his tears of rage.

Each rock he hurled was at Vanderveer.

And each went straight to hell.

THE ADMIRAL
AND BUNKIE

THE MOTOR HOME'S ENGINE FALTERED ON THE BRUTAL Carson grade. The admiral cocked his head and listened. It sucked at the thinning air, knocked, coughed, and caught again.

The towering peaks leaned toward them. There were granite walls everywhere, across the raging river on their right, past the canyon on their left, blocking the pass beyond. It seemed impossible that a way existed through the pinnacles ahead; he thought of Morgan, who had been uncertain that he'd picked the proper canyon, despairing, searching for a niche.

Here the narrow highway clung to the southern wall of the Carson River canyon. The road soared, in less than seven miles, from the flat Nevada plain to eighty-five hundred feet at the final summit of the pass.

The admiral glanced at the dashboard. From adolescence on, he had learned to fear an overheating motor on this vicious stretch of road. The panel told him nothing. Idiot lights—designed by morons—never did, until too late. He'd fought the trend away from gauges in Navy cockpits all his flying life.

He hoped they'd crest the first summit before the radiator boiled. He knew precisely where he wanted to park to start his plan to save Bunkie; if he were forced to stop too soon, his scheme would die.

The windshield wipers rose and fell, rose and fell again. Their pendulum beat was hypnotic in the overheated air.

He felt his eyelids growing heavy with the altitude. If Margolis, his cardiologist in Grass Valley, knew he'd planned on *this* Sierra pass to end their trek, he'd have had a heart attack himself.

He began to breathe more deeply, fighting, like the engine, for oxygen in the thin mountain air. He must stay alert, no matter what, until the job was done.

The snow was falling so swiftly now that it no longer melted on the road: as they climbed, it turned to mush.

On a high-banked curve, the rear end slid; he steered into the slide and straightened. The wipers gestured, the heater whirred, the engine pinged. The accelerator was floored, and they climbed at hardly thirty miles an hour.

Out of the corner of his eye he could see that Bunkie was simply sitting, waiting. She had not read his plan, on Morgan's letter, fearing to be caught, perhaps.

He cleared his throat and shot his eyes toward her, and then the map, folded in her lap, in which she'd hidden the letter.

She must read it, and obey it, or she'd die.

Bunkie stared out at the floating snowflakes. She thought of a glass ball on her dresser at home. When you turned the ball over, it snowed inside. Grandma had bought it at a roadside gift shop for her when she was very young.

In the ball was a minute cottage, hidden in the trees. In its doorway stood a tiny angel. Bunkie sometimes imagined joining the angel in her secret hut, and starting a blizzard to hide them both from people who were mean.

Now she made a wish. Around the curve would be the little cottage, and the angel would see that they got inside, and the snow would hide their tracks.

The windshield wipers waggled. They were the fingers of twin ogres, cautioning her to be careful, or they'd drag her to their den.

She heard Pops clear his throat. He wanted her to read the note, and she hadn't yet dared to open it. She glanced at the mirror on the sun visor: the Mexican was asleep in the armchair; the blond man sat at the table, facing them but busy fiddling with her Rubik's Cube.

Hands trembling, hiding what she did, she uncreased the roadmap on her lap and unfolded the letter inside. Beneath the browned handwriting that she found so hard to read, her grandfather's simple, rounded letters stood out boldly.

When we stop to put the chains on, I'll get both these bastards out. Will leave engine running so heater will stay on. When I bang on back of motor home, you will drive away.

Drive away? She looked swiftly at her grandfather. Never!

He cleared his throat again. She dropped her gaze to the paper: *Procedure: Pull parking brake handle to release. Put shift lever in drive. Press gas pedal (next to footbrake), drive very slow to first gas station, call police on phone. I love you, Pops.*

She gasped. He should *know* she'd never leave him all alone.

Slowly, positively, she shook her head.

He flicked his eyes at her. They were hard as stone.

A billowing snow cloud burst over the pass, swirling down the canyon, and hid the highest peaks.

She carefully folded the letter and replaced it in the map.

The admiral's heart fell. He knew that Bunkie understood the message but intended to disobey him; it was clear that she'd never leave him on the road.

The blizzard thickened. They crested the first of the summits. Hope Valley lay below, where Morgan's mule had almost frozen, and Morgan had nearly died. As the road descended, a sign appeared: SUMMIT THREE MILES AHEAD. CHAINS REQUIRED PAST THIS POINT.

It was time to pull off the highway. There was no way to get her to obey him, unless...

What if he convinced her he could get back aboard? And he might get back, indeed, if she caught them by surprise and he could reach the ladder to the roof. At least he'd promise to try.

The admiral pulled to the turnoff and parked, carefully,

on a gentle downgrade. He turned the heater up and left the engine on. There was not another vehicle in sight. The road dipped into the snow-covered Valley of Hope, as the emigrants had called it. In the distance he could see it climbing another thousand feet to the true summit and the pass.

"Chains," he called to Jeff. "We need them now."

Jeff moved forward, looked out at the snow, motioned the admiral to leave the driver's seat.

"Come on," Jeff growled, "you're going to help."

The admiral feigned surprise. "It's seven thousand feet up here! You know about my heart!"

"You think I'd leave you in this thing? Now, move!" Jeff turned, drew the admiral's flight jacket from the closet, and put it on.

The admiral stared into Bunkie's eyes as he slid out from his seat. "I'll hang on to the ladder," he murmured. "Just do it like I said! Goddamn it, that's an *order*!"

Jeff barked from the table: "No *talking*, damn it—"

The admiral looked into Bunkie's face. She nodded imperceptibly. Thank God, at least she'd try....

The Mexican donned the admiral's sweater, leaving him to step shirt-sleeved and shivering into the blowing snow. The two followed him to the rear of the Winnebago. He opened the generator compartment. By the bright yellow diesel generator lay the tire chains. Miguel dragged them clanking to the highway, and Jeff began to lay them out.

The links were snarled and the admiral stooped to help him. The chains were cold and turned his fingers to ice. His knees were shaking and his breath heaved; for a moment he thought he might have a real attack, instead of a fake one, but the moment passed.

It was time. He clutched his chest. "Wait..."

Jeff looked up. "You look like hell!"

"I...Heart..."

He staggered to the back of the motor home, grasped the ladder which led to the top, stood panting and clutching at his chest. "Can I go inside?"

"No way."

He took a deep breath. Bunkie had had time to shift

202

seats, the moment had come. He slammed his palm against the rear, and shouted: "Bunkie! Now!"

For an instant all was still. He saw Miguel unfolding from his squat, Jeff reaching for his gun.

Then the motor home lurched forward, almost yanking his arm from its socket. Miguel fell backward in a shower of snow, and the admiral glimpsed Jeff leveling his gun.

He clung to the ladder, somehow, as the vehicle picked up speed. He was stumbling, feet dragging, fighting to stay erect in a needle spray of crystals. The rear tires whined on the icy road and the tail of the motor home wagged like an elephant's rump, slamming him from side to side.

He grasped another rung with his right hand, felt the scar at his pacemaker stretching, somehow got a knee to the rear bumper, and hoisted himself up.

A shot rang out. Plastered against the motor home, he craned back. Jeff was aiming his .45 again. He heard Miguel shout at him not to fire: "¡No! ¡No dispares! Teresa!"; saw the Mexican knock the weapon up, heard it discharge in the air.

He clung panting for a moment to the ladder. The vehicle was skidding, lurching sickeningly. Bunkie had already lost control. He peered back. The two men were running down the road, but as he watched, they faded into the blowing snow. If he could get to the wheel . . .

"Get it stopped," he shouted. "Bunkie!"

The motor home picked up speed, fishtailed, and then began to slide.

Bunkie had released the brake, been ready when she heard her grandpa slam his hand against the rear. She jammed the gearshift lever into Drive and jerked the motor home into motion. She pressed the gas pedal, felt it accelerate, and clung shaking to the wheel. The first sickening sidewise lurch felt like skiing, when you caught an edge.

She heard a gunshot. Had they killed him?

Ahead, the road led dimly down to a valley, before it climbed again to greater peaks. To the rear, she was blind, too short to see in the side-view mirror. She could barely reach the gas pedal or the brake.

Half-standing behind the wheel, she peered into driving snow. Where was Pops? Aboard, or lying on the road behind? Had they killed him, or had she?

"Pops!" she yelled.

She was going too fast. "Drive very slow," he had written. She glimpsed the speedometer: already twenty, and climbing. She took her foot from the gas pedal and jabbed at the brake. The motor home skidded left. She turned the wheel to the right. The skid got worse.

To the *left*, then. She tried it, and it worked.

"Pops?" she screamed. She managed to roll down the window. *"Pops!"*

She heard nothing. She pictured him flung from the ladder, dislodged by her stupid skid.

But every time she tried to slow, the motor home skidded again.

Twenty-five miles an hour, and going faster....

The admiral knew suddenly that Bunkie could never control the heavy vehicle on the icy downhill slope.

He fought his way up the last rungs of the ladder, dropped to his hands and knees on the icy surface of the roof. If he could work his way forward, get a foot in her open window, and slither down beside her on the seat, he could take control.

The Winnebago slid toward the shoulder, lurched, re-covered, skidded as Bunkie spun the wheel, steadied and spun again.

She was jamming the brakes, skidding, and jamming them again. And all the while her speed was building, building, building....

He dropped to his belly, grabbing for the air-condi-tioner housing. He clung while she swung around a curve, then inched forward along the swaying, slippery surface when he could.

"Go easy on the brake!" he screamed, and pounded on the roof.

* * *

She heard him yell from the roof. Her heart leaped. If he was aboard, then they were safe. If she could just get the dumb motor home stopped!

He had shouted to go easy on the brake, so she ignored it and concentrated on the wheel. All she had to do was steer, now, and somehow stay on the road. She'd stop when they reached the valley below.

A curve loomed ahead. Tongue between her teeth, she began to guide the motor home around it. When she felt the skid start, she was ready: she steered toward it, not away, and the motor home obeyed her.

Another curve, to the right; then one to the left...

Like a video game. Right, left...

All at once she was heading for the snow-filled ditch on the wrong side of the road. She steered back. But now the wobbles were wider, the grade steeper, the curves narrower.... Again, she swung to the wrong side of the road.

And then she glimpsed, through blowing snow, a massive silvery shape ahead, climbing toward her in a shroud of white.

And suddenly, through her open window, she felt a groping foot.

"Pops!" she screamed. Panicked, she spun the wheel and jammed the brake.

As a mighty airhorn bellowed, the motor home ignored it, and her, and began to spin.

Somewhere, in the midst of it all, she glimpsed her grandfather in midair, arms and legs all floppy, flying like a giant Raggedy Andy doll through the falling snow.

Feeling with his foot for her open window, the admiral touched her with his toe and heard her scream; her cry was drowned in the roar of an airhorn; he clung to the roof antenna and stared ahead.

Ghostlike in the driving snow, a semitrailer loomed, crawling up the grade.

She was over the line, half in the other lane: he braced

for the shock and cringed. The motor home swung, somehow, and avoided the truck.

But now she'd truly lost control: he felt it in his gut.

He'd had the feeling in a Panther jet, as he fell into a spin. The motor home wheeled ponderously, pirouetting down the slope. One full circle, then another. He swung his foot back to the roof, clutched the antenna, felt it break, went sliding across the icy top, fingernails tearing at vents, seams, rivets.

Then he was flailing at empty air, lost in a blank white void.

Before he struck the snow-filled ditch, he knew that he had failed.

MORGAN

WHEN HE HEARD THE GUNSHOT, MORGAN WASHBURN was dozing in the shade of the carriage. The Pioneer Line was nooning. The mules were grubbing, fifty yards away, under a heartless sun. They were trying to graze on bulrushes along the last traces of the Humboldt River. Ahead lay the shimmering expanse of the endless Carson Sink.

The shot rang loudly in the arid desert air. He thrilled in anticipation; his tongue grew moist.

Meat? A teamster had reported a deer in the rushes. Stein had rushed down to the brackish stream with his repeating rifle and was hunting it afoot.

Perhaps he'd sighted it? *Hit* it?

Morgan's heart raced. Fresh venison, here, would be

a godsend. They all had traces of scurvy; Isaiah was in the sick-wagon; it could literally save his life.

He started to rise. So fiercely did his body hunger for meat, he could not help but hope.

Then reason intervened. Stein was a poor shot; the odds on his filling their larder, in country so hunted-over, were the odds on filling an inside straight. Those who had passed before had feasted on what deer there were; previous mules—and oxen—had eaten the grass; the August sun had swallowed up the tepid water.

It was September—September what? Since he had quit his daily journal entries, and they were weekly entries now, he was always forgetting the date.

September . . . something.

He sank back. He'd wait to hear another shot: Stein could never drop a deer in one, he knew.

It was too hot to move.

"¡Ay! ¡Ay! ¡Ay!"

He sat up, banging his head on the carriage spring. A Mexican herdsman crashed through the underbrush and rushed to the circle of carriages. He was wild-eyed, red-faced, waving his arms and shouting in Spanish. Isaiah's head appeared at the circular opening in the rear of the sick-wagon's canvas top.

"¿Qué pasa?" Isaiah called. The herdsman jabbered, and Isaiah turned white.

"Dr. Washburn! Dr. Marshall! Mr. Stein is shot!"

Morgan rolled from beneath the wagon, grabbed rags from his medical kit, and a bottle of laudanum, and loped behind the Mexican toward the stream. Stein lay crumpled on the bank. A teamster stood staring down at him; a mule, braying wildly, was mired in the alkaline mud below. The Jennings repeater lay three feet away, its muzzle smoking; the smell of black powder lay heavy on the air.

The teamster was breathing heavily. "Jesus Christ, Doctor! He laid that goddamn Jennings down to help me with the mule! And now he's kilt!"

A tide of blood was blackening the front of the stocky Jew's red shirt. Morgan groaned. Gut-shot, badly, and hell awaited him if he awakened. Swiftly, he checked the pulse, lifted an eyelid, chilled when he found life still. "Get blankets from the sick-wagon! And men to move him up."

Marshall arrived panting, his scrabbly beard tangled, his cheeks all streaked with dust. His popping eyes were bloodshot from the trail. He carried his bag: in it, no doubt, was a lancet and cups to bleed him.

"Gone, Doctor?" breathed Marshall.

"No."

Morgan placed a hand upon Stein's brow, willing him to die.

Not killed. Not gone. Not yet.

Within the hour, he hoped.

He prayed to a God he did not know that Stein would not awaken.

The eyelids trembled, and Stein was staring up into his eyes.

"Doctor..." he whispered. *"Dr. Washburn?"*

"Yes, dear comrade. Rest..."

The mule scrambled from the mire and laughed. A cricket sang.

Morgan opened the bottle of laudanum. In a moment, he knew, the screams would come.

They laid him in the shade of the sick-wagon: to try to lift him in would kill him, and if that did not, the jolting of the moving wagon surely would.

Now, as Morgan sat by the dying man's head, the Mexican's shovel grated ten feet away, biting into the sandy soil. They were certainly digging it close enough, in their hurry to be gone: if Stein regained consciousness, he would hear them digging his grave. Captain Turner stared down at them.

"Well, Doctor?"

"He's still alive," murmured Morgan. He squinted up at the little man, into the afternoon sun. A slow rage was building in Morgan, against Turner and the teamsters shuffling their feet by their wagons, mumbling to be gone.

Turner sighted at the sun, then squatted, peered into Stein's face. "You're sure? He looks—"

"I told you, still alive," growled Morgan. Stein's eyelids flickered. "He's coming to again, I fear, so if you'll stand away..."

He took Stein's hand, all slippery with his blood. The *chng...chng...chng...* of the shovel and the ring of the pick on rock continued. He could read in Stein's eyes that their message was heard.

Stein began to squeeze his hand, harder and harder. Morgan waited, dreading what was to come. He had dosed him with four grains of Dr. Marshall's pulverized opium, in water, at the site of the accident, and another four grains after they had moved him to the road. Over the past half hour Morgan had managed to get six ounces of laudanum down his throat, but the bullet had apparently ripped through his stomach from colon sigmoideum to intestinum tenue and each time he regained consciousness the pain seemed fiercer still.

Morgan heard Stein moaning. "Doctor? You are still here?"

"I'm here, Benjamin."

"It's...It's...coming!" Stein's face contorted and he began to writhe. All at once he screamed, a long, singing wail that tore at Morgan's heart and made Turner spin on his heel and walk away.

Stein clung to Morgan's hand like life itself. Morgan could not bear to watch his agony. He turned his face. He saw Turner talking to his teamsters, who began to hitch the mules.

He measured two ounces of laudanum and held the measure to Stein's lips. In a few moments Stein's eyes closed. Turner returned. "Doctor, we're near to rolling now."

"You should," Morgan said bitterly. "You've seen to it that we're far enough behind!"

Turner flushed. "I told you, if you want, we'll carry Stein."

"To what purpose? He's in agony enough."

Turner jerked his head toward the Mexican, who was inside the grave and shoveling fast. *Chng...chng... chng...* "That Greaser's near got it done now, Doctor," Turner said uncomfortably. "Will you be ready to go?"

"No. Your passenger's not dead."

Turner cleared his throat, measured the sun again. He stooped, picked up the laudanum, and glared into Morgan's eyes.

"Well, damn it, then, why don't you just—"

Morgan sprang to his feet, towering over the little man. "Why don't I *what,* you son of a bitch?" He grabbed Turner's shirt and shook him like a rat. "Just hurry him along? All right, sir. Why don't *you* just put a bullet through his brain?"

Turner grabbed at Morgan's bloody hand, tried to tear it loose. "My shirt, goddamn it. You've bloodied it! Just watch what you're about."

"To hell with your shirt, to hell with you, and to hell with your goddamn train!"

He shoved him and Turner stumbled on the dirt piled by the grave. He glared at Morgan and headed for the front of the train. In a moment Morgan heard his cry: "Roll, goddamn it! Roll 'em!"

Morgan untied Isaiah's horse from the sick-wagon and tethered it to a bush. He told Isaiah and Cantrell that when Stein died, he'd bury him, and soon catch up.

Cantrell wanted to stay to help, but Jo could not carry two. Morgan cut a piece of canvas off the sick-wagon's top, ignoring its teamster's protests, and propped it up by Stein to give them shade.

He left his medical kit in Carriage Eighteen, but packed his fishing rucksack with canteens and laudanum for Stein. For himself, he packed his journal: he would catch up on its entries while he passed the deathwatch.

Sitting by his dying friend, he watched the wagons start their crawl across the shivering desert sands.

To the southwest he noticed a cloud of dust.

Another train? Or wind?

He didn't know.

Stein groaned, moved slightly, and slept on.

The sandstorm began at midnight, whipping away the shelter with its first angry gust. Morgan heard Jo neighing in panic, and then the sound of her hooves as she bolted

210

and slipped her tether. The hoofbeats grew fainter as she galloped away, after the Pioneer Line.

Still the little saddler lived on. Morgan huddled by him miserably, to windward, to protect his wound from driving sand.

Stein clung to life until dawn, muttering at times of his sweetheart Hannah, and of saddlery: pommels and cantles and stirrups and leather curing in the sun.

At dawn he turned lucid.

"Have they gone, Doctor?"

Morgan nodded.

Stein tried to smile. "I thought so. They have ceased to dig my grave." Tears came to his eyes. "And you stayed?"

Morgan shrugged. "You'd have stayed with me, I think."

"Who knows?" His breath was short; he would not live long. "Laudanum, you have?"

"You've had a lot. And I'm going to give you more, if the pain—"

"Enough to end it, Doctor? I've tarried far too long."

Morgan chilled. There was an oath he'd taken...

"Benjamin, lie back..."

Stein held out his hand. "The bottle, sir..."

He'd sworn the oath at Geneva, on a Bible. It had served to bind physicians—good ones, anyway—from Hippocrates to himself.

"I cannot, Benjamin. You know that."

"I beg you, sir...For you must *go*."

I will give no deadly medicine to anyone if asked...

"Lie back, and sleep..." He felt Stein's brow. It was very cold. He would not last long.

Stein's eyes grew wide. He grabbed Morgan's arm, writhing from side to side.

The scream, when it started, silenced the crickets in the slough. It was high, and wailing, and hellish in its pitch. And it remained, when Stein had quieted, on the breathless morning air.

"I cannot stand it. Doctor...*Morgan! Please! I beg!*"

Morgan could not reject the plea. He put the bottle to Stein's lips and held it there. Before he had half-emptied it, his head fell back. In thirty seconds, his breath went out, in a butterfly-wing flutter. He was dead.

Morgan dragged him to the graveside. It had filled with blowing sand. He was scooping it out with his hands when two wagons creaked by. They were from the Michigan Wolverine Company, and their comrades were days ahead. The drivers were desperate men and hardly glanced at Morgan scooping sand by the body at the side of the road. They never even answered when he shouted to them, begging for help in burying Stein.

Lashed to the rear of the second wagon was a shovel. Morgan did not bother to ask for it: they would never have given it over. He slipped it loose as they passed.

He shoveled the sand from the grave and rolled Stein's body in. In half an hour he had it filled. He marked it with stones arranged in a cross. He bowed his head while he tried to recall an appropriate passage from the Book of Common Prayer.

"I commend my brother to the ground, earth to earth, ashes to ashes, dust to dust," he muttered. "Good luck, my friend."

He hoisted the rucksack to his back and started down the ruts. He paused, thinking, then turned and went back to the grave.

He rearranged the stones into a six-point star, like one he had seen on a synagogue in New York.

Then he trudged out on the Forty Mile Desert, across the Carson Sink.

Five hours later, under the brutal midday sun, Morgan stood trembling at a fork in the ruts, confronted with a myriad of signs.

Left fork or right? Right fork or left?

Scores of messages were painted on boards; many more were jammed on sticks, some seemed to have been left there months before. All seemed written hurriedly, the spoor of frantic, tortured men, racing their doom to the Carson River, somewhere up ahead.

JEREMIAH BIGGS TOOK LEFT FORK HERE, BEGS EPHRAIM BIGGS TO FOLLOW   SUPPLY WAGON OF JACKSON

COUNTY COMPANY! TAKE THIS BRANCH! GOD WILLING, WE
AWAIT YOU AT THE CARSON!   LIPPENCOTT TRAIN TURN-
ING RIGHT HERE: JULY FIRST, 1849   RIGHT FORK IS A
HUMBUG! TAKE THE LEFT!   WILD ROVERS COMPANY
PASSED HERE AUGUST 16, OUT OF WATER, NO MORE
FEED

In mounting panic, he read them all, stumbling from
crumpled sheet to faded clapboard, read them by the score,
all those papers on which the ink had not already faded,
the signs not yet erased by the heat of the sun. When he
had finished, he got himself together, then systematically
forced himself to do it once again. All the messages were
weeks old. None mentioned the Pioneer Line.

He had slogged for perhaps fifteen miles through sagebrush since he had buried Stein, seen nothing but whit-
ened bones of oxen, and, finally, poor Jo dead and swelling
on the trail. He was nearly out of water: he had passed
the two Wolverine wagons two hours back: the men were
badly frightened, and out of water too.

If he did not soon catch his outfit he would die.

Surely they had left a note to guide him: if not Captain
Turner, then Isaiah or Cantrell.

They had! he knew suddenly. *And the sandstorm had
whisked it away!*

He saw an errant slip of paper, snagged by a sagebrush
far from the ruts. He staggered to it, plucked it, and read:
PEAR SOAP FOR INFANTS. He turned it over.

The back of it was blank.

He looked ahead. Right or left, left or right?

He was lost.

He was suddenly dizzy and strangely chilled. Heat-
stroke! He retreated to an abandoned, wheelless wagon,
a hundred yards back from the fork. He found shade
behind it, though two oxen carcasses shared the shadow
with him; the heat had burst their bellies and their hides
lay loose on their ribs.

The tattered rags of the wagon's canvas top hung
scorched in the furnace heat. He sat in stupor, desiccated,
and too tired to think.

The sun peaked and began to sink, drawing the shadow

closer to the oxen; soon he must draw nearer to them too, or abandon the shade to the dead.

He drifted into a dream. He was flying high above the desert, peering from the porthole of a marvelous balloon. It was shaped like a giant cigar and speeding at a hundred miles an hour straight toward the sinking sun. He drank cold, clear water, poured by Mary from a silver pitcher, beaded with icy sweat. He lifted his glass to Captain Turner, sitting in front, guiding the balloon with reins steady in his hands. Then Morgan motioned Mary to his window, to pity a dying emigrant—himself—hiding in the shelter of a wagon, below on the burning sands.

He awakened, heartsick that the dream was only that. He lifted his canteen and rocked it, listening. Almost empty. He finished the last swallow. His throat seemed to absorb it all, and he wondered if any had reached his stomach.

By his side lay his canvas knapsack, with the laudanum he had taken from his medical kit for Stein. Tied to the knapsack was Stein's canteen, dry as the air he breathed.

He would die here. He could not go on. He took his ink bottle out and set it on a rock; tore a rough-planed board from the wagon seat to use as a desk.

His lips were split; his knuckles too; his palms, blistered from shoveling poor Stein's grave, seemed filled with glowing coals.

The sun probed through the wagon top, scorching his booted legs. It touched the journal on his knees. The pages crinkled, squeezed of life as ancient parchment, hot as hammered metal on a blacksmith's forge. The ink dried on his pen, almost before he could touch it to paper. He stirred uncomfortably, looked southwest, and bent to write.

The whole atmosphere glows like an oven! Off to the southwest, as far as the eye can extend, nothing appears but a level desert. This I must cross. The trail branches here. I know not which branch to take. The right branch or the left?

He touched the page before him. At Mary's insistence, he had bought the journal in Rensselaerville at Jeremiah

214

Mulford's store; she had wanted him to keep a diary of the great adventure, so that she could know it too.

Having stocked no proper diary, Jeremiah had sold him an account book instead. Well, the account seemed close to settlement. Even if he found strength to go on, the odds were one in two against him. If he picked the wrong ruts to follow, he would never rejoin his companions; without water, he could never reach the Carson alone. The diary would be his final testament.

Which no one would ever read. . . .

He wrote a plea on the inside of the cover that, if found, the journal be posted to Mary. Conceivably, some Good Samaritan might mail it, if he left it here. If not, she might never know his fate.

He had hoped to wait for dusk before marching on, to avoid the heat of the sun. But the moving shade was driving him closer to the oxen and the awful smell of death. He capped his ink, put pen and ink into the knapsack, and struggled to his feet.

He placed the journal in plain view on the seat of the wagon and weighted it with a rock. He stepped from the shade into sunlight.

The sun turned to a massive ember, tearing at his brain. He retreated to the shadow. Better to bear the stench of the oxen and sip the laudanum until he passed away, than to face such burning heat.

No. Damned if he'd burrow like a prairie dog and die! And damned if he'd leave the journal here! To abandon it was to admit that he would perish.

He'd survive, or not, but the journal went with him!

He jammed it into his pack, shouldered the rucksack with the empty canteens, and moved to the fork in the road.

Right or left, left or right?

He was all at once in Rensselaerville, dozing next to Mary in her family's pew.

"Morgan," she chuckled, "Morgan, wake up!"

Reverend Thistle was impaling him on his stare: "Blessed are they, Dr. Washburn, which do hunger and thirst after righteousness: for they shall be filled."

Well, he hungered, and God, how he thirsted!

He picked the righteous, right-hand fork, and plodded on, southwest toward the blazing sun.

He walked all afternoon, and half the night by starlight. At dawn, he saw a cloud of dust: by noon he'd caught the stragglers of the Pioneer Line: Captain Turner and the leaders were thought to be an hour ahead, racing for the Carson at a brisk two miles an hour.

The last three carriages had no water to give him, the next he asked gave grudgingly. His own carriage, when he came upon it, had no food. Dr. Cantrell was driving: he embraced Morgan, gave him the last of his water, and sent him ahead for food. Isaiah, in the sick-wagon, cried when he saw him, and passed him his mirror: Morgan gazed at his own reflection, a death's-head with rotting gums, staring with burning eyes.

To climax his homecoming, Morgan had to trudge to the head of the column to beg Turner himself for biscuits.

At evening they reached the tail of the Carson, which had sunk into the sand. They drank from a salty pool. Turner decreed that the teams were too tired to proceed: tomorrow they'd rest once more.

"Christ," growled Morgan, when he heard. "Is it Sunday, once again?"

No one knew. Morgan examined Isaiah. His teeth were loose, his skin was flaccid, his hair was falling out.

He was good for less than two weeks, he reckoned, and Dr. Cantrell agreed.

It was pack him over the passes, or dig another grave on the desert, and Morgan did not want him to die. He confronted Captain Turner, who refused to sell him a mule.

"But your wagons and your carriages will kill us! *Unhitch!* Leave the vehicles, pack the mules, and climb it! Or we'll die down here in droves!"

"No. We're a wagon company, not a packtrain!"

The little man was bristling, spoiling for a fight. Morgan looked at him and smiled.

"All right, sir," Morgan murmured softly, "I expect you're right."

* * *

At midnight Morgan crept by moonlight into the center of the ring of wagons and carriages, which formed a corral for the herd of mules. He found Cantrell, who had the night watch, sitting on a rock by a glittering, stagnant pool of gray water, staring at the enormous mountains to the west.

"Sir, I'd like to steal a mule. What would you think of that?"

Morgan saw his teeth flash in the moonlight. "Nothing, sir. For I'd not see it. My eyes are dim with age."

Morgan squeezed his shoulder. "I'm going to try to get Isaiah through alive. Doctor, would *you* want to come?"

"I cannot," sighed Cantrell. He stood suddenly, searched the herd with his eyes, found Icarus, and led him to Morgan by his bridle.

"Why not, sir?" Morgan asked uncomfortably. Stealing the mule was hardly theft. "For Isaiah—maybe for me as well—it's a matter of life and death!"

Cantrell laughed softly. "I'd steal every goddamn mule he had, to get over that mountain range! That's not it, Doctor, believe me."

"Why not, then? Why let Turner trap you in the snow up there, and die without a fight?"

"You have young legs. I'd slow you down. 'He travels fastest who travels alone.' Mr. Hollister will be burden for you enough."

He was right. Throat tight with emotion, Morgan clasped his hand, looked into the bleary eyes, and said: "In the Mother Lode, then, sir?"

A coyote howled in the distance. Icarus snuffled and stamped. From the teamsters' campfire Morgan heard a Mexican singing plaintively. He knew no Spanish, but the melody spoke of partings, sweet and sad.

Cantrell nodded. "I hope so, Doctor. God willing, in the Mother Lode."

Morgan crept into the mess wagon and stole a five-pound tin of hardtack biscuits. The smell of the rotten onions set his belly's juices alive, but when he found one that had fallen between the wagonbed's boards, and tasted it, he gagged.

A half hour later, passing silently, with Icarus saddled

217

and Isaiah mounted astride, Morgan could see the doctor standing sadly by the herd. Morgan lifted a hand in the moonlight, but Cantrell did not see.

By moonlight they followed the Carson's dry bed. At dawn Icarus smelled water by an abandoned campsite. It was tan and brackish, but better than yesterday's, and the next pool better still.

The tail of the Carson River seemed to appear, disappear into the earth, and reappear again. They followed the stream where they could find it, and when it vanished into the sand they sometimes went by chance. In three days they were staring up at the Sierras, as storm clouds gathered above.

The mountains were immense: Morgan craned to see their peaks. They utterly dwarfed the Bighorn, Wyoming, and Grand Teton ranges they had passed in the Rockies. As he gaped at their heights, the clouds grew thick, and hid the crests from sight. He heard thunder in the passes and was frightened at the sound.

He could not tell from Bryant's guidebook which canyon to enter, so he picked the one down which the Carson—now a torrent—roared. They began to climb, Isaiah astride Icarus and Morgan's hand on the mule's bridle.

For three days they struggled up the pass, slipping and sliding with the mule along the raging stream. For food, they had the biscuits. They could not chew them with their bleeding gums, and soaked them to mush when they could. Scurvy struck harder: Morgan lost a tooth, and Isaiah lost three. And when they finally stood, on the third day, at what they had thought was the crest, it was a false one and another rose ahead.

Storm clouds billowed at the true summit, which rose beyond a long green valley below them. From the guidebook, Morgan learned that was the Valley of Hope. There seemed little enough hope, for it would be a full day's journey across, and the clouds over the true summit seemed packed with snow. They descended into the valley and started.

218

By dusk, halfway across it, they were ravenous with hunger, half-insane. They decided to sleep in a grove of scrubby pines near a lake in the floor of the valley. Morgan helped Isaiah off Icarus.

Morgan had reached an awful decision. He patted the mule's brown jowls. "Old friend . . . Icarus, you must die."

Isaiah was staring at him. "What?"

"We have to eat, Isaiah."

Isaiah took his arm. "Are you mad?"

Morgan pointed to the summit. "There's snow in those clouds. Tomorrow, if we survive tonight—we're going to need our strength." He began to charge his pistol. "I can't go any longer without food. Can you?"

Isaiah shook his head. "I'll starve before I touch that animal! My God, he's saved my life!"

"Your life's not saved yet! And I didn't haul you this far to hear sentimental tripe! He's just a goddamn *mule*!" His voice broke. He was close to weeping. He grabbed Isaiah fiercely. "Beyond that crest—beyond that pass—lies all we've come to see!"

Sick at heart, he yanked the saddlebags and his medical kit from Icarus's pack, tugged off the crude saddle they'd made from blankets for Isaiah, and piled them on the ground in the shelter of a pine.

Avoiding Icarus's patient eyes, he capped his Navy Aston. Suddenly Isaiah cocked his head. His face lit up with hope. "No! Morgan! Listen!"

Morgan listened. From the meadow lake he heard the lowing of an ox, faint and plaintive. His heart leaped. Cautiously, he uncocked the pistol, jammed it into his waistband. He grabbed Isaiah's Bowie knife, and stumbled to the lakeshore.

Mired in mud, moaning softly, was a half-starved, half-dead ox. A wooden yoke lay near him, and an abandoned wagon with a canted, shattered wheel. Morgan slogged through the mud, took a deep breath, and dispatched the poor creature. He cut all the meat they could pack from the animal's loin with the Bowie, ripped slats from the sides of the wagon for firewood, and that night they gnawed on beef.

They awakened at dawn in a blizzard. Morgan cinched

Icarus's pack on, helped Isaiah mount. A howling wind down the pass piled snow into drifts in the lee of boulders; Morgan, blinded in the white shroud, led Icarus into drift after drift and had to haul the floundering animal out.

His boots, dried out on the desert floor, began to rot on his feet. He had only the remnants of his greatcoat to wear for warmth: Isaiah, mounted, was hooded in both their blankets. The stitchings on Morgan's right boot gave way, and its sole separated: his toes became frostbitten.

After eight long hours they began the climb to the final summit. Morgan could not see five feet ahead of him: he marched from one pine, scarred by the ropes of emigrants hauling their wagons up the sheer granite cliffs, to the next, pausing at each.

His breath shortened. He fought for air. Isaiah fell from the mule and had to be hoisted to its back again. They traversed a slope of shale, slippery as ice. Icarus kept his feet, though Morgan fell a dozen times. They picked their way through a white hell along a narrow path traversing the Carson's gorge: when the wind, for a moment, swept the veil of white aside, Morgan saw a drop of a thousand feet below.

They struggled through drifts like flour, as the snow-flakes floated down. They became lost, and could not tell in the driving snow if they'd reached the summit's crest.

When they dropped, exhausted, in a grove of trees, under a mighty pine, each was too tired and numb to care.

At dawn the sun rose behind them, bursting over the crest. To the west lay the Valley of the Sacramento, bathed in golden haze.

During the night the snow had stopped falling. The pass was blocked behind them: God help Cantrell, and the Pioneer Line.

Isaiah stared into Morgan's eyes. "My friend," he swallowed, "Morgan..." Suddenly he hugged him close, and swung away. Morgan saw his shoulders shaking. Embarrassed, Morgan fumbled in his knapsack, taking refuge in his journal of the trip. He sat beneath a pine in the warming morning sunlight, and he wrote:

The Summit is crossed! We are in California! Far away in the haze, the dim outlines of the Sacramento Valley are discernible! We are on the downgrade now and our famished mule may pull us through. We are in the midst of huge pines, so large as to challenge belief.

A drop fell on the page, smearing his words. He frowned up at the pine tree, saw nothing that could have dripped...

If there is a hospital in Sacramento, Hollister may live. He was overcome with the greatest weariness he had ever known. He was sicker than he knew. *And so may I...*

Astonished, he doubled over suddenly, sobbing like a child. He was mortified. Isaiah had known him a full five months, and never seen a tear.

Morgan finally drew a shuddering breath, closed the journal, and arose to saddle the mule for Isaiah.

So much, he thought wryly, *for the hardy pioneers.*

They were a full hour down the trail before he trusted himself to look his comrade in the eye.

THE ADMIRAL

"POPS...OH, POPS, OPEN YOUR EYES, *PLEASE*..."

The admiral clawed his way to consciousness. Snow-flakes were landing on his face. He was shivering, frozen to the core, on his back in the snow, with his head in his granddaughter's lap. He heard the squeak of footsteps on soft-packed powder, growing closer.

He opened his eyes. Bunkie was looking down at him. Her cheeks were wet with tears. The admiral raised his head. He lay in a snow-filled highway ditch. A few feet away sat the motor home. Wherever it had come to rest, it was now parked neatly at the side of the highway. It

221

seemed undamaged. Jeff was crunching toward them across the snow.

"Bunkie?" the admiral croaked. He tried to sit up, fell back, panting. For a moment he thought that he might have broken his back. He seemed incapable of stirring, except for the damnable shivering.

"Oh, Pops," she moaned. "I *tried*..."

"Not your fault," he grunted. "Mine..."

Jeff was suddenly looming over them, haloed against the clouded sun, staring down with icy eyes, automatic in hand. His foot lashed out and the admiral felt a searing pain in his ribs as he kicked him, once and once again. "OK, asshole, on your feet."

"I...can't," he mumbled. "Look, don't blame her! I told her to! I *ordered* her—"

"Get on your fucking feet!"

He struggled to his knees, rested, rose, grabbed at Bunkie for support. Jeff prodded them toward a grove of mammoth pines. Bunkie's grip on his hand was viselike; he could hear her gasping in fear.

"Pops," she sobbed, "I'm *scared!*"

Jeff's hand slashed out and caught her on the cheek. She stumbled and fell, fought back to her feet. Her eyes were wide with fear.

The admiral's instinct was to brave the gun and go for the man: he forced himself to hold back.

If he could just buy her back the time he'd snatched from her...

"You still *need* her," he pled to Jeff. "You said you'd let her go!"

"You're both more fucking trouble than you're worth."

The giant pines hovered, sighing in the wind. Bunkie seemed wobbly, on the point of collapse. Jeff pointed toward the largest of the trees. "Over there."

The admiral heard a truck grinding up the hill from Hope Valley, cresting the pass, downshifting as it began the long descent to the foothills below. Finally there was only the fading rattle of its chains.

Time stopped. The rustling of pine needles stilled. The snowfall was over; sound seemed deadened in the air. All at once he heard a scream of pain from the motor home. It was Terry, wailing like a frightened child.

"On your knees, and face the tree," said Jeff.

He was damned if they'd be slaughtered like pigs. He squeezed Bunkie's hand. "We can face *you*, you son of a bitch. You can goddamn well face *us*!"

Jeff raised his gun, leveling it at Bunkie. The admiral lurched forward to grapple with him, slipped on the snow, and stumbled to one knee. The gun swung to his head. He closed his eyes.

Miguel's voice cut through the air. "¡No!"

He opened his eyes. Miguel was running toward them, crunching across the snow in giant, loping strides. The Mexican grabbed Jeff's arm. His face was white, and his eyes were wide with fear. "¡No! ¡No lo mates! Ella lo necesita ahora."

"You can't kill him! She needs him now."

"Shit," Jeff breathed. "¿Qué pasa?"

"¡El dolor la matará si no le saca la bala!"

"She is going to die of pain if he does not take out the bullet!"

Jeff looked at Miguel, started to speak, flicked his eyes at the admiral, and seemed to change his mind.

"OK," he said, "she's bad. You stirred up her shoulder. He wants you to get that bullet out." He grabbed Bunkie roughly, squatted to look her in the eye. "Now, look, you little shit, I'll *kill* you if you make another move! You *got* that?"

She whispered: "Yes."

"Yes, *what*?"

She swallowed and licked her lips. Finally she got it out: "Yes, sir."

He jerked his head toward the motor home. Clinging to Bunkie's hand, the admiral stumbled back.

The admiral looked down at Terry. She was writhing in bed, uttering little cries; her face was flushed and greasy; she could not seem to bear the pain.

"There's a hospital in Stockton."

"If we take her to a hospital," growled Jeff, "we'll leave you two right here!"

The admiral rubbed his eyes. Fate had drawn him to this moment: he felt helpless and adrift. To introduce this monster deeper into his life frightened him, almost more than death itself. But he had to buy some time. . . .

"We're within two hours of my house," he said slowly, in a low monotone. "It's got a surgery—"

Jeff stared at him. "You mean an *operating* room?"

"My great-grandfather—"

"You got your own *operating* room? Two hours from *here*?"

Jeff's lips were taut with anger, his jaw outthrust with rage. But when the admiral read his eyes, they were passionless and cool. Jeff was acting out his own charade, but why? "You dirty son of a bitch," Jeff growled, "isn't this a little *late*?"

"It's a historic monument, restored," the admiral explained. "Old instruments, old-fashioned equipment. It's all one hundred and thirty years old! I've got nothing there myself." He explained that everything modern had been gone for twenty years, that he seldom went near the room himself. "It's primitive, and dirty, but I'll try to do it there."

Bunkie was staring at him as if he were mad. Jeff grabbed her arm. "Look, is this bullshit, or the truth?"

She looked him square in the face. "My grandfather never lies!"

Jeff thought for a moment, then seemed to make a decision. He translated into Spanish what the admiral had said: Miguel's eyes began to shine with hope.

But the admiral saw on Jeff's face a tiny smile, too quickly hidden.

Something was wrong. Treachery was in the air and the admiral knew that he was somehow being used.

They crested Carson Summit, the admiral at the wheel. The sun burst out ahead, fringing the enormous pines with fire. Across the Sacramento basin another storm was

224

gathering, but the Sacramento Valley lay before them in a haze of golden light.

Morgan had crossed on such a day, hoping his dangers were done. *The Summit is crossed! We are in California! ... We are on the downgrade now ...*

Morgan had erred. His danger had lurked ahead, in Nevada City. Their danger lurked there too, northwest along a winding highway that the admiral knew well.

He'd bought Bunkie two hours more, and that was all. He had lost all hope himself.

SUNDAY

NIGHT

MORGAN AND MARY

THE PRESENCES OF MORGAN AND MARY HOVERED CLOSE
to the speeding motor home, and past the Milky Way; in
the mountains they had loved, and in stars no man had
seen.

Their seed had beaten the first of the snows, as Morgan
had before. But now the motor home turned northward,
away from Morgan's track. Swooping, speeding, climbing, it wound along the alpine crests.

Morgan and Mary had watched their tall descendent,
in the Valley of Hope, as his shrewdness saved the child.
From the very edge of the Spheres of Thought, the man
had snatched her back.

His fight for the child he loved was in the long run
useless. Morgan would ordinarily have been easy with
such a thought, for all such efforts failed. Those he'd
saved in earthly days, like those he'd failed to cure, had
all died in the end.

But behind the home he'd built for Mary they'd planted
a cherry tree. They had planned to start an orchard, but
she'd died as their son was born. In the eternity before
he joined her—which was really the blink of an eye—he
had not found, in all the years, the heart to plant again.

The child in the motor home was the last leaf on their
tree. Until she'd flowered, he hoped she need not fall.

* * *

Mary knew Morgan's thoughts as well as she knew her own, and wanted the child to live. But what would be, she could not change, any more than what had been.

The motor home was winding north toward Echo Summit, high above the lake. It braved another flurry of snow, then swooped down Meyers Grade, and took the western shore of Tahoe. It skirted sapphire waters and climbed the Donner Pass.

She knew that it was making for the home that Morgan had built for her, and that she had loved so well.

Watching all, though powerless to change it, she saw another thing as well. A graceful silver airplane, swift as a morning dream, was racing over storm clouds above the Great Divide, speeding, one day's full march to a pulsebeat, into the setting sun.

In it, the child's mother—her own great-great-granddaughter—sat reading next to the child's father.

Their destination was her home in Nevada City, but she knew their fate no better than she knew their child's.

THE ADMIRAL
AND BUNKIE

THE ADMIRAL SWUNG OFF INTERSTATE 80 SHORT OF EMIGRANT GAP and cruised along the ridge south of Bear Valley between columns of stately pines. Beside him Bunkie sat like a stone.

The sun was touching the tips of the trees ahead. Slanting pillars of golden light held fat-bellied clouds aloft.

He'd dreamed of this return, with Bunkie at his side.

If he had not stopped for the felons on the highway, he would be pointing out the places of his youth to her now, as he always had before: ancient mining flumes he'd skidded down on boards, lakes he'd swum, secret streams in which he'd panned fool's gold, seldom finding color....

Now each mile through his childhood was a minute closer to the end.

Across the valley, scarred with the yellow stains of old hydraulic diggings, the Sierra Buttes were smothering under billowing clouds of rain.

The woman's groans were becoming unbearable. Every dip in the highway brought a cry of agony and every curve a moan.

They had less than ten minutes to drive.

He'd been an idiot to try to escape. Tijuana would have given them five hours more; anything might have happened on the way.

He was very weary. His back ached, and his pacemaker scar seemed torn inside. Despite the device, his pulse seemed erratic, too.

He switched on the headlights. Jeff grabbed the map from Bunkie to check their route. From it fell the note to Bunkie that had almost got them killed.

"Well, well," Jeff said, "what have we here?" He began to read, a note of amusement in his voice. "'When we stop to put the chains on, I'll get both these bastards out.'" He read silently, then chuckled. "'...drive *very slow* to first gas station, call police on phone. I love you, Pops.'" Jeff laughed. "How sweet, 'Pops.' Who wrote the letter on the top?"

"Just an old letter, it doesn't matter," muttered the admiral, swerving to avoid a skunk mashed on the highway. Terry shrieked, and Miguel cursed from the rear, yelling at him in Spanish to take care.

"*My dearest Mary...*" read Jeff. "Who's Mary?"

Bunkie turned in her seat. "She's my great-great-great-grandmother! And—"

The admiral stiffened. There was a note of hysteria in her voice. "Quiet, Bunkie," he murmured. "Cool it."

Jeff seemed amused. "Great-great...Christ, I wouldn't know my *mother's* name, except the foster home fucked

231

up." He continued: "*I am arrived in a town called Ne-vada. So much has occurred in the past two weeks that I scarce* ... Jesus, who *wrote* this, anyway?"

"Morgan did!" cried Bunkie. "Her *sweetheart*! And you can't read it!"

Appalled, the admiral glimpsed her sliding from her seat. She turned and lunged for the letter. Jeff, startled, pulled it away.

"Bunkie!" called the admiral, slowing the motor home. "You sit down!"

She ignored him. She was glaring up at Jeff. "It's *hers*," she sobbed, "now give it back!"

"Tubby," Jeff said coldly, "get your ass back in that seat, or I'll goddamn shoot it off!"

"Pops! That letter was to *her*!"

The admiral took his hand from the wheel, reached back and grabbed her arm. He pulled her forward and pushed her, as gently as he could, into the passenger seat. "Now Bunkie," he murmured, a catch in his voice, "you stay *there*."

"But Pops—"

"Pipe down," he said softly. "Just let the letter be!"

She was crying. He patted her knee.

Breaking. Finally she was breaking.

Who could blame her? He was breaking too.

Bunkie sat burning with shame. She'd cried again, in front of the man. He seemed to like to see her cry.

She had sat quietly when he started the letter, braced for the part that was coming. And still, the outrage when she heard him read it had forced her from her seat.

Now the man knew he could make her cry, and he probably would again. But it wasn't fair, it wasn't right! Morgan's letter was to Mary, and they shouldn't let him read it, it was wrong.

He was reading aloud again: "*...a town called Ne-vada. So much has occurred in the past two weeks that I scarce know where to commence. So I shall begin, my darling, by penning you what I could never bring myself* *to say, beneath your father's cherry tree—*" He laughed. "A real stud, Admiral? Run in the family?"

"Just a country doctor," Pops answered softly. "Look, it's time we gave Terry another shot—" He began to slow the motor home down.

"Keep going," ordered Jeff. "*. . . beneath your father's cherry tree. But in that hospital in Sacramento, under the care of strangers, a vision entered there. She wore a pale green robe of silk, and beneath, her sleeping gown. She walked as in a trance—*"

Bunkie's face was flaming. She felt as if the man were . . . well, *undressing* Mary—as Angela said her boyfriend Mel had tried to do to her. *Stop him, Pops, please stop him . . .*

But Pops, who could do *anything*, could not.

Blessedly, she heard him crumple up the paper. He reached past her and threw it out her window to the winds.

"What shit," he said, "what a pile of shit! How long we got to go?"

"Five minutes," sighed Pops, glancing out the side window. "Just about five minutes; here's Scott's Flat."

And then what? Bunkie wondered. What was next?

The admiral drove onward, growing more frightened for Bunkie with every passing mile. Lake Vera lay to the north: one stormy night like this, swimming bare-assed in it with the queen of Grass Valley High, he'd almost drowned.

Tonight, he wished he had.

"Nevada City," he announced reluctantly. In the dusk, the lights of the tiny town were coming on. He turned down the highway exit ramp, then turned left on Coyote Street, heading toward the center of town.

"'Nevada City,'" Jeff said thoughtfully. "In California? Why is that?"

Because, on the eve of statehood, Nevada had stolen its name.

233

But he felt no need to tour-guide the son of a bitch, and didn't answer. Rain splattered on the windshield. He turned on the wipers and headed for home, on the longest route he could.

MORGAN

MORGAN WASHBURN, SWEATING UNDER A FIFTY-POUND pack, climbed Tribulation Trail to the mining camp of Caldwell's Store, smelling woodsmoke on the path. He stopped at a crudely lettered board nailed to a pine tree. Faded letters read CALDWELL'S STORE— 1 MILE, but a line of fresh paint ran through it, and above it was written NEVADA. He was not surprised: all through the Mother Lode this spring, stores were changing to camps, camps to villages, villages to towns. All California was abroil: delegates were on their way to Washington City to assure its admission as a state. Everything was changing overnight. Someone here with a poetic bent had simply seized the opportunity to improve his new community's name.

Isaiah, carrying a burden as heavy as his own, arrived and collapsed at the side of the trail. His glasses were streaked with sweat and his face with trail dust; his forehead was blistered from the sun. He glanced at the board on the tree.

"Nevada?" he mused. "'Snowy,' I think, in Spanish."

"Snowy" seemed appropriate to these lower ranges of the Sierras. They must have been deep under drifts all winter. Though it was late in April and the two were far below the timberline, a patch of dusty snow still lay in the shade by the side of the trail. Morgan scooped up a handful, and pressed it to his brow.

His head ached. Gambling and rotgut whiskey had damaged him the night before. He was panting from the hike, too tired from the climb from Rough and Ready camp, the site of last night's debauchery five miles back, to take his knapsack off. It was stuffed with medicines, a few medical instruments, and food. His bedding was in a roll on top. What gold dust he had was all gone.

He backed against a fir to rest his pack. His four months in Sacramento had softened his muscles, as the scurvy had surely enfeebled his heart and lungs. Hollister seemed even weaker.

Sacramento City, the haven they had sought as they raced the snows through Carson Pass, had seemed at first to succor them, but then turned into a watery hell. Tempestuous rains flooded the tents and shacks in January, and the Odd Fellows Hospital nearly slipped its moorings. They were rescued from an upper window by a boatman who charged them eight dollars each to ferry them to a brigantine tied to the city dock, where they rented a stateroom at nineteen dollars a week. At least their new home floated, but there both caught "Sacramento Fever"— Morgan thought it a strain of typhus—and nearly died again.

A bad winter, one that would live in his memory—and perhaps his body—for all the years to come. Still, they escaped lightly: Dr. Van Ness, who treated them, told them that one of ten of his patients died of it.

Although Morgan might have prospered in Sacramento City, medical fees being high—Van Ness was charging an ounce of dust for a consultation and one hundred dollars for a "house call"—he learned to hate the town, with its piles of rotting garbage, muddy streets, and filthy docks.

He extracted from his medical kit a few medicines and instruments which might help him to establish a practice, and left his kit as security for their eight-hundred-dollar medical bill to Van Ness. He struck north to the mountains with Isaiah, determined to escape the miasmal slough of Sacramento and do better.

After winter rains and Sierra snows which surpassed

235

any in the memory of natives, the spring brought even more chaos to mining. Rumors of goldstrikes in northern camps were sending southern miners north; tales of finds in Mariposa were drawing northern miners south. Weary prospectors were leaving claims, meeting others on the trail with new stories of riches elsewhere; lines of men were moving antlike, east and west, everywhere along the dusty trails.

In the Mother Lode, no one was immune to gold fever. Doctors, lawyers, soldiers—above all, sailors and their officers deserting the ships on San Francisco Bay—all had abandoned their pasts to work the gravel bars of rivers raging from the hills.

The gold fever had suddenly infected Morgan and Isaiah. They found themselves, almost without willing it, building a rocker and staking a claim near Oro, on the River Bear. Whether or not they struck it rich, Morgan rationalized, it would be salubrious to sweat the fevers of Sacramento from their bones.

Instead, they had nearly killed themselves. Sloshing in icy water, in knuckle-scraping, muscle-tearing labor, lifting, always lifting, scrabbling in gravel, shoveling, they labored on a gravel bar from dawn to dusk, one wobbling the rocker like a demented nursemaid, the other shoveling gravel from the riverbed, both peering continually into the wooden box for color, like the two fools that they were.

The excitement lasted for barely half a day, but they were too proud to quit. Living in an abandoned cabin with a roof of green cowhides, they netted, at the end of two weeks, a full four ounces of gold. At the assay office in Plumas City, where they weighed it out, they got fourteen dollars the ounce, for a total of fifty-six dollars.

Prices were soaring along the Mother Lode—a red shirt, badge of the miner, cost sixteen dollars at Plumas, and their breakfast of sardines, bread, butter, cheese, and two bottles of ale cost forty-three dollars. They calculated that they would have to squeeze four ounces of dust a day from their claim to stay alive. Isaiah reckoned that they would have profited better for the past two weeks had they sat by the side of the river, feeding it silver dollars, at the rate of one each hour.

So they abandoned their new profession and the claim, and left to seek a place where they could practice what they knew.

They traveled from Plumas up the Feather River to Marysville on the *Linda*, a steam-powered scow which a Mormon had bought for forty thousand dollars and which, according to rumor, had earned back her price in a month. In Marysville—a hodgepodge of Digger Indian huts and a corral—men were selling "city" lots for two hundred and fifty dollars each, and seventeen houses were under construction, to be completed in the next ten days. There being no place to stay there, they decided to inspect the northern camps.

They went afoot, too broke to afford horses. They slipped and slithered along the Yuba River trail to Yuba City. They found the town a morass from the winter's rains. Long's Bar, Park's Bar, and Rose's Bar were miserable tent villages, with harrowed, scrabbling miners working gravel bars in the raging Yuba under a blazing sun.

Union Ranch, a digging near the junction of the Yuba with Deer Creek, was inundated; they passed on. Last night in Rough and Ready, which had jocularly "seceded" from the United States the week before and was operating under its own constitution, they had rented a room above a gambling hall. The establishment, complete with a ten-pin bowling alley, was run by a portly, hard-drinking minister, Reverend Royce Thornberry. Encouraged by Isaiah and the reverend's whiskey, Morgan lost what remained of their stake at euchre.

The reverend, a potbellied, gray-haired Methodist with beady eyes of green and jowls overrunning his minister's collar, beckoned to Morgan and Isaiah from behind his bar.

"Whiskey, Doctor? And your friend?"

"Please."

"Doctor, you got tooth forceps in that bag?"

Morgan nodded, sensing a windfall.

Thornberry put a bottle and three glasses on the bar.

"The good Lord, sir, in his wisdom, has visited on me a toothache."

The minister leaned across the bar, opened his mouth, and pointed. Morgan grabbed the jaw and turned his head to the light. The teeth were brown with tobacco. He sniffed and caught the odor of decay. The upper gum was inflamed. Morgan stuck in his forefinger and wobbled a molar. Thornberry yelled: that was the one. It was loose and quite ready for extraction.

"Bad, sir," decided Morgan. "Has to go."

"How much, sir? In dust?" the reverend demanded.

"Marysville rates," answered Morgan. "Two ounces, fine or coarse."

"Thirty *dollars*?"

"That's right, sir."

In Rensselaerville, he and Mary's father would be lucky to get five.

Thornberry pursed his lips: on so full a face, they looked quite small. "Dr. Cantrell, up at Caldwell's Store—"

Morgan's heart bounded. "*Cantrell?* He made it over!" He clapped Isaiah on the back.

The reverend nodded, making his jowls quiver. "He's at Caldwell's. Or 'Nevada,' if you will. *He'll* pull a tooth for an ounce."

Morgan was overjoyed. He'd given up Cantrell for lost when the snow blocked Carson Pass. "He asks only an ounce?" he repeated. "Of whiskey, or of gold?"

Thornberry frowned. "He's a man of some years, Doctor. The Lord bids you respect your elders. An ounce of gold, of course."

"Then use him, by all means."

He heard Isaiah sigh. They needed the money: Isaiah was right: he must learn to be discreet.

But the minister was fingering his jaw.

"One ounce, two . . . It isn't that." He looked at Morgan's hands, calloused and red from moving river rocks. "There are some don't hold with doctors that got to work the rivers."

The hell with him. "There are some who don't hold with ministers who serve whiskey in their church."

Thornberry flushed angrily. "The Lord moves in mysterious ways. At least my church is full."

Isaiah cleared his throat. "He means no disrespect, sir. He's a very pious man."

Morgan succumbed to the laws of survival. Feeling like a hungry quack, he pointed out that he was a graduate of Geneva Medical College, in the State of New York. "And begging your pardon, sir, that's your third upper *molar*! The most dangerous tooth in your mouth!"

"What can happen to a tooth?"

"It's not the tooth, sir. It's the pus. I've known men to die."

Thornberry frowned, thought for a moment, and capitulated. They finished off the bottle, to properly anesthetize the patient and inspire the practitioner.

Morgan pulled the tooth in Thornberry's office, with Isaiah holding the reverend in his swivel chair. He got it out quite handily, with a transverse flick of the wrist, causing only a few bellows in a minor key—a most important matter, should there be other sufferers in the bar.

Morgan handed the reverend the bloody molar, as the minister sat dabbing his lips with a red kerchief.

"I prescribe another pint of whiskey, Reverend," Morgan said, "before your vesper services tonight."

Thornberry regarded him blearily, unamused. Reluctantly, the minister weighed out two ounces of gold dust on his assay scales, poured them into a bag. He jiggled the bag in his hand, rested his green pig-eyes on Morgan's.

"Perhaps you'd like to double it, Doctor? *Four* ounces, or none?"

"No, Reverend," exclaimed Isaiah, "he would not!"

Fuzzily, Morgan eyed the bag. It looked very small. Two ounces would hardly get the both of them fed tonight.

"Reverend, I think I shall."

Thornberry slid a pack of cards across his desk. Morgan shuffled and the minister cut. He held up the ten of hearts. Morgan cut and got the eight of spades.

Isaiah groaned and Morgan shrugged. They retired to their room and spent a sleepless night in the din of the bowling pins below.

Now, on the trail to Caldwell's Store, they were dead

broke, and, even after eight hours, still queasy victims of the Reverend's awful whiskey. Morgan could feel it oozing with his sweat from every pore. He removed his wide-brimmed miner's hat, wiped his forehead with the bandana around his neck, and moved from the tree, taking the strain of his pack onto his shoulders again.

The camp ahead—Caldwell's, or Nevada, or whatever its citizens had decided to call it—would be the last on their itinerary. If prospects for medicine and law did not pan out, they would go down to San Francisco, which—though it was said to have a hundred doctors already and over fifty lawyers—was building a city hall and possessed, at least by all accounts, a hospital and a courthouse.

He glanced again at the sign. At least the camp had a name; some had none at all.

A prospector clanked by, leading a mule. The pack bristled with shovels and picks: atop was lashed a rocker. The miner was a gaunt young man with high color on his cheekbones and a narrowed, hollow chest. Consumptive, Morgan guessed, prognosticating a year of shoveling gravel in icy waters before he left this earth.

How would Mary fare in this land of rain and dust and mud?

The man raised a hand in greeting and smiled toothlessly. Scurvy, too. From the trail or from the sea? But the miner did not stop to talk.

No one had time for chatter; there was only so much gold.

"Let's go," said Morgan. "It says one mile to Nevada, and I think I smell its smoke."

Isaiah groaned and held out a hand. Morgan hauled him erect, and they resumed the path.

They stood on the trail staring down at the town. It was already bigger than Rough and Ready, Plumas, or Marysville, bigger than Rensselaerville by far. Behind it, tall pines climbed three hills; behind those hills soared another, shaped like a sugarloaf.

Already three rudimentary streets splayed out, like tines

240

on a pitchfork, from a bridge over Deer Creek. Upwards of a hundred structures—large and small, houses and hotels—lined the streets. Morgan could see a half dozen more under construction: the hammering was music to his ears.

He heard the chuffing of a steam sawmill: hence the smoke he had smelled along the trail. A faint blue haze hung over the buildings below. A spinning saw was singing out a long, shrill wail.

The sound evoked another. His heart beat faster. Two years before, he'd galloped out from Rensselaerville, one night, north through the Helderberg Mountains on the Albany Road. He'd arrived at a French-Canadian farmhouse, with the farmer who had fetched him far behind. He'd delivered a child, his first. When she wailed a shrill long cry, he grinned and held the child aloft, a gift to the wife and her man.

This town, like the child, would live; he felt it in his bones.

Morgan's eyes swept the crystal-clear mountains and dropped to the center hill. On a knoll above the pines, he fancied a house like Mary's father's, alone, where no other house would be for years.

He took a deep breath. The air seemed fresh; even the smoke seemed clean. The sun was warm and the breeze was dry; the ground was springy with pine needles; they would ride the hills and scale the mountains, and some day she would be well.

"Isaiah," he breathed, "I like it."

Isaiah removed his spectacles and squinted down at the place. His eyes had been weak when he'd started on the Great Platte River Road, and had weakened even more from the scurvy. "When you're blind as a bat at a hundred yards, it's just another camp."

They moved down the hill and found lodgings on credit at the Nevada Hotel. It had been built the month before, of wood from a single pine, by a Tennessee couple named Turner—no relation, Morgan hoped, to the captain. It was forty feet wide by fifty feet long and two stories tall. They rented two cots in a garret which contained a dozen more.

241

The hotel was conveniently next to the Empire Saloon, where miners were swaggering continually in, and drunks were staggering out. From the shouting therein at high noon, and a claim jumper being thrashed outside, it seemed an appropriate source for patients for Morgan or clients for Isaiah, or both.

Morgan left Isaiah on his cot, sleeping off his excesses of the previous night, and went to poke around Nevada's streets and see if he could find Cantrell.

In half an hour he was in love with the little town. He found two hotels—the Placer and the Missouri—besides their own. He saw a boarding house—the Eldorado, offering room and victuals for eleven dollars per week—to which they'd probably move. He discovered a laundry run by a skinny Chinaman named Li: it was the first such he'd seen in the Mother Lode, where miners sometimes had to ship shirts via San Francisco to Australia to be washed. At Clark's Pharmacy, near the end of Broad, he posted his name on the wall, should a patient wander by.

He walked Broad Street from end to end, and Main and Coyote too; everywhere he felt energy, cheer, and optimism. The air was bracing and the sun quite warm.

He inspected "coyote" diggings, which he'd seen in no other camp, where men were being lowered by bucket a hundred feet straight down, and were said to scrape at veins of gold in tunnels hardly wider than their shoulders. The diggings were mere tunnels, such as animals might burrow, but they gave a feeling of permanence that the placer camps could never match.

Finally he climbed the hill they called Oregon, the central of the three. He found the knob he'd seen from the trail. A fine oak tree grew on it. He did not know who owned the land, or if anyone had claimed it. For a long while he gazed upon the town, soft in golden sunlight slanting down from American Hill.

He looked furtively around, dropped to one knee and sifted acorns through his fingers. He made a promise to Mary. If she would come to join him here, he would build her a home on this spot.

242

* * *

The Empire Saloon reeked of rotgut whiskey served too green, and the sweat of working miners, who were jammed two-deep at the bar. Morgan, sitting on a flour-barrel chair at a table, regarded his friend Cantrell.

He'd found him bartending here. They embraced; then, embarrassed at the display of affection, the older doctor abandoned his post to another bartender and dragged Morgan to a table to talk. What he had to say was shattering.

"Vanderveer?" breathed Morgan. "He's here? And owns *this*?"

"Free and clear," said Cantrell.

He was dead serious. His pockmarked face was drawn, and his eyes were laced with red. He'd gained weight since Morgan had bid him farewell by Carson's miserable Sink. But he had good news to give: the Pioneer Line had conquered the pass, wagons and all, two weeks after Morgan and Isaiah, though eight men had died of scurvy and forty of Turner's mules had frozen in Hope Valley, short of the pass.

In those two weeks, the two agreed, Isaiah would surely have died.

Their table was a pine tree trunk, a good three feet in diameter, already stained with spirits spilled from a hundred sawed-off bottles serving as glasses. Between them sat a bottle of the house's best bourbon, snagged by the old doctor himself from behind the rough pine bar, which he tended every morning.

Cantrell explained his exalted station as a bartender: there were eight doctors in town already. He counted them off: "One is an eclectic, just like me, only he got here first. There's a homeopath panning at Gold Run, and a botanic physician trying to practice at Grass Valley: that damn fool Marshall's built a surgery at Town Talk. There's a Thomsonian quack clerking at the Missouri Hotel, and two surgeons trying to cut each other's throats at the Eldorado Boarding House."

Caldwell himself, who owned Caldwell's Store and after

whom, until last week, the town itself had been named, also claimed to be a doctor.

"If Vanderveer hadn't hired me, I'd be treating horses for the heaves." Behind the bar Cantrell reigned supreme, he told Morgan.

Like a wolf guarding the sheep, thought Morgan. "How do you get along with your employer?"

"I stay well shy of the son of a bitch, and he pays me in dust every day." He promised to see that Morgan never went thirsty between dawn and noon, at which time he was relieved by a German professor of literature, who knew barely enough English to take orders.

Morgan studied the lofty ceiling and rough-hewn beams. "It's a *palace*!"

"He's made his pile." Cantrell had found Vanderveer already established when he had arrived last November. The lieutenant swore that he and Oglethorpe had made California less than thirty days after they left the train at Beer Springs. "When he settled here, everybody else was panning on Deer Creek, so he went dry and staked coyote diggings out on half of Buckeye Hill." Cantrell poured Morgan a drink, lifted the bottle to his lips, took a long gulp, and set it down. "Then he and Alston Oglethorpe went down to San Francisco and borrowed twenty thousand dollars, at ten percent a month."

"On what security?" wondered Morgan.

"On the deed to Oglethorpe's plantation, and his own goddamn commission in the Navy! But you'd best not mention *that*. It's 'mister,' not 'lieutenant,' now. The *Somers* hanging ain't quite popular with deserters from the ships. In this saloon, you'll hear no word about the Navy from the boss."

Vanderveer returned from San Francisco and hired Cousin Jack tin miners from Wales and men who had mined iron in Wisconsin to work underground. They dug straight down to bedrock, and shored the shafts with logs.

"Some say he's found the Mother Lode," said Cantrell.

Vanderveer used Indians and Darkies to winch up the dirt and pile it by the entrances. He devised a way to ventilate the tunnels by laying tubes connecting the bottom to fire pits on the surface, so that the hot air, like that in a steamship's funnel, drew a draft up the hoses, sucking foul air from the miners at the bottom of the diggings; fresh air from above rushed into the vacuum and replaced it.

"Then the rains came and washed out Vanderveer's dirt for him, and left the goddamn gold piled high: he just scooped it off the ground." He shrugged. "That wasn't enough, so he built *this* place to wash gold from the miners on the Yuba. He grubstakes half of them already. He's paid off his loan to the San Francisco bankers and staked out Oregon Hill."

Morgan's spirits dropped. So much for the knoll, under the oak, and the home he'd build for Mary above the thriving town.

"He'd like to be alcalde," finished Cantrell. "There's a preacher named Thornberry, in Rough and Ready—"

"I know, I pulled his tooth."

"He's with Vanderveer, and Oglethorpe. He owns half the miners down there now. With his miners behind 'em, and Vanderveer's too, some day those three will own this town."

Morgan found himself too sick at heart to even talk of the matter. Under California law, inherited from Mexican, the alcalde was a mayor and justice of the peace combined. Morgan had already picked this village for Mary: a man like Vanderveer as alcalde could turn it into hell.

Cantrell glanced up. "And speak of the devil," he muttered, "here's the son of a bitch right now."

Morgan felt a heavy hand upon his shoulder. "Hello, Doctor! We meet again."

He shrugged off the hand and turned. Vanderveer was cleanly shaven. He wore a cream-colored waistcoat, swallowtail, and stovepipe hat. Morgan looked into the cold gray eyes impassively, saying nothing.

Vanderveer swung a barrel chair around and sat in it backwards, legs astraddle the back, chin resting on his hands. "You should have come with *me*, sir. We made it in a month."

"Not too close, please," said Morgan. "There are onions on your breath."

The granite eyes went dead. "I see. Onions..." Vanderveer leaned forward, smiling coldly. "Do you imply, sir, that I didn't pay for them?"

"You'd have paid more, had I laid hands on you."

"Perhaps, perhaps not. Well, you made it over anyway. Are you mounted?"

"No, thanks to you."

"That's why I came over," said Vanderveer. "What was your horse's name? 'Colonel'?"

"'Major,'" murmured Morgan. "'Major' was his name."

Vanderveer shrugged. "I'm promoting him posthumously, for valor on the trail." He beckoned to the bartender. "Herr Professor! Holen Sie schnell eine Tüte Gold!"

A sad-eyed man with a bushy beard, in a vest well-stained with whiskey, tottered from behind the bar. He had a bag of gold dust in hand. Obsequiously, he placed it on the table in front of Vanderveer. The lieutenant hefted it, opened it, as if to pour some out. He stopped.

"Is Mr. Hollister still with you?"

"Yes. He nearly died of scurvy. Also, thanks to you."

"Has *he* still his horse?"

"She died on the desert."

Vanderveer drew the string tight again, tossed the whole bag across the table. "There's a livery on Coyote Street, behind Masonic Lodge. They sell horses. Buy a couple."

Morgan took the bag. It weighed easily two pounds: close to four hundred dollars of dust. "Thank you," he said dryly. "It seems time."

Vanderveer nodded briefly. "I have a piece of advice," he said. "There are—how many doctors hereabout, Dr. Cantrell?"

"Eight at last count," said Cantrell. "He already knows."

"And over twenty lawyers. We've quite enough doctors for an epidemic, and the lawyers to write a constitution, if need be."

"Interesting," said Morgan softly. "Well, you'll have another doctor, and another lawyer, I think, as well." He downed his drink, studying the label: Old Crow. It clutched at his belly with talons of fire. He poured another. "Now, what is your advice?"

"It's a small town, Doctor. I doubt it's large enough for you and me."

"I've seen the town. I asked for your *advice*," persisted Morgan.

"Ride west, Doctor. Ride west to the setting sun." The lieutenant turned away, began to make his passage through the gambling tables.

Morgan felt his pulses racing. "Mr. Vanderveer!" he called. "Lieutenant?"

The room fell silent. Vanderveer turned.

"Yes?" His eyes were chilling.

"It seems you've become quite the gambler," said Morgan loudly, nodding at the faro tables. "I'd like to double this. Do you still play poker? Or are the odds too poor?"

The faro dealer froze, hand in the air. Outside the open door, a train of pack animals creaked by. The sawmill screamed distantly, and a dog barked.

"The odds are fine," called Vanderveer. He moved back across the room. He took the faro dealer's cards, sat down, shuffled the deck, and pushed it across to Morgan.

"Perhaps you'd care to cut?"

They played until dark, as a ring of miners gathered round. At midnight Morgan was down to two ounces; at dawn he had three full bags and could barely remember his name.

When he stumbled next door to the Nevada Hotel, he had filled an inside straight, with the table hidden under bags of dust and men standing on crates to crane from the door.

Lurching back to the hotel with a crowd of cheering miners following him, he had one twelve-ounce bag of gold dust in his hand and a receipt for sixty-one others that lay in the Empire's safe. He had won over ten thousand dollars since daybreak, and the knoll on Oregon Hill.

He climbed the ladder to the loft. The other cots had emptied, for placer miners began work at dawn to avoid the heat of the day. But Isaiah had slept the night away. He opened his eyes as Morgan tossed his boots onto the pineboard floor.

"Where you been?" he asked sleepily.

"Playing poker." Morgan padded to the window, looked out at the hills. On his knoll—and Mary's—the pinetips were shimmering in early light.

"Did you win?" yawned Hollister.

Morgan was drained, and still half-drunk; it would be days before he truly believed what he had done, and he would never gamble again.

"I won some land," he murmured. "And enough to build a house. And passage money on a ship: home for one, and back for two." He yawned. "Yes, sir, I'd say I won."

He crawled onto his flimsy cot and slept the whole day through.

THE ADMIRAL
AND BUNKIE

THE ADMIRAL DROVE THROUGH HEAVY RAINFALL DOWN Coyote Street to Broad. He could easily have taken a shortcut to his home, but he could not bring himself to use it; his deepest instincts demanded delay. Each stroke of the windshield wipers seemed a heartbeat added to their lives; each block they passed, another they would never see again. Familiar streets, glittering in the rain under antique streetlamps, etched themselves in his mind.

He peered out at the town he'd been born in. Every slab of pavement was part of him: on errands to town as a little boy, he had hopped over every seam. *Step on a crack, you'll break your mother's back.*

He'd had a fight with a Grass Valley interloper on this corner, where Church met Main; here outside the National Hotel, he'd crumpled a fender on the big La Salle he'd "borrowed" from his father. He'd been picked up by the sheriff here, outside the Golden Nugget, half-drunk on beer at eighteen; he'd proudly driven his dad on house calls to this house and that one, when he'd first bought the Model A.

He found himself searching everywhere for one familiar face, to reassure himself that help lay somewhere near.

If he could find a sheriff's car . . . Or drive up to the teenagers that idled at tables in the court beside Framastnyls Restaurant and Bar, then quickly reach across, open her door, and push Bunkie into the crowd . . . Or crash the motor home into the courthouse wall, and hope for a quick reaction from police . . .

He drove past Framastnyls. The teenagers were all indoors: he could see them through the windows. The streets and sidewalks were bare. It was a rainy Sunday evening in a little town: everyone was inside with frozen pizza dinners, "60 Minutes" on TV.

He turned northwest on Broad Street, past the site of the Nevada Hotel, where Morgan had stayed. He was praying for the normal Sunday-night traffic jam: sightseers, up from San Francisco to shop for nonexistent goldrush antiques, usually deserted en masse on Sunday nights, causing a tie-up on the narrow streets that natives avoided like the plague.

But tonight the rain had driven tourists away early and there were actually empty parking spots on Main Street, a rare and wondrous thing.

He saw no police, though he drove past the garish courthouse that—with the freeway—defaced the town he loved and housed the sheriff.

Jeff loomed in the shadows behind them. "Look, you trying to run up the meter? Or are you lost in your own home town?"

"Just heading home," he murmured.

"*Don't* dick around," Jeff threatened, "get us there!"

It was no use. There was no help. He turned up a narrow, cobbled street and headed for Oregon Hill.

Passing the old Miners' Foundry, which had cast stamp

249

mills and ore cars for all Nevada County, he hit a rut in the pavement, and Terry yelped in pain.

He was trapped. The Washburn house—and surgery—were a few short blocks away.

His home loomed cold and dark on Oregon Hill, silhouetted against the lights of the town below. It was immense, even for the age in which it had been built. Morgan Washburn, MD, was said to have won the money to build it in a horse race, or at cards, depending on which tourist pamphlet one might buy. The admiral slowed. A single light shone on the screened-in porch, and another in the living room; he had left them on when he left three weeks ago, to discourage intruders.

The huge front yard was dominated by a massive oak. The last wooden sidewalk in town ran in front of the house and its neighbors. Great elms sheltered the sidewalk and the street below, which had sunk a good ten feet in the last century. Wooden steps at the end of the block were the only means of mounting from street to sidewalk: they'd never get the woman up the steps without half-killing her.

"That it?" demanded Jeff.

The admiral nodded.

"Jesus! You live there *alone*?"

"Yes."

"There's got to be a back way in. Use it."

As always, he had left the house in the care of the Hanifans, who lived behind it in an ancient frame house across the lane. Chuck Hanifan was a retired postman, who treated the admiral like an ex-president who'd returned to honor his birthplace. They had been playmates as children and teammates at Nevada City High.

Shirley Hanifan had been a schoolmate too. The admiral remembered her as a bright, bespectacled girl whose mistake had been in marrying the first man who asked her. Now she cleaned the Washburn house—refusing payment—and guided tours through it for the Nevada County Historical Society, cherishing the place as much as the admiral did himself.

He circled his home and drove up Isaiah Lane. Water

was rushing down it already; it had always lacked proper drainage. He passed the stable where Morgan had kept his horse. Inside it, he knew, sat his own Datsun 280, on blocks to save its tires. Next to it was Morgan's buckboard, newly painted by Hanifan, with its brass carriage lamps all polished, no doubt, for the next of Shirley's weekly tours.

The headlights swept the cherry tree planted by Morgan and his bride, then glared at the stable in the rear and glinted off the green-roofed woodshed near the kitchen entrance. Rain was pouring from the roof gutters.

He had a sudden recollection of a dream: dripping eaves, a pumpkin pie . . .

"Home, Bunkie," he murmured. She had fallen asleep, pale in the light of the dash. "We're home."

Bunkie tried not to hear the voice. When she was little, heading home from Long Island after weekend visits to her aunt's, they would put her in the rear seat of the VW and she would fall asleep—or half-asleep. When they'd come close to home, she'd feel every turn and bump, hoping the ride would go on forever, so she wouldn't have to face the cold walk down the street from the garage, and the elevator ride.

She'd wish harder at every familiar corner in the neighborhood, and it never worked.

"Home, Bunkie. We're home." Her grandfather's voice, not her dad's. She sat up, blinking.

For a moment she didn't know where she was. Then she did.

They were parking behind the house in Nevada City. She'd been here half a dozen times before. On her summer visits to Coronado to her grandfather and grandmother's, whenever Pops decided he wanted to fish in the Sierras, or camp, or pan for gold, they'd drive north and start from here.

The headlights swept the stable in the rear. When she was small she'd loved it. Pop's father—her great-grandfather—had made the hayloft a gym for Pops when he was young. It was full of dusty dumbbells, trapezes, rings, and bars to hang on upside-down. You could slide down a hay chute into a pile of straw: she and Pops did it all the time.

Inside the house was even better. There were corners and places she could hide where no one would ever know. The attic was full of strange lavender smells and clothes that were really gross: there was a wire shape like a woman that could be used to make a dress.

There were trunks and umbrellas and dolls and pictures of people from a million years ago, and bureaus lined with newspapers about the War. Not World War *Two*. World War *One*.

There was even supposed to be a picture of Morgan Washburn as a surgeon in the Civil War. She and Pops looked through everything for it one rainy day, and couldn't find it.

She'd played hide-and-seek with her grandmother in the dark and gloomy halls, crept into a hiding place beneath the creaky stairs. She'd played doctor in the surgery, where Morgan, and Morgan's son, and finally Pop's father had operated. She knew every corner of the place.

She blinked. The headlights were shining on the woodshed, and swept to rest on the wall near "Madam's Door."

"Come on, Doc. Kid, you stay right there."

She whimpered in protest. With Pops near, she felt safe. And what was going to happen to him when they found out the truth?

The admiral hesitated. He found himself staring through the steaming windshield, straight ahead. His headlights glittered on the back of the house. Inside this gray wooden wall lay the surgery.

Behind the wall was a bathroom. It was tiny, but had been Morgan's pharmaceutical storeroom and laboratory. When surgeons had quit mixing their own drugs in the 1890s, and inside plumbing became fashionable, Morgan had installed a pull-chain mahogany toilet in it and turned it into a bathroom.

History said that at certain times, for certain people, it had been a waiting room.

Quickly he punched off the headlights.

Usually, firewood was stacked against the surgery wall. When the admiral had left for New York, the woodpile had been high, half-hiding the back of the house from the alley they called Isaiah Lane. Now, thank God, the stacks were gone, each log probably tucked neatly into the woodshed. Hanifan had beaten the winter rains.

With the back of the house clear of firewood, there was the barest chance . . .

Bunkie knew the house inside out.

She knew, and had used, Madam's Door . . .

"Come *on!*" barked Jeff from the rear. "I want to see what you got."

The admiral climbed out in the rain, led Jeff down the slippery pavement between the woodshed and the kitchen door. He reached up for a key hidden in the eaves, and found it. Automatically, he scraped his soles on an iron boot-scraper, unlocked the door, and stepped in.

On the kitchen table was a birthday cake, with a single flickering candle. A light switch snicked. He was suddenly blinking in the kitchen's glaring light.

"Happy birthday!" yelled Kelly, a blur at the sink.

"Many happy returns!" called Howard, from the refrigerator, and then yelped: "Oh my God!"

"Nobody," growled Jeff behind the admiral, "make a single fucking move!"

MORGAN

MORGAN WASHBURN, MD, PEERED OUT THE WINDOW OF
the Sacramento–Downieville Coach and saw that he and
Mary had reached Rough and Ready, on the Gold Run
Road.

Their carriage—a new red Concord with bright yellow
wheels, built by Abbot-Downing of New Hampshire and
freighted around the Horn for the California Stage Lines—
creaked down a street of false-front stores. Their driver
was the famous Charlie Parkhurst, a slouch-hatted whipster with the gentlest hands in all the Mother Lode, who
had once blasted the heart from a highwayman just outside
this very town.

Morgan had last year treated Charlie for piles, an oc-
cupational disease among "whips." He applied bella-
donna, lard, tallow, and sweet oil. Morgan was possibly
the only soul in California who knew that "Charlie"—as
deep-voiced and profane as any other driver—was a
woman in disguise.

Just another crazy secret of the jumbled Mother Lode.
Another forty-niner might believe it—the lure of California gold had so upset the scheme of things that there were
transvestite women working the gravel bars as hard as
any man—but if Morgan ever told Mary, she would think
he was teasing her.

The trail had widened to a roadbed, but otherwise hardly
improved, since he had hiked it with Isaiah two years
before. The coach had let off the last of their fellow pas-

254

sengers at Park's Bar, some few miles back, and now they had the Concord to themselves.

In an hour they would reach the much finer streets of Nevada City, and Mary would first glimpse her home, which he had refused to describe since he had built it. They had traveled fifty-five miles from Sacramento since 5 A.M., and had another ten to go before they reached their destination. He hoped to arrive before tea.

Carefully, he eased his arm from around his sleeping bride: married or not, he'd be embarrassed if some Rough and Ready miner should notice such affection in front of God and man.

She was sound asleep, her straw bonnet thrown to the seat beside her, hair bunned modestly for the road. She wore her calico traveling dress: her black silk gowns were still in their trunk, to follow by ox wagon from Sacramento. He hoped she would not miss them when she entered Nevada City's social whirl.

He studied her shyly. She had suffered from seasickness en route. Soon after they had stepped from the steamer *Cortes* in San Francisco, she had stepped onto a scale at the Nyantic House, where they lodged. The passage south by steamship from New Orleans, the crossing of the Nicaragua Isthmus on a scrawny gelding, and the voyage north to San Francisco had cut her weight to ninety-two pounds.

But two weeks in the city had filled her oval face again. He had been frightened by the high color in her cheeks, but it had lessened; she was pale, now, from fatigue, but she had coughed hardly at all since a spell she had on a river steamer crossing Lake Nicaragua.

The rosiness in her cheeks in San Francisco must have been excitement, nothing more.

He glanced out at Rough and Ready. In the two years since he had first seen it, the place had not improved. He saw that the bench in front of Reverend Thornberry's bowling alley and gambling hall remained the cultural center of the town. The camp had rejoined the Union three months after its private secession—in order not to miss the Fourth of July—but it was still under the thumb of

Thornberry. It was, in Morgan's eyes, a cancer on the Mother Lode.

To awaken her to see it was hardly worth the candle. She would need all the strength she had to absorb her shock at what he'd built her in Nevada City, up ahead.

For weeks after they arrived she would be receiving callers daily, from noon to dinnertime: ministers' wives, the banker, storekeepers' wives and daughters, the superintendent of the Northern Cascade Mine. She would find that he'd become a citizen of substance, more quickly than she could have dreamed.

Despite Dr. Cantrell's pessimism, Morgan had been lucky in his work. He had begun his practice from the Nevada Hotel. He had saved a Welshman's mangled hand, crushed when a shoring in one of Vanderveer's coyote diggings had collapsed. His fame grew, and when the Great Fire struck last year—the downtown section having been torched by an angry miner—the two other "surgeons" in town became discouraged and departed for greener pastures. His nearest competitor was Dr. Marshall, who had settled in the tiny village of Town Talk.

Morgan had guessed correctly that Nevada would rise phoenixlike from the ashes and live again. He had stayed, watching it reborn in brick and stone to become the county seat.

He kept his fees as low as he could. He treated Indians, Darkies, and Greasers, whom most other doctors refused; he welcomed Chinese as patients, and found that—unlike most other miners—they always paid their bills.

After the fire he'd cleared two acres around the oak on Oregon Hill, and saved the rest of his Empire winnings until October's rain and snows. The heavens opened, the rivers swelled, and placer mining stopped. When prices plummeted at the lumbermill, he bought his wood. He found that thirty-four-dollar-a-day miners would suddenly work for sixteen dollars, to build Mary a house, and him a surgery on the hill.

He used the rest of his ten thousand dollars to order furniture and a piano to be sailed around the Horn. It arrived by clipper in less than six months. Only then did he set sail himself, to go and fetch her back.

Only two houses in the town were bigger: the enormous wooden castle Vanderveer had built, painted red like his stamp mill, and the whorehouse of a certain Madam Lenoir upon American Hill. His bride would find herself presiding over the third grandest house in a thriving little city that, some thought, might rival San Francisco in the end.

He moved impatiently on the coach's velvet seat. His excitement had been growing all day long, as the carriage's fine new leather thoroughbraces cradled them like royal travelers along the prairie road from Sacramento behind the California Stage Line's great white teams—changed every twenty miles—then wound into the Sierra foothills, and finally came upon the mountains that he had grown to love.

Mary had begged him to describe their home, cajoled, and threatened him, but he had stuck to his guns. She had no idea of what awaited her, splendid in fresh gray paint, with gables trimmed in white and a roof of forest green, behind the great oak tree ten miles from here in Nevada City.

Their driver pounded on the roof of the carriage, a signal that they were stopping at the Rough and Ready Livery to change teams. The brakes screeched. Mary awakened with a start. "Are we there?"

"Certainement!" he said mischievously. "Nous avons arrivés!"

"Nous *sommes* arrivés," she corrected absently. Her eyes widened. She leaned out the window. "This...is *Nevada*?"

"Nevada City, in the flesh," he assured her. "Just as I described it."

"Not exactly, sir," she protested. "But let me see...."

Leaving her spoon bonnet on the seat, she flung open the door and squirmed out before he could help her. They were drawn up before a mud-splattered livery stable, across from Reverend Thornberry's saloon.

"Here," he murmured modestly, handing her the bonnet, "you'll probably cause a riot here, you'd better put it on."

He looked at Thornberry's saloon. Sure enough, she'd been seen, and the word was out. A crowd was gathered in the door. Thornberry, in his clerical collar, pushed his belly through the mob, and the red-shirted layabouts left the bench to stroll across the street.

She tied her "ugly" over the front of her bonnet to shade her eyes and regarded the advancing horde, astonished. "My goodness, Morgan," she breathed, "who are *they*?"

He told her that the fat minister owned the saloon, a ninety-two-foot bowling alley, and dealt faro and monte. "You'll love his sermons on Sundays in the bar. That first man—with the red braces—is our alcalde—'mayor,' you would say."

"I think you're teasing! Are you, Morgan? Are you?"

The reverend was well in his cups. A drop of spittle rolled down his chin. Morgan cringed but introduced him to his wife.

The minister bowed. "I'd *heard* you were returning from the States, Doctor, with a treasure you'd left behind."

"Well, Reverend," said Morgan. "This is she."

"Welcome, ma'am, to our humble town. I wish that you were staying."

Mary curtsied lightly. She glanced at Morgan, and there was a mischievous glint in her eye. "I hope to, sir, since this is Nevada City—"

Thornberry stiffened. "It isn't, ma'am. Now, did he say it *was*?"

Morgan sighed. "A little joke, between us."

Thornberry glared at Morgan. "The Scripture bids you love your neighbors, not deride us, sir!"

"All right, Reverend, I'm *sorry*. I meant no—"

"We have not your fine houses, down here in the flat. But there's one house you have *there* that we'll *never* have here, and that—begging your pardon, ma'am—is one of ill repute. I've heard their doctor's been gone these months, and I've heard he's sorely missed!"

"That'll do!" growled Morgan. "You've had *my* apology. Make sure I don't need yours."

"If you do, sir," belched the reverend, "I'll be here."

He turned and weaved back to his saloon.

"Ill *repute*?" asked Mary, when they were back in the

carriage, and swaying up the Deer Creek Road. "*Their* doctor?"

"I treat them," muttered Morgan. "Someone must."

"Do you play the piano there, too?"

Morgan looked into her eyes. They were twinkling with glee. He shrugged. "There's just one piano in town, my dear. And I play it all the time."

The laughter left her eyes. "Morgan! Are you serious?"

"Yes."

"Hmm . . ." she said, watching the pine trees crawl by outside the window, and when he touched her cheek she turned away.

He pulled his gold watch from his velvet vest. Half an hour to go.

He asked the coachdriver to stop before descending the last hill to Nevada City, so that Mary could appreciate the prospect from on high.

He helped her from the carriage and led her across the pine needles to a viewing point. He had been gone only six months: he had sailed to Nicaragua, crossed the Isthmus on horseback and married, and returned in scarcely more time than he had crossed overland in '49. Most of the trees which had hidden the houses when first he'd seen it had disappeared in the fire of '51; the rest had been removed for timber while he was east.

Still, Nevada City lay clean and white before them, with a brand-new church standing whitest of all against the forest-covered slopes.

"We've got a new church since I left!" he exclaimed.

"I doubt I'll ever get you there, but it's a pretty one, indeed. Now, where's our house?"

He gestured toward Buckeye Hill, slashed and scarred with mines. "It's one of the shacks on that slope there, hidden in the trees," he lied. He could hardly keep his eyes away from Oregon Hill. Their home sparkled next to the oak tree, in full sight but far away. He tried to keep the excitement from his voice, pointing it out: "That one there, up on the hill, is new. It belongs to a fellow you'll get to know, before too very long."

259

"It's most beautiful," she agreed. "And this 'house of ill repute,' at which you entertain. Where would that one be?"

"I've forgotten," he smiled. "Mary?"

"Yes?"

He glanced at the driver. Charlie Parkhurst, who had put down the reins to fill a pipe, was gazing politely away across the trees. Morgan took Mary's hand, quickly pressed it to his lips. "Will you be happy here?"

She looked deep into his eyes. "I think I should be happy, Morgan, wherever you were." She blushed. "I ... I love you, Morgan. Truly do ..."

She had never said it so before, nor had he told her how much he loved her.

"I, too, feel ... *great* love for you," he said. "Now, dearest, shall we go?"

They sat at a window table in the dining room of the new Nevada Hotel, sipping tea from silver service, with biscuits and sweetcakes galore.

The arrival of a lady in Nevada City was nowhere near the event that it was in Rough and Ready; still, Morgan noticed that Mary created a sensation outside. Chinese gathered at the edge of Chinatown to glimpse their doctor's woman, and miners continually left Vanderveer's Empire Saloon, to stroll the street and glance into the dining room.

Isaiah Hollister had driven Morgan's new buckboard to the Nevada Hotel to meet the Downieville Coach. Its splendor had astonished Mary. Now it shone in ebony brilliance behind Morgan's big bay gelding, with the reins draped through a new iron hitching post on the wooden sidewalk just outside.

Isaiah had yesterday moved out of Morgan's house on Oregon Hill. Though there was plenty of room, he didn't wish to intrude on their privacy. He seemed bedazzled by Mary's beauty. He was privy to Morgan's plan to surprise her, and said nothing of the home.

Isaiah had a copy of *The Young America*, the town's

260

Democratic newspaper. He slid it across the table to Mary.

"'From our San Francisco correspondent, we are happy to report,'" she read, "'that our esteemed townsman, Doctor Morgan Washburn, MD, has arrived in that city on the steamship *Cortes,* with his bride of three months, the former Miss Mary Cornelia Cullen, of Rensselaerville, in the State of New York. Mrs. Washburn had traveled to Philadelphia to study at the Female Medical College and we have it on good account that had she not been diverted from it by the higher calling of matrimony—'" She chuckled. "Higher? Well, all right . . . 'she would have followed the notorious Elizabeth Blackwell into the practice of medicine itself.'" She looked up in surprise. "Now, who could have known that here? Or in San Francisco?"

Isaiah smiled and swirled the tea in his cup. "I am the distinguished editor, Mrs. Washburn—Mary—of the publication you hold in your hand. Also its sole journalist, correspondent, and newsboy. All, I may add, against your husband's good advice."

Before Morgan had sailed for the East, Isaiah and Niles Searls began a law partnership, operating from a flour-barrel desk and barrel-stave chairs in the rear of a bookstore that Charlie Mulford built on Main Street. There were hardly enough clients for both and their practice did not prosper.

But an opportunity came for Isaiah, who had a talent for writing more lively prose than that in briefs and contracts. An editorial quarrel had begun between the owner-editor of *The Young America* and the editor of the Whig paper, owned by their former messmate Oglethorpe. *The Young America* was antislavery and supported the right of Frenchmen and Chinese to stake claims along the river; Oglethorpe's paper objected.

When Oglethorpe threatened to shoot *The Young America*'s editor in the street, the latter, a reasonable man, decided to move up the Yuba River to Downieville, offering Isaiah the editorial seat. Morgan had foreseen trouble from Ogelthorpe, who obviously suspected their part in the defection of his slave. But apparently Isaiah had not taken Morgan's counsel to stick to the law.

"Isaiah," said Morgan now, pouring him tea, "you're not a newspaperman!"

"I still practice law, what there is of it."

"But what possessed you to risk *this*?"

Isaiah shrugged and said he didn't rightly know: a hundred dollars a month, perhaps, from the exiled owner; a chance to save the town from going secessionist. He sipped his tea, and looked Morgan in the eye. "Maybe, to save the place from Vanderveer?"

Morgan's heart sank. "He's running for alcalde?"

"Justice of the peace, we call it now. Against Albion Olney, the incumbent. Half of Reverend Thornberry's miners will be up from Rough and Ready to stuff ballot boxes, but we'll beat the son of a—" He blushed. "We'll thrash him somehow, wait and see."

"Politics," sighed Mary. "I thought I'd left them behind." Morgan felt her hand fall lightly on his wrist. "I want to see where we shall live! Are you trying to *torture* me?"

He grinned, arose, pulled back her chair, and bowed to Isaiah. "By your leave."

Isaiah winked at Morgan and arose. "Mary," he warned, "a caveat?"

She smiled. "Go ahead, sir."

"Don't be disappointed in your home. Morgan is a persuasive man, and he wanted you here very much. The house . . . Well, this is hardly more than a mining camp, and he did the best he could."

She took Morgan's arm and smiled. "I'm sure it's small, and roughly hewn, and needs a woman's touch. But I came for *him,* not for his house, and so I'm quite prepared."

Morgan picked up their carpetbags, slung them into the box of the buckboard, and then helped Mary to the seat. He took the reins from the hitching post and flicked his bay into a trot.

A passing miner doffed his hat, and they headed for Oregon Hill.

* * *

They stood beneath the big oak, looking up at the house. The sun was burnishing its cupolas, glinting golden on gabled windows. A mountain canary began to sing, from a tree somewhere in back.

She clutched his arm. "It's the one we saw, the one from the hill!"

"I told you it belongs to a fellow—"

"—I'll get to know, before too very long." She punched him in his ribs with all her strength. "You monster!"

Mary ran for the door, and he followed her. She was in the parlor, caressing the pianoforte. She whirled in the dusky light, her face ecstatic. "And this is the only piano in town?"

He began to light the lamps throughout the house. "The only one," he nodded, "so I've been maligned."

"You have indeed: I know that fellow better already," she murmured, and ran upstairs. He could hear her rushing from room to room, and she hurried down again.

"Morgan, it's *beautiful*! And I never, never dreamed!"

He led her to her kitchen, to his waiting room and surgery, and suddenly grinned. In the back of the surgery was his apothecary, a lean-to addition to the home, where he mixed his potions and drugs. He brought her into the tiny room, and slid a clapboard sidewise on the back wall, under the slanting ceiling. He pushed on the wall, and a secret door swung open.

"What is this?" she asked.

"For the ladies from Madam Lenoir's. Isaiah calls my pharmacy 'Madam's Waiting Room.' It's for her and her girls and the Mexicans, and some Darkies and Chinese, too."

She stared at him. "You make them wait in here?"

He jerked his thumb toward the parlor, where his other patients would be sitting when they knew that he was back. "The storekeepers' wives wait in front. As do those pillars of the church, their husbands, who sometimes suffer the same complaints as the girls on the hill have got, but call it something else." He shrugged. "It's sad, but it's that, or my practice would die."

"It's all so strange!"

"Stranger than you think." He was sure that she wanted

263

to help him in his work, but there were things she had to know. He told her of Charlie Parkhurst, the woman stage-driver. Mary was not nearly so incredulous as he thought she'd be. Her eyes melted with pity. "Poor thing...To have to live that lie." She toyed with a mortar and pestle on the counter. "So, through that door come prostitutes and Chinamen and women dressed as men?" She chuckled. "What would Father say?"

He closed the secret entrance. "I don't know what he'd *say*. But out here, he'd do the same."

She nodded. "I know he would. And Morgan?"

"Yes?"

"You've kept me from becoming a *real* doctor—"

"Thank the Lord!"

"But I'll make a damn good nurse."

He hid his shock at her language and took her into his arms. "You want that?" he murmured into her hair. "You truly, truly do?"

Her voice was muffled. "Yes, I truly do."

God knew what the town would think, to see her working beside him, but he somehow didn't care.

"Then that's how it will be."

THE ADMIRAL

THE CANDLE ON THE BIRTHDAY CAKE BLEW OUT AS JEFF slammed the door. With the gun he motioned the admiral and Howard to the sink, next to Kelly.

"Who are they?" he demanded.

"Who are *we*?" Howard asked. His voice shook, but

he had not moved. "Where the hell's my daughter, and who the hell are *you*?"

Jeff moved so swiftly across the kitchen that Howard never raised a hand. The blue-steel of the automatic glittered in an arc; there was a sickening *splat* of metal on flesh and bone. Kelly cried out, and Howard went spinning across the room. He crashed against an ancient iron stove, and lay moaning, blood streaming from a gash in his temple.

"Oh, God!" murmured Kelly. She snatched a dishtowel from the sink and kneeled beside him, cradling his head and pressing the towel to his wound. "Dad! What—"

"Shut up!" Jeff barked. He faced the admiral. "You said you lived alone!"

"She's my daughter, he's her husband, it's a surprise. I didn't expect—" He moved to help Kelly, found the gun jabbed into his ribs. He stopped.

"Dad, he's bleeding. *Call* somebody!"

"*Sure*, he will," Jeff said tonelessly.

"Honey," muttered the admiral, "I can't."

She was staring at his face. "You *can't*?" She started to rise.

"Rip out that phone," Jeff ordered him, nodding at the kitchen extension. Without hesitation, the admiral tore it from the wall.

He felt the gun leave his ribs as Kelly scrambled to her feet, eyes blazing. Howard and Kelly were wild cards, of no use at all to Jeff. He might kill them where they stood. "Kelly!" he barked. "*As you were!* Stay where you are!"

She froze. Their eyes met. "Now darling," he said softly, "you do everything he says."

"You got it," said Jeff briskly.

"But Bunkie?" she whispered. "Where's Bunkie?"

He held her eyes. "Bunkie's fine." Kelly was crying now, and he must somehow calm her. "Bunkie's OK. We can keep her that way. There's a woman I have to operate on, and you'll have to assist."

She was gazing at him incredulously. *Think, my darling, think!* To Jeff, to give her value, he lied: "She's a nurse."

Jeff held him with the cold blue eyes, and jerked his thumb at Howard. "What's he? A brain surgeon?"

The admiral chilled. What was that supposed to mean? He said: "A college professor. Kelly, I'm going to extract a bullet from the left—I haven't got time to explain. Bandage his laceration with what you've got. And then you'll have to scrub."

Think, Kelly. Be cool. No questions, please.

Thunder muttered from somewhere beyond American Hill. He heard hail peppering the roof. Howard murmured something and was still.

She studied her father narrowly. She had no hint of what he'd done, but she would go along.

"Yes sir," said Kelly. "Bandage his laceration, and then scrub."

Carefully, coolly, as her mother—or great-great-grandmother—would have done, she bound the dishtowel around her husband's head.

MORGAN

MORGAN WASHBURN SAT AT THE HEAD OF HIS POLISHED walnut dining table, presiding over the little group of Pioneer Line survivors at noonday dinner on Independence Day, 1852.

He was deeply troubled with a premonition that all would not go well today, that the fabric of Nevada City was tearing while he ate.

Through the open window behind him he could hear the bells in the fire tower and the church steeple competing for attention, borne on the crystal mountain air: the firebell was chiming an invitation to the miners to hear a patriotic speech by Vanderveer in front of his Empire Saloon, while the churchbell summoned them to special services at Reverend Lamden's church. All last night, drunken gunfire from the streets of town had hinted which would win.

He got up from the table to pour the wine. The meal, cooked by Mary with her hired girl Juanita, was a far cry from that which they'd spread on canvas on the banks of the Platte three years before.

Mary's silver service—arrived only last week from Rensselaerville via clipper ship and the new Wells Fargo Express—glittered on the table in the shuttered light from the tall, thin window behind him.

Before each guest stood a tiny American flag, supplied by Charlie Mulford from the stationery counter of his bookstore. A bouquet of red roses, white carnations, and blue azaleas sat patriotically as a centerpiece. He asked Juanita to move it to one side so that it would not block his view of Mary.

He lifted his glass of claret. It was cloudy, but he was accustomed to that. Shipped without harm all the way from Marseilles to San Francisco, even the best of the traveling wines seemed finally to meet their doom on the ox trains from Sacramento to Nevada City; one simply learned to accept the loss.

Isaiah, Dr. Cantrell, Niles Searls, and Charlie Mulford had come: the conversation dealt mostly with Isaiah's powder blast on the Platte and the stampede it had caused on that long-past Fourth of July.

Morgan studied the wine in the glass. He swirled it. It did not improve. He considered throwing it out the window. His head ached already: he had consulted with Dr. Cantrell in his surgery, before dinner, on the advisability of using a lithotrite on a middle-aged French miner who was trying to pass a stone. The two had finished half a bottle of good medicinal bourbon, and decided that the course of wisdom was to wait. So for all the medicine his doctors had ingested, the poor Keskedee was no better for it yet.

267

Here at table they had toasted their departed messmate, Stein, and touched glasses again, wishing Vanderveer ill health. They had toasted Morgan's announcement of news that the Pioneer alumni were the first to hear: that Mary was four months with child. Now Cantrell raised his glass again, in celebration of the Fourth.

"To our Great Nation, on this day of celebration," he rumbled, stifling a belch, "may it not be ripped asunder by abolitionist or secessionist, either one."

"And to our little city," said Mary. "May it not be ripped asunder by your messmate who's not here."

Vanderveer had run for justice of the peace, and true to his word, Isaiah had impaled him on the pen: *It is high time that we ask ourselves, in this fair community in which, comforted by family and loved ones arriving almost weekly from the East, an honest man may soon take ease at sundown unassailed by fears that he may not survive the night—that we ask ourselves if we wish our miscreants judged by a man who seized upon Nevada's infant days to infect it with a gambling hell, with which to pluck from miners the precious dust so arduously won in the raging river's rush.*

Neither Vanderveer's own miners nor Thornberry's mob—which had invaded Nevada City to stuff ballot boxes—had been enough to swing Vanderveer the vote. Albion Olney, nearly forty years old and one of the patriarchs of the town, had won the office of justice of the peace by a margin of twenty, and Niles Searls had become an alderman.

Isaiah's editorials were too ornate for Morgan's taste, but without them Olney and Searls would never have won.

Morgan knew that the last shot had not been fired. Implacably, since the election, Vanderveer had waited for a crusade he could lead.

Vigilante "justice" and vigilance committees had been bound to come, for the Mother Lode had turned lawless. The trustful days of '49—when a man could leave his cabin unlocked and his bag of dust on his bedroll—were over. Emigrants from Australian penal colonies were everywhere this year; ruffians from Eastern slums joined the rush; native, Spanish-speaking *Californios*, proud, harassed, and dispossessed, were turning into highwaymen on the trails. Mexicans' wives were raped by whites; Digger Indians—thought to steal horses—were being shot on sight; bodies of Chinamen, grabbed by their queues and scalped by drunks, rotted on the trails.

Americans were running Mexicans—and French and Germans, too—off the foreigners' legal claims. The battle for good government had hardly started, though the constitutional convention in Monterey, heavily skewed with New York lawyers, had produced a mirror-image of the New York Constitution, forbidding slavery and dueling, and strengthening women's rights.

But even New York lawyers like Isaiah Hollister and Niles Searls held little hope for quick improvement in California's criminal courts.

Miners' Law still reigned throughout the Mother Lode, and Judge Lynch too often overruled a justice of the peace. In the northern camps, vigilantes drove the criminals to Los Angeles, which—in self-protection—had to form a committee of its own. Morgan had read in the *California Star* that Boss Sam Brannan of San Francisco had declared before his Vigilance Committee that: "We are the mayor, the hangman, and the laws! The law and the courts never hung a man in California yet!"

Brannan, for once, spoke the truth, thought Morgan. The official courts of California had never hanged a man, but they would soon decide the fate of women—two of them—and both had been patients of his.

One was Madam Lenoir, and the other her famous prostitute, Cristina Lopez. They were spending their Independence Day in the Nevada City jail.

Last Wednesday Cristina had been attacked in the madam's bordello by an admirer, one John McCrae, a popular young Scots miner from Rough and Ready. The Scot had gotten raging drunk, armed himself with a blacksmith's mallet, and found Cristina, understandably enough, in bed with another man.

As Cristina's client dove from a second-story window to the stableyard outside, the madam had grappled with McCrae while Cristina, known from Downieville to Volcano Diggings for her beauty and hot temper, had yanked a stiletto from beneath her mattress and stabbed the Scotsman in the chest.

McCrae was hanging on to life at Dr. Marshall's surgery in Town Talk.

Isaiah had taken the two women as clients. He had visited them in the single-celled, windowless town jail, and found them as comfortable as could be expected. Every day last week Mary had called on them, to see that they lacked nothing. She reported that they were quite content, though nervous at certain rumblings, from Rough and Ready, orchestrated by Reverend Thornberry, Vanderveer's political ally.

Isaiah and Searls were certain that they would be freed by Justice Olney. In a town where—recently—a miner seemed to be shot every week and where the murders of Darkies, Chinese, and Greasers were not even reported in the newspapers, a knifing in a whorehouse seemed a trivial affair.

But Vanderveer was stirring the miners. He had called for a public trial of the madam and Cristina at a meeting last week at the Empire Saloon and had organized a chapter of the Committee of 601, a vigilante organization spreading through the Mother Lode from Mariposa in the south to the camps on Yuba Pass. He was doubtless offering free advice to McCrae's friends, with the free whiskey he was dispensing today to celebrate the Fourth.

Morgan raised his glass, smiling into Mary's eyes. "Mary's right, my friends. Let us never be torn asunder, or our little city's doomed."

Juanita padded in. She was a stolid Mexicana, who lived above the woodshed; her husband tended the orchard. She was ordinarily a cheerful, smiling woman, but now her face was heavy with distaste. She marched to Morgan and bent her head to whisper, lower lip outthrust.

"Una puta, Señor Doctor," she announced, casting her eyes toward the kitchen.

A whore? On this day? Surely an emergency, or she would never have dared to come. If Madam Lenoir found out, she would have her drawn and quartered.

Juanita frowned. "I said to her, go to Madam's Door,

she says no, she will wait in my kitchen: ¡es muy importante!"

He excused himself and found Madam Lenoir's daughter, Helene, a pretty blonde of twenty-three, in the kitchen, gnawing at her nails. She was heavily rouged, but dressed in a black silk gown as sedate as a minister's wife. Her English, like her mother's, was poor.

"I 'ave just go in ze town, monsieur. They say 'e has *die* last night! On dit qu'il est *mort*!"

"McCrae?"

"Oui! And his friends, at first light, they 'ave break in ze jail! And 'ave take—"

Her eyes filled. She held on to the sink's iron rim, and looked out the window, fighting for control. Her mother's landau, driven by the little Darkie who tended the bordello's door, awaited outside. The lad was standing on the driver's seat, peering back at the town. Morgan could hear gunfire through the open kitchen door: it seemed to have increased.

"—Zey 'ave take my mama . . . and Cristina . . . to ze Empire! Monsieur, zey talk of *'anging!*" She swung and faced him, sobbing. "You 'ave here Monsieur 'Ollister? Or Monsieur Searls?"

"They're both here," he said, heart sinking. He took her hands. They were ice cold. "We'll go."

"Et vous, attendez ici," said Mary from the door. "She'll stay with me, Morgan, till you come back?"

He nodded, gathered his friends, and crowded into the landau as the Negro whipped the team into a trot.

The carriage, quilted in rose-colored silk, smelled strongly of perfume. "They'll never hang a prostitute," muttered Morgan, clinging to the carriage strap as they jounced down Isaiah Lane. "Hell, they *need* them here too much."

Isaiah looked him in the eye. "There are plenty more to take their place, and every man jack knows it."

The crowd of miners on Main Street was so thick they had to climb from the carriage a hundred yards short of the Empire Saloon.

The firehouse bell tolled madly, but the bell in the steeple had stopped.

271

Morgan, Isaiah, and Cantrell fought their way through the crowd, in a miasma of rotgut whiskey and unwashed bodies. Searls pushed his way through, too, but Mulford was lost in the mob outside the Empire.

The entrance was guarded by Vanderveer's faro dealer, a tall, hook-nosed Australian with bloodshot, close-set eyes, wearing a brown bowler hat. On his waistcoat was pinned the sheriff's star.

"Who the *hell*," demanded Searls, "gave you that?"

The dealer regarded Searls blearily. "We've had a new election, mate. You ain't alderman, no more."

"Where's Judge Olney?" protested Searls. "Where's the justice of the peace?"

"He's with the sheriff. They seemed of a mind to contest the election. They got locked in the jail and somebody lost the key."

"I'll ride to Camp Far West," Searls murmured to Isaiah. The Second U.S. Infantry had an encampment on Bear River, almost fifteen miles away. Two hours at a fast trot on the trail, thought Morgan, if Searls's horse would last; another two hours back. "Just try to slow things down," Searls urged, and squeezed back out of the crowd.

"You're in our way," grated Isaiah to the dealer. "Stand clear!"

The dealer opened his greasy frock coat and Morgan glimpsed the sheriff's new pearl-handled Colt in a gunbelt around his waist.

"Too late. The jury's hearing the case. And there just ain't no more seats."

"'*Jury*?'" Isaiah's thick glasses glittered in the sun. "Well, I'm their lawyer, Dr. Washburn's their physician, and we're coming in!"

They shoved past the dealer and stepped through the swinging door, blinking in the smoke.

Morgan had not been in the place since he had won his stake. It had hardly changed. Every one of the tree-trunk tables was filled; twelve tree-stump chairs in front held the jurymen: one was being sick on the sawdust floor.

Madam Lenoir sat at a green-baize faro table. Her orange-dyed hair hung limply in curls; she wore a pink bonnet and a pink silk gown. A pink parasol hung from the table. Her blue eyes were streaked with red. She was a stout woman, and her face was sweaty. In her brothel during his house calls, or in his surgery, she had seemed unsinkable, like a sturdy man-of-war; here she was a battered dinghy, gone adrift.

Next to her sat Cristina, a slender young Mexicana in a red brocade gown, scornfully combing her hair. On the green felt table before her lay her jaunty hack hat of straw, with a scarlet ribbon tied around it. Her dark brown eyes were shining; she seemed almost amused.

She either failed to know her peril, or was too proud to show her fear.

Thornberry presided behind the bar, in his soiled clerical collar, apparently acting as a judge. Before him sat a bottle, nearly full. Vanderveer, cold-eyed and immaculate in a gray frock coat, leaned against the bar, questioning the accused.

"So, Cristina, you came to the States *intending* to ply your trade?"

"When I come, California is not the 'States.' Is rather my own country, is *Mexico!*"

"Oh, Jesus," muttered Morgan, as an angry mumble swept the saloon. "On the Fourth of July?"

"They'll hang them," muttered Isaiah. "No matter what we do. Unless we give Searls time to get to Camp Far West . . . Reverend!" Isaiah called.

Thornberry squinted blearily across the room. "Hollister? You're a lawyer! You must know how to address the bench."

"Your honor," said Isaiah, quickly, "these ladies are my clients, and I haven't conferred with them. I ask for a recess."

"This ain't a schoolhouse!" shouted a beer-bellied, red-shirted juror. "We're hangin' them from the bridge before it's dark."

Cristina swung her eyes to the juror. "I know *you*, Enoch: too quick to speak, too quick in bed!"

The miners in the rear laughed; a grizzled prospector

273

lurched to Cristina, tried to kiss her; she kicked him in the ankle, and he hobbled off, howling in mock agony. Thornberry gaveled the place quiet with the butt of a Colt .44.

"The District Attorney will proceed."

Morgan chilled. Vanderveer, *District Attorney*? Not now, certainly, but later? If they hanged the women, with the connivance of half the county, Vanderveer could easily exploit their hangover of guilt, in a real election, to legitimize everyone's part.

Vanderveer continued trying to prove that the deceased was not merely a customer, but a heartsick lover trying to save her from herself.

"Is *not* true, Señor." She smiled. "*My* man is in Monterey. McCrae, he pay his ounce, like..." She jabbed her finger around the room "...like you, and you, and you!"

Her dark eyes fell on Morgan's. She shrugged and shook her head. He moved to her across the room. "Searls has gone for the Army," he whispered, "they'll be here."

He had examined her breast for a lump in his surgery a month ago, at the madam's request, with Mary at his side. He found nothing but a harmless wen, which he removed by knife.

He had never been tempted by the other girls Madam Lenoir had sent for treatment, even after his womanless trek across the plains. But Cristina's lustrous, supple body and proud bearing aroused him, as few women had before.

Mary sensed it. When Cristina was clothed and on her way, she chuckled: "You *are* a saint."

"With you around, at least," he conceded.

"Could you not have found me an errand?"

He was writing up Cristina's history at his rolltop desk. He put down the quill.

"I didn't try to think of one, my love."

"On religious grounds? Or ethical?" she asked.

He had not touched another woman since they'd met, but he dearly loved to tease.

"Medical," he said. "Half those prostitutes are infected, and you never truly know."

"And that's the only reason you can give?"

She turned away. Her shoulders trembled. She never

274

cried: *My God*, he thought, *she must be pregnant*. He arose and took her into his arms. "I would never touch another woman! I love *you!*"

He looked into her face. She wasn't crying, but laughing. She giggled: "Well, you said it! At long last!"

He blushed. Why must she always know his innermost thoughts? "That I love you? I've said it many times before."

"Not precisely: '*I . . . love . . . you.*'"

"Anyway, you gave me a turn. You seldom cry. I thought . . ."

She grinned. "Thought what?"

"That you might be . . . never mind."

"With child? Expecting? Enceinte?" She chuckled. "'Pregnant'? Say 'pregnant,' Morgan! I'm your wife, and I've had a year in medical school, it's all right."

He looked into her eyes. "Well, Mary, are you? 'Pregnant'?"

Mary grinned and kissed him. "You're the doctor," she whispered. "And so you must tell *me.*"

Now, in the Empire Saloon, Cristina smiled into his face. "I think your Army, they will be late."

"Leave off talking to the prisoners," ordered Thornberry from the bar. Morgan moved away, thinking of the lithe body twisting on a rope, and the firm proud breasts and rounded hips decaying in an unmarked grave in the cemetery on the hill.

Such a thing must not happen, to her or the madam. But she was right: Searls was hardly down the trail.

"Come on, Reverend," growled Enoch from the line of jurymen, "let's get 'em tried and hung!"

There was a mutter of assent from the watching miners. Outside a chant began. At first, Morgan heard only the rhythm and could not make out the words, and then he caught them: *Hang 'em now . . . hang 'em now . . . hang 'em now . . .*

The reverend rapped with the butt of his pistol, the sick juror gagged again. Outside a fusilade rang out, and cheers, as a whiskey keg was breached.

Vanderveer finished his case: the blacksmith's sledge which McCrae was supposed to have flourished had somewhere disappeared. Why? Because it had never existed at all. So McCrae, far from his native Scotland, had been helpless, struck down in the flower of his manhood by a Mexican devil, in a house built by a foul French woman to bleed miners of their dust.

Hang 'em now ... hang 'em now ...

Isaiah countered as best he could, while the minutes ticked away. Light slanted through the saloon windows as the sun dropped to the pines on American Hill. Isaiah pled that Cristina had acted in self-defense, citing case after case of New York law, and California precedent too. And when he saw that he was losing the "jury's" attention, he switched to an attack on Vanderveer. "Let us ask why he is here, why he does not let law prevail. Let us ask who *Vanderveer* is!"

Morgan's heart sank. Isaiah was flailing, playing for time, and treading treacherous ground.

Morgan, finding a tree-trunk table next to Dr. Cantrell to rest his haunches against, began to sweat in the heat. A fly buzzed at his forehead; he slapped it away. He longed to breathe fresh air.

Hang 'em now, hang 'em now ...

"You should know," cried Isaiah, "that this man Vanderveer, who has gathered you here to hang helpless women—"

"Helpless, hell, they killed Johnny!" called someone from the crowd.

"—this man is no stranger to the hangman's noose!"

"Oh, shit," groaned Cantrell, "no!"

The chant outside went on, but the mumble ceased inside. Holding their attention now, Isaiah faced the crowded hall.

"Many of you were seamen. You said to *hell* with your bully mates, *farewell* to the lash and the brig. You left the rotten hulks to seek your gold. You were right. Let the worms gnaw at their hulls, and Seaman's Rights forever!"

There were cheers, and someone yelled thickly from the rear: "Hurrah for Seaman's Rights!"

Isaiah had struck a vein of gold. In New York and Boston and even San Francisco, seamen were in revolt against laws and ships' articles that made them little more than slaves.

Isaiah pressed on: "Well, Vanderveer served on a rotten ship, and no merchantman was she." He peered around the barroom. "Jake? Abe? Harrigan? McCloud? Have you heard of the *Somers* affair?"

Morgan stiffened. His hands were suddenly cold. Vanderveer's voice cut across the saloon. "Mr. Hollister, I warned you on the *Michigan!*"

Isaiah polished his glasses, replaced them, and turned to the twelve men on the stools.

"Mr. Vanderveer has asked these fallen women questions, half the afternoon. Enoch, you were on a whaler. Now ask *him* if he served—not in the fo'c'sle, but the *wardroom*—of a goddamned man-of-war?"

"Hollister," growled Vanderveer, "I've told you—"

Isaiah's voice rose. He swung to face Vanderveer. "Ask him if he hanged two common seamen, and a youth of just eighteen, only ten days off New York! Ask of the *Somers* 'mutiny,' men, and see what he will say."

The saloon was deadly silent. Outside, the firehouse bell had stopped.

Only the chant went on, and it seemed to Morgan that it was louder: *Hang 'em now, hang 'em now . . .*

"Vanderveer," someone called. "That true?"

Vanderveer peered into the crowd. "I sat on the *Somers* court-martial, yes."

"Well, *damn* you," shouted another voice. "Navy, whalers, merchantmen officers: damn you one and all!"

"Who's that?" Vanderveer called, squinting. "Harrigan?"

There was no answer. Vanderveer stepped behind the bar, turned and tossed a bag of gold dust to the rear. "Your wages, Harrigan! Anyone wanting steady work, see me tomorrow. I'll need a new hoistman on the Jenny Lind shaft." He smiled. "Yes, I sat on the *Somers* court-martial."

"You hanged three seamen!" someone belched.

"Not seamen." He looked at the group in the back. "Jake, Abe, McCloud? Would you like to know who they were?"

"We know!" called a voice. "They ain't a seaman in here ain't had *Somers* jammed up his ass! By some ape like you on the quarterdeck trying to cheat us of our grog!"

"Well put, Jensen." Vanderveer peered into the crowd, tossed back another bag. "When you've spent that, try panning on Deer Creek again. You're through on Buckeye Hill."

But the muttering persisted.

By God, thought Morgan, *Isaiah had done it! Now, if he could get him out of town alive . . .*

Vanderveer stuck his hands in his trouser pockets and addressed the group in the rear. "Would you like to hear the truth, my friends? By one who started in the fo'c'sle as a common seaman?"

The mumbling quieted.

"And found himself in the wardroom," Vanderveer continued, "passing judgment on his mates?"

The hubbub stilled. "Go on, Boss," called a seaman-turned-miner named McCloud.

"*One* mutineer was our boatswain's mate, who used his cat-o'-nine-tails on every lad we had. *Another* served on a slaver and would gladly knife his mates. And the third . . ." He turned to Isaiah. "Tell them who the third was, Mr. Hollister."

"A boy of just eighteen!" cried Hollister.

"A 'young *gentleman*,' you'll recall," Vanderveer said tersely, his voice cutting through the murmur, "whose father was the Secretary of War. And who held a midshipman's warrant which his daddy got for him! A fine young gentleman who thought he'd try to pirate from a U.S. man-of-war!"

Vanderveer studied the crowd. His eye fell on a group of Welshmen sitting at a pine-trunk table, smoking stolidly. "You Cousin Jacks! Do *you* have questions about the *Somers*?"

An iron-jawed Welshman knocked out his pipe. "Never heard of her before, Cap'n. And don't much care."

It was clear that Vanderveer had won, but Hollister would not quit.

"Ask him why they couldn't wait to give them a proper

trial ashore!" he cried. "Ask why they tried those men at sea! Just ten days from New York!"

Vanderveer strode to Isaiah, grabbed his lapel, and slapped his face. Isaiah's glasses went flying, and shattered on the floor. Vanderveer shoved him violently away, and Isaiah stumbled against the bar.

Vanderveer faced the crowd coolly. "Ask *him* where he'll be at dawn. Facing me, at ten paces? Or hiding up in Downieville, with his yellowbellied boss?"

"Hold on!" said Morgan, moving toward the bar. He felt the sawdust squealing under his feet; his fists were cocked and ready, hands shaking with anger. His voice resounded from the walls. "What in the hell kind of town *is* this? And I brought my wife here to live! Another Rough and Ready, do you want?" He glared at Thornberry. "There's one man dead already: Johnny McCrae. Do we let another die in a duel tomorrow, just because it's dawn?"

"That's between the two of them," said Thornberry. "We're here to hang the Jezebels. Sit down, or get thrown out!"

"Don't worry, Doctor, I won't fight." Isaiah motioned him away, picked up the frames of his spectacles, and pocketed them.

"Then I'll post you as a coward," Vanderveer said coldly, "in every goddamn stage stop from here to Sacramento!"

"Enough!" belched Thornberry from the bar. "I want the jury to vote! Enoch Wells?"

"Hang the Greaser and the Frog-eater," yelled Enoch. "They killed our Johnny-boy."

And one by one, as glasses clinked, the other jurymen agreed.

"May God," intoned the reverend, "have mercy on their souls."

As Master at Arms of the Committee of 601, Vanderveer drove the madam's landau, like a tumbrel from the French Revolution, to the center of the bridge. Thornberry rode beside him. Inside sat the two women; Morgan and Isaiah walked behind.

"When the Marysville stage leaves," murmured Morgan, "I want you on it, heading west. If Vanderveer can't kill you on the field, he'll gun you in the street."

"I may go farther," Isaiah agreed. "I've never set up as a hero. If he posts me, I may move east. I'll get fired as editor, and as for *law,* who'll retain a yellowbellied lawyer, here in the Mother Lode?"

"You're no 'yellowbellied' lawyer! You smoked him out in front of the mob. You *couldn't* fight him, Isaiah, you're half-blind!"

"*Justice* has gone blind! And where's the Second Infantry?"

They had reached the center of the bridge. Vanderveer reined in. His posse—the jury—had to half-support the madam to the railing. Thornberry, who'd finished his quart of whiskey while the parade began, was waving his Bible at her; he sought to offer them a prayer, but the noise was overwhelming, and no one heard the words.

The madam did not choose to speak. She was forced to mount a crate drawn close to the rough-cut railing, then to turn toward the mob and sit on the rail. She sat there briefly while Enoch Wells adjusted a noose around her neck. Then Enoch and another pushed her off.

She disappeared with a scream in a flurry of skirts and petticoats. Morgan flinched as he heard the rope snap her neck below the bridge with a crack like that of a breaking branch.

Shaken, he rubbed his temples. He would carry the memory of her astounded blue eyes, as she was shoved backwards to eternity, all the rest of his life.

Cristina watched the madam's execution coolly, standing on the step of the landau. She shook off the miners' hands as they grasped for her, removed her red-ribboned straw hat, swept back her hair, refused a hood, and stood by the railing as they slipped the noose around her neck.

Morgan's mind was casting desperately, seeking for delay. He had a sudden blinding thought, an ace that only a doctor might play. There was no time to plan a speech, only time to say his piece. "Wish me luck," he muttered to Isaiah, and climbed onto the crate. He took a breath, and bellowed into the faces of the crowd: "Wait!"

"Get down, Doctor," growled Thornberry, "before we hang you too."

He ignored the reverend. His eyes swept the mob. "Enoch, Adam, Philips, House! I've treated you all, and she has too!"

"'Treated,'" smiled Enoch. "Well put, Doc. Let's hang her!"

Morgan braced himself and shouted out: "Will you murder an unborn child?"

The miners froze. He saw Cristina's eyes widen. The bridge was suddenly quiet. He went on, hoarsely: "A child who could be *yours,* Enoch, or yours, Rebard? Or anyone's, of half a dozen here?"

A buzz of conversation started. "What's that?" asked Thornberry, climbing down from the driver's seat. "What 'unborn child' is that?"

"She's three months gone with child," lied Morgan.

On the outskirts of the crowd, as the word passed to them, men shook their heads; Morgan saw some walk away.

"How do *you* know?" asked Thornberry. He sidled through the mob. He seemed suddenly to have shrunk. His bleary eyes held Morgan's. "How is it you know this, Dr. Washburn?"

"I examined her on the second day of June, with my wife present." He scanned the crowd, and found Cantrell. "And Dr. Cantrell, too."

"He's right," lied Cantrell, instantly. "I was there; she's three months gone."

Thornberry handed the Bible up to Morgan on the crate. "Put your hand on that, and swear it's true, or may Heaven strike you dead."

Morgan touched the greasy leather binding and intoned: "I swear she's three months gone with child, or may Heaven strike me dead!"

"Ask him why he waited so long," laughed Vanderveer, from the driver's seat. "Why *did* you, Dr. Washburn?"

Morgan flushed. "Because I don't discuss my patients' symptoms in public."

"Thank God for that," someone said, laughing, "or they wouldn't let the half of us in the whorehouse on the hill!"

"There'll *be* no whorehouse on the hill," warned Morgan, "if you hang her!"

He studied the faces before him. He had given them pause. Some seemed more sober. They were talking one to the other. He looked at Cristina. The hemp had reddened her ivory neck; she moved to ease the weight. Her eyes were downcast. *Say something*, he begged her. *Back us up!*

"Humbug!" someone cried at him, without conviction. Thornberry, strangely quiet, was standing at her side. He seemed transfixed. He was rubbing his jaw indecisively, when Vanderveer spoke from above.

"Cristina?"

"Yes?" she answered from the rail.

"Why do *you* not speak up?"

She shrugged and said nothing.

Thornberry looked up at Vanderveer. "We might leave her jailed, and wait?"

"Yes!" called Morgan, heart leaping with hope.

"If we wait, we'll find the Army here. There *is* no child, goddamn it," laughed Vanderveer. "Can't you see?"

"Tell them, Cristina," Morgan urged her. "Tell them now!"

Thornberry nodded: "If there *is* a child, speak up, Cristina! I ask you in God's name!"

"God's name?" For a long moment, she studied her straw hat. But when she looked up her voice cut through the hubbub, and she spoke to the whole mob:

"Why should I beg with you? To make hard your pricks? If men are going to hang *me*, who make love with them, why do they care if they kill a baby they never seen?" She tossed her head. Her full tresses shimmered like ebony in the sun.

The crowd grew quiet. "Cristina," murmured Morgan, "that's enough."

She laughed. "I theenk, is waste of breath to beg you for my life! You sure to hang me anyway. Madam's life, mine, little baby's . . ." Her eyes were heavy with scorn. "You have stole our country. You are stealing our gold.

Now you steal little Mexican bebé's life! On your 'Fourth of July,' with your guns *bang bang,* life no importa! Not to you Gringos, no!"

- Not "Gringos"! Cristina, please... Morgan squeezed her shoulder, too late.

"*Gringos?*" a drunken miner bellowed, struggling to mount the landau's wheel. "Hear *me,* you Greaser puta! I was at Buena Vista with the Mississippi Volunteers! I seen Colonel Jefferson Davis take a poisoned rifle ball! I seen Santa Anna bayonet our wounded in the pass. I seen Mexican dragoons cut off a Texas Ranger's balls—" He fought to retain his balance on the landau's hub. "*I* know what to do with Mexican babies! And their goddamn mothers too!"

The drunken miner flailed his arms. "Hang 'er!" he yelled, and fell from the landau.

"Hang 'er!" screamed another, and the crowd began to roar. "Hang the puta! Hang the puta! Hang the puta now!"

All his efforts, thought Morgan, and Isaiah's... gone for naught.

Thornberry's hands were up for quiet. It was useless. The din increased. "You should not have called them 'Gringos'!" He seemed all at once contrite. "We might have... Have you anything else to say?"

"No."

Thornberry's eyes pled with her. Someone jostled him, and he nearly fell. "Not even to *me,* as a man of the cloth? In private? To save your soul?"

"No, Señor 'Man of the Cloth,' not you." She had to shout to be heard. "But to Dr. Washburn, yes."

Someone pushed Morgan off the crate. Morgan grabbed Cristina's arm. "I'm sorry we could do nothing, and I'm deeply shamed for them."

"You did whatever you could, you are one of the good," she said, up into his face. "I have favor to ask, por favor?"

"Anything you wish."

She drew him close, until her lips were at his ear. "You must never, never tell them that you lie.... You promise?"

He nodded, speechless. She suddenly mounted the

wooden crate, grasped a piling on the bridge, and pulled herself erect to balance gracefully on the railing. She brushed her hair from her eyes, and shaded them against the setting sun.

"Thornberry?" she called down, above the yelling. "Señor Reverend?"

Enoch Wells and the other executioner were clawing for her legs.

Thornberry lurched forward, Bible extended, his face as gray as stone. "We will offer a prayer, before you go."

"No, señor." She spun her straw hat toward Thornberry. Instinctively, the reverend caught it by the rim. "I thank you, though. And, Señor Reverend?"

"Yes?"

"Your child, he thanks you too!"

She blew a kiss to all, stepped back one pace, and disappeared from sight.

There was a roar from the crowd that mercifully drowned the sound of her snapping neck. Thornberry stared after her, put his elbows on the rail, and hid his face in his hands.

Morgan turned away. He saw Vanderveer, on the landau's seat, smiling coldly down at him. The mob had surged to the rail and craned to see her fall.

The roar of the crowd was suddenly gone. The bell in the firehouse began to toll again. Vanderveer broke the silence. "Dr. Washburn," he called down, "you said she was with child. And I called you a liar for it. Shall I post you as a coward too, with your friend?"

Morgan felt the blood rush to his face. He thought of Mary sitting at home with Madam Lenoir's daughter: he owed it to his wife and unborn child to hold his tongue in check.

Instead, he found himself calling clearly: "*You're* a goddamned coward to challenge Hollister. But we knew that all the time."

The miners leaving the bridge rail froze: for a moment the world stood still. Vanderveer swept the whip from the landau's socket and raised it high.

"A coward? Will you stand for him tomorrow, or bear

the lash instead?" He jiggled the whip in the air. "Now which is it to be?"

Morgan looked up into Vanderveer's face, and studied the whip held high. "*Touch* me with that," he growled, "just *once*—"

Slowly, mockingly, Vanderveer brought the whip down and tapped him on the cheek. Morgan tore it from his grip and hurled it away. It spun lazily in the afternoon sun and splashed into the river.

"You were touched, sir," grinned Vanderveer. "Will you challenge?"

He thought of Mary as a widow far from all she knew, alone with a fatherless child.

"I *cannot*, you rotten son of a bitch! I have a wife to keep!"

"Well," Vanderveer shrugged, picking up the reins, "there's a vacancy in the whorehouse...."

"*What?*"

Vanderveer smiled down on Morgan. "Perhaps she'd keep herself."

The mumble of the crowd was stilled. He was suddenly the center of a tableau, frozen in time. He felt a hundred eyes, probing at his face.

Never challenge, but never refuse. He'd refused too long, and—his father was right—escaped nothing in the end.

He sprang to a spoke on the forward wheel, hoisted himself to the driver's box. He slapped Vanderveer with all his strength, across his square-set jaw. The lieutenant fell sidewise on the seat. Morgan heaved him to the mob below, and took the reins himself.

"Tomorrow, then, at dawn, sir," Morgan called down. "Mr. Hollister will second me. So choose your weapons now!"

Vanderveer arose, coolly brushing the dust from his gray frock coat. Instead of fury in his eyes, Morgan saw delight.

"Pistols, sir," grinned Vanderveer. "My flintlocks. Mr. Oglethorpe will call on Mr. Hollister tonight."

Blindly, Morgan wheeled the carriage around, waited for Isaiah to climb up, and clopped back across the bridge.

285

He'd been a fool. As challenger, under the Code Duello, he'd dealt him all the cards: choice of weapon, terms of firing, pick of judge and place.

Vanderveer had played an expert hand, from the moment in the *Michigan*'s saloon, a full three years ago.

Now the cards lay on the table.

He'd been trapped.

THE ADMIRAL
AND BUNKIE

THE ADMIRAL SAT ON THE SIDE OF THE BED. LYING UNder a carved headboard which had come around the Horn, Terry drifted in and out of consciousness. In the amber light from the bedside lamp her cheeks were pale as the sheets. She and Miguel seemed so foreign in this familiar room that the admiral was disoriented. He must remain cool. He took a deep breath to steady his nerves.

Rain dripped into the zinc gutters outside. A distant roll of mountain thunder rattled a stained-glass pane. He choked on the mustiness of the place, closed for almost a month.

Behind huge walnut sliding doors dividing this bedroom from the ancient parlor, Kelly and Bunkie waited, with Howard, under Jeff's gun.

He heard the slosh of tires on Isaiah Lane: it was Hanifan, undoubtedly, whose garage opened onto it opposite the Washburn stable. He was probably weaving home from his Sunday night at Odd Fellows Hall.

Terry moaned, still comatose from her last shot, but awakening. She stirred, childlike in the mammoth bed.

286

According to Washburn family lore, this bed had been used for convalescing patients, sometimes occupied for days or even weeks by survivors of surgery in the adjoining room.

The bedroom had always depressed him. God knew how many men—and women—had died in it. It had seldom been used in his own lifetime except for guests. He remembered, at the age of eight, hiding in the monstrous armoire in the corner, emitting deathly groans in a futile effort to exorcise from the house a female cousin who came to stay too long.

Jeff had relieved himself in the toilet off the surgery, obviously spotting no evidence of the secret door. Now, from the parlor, the admiral could hear his voice questioning Kelly. The admiral hoped she'd understood the charade, but wasn't sure. Nervous as to what she'd say, anxious to be with her, he quickly lifted Terry's arm and wound the blood-pressure cuff around it. He had found the sphygmomanometer in the kitchen, a relic of his pacemaker operation. He'd been supposed to take and record his own blood pressure twice a day. Finding the instrument was a godsend: another way to stall, until he could think of a way to get Bunkie—or Kelly—into the toilet in the surgery, where they might leave through Madam's Door.

And using it was convincing to Miguel. There was no way to judge how many doubts the Mexican had of his competence by now, but taking Terry's blood pressure seemed to provide magical comfort: Miguel was watching him like some anxious Aztec warrior chief worshiping a god.

The admiral muffed the reading, distracted by a sudden feeling that he should be in the parlor with the rest. The intuition grew. He shook it off, pumped the cuff around Terry's arm, and started again.

Terry's eyes flicked open. Her breathing seemed shallow. Her blood pressure was 140 over 80. Lower than his, but he had no idea of what was normal for her age. He would simply claim it was too low to operate, and stall.

287

He nodded wisely, for Miguel's benefit, placed his hand on the woman's moist forehead, and arose.

At least he had found an excuse for telling Jeff that he must delay.

Bunkie sat on the couch in the parlor, trying to be somewhere else.

Her face was flaming, and her heart was beating crazily. She knew exactly what Jeff was saying to her mother, and saw its effect on her father, but it was all such a nightmare that she couldn't believe her ears.

Pops, Pops, hurry back. Something awful's happening here!

Her father, head wrapped in the bloody dishtowel, was sitting deep in the old leather chair. Her mother sat on its arm, her hand gripping his shoulder.

Jeff stood before them, grinning. "Kelly? That your name?"

Her mother was looking at him as if he were a cockroach in the kitchen sink.

"Sexy name, sexy woman." He reached out and turned her face to the light. "Well, Kelly, I been locked away. If we don't get through to T-town, I'll never get laid again."

Bunkie, face flaming, could not watch any longer. Her eyes darted about the room: a picture of Morgan and Mary—he seated, she standing—on their wedding day; a moose head mounted on the wall—as a child, she'd run outside the house, trying to find the rest of it; the grandfather clock, pendulum motionless because no one had wound it for a month.

Jeff's voice droned on. "Now Kelly, if your daddy don't quit fartin' around, I'll never get past here. So you and I, you know what we're going to do?"

Hail began to fall outside, Bunkie could hear it on the roof. The grandfather clock watched silently: she wanted to wind it, to start time up again.

Jeff was passing his hand down her mother's cheek. "We're going to get that shit-eatin' look off your face." She saw her mother flinch. "Kelly, you ever fuck a man's been locked up for four years?"

288

Bunkie's father grunted as if he'd been struck, and tried to rise. Her mother, face closed in fear, absently pressed him back. Jeff bent closer. "Well, *have* you?"

Her mother's eyes were full of terror. She did not move or speak.

"Then stand up, Florence Nightingale," Jeff said quietly. "Let's see just what I got."

Her mother started shakily to rise. Suddenly her father was lunging at the gun. "You got *nothing*, you crazy son of a bitch!"

Bunkie screamed a warning. "Daddy, no!"

Jeff jerked the gun back, stepped aside. A magazine rack toppled and a chair fell over, as her father grappled for the gun. Jeff simply held him off, slashed it across his face, and pushed him back into the chair. Blood dripped from his cheek down his checkered lumberjack shirt. She had shopped for it last Christmas all day long, and paid for it from her allowance.

She found herself across the room, holding his head to her breast to stop the flow, as if shirts were all that mattered, pain didn't hurt at all. Crazy, crazy, what was wrong with her?

"Daddy, Daddy, Dad . . ."

She felt Jeff's hand on her arm and was all at once flung back to the couch, with strength she'd never known. Her mother dabbed at her father's cheek with the hem of her skirt and retreated when Jeff shoved her aside.

Jeff yanked him off the chair, threw him to the floor, and began to tie him up, bending him all backwards, with a lightcord he ripped from the floorlamp.

Bunkie flew to her mother's arms.

Where was Pops?

The admiral opened one of the massive rolling doors between the sickroom and the parlor.

He froze, staring. Jeff was kneeling by Howard, bending his son-in-law's legs backwards and trussing his hands to his ankles, gangster-style, with a lightcord ripped from the floorlamp. A chair lay on its back. Magazines from an overturned rack were scattered on the rug. Howard, head bandaged in the dishtowel, lay with his back to the TV console below the great iron stove. A new gash on his cheek was oozing blood. Jeff finished and stood up.

Howard's face was blank with shock, but he was conscious, watching everything. Morgan caught the accusation in his eyes. He dropped to his knees beside him. "Howard, what happened?"

"Get up!" growled Jeff. "Just leave him be."

"Yes..." breathed Howard. "Just goddamn leave me be."

He thinks it's all my fault, the admiral thought. *And he is right.*

"Don't sound as if he likes you much," Jeff grinned down at Howard. "Maybe for giving us a lift. What *do* you like, Professor? Television?"

Howard glared at him. "You rotten bastard, you're all gun! Put that away and—"

Jeff touched the tip of Howard's nose with his toe. "And what, Professor?"

"And I'll kill you, you son of a bitch!"

"Howard," ordered the admiral, "shut up!"

"You're off your flagship now, Stretch," groaned Howard. "I wish to God you weren't."

Flagship! A medical admiral with a flagship! Oh, Christ! He suddenly remembered that Howard had been unconscious in the kitchen when he clued Kelly on the fatal charade.

He cut his eyes to their tormentor. Jeff was studying the TV controls, and hadn't seemed to notice. He flicked it on and shook his head. "Brains," he scoffed. "He's a goddamn *college* professor, and he tried to grab this gun!"

"He—*what?*" The admiral's throat tightened. He stared at his son-in-law. Guts?

"Too much John Wayne," smiled Jeff, jabbing Howard in the stomach with his toe. "Hell, Professor, even this old fart's got better sense than you!" He turned on the TV. The staccato *tick-tick-tick-tick* of "60 Minutes" filled the room.

Jeff measured the distance to Howard as if setting a football up for a field goal. He prodded him in the groin with his foot. Howard paled and the admiral flinched. Jeff turned up the volume.

Jesus, he was going to kick him to death: the sound was to drown Howard's yells!

Tick-tick-tick-tick... "I'm Mike Wallace..." The volume rose further. The daguerreotype of Morgan and his bride began to dance upon the wall; the woodstove rattled; the streaming windows shimmered, vibrating with sound.

"I'm Morley Safer..."

Howard lay writhing, back near breaking, teeth gritted. The flickering colors off the screen were haloing his hair. His stomach curved, exposed, distended, tensed for the blows to come.

"I'm Harry Reasoner..."

Jeff, automatic loose in his hand, slammed his foot into Howard's distended stomach. Kelly shrieked, Bunkie screamed, Howard turned white, gagged, but made no other sound. The foot came back, lashed out again, harder. Howard grunted.

"Watch it!" yelled the admiral, "you'll kill him!"

"All this and more tonight on '60 Minutes'..."

"¿Qué pasa?"

The admiral swung around. Miguel was in the doorway, staring at the scene.

The admiral knew that he must start the operation or watch Howard kicked to death. He could no longer stall. He jabbed Miguel, pointed to the surgery, then at Terry in the bedroom. Then he made a knifing motion, touched the back of his wrist to indicate time, and pointed to the surgery again.

Miguel nodded, strode between Jeff and his victim.

Jeff tried to push him aside, his eyes on the target below.

"Not now!" Miguel yelled in Spanish, over the TV. "¡El doctor! ¡Mi hermanita! We have better things to do!"

Jeff's foot came back again. For a moment the two faced each other. The Mexican reached out slowly and turned the TV off. "Más tarde," he said softly. "Jeff, ahora, no!"

"Later, Jeff, not now..."

Jeff turned to the admiral reluctantly. "You ready?"

The admiral nodded, sick at heart. But better to kill the woman on the table than to stand and watch Howard die.

Howard was moaning, writhing on the rug. Kelly left Bunkie, kneeled by his head, and looked up at Jeff.

"Can I untie him? *Please?*"

"No."

She looked up at his face. "I'll do anything you say."

Jeff grinned. "Your fuckin' right you will, later. Now, leave him there. Get up."

She arose. Bunkie was crying. The admiral wiped his granddaughter's face with his handkerchief and for a moment pulled her close. Her hair smelled dank and damp.

"*Madam's Door*," he whispered into her ear. "Remember Madam's Door?"

"Knock off the shit!" barked Jeff. "Let's go!"

Thunder rumbled distantly. Rain pelted the porch outside. Had Bunkie heard, and understood? Or was she too distraught?

Bunkie drew in her breath in a long, shuddering sob. She looked at her mother. "I've got to go to the bathroom, Mom."

Kelly looked at Jeff. "Ask him."

Jeff pointed to the surgery. "The one in there."

In a moment the admiral heard her bolt the toilet door.

She'd heard the message, loud and clear. Now all he could do was hope.

MORGAN

MORGAN WASHBURN STOOD AT THE WINDOW OF ISAIAH'S second-story lodging at the Nevada Hotel. From the window he could see the Deer Creek Bridge. In its center an Army lieutenant, his horse tethered to the rail, was hanging an oil lamp on a piling. In the shadows, a squad of blue-coated Rifles from the Second Infantry was disembarking from an Army Dougherty wagon that bore a similarity to poor old Carriage Eighteen.

He sensed Isaiah behind him. Isaiah was bitter: "In time to hoist the bodies up! If they'd sent cavalry—"

"Well, they didn't," Morgan said sharply. He was nervous, and a little scared. There was a knock on the door. "Come in," called Isaiah.

Alston Oglethorpe walked in. He carried two pistol cases: Vanderveer's, certainly, and perhaps Oglethorpe's own. His eyes widened to see Morgan there.

"*Your* presence, Doctor, is hardly tolerable. This is a matter for seconds."

"Mr. Hollister's unfamiliar with the Code."

"Perhaps you'll find yourself another man, then?"

Morgan pointed out that Nevada City wasn't Charleston; experts in the Code Duello were a trifle hard to find. "Isaiah's my second, he remains so. I'm here, and here I'll stay."

Oglethorpe shrugged, tossed his gray tophat on a chair, and set down the cases on the bed. He handed Isaiah a Seconds' Agreement. Isaiah brought it close to the oil

293

lamp on his bureau, squinted, and pronounced it a contract for mutual murder, and without any legal standing at all.

"Initial it," murmured Morgan, "and pass it over."

"No! For it's without equity, as well! Morgan, listen: '...the said Morgan Washburn, MD, having demanded at the hands of Guert Vanderveer, passed lieutenant, United States Navy, immediate personal satisfaction, the choice of weapons, place, judge, and terms of firing shall be the latter's—'" Isaiah looked up, aghast. "All the choices are *Vanderveer's!*"

"Not *all*, sir," Oglethorpe pointed out mildly. "Your man was free to choose *you*, for instance. He may choose his surgeon. The *distance* is yours to choose—"

"We choose a hundred paces," said Isaiah swiftly.

"'—unless the chosen distance is bizarre,'" sighed Oglethorpe. "Mr. Hollister, I reckon you should take this seriously, or I'll be forced to call *you*." He smiled thinly. "Your principal has even one *more* choice. *I* think he should use it."

"What's that?"

"To cut and run."

"I think not," said Morgan tersely.

Morgan took the agreement from Isaiah and signed it with a scrawl. He walked to the bed. One of the pistol cases was of battered mahogany, with Vanderveer's name engraved in a brass plaque on its lid. He opened it. In the background he could hear Oglethorpe instructing Isaiah in his duties as a second.

"You'll be armed with a Henry Derringer, or better, I presume—"

"Me?" he heard Isaiah gasp. "Why?"

"To dispatch my principal if he fires off-signal or moves. As I'll certainly dispatch yours. . . ."

Morgan put their conversation from his mind and studied Vanderveer's brace of pistols. They were made by J. Cooper, of New York. The two weapons nestled, facing each other, in faded, salt-streaked velvet. The ramrods bedded beside them were of hickory capped with brass. Between them was cradled a brass snuffbox with spare flints, and a tarnished powder decanter, green with age. The pistols had a well-worn look, as if they'd been to sea.

In an age when even the U.S. Cavalry finally used percussion caps, only dueling pistols depended on the flint of yesteryear to strike the flame. He touched the flints clamped in their cocks; they were hardly worn, apparently replaced for just this affair.

He lifted the weapons from their velvet nests. They seemed perfectly matched. They had neither front sights nor rear ones; dueling pistols seldom did. They weighed some two and a half pounds each, with graceful swan-neck, checkered stocks and octagonal barrels ten inches long. He peered into the muzzles: they were rifled. The lands were worn with use, but the grooves were quite unfouled. Vanderveer kept his instruments as spotless as he himself kept the scalpels in his surgery.

He cocked the hammer of the first pistol and touched the trigger. Unexpectedly, the hammer snapped: he almost dropped the piece.

"My God," he breathed. "A breeze could fire that gun!"

"A trifle light," smiled Oglethorpe. "I found them so myself. But he preferred his own to mine, and the choice is up to him."

Morgan cocked and snapped the second pistol: equally touchy, as hair-trigger as Vanderveer himself. Three tiny notches were filed on the butt of one, one notch on the other's.

Four victims already on Vanderveer's soul, or were the notches simply a bluff? He did not intend to ask.

He tested the pull again, and decided to pick the pistol with three notches, if tomorrow he won the call.

He inspected the reserve set: Oglethorpe's percussions, bound in silver, made by James Haselett of Baltimore, and beautifully engraved. There was little to choose between the two reserves, should the duel go beyond the first shot.

"Morgan, your help?" asked Isaiah.

He moved across the room.

"Frenchman's Flat, they've decided." Isaiah showed a sketch. "He wants the eastern end."

To make me aim at a silhouette, into the rising sun.

He had expected nothing less, and shrugged. "His choice, I fear."

"He wants firing to continue until you or he is down," complained Isaiah. "Flintlocks, then percussions, then flintlocks once again. Fire and load, fire and load, if it takes all morning long."

He'd expected that as well: a blow had been struck, there was no greater sin. *There shall be no verbal apology accepted for a blow upon a gentleman, and in such case firing shall be continuous until one or both principals are disabled.*

"Agreed."

"Dear God," breathed Hollister; there were tears in his eyes. "It's barbaric!"

"So's a hanging from a yardarm." Morgan moved back to the window. "Or a bridge..."

The Army lieutenant, already mounted for the return trip and watching pensively from the flickering shadows, had apparently decided not to dirty the Army's hands. Under the guns of his men, a half-dozen miners from the saloons on Main Street were drawing Cristina's body over the rail.

"Further questions?" asked Oglethorpe.

Morgan was suddenly twelve years old, out by the stables with his father, firing at the white oak tree. "And then you ask his terms of fire.... Turn and fire, or stationary?"

He turned back to the room. "The terms of fire, sir?"

"Stationary," said Oglethorpe. He read from the Agreement: "'Principals to face sideways, the firing shoulder of each toward the opposite party, pistol pointed toward the earth, arm straight, extended downward. Seconds, having placed their principals, are to station themselves on a line which shall be the perpendicular bisector of that joining the principals, and at a distance of twenty feet from each other. The judge to give the firing signal loudly, from a position by the second of the challenged man. Neither principal to raise arm or pistol from said downward position, or make any motion whatsoever before the firing signal, under penalty of a ball from the other's second.'"

"And what is that signal to be?" Morgan's voice seemed to echo in his ears, as if from a distant place.

"Pre*sent*! One, two, three! No movement before the word 'pre*sent*,' no firing after 'three.'"

Morgan raised his eyebrows. "'Pre*sent*'! Why not '*fire*'?"

"Vanderveer says it's the Navy way," explained Oglethorpe. "I find it odd, myself. He cites the Decatur-Barron duel, and one his father had. He's strangely adamant. Again, it *is* his choice."

"You sound like a pair of law clerks," Isaiah exploded. "It's proper to blow a man's head off, as long as the wording's right?"

Oglethorpe studied him. "Mr. Hollister, I've warned you! This is an affair of honor, do not make light of it!"

"You make light of murder, sir, not I!"

"The judge?" asked Morgan swiftly, to cut the argument short.

"Reverend Thornberry, if he's sobered up. Otherwise, your choice."

Oglethorpe moved to the bed, picked up the dueling sets, and started for the door. He paused.

"I almost forgot, Dr. Washburn. What distance do you choose?"

His father's voice came back: *"Write your will, and say your prayers, but hold back what you can. Let the other party toss and turn, duels make for sleepless nights."*

"Tell the lieutenant I shall sleep on it tonight, and decide tomorrow on the field."

Oglethorpe stared. "You can't do that!"

"Indeed I can," Morgan smiled. "You'll see it in the Code."

Morgan returned home. He gave pulverized opium and what comfort he could to Madam Lenoir's daughter and watched her leave in the landau.

There was no drug to ease his guilt toward Mary—for he could not tell her of tomorrow or of his fears for her if he should die. He watched her sorrowing at the details of the hanging, which he had not brought himself to tell the daughter. He sat with her, trying to drown her distress by reading Emerson to her by the stove in the parlor. He enticed her to bed early. They made love, but when finally she slept, he could not. At last he arose, brushed her lightly with his lips, and stole away from the one he loved like a thief in the black of night.

He dressed in dark clothes—to make a poorer target—donned his black greatcoat, and went to his surgery, where he wrote her a letter, trying to explain.

Since there was no excuse for his foolishness, short of the romantic twaddle they laughed at together in Scott or Malory, there was nothing he could write. Her grief would so outweigh his "honor" that no words could balance the scale.

Still, he must be ready to stand at Frenchman's Flat at dawn. *You cannot escape in the end....*

If he survived, the letter would be unimportant: if he died, she'd know he'd tried. He wrote: *It seems I have not lost Southern roots, dislike them as I do. But this letter I cannot finish. You, I love with all my heart, as I love the child you carry; if there is a life beyond, we shall never be apart.*

He left the sheet on his desk unfinished, and rolled the desktop down.

Then, not wishing to alert Juanita or her husband above the woodshed, he stepped into his apothecary, pressed the secret wooden knot, and escaped through Madam's Door.

Seated in the hired brougham in the first faint light of day, Morgan heard the leather thoroughbraces squeak below as Isaiah moved. "Morgan," he said, "they're here."

Morgan shivered in his Inverness greatcoat. The carriage—hired and driven by Cantrell—had been resting for half an hour in crystal starlight under a walnut tree just fifteen minutes from his home. He could not tell if his trembling came from fear or the predawn chill. He found himself feeling his pulse, trying to estimate its rate without looking at his watch. He could not.

He peered out the window. The walnut's twisted limbs

framed a gray-streaked sky. A surrey and two horsemen had arrived; Vanderveer's stolid silhouette loomed against the trees, across a pea-green meadow smoking with tule fog. The lieutenant wore a cloak.

"It's growing late," Isaiah reminded him. "Have you decided on the distance?"

"No."

His eyes were dry with fatigue, and his muscles tight with fear. He began to take deep breaths to relieve the tension before it gripped him further.

Fifty feet away growled the Bear River. He'd fished the stream often with Isaiah; they'd panned its banks one day and found color in the black sand on its bars.

He pulled his gold watch from his vest pocket. "Light a match, Isaiah?" he asked.

A sulphur match flared, acrid in his nostrils. It might be the last match he would smell. He savored the bite of it in his nostrils, and the warmth of its flare on his face. He snapped open the watch. Four thirty-two. Dawn would break in ten or fifteen minutes.

He closed the watch and handed it to Isaiah. "You're to keep this, my friend."

"Morgan!" groaned Isaiah. "Don't say that!"

"That isn't what I mean," said Morgan sharply. "My chances are as good as his. It's that . . . Well, it's against the Code to have it in my waistcoat, and Oglethorpe will be feeling my chest for body mail."

"'Body mail'! My God, it sounds like the Third Crusade!"

"Someone's tried it, I assume. Or it wouldn't be in the Code."

"The 'Code,'" Isaiah muttered bitterly. "*Damn* the Code!"

"We've got to play by their rules, Isaiah, or he'll simply provoke another duel, and then there's nothing solved."

Morgan surveyed the field. His mind was awash in precepts from his father: "*Recoil carries up the ball; aim for the belly, hit the chest; squeeze butt and trigger together; shake hands with your piece, never pull. Stand sidewise, and keep your gut pulled in; hurry, but take good aim.*"

He climbed from the carriage, looked up at Cantrell. The old doctor sat like a character from Dickens, deep in a muffler and a Mackintosh which smelled of India-rubber. His nose was red and running: he looked half-frozen from the trip. He handed down a whiskey bottle. Morgan took a fast swig, and let the liquor warm his gut.

"Good luck, Doctor," said Cantrell. "Keep your belly in."

Followed by Isaiah, Morgan moved across the field. He felt already dead, floating above the tule fog, untouched by fear or hate.

"The distance," urged Isaiah. "You have to decide it now."

His uncle had been murdered from afar, at a full twenty paces, by a horse-breeding squire who'd loosed a dozen rounds every morning of his life. The horse breeder waited until his uncle's ball had passed, then took good fast aim and shot him—at the count of three—dead center between the eyes.

The distance, distance, distance . . .

Dr. Marshall, Vanderveer's surgeon, spread his instruments on a canvas under a live oak tree. Oglethorpe looked fresh, and happy to be there. Thornberry seemed gray and haggard as the sky, but sober enough to be judge.

"How many paces, sir?"

"First toss the coin," said Morgan. Thornberry flipped it. As it spun in the silvery light, Morgan called it heads.

It was tails. Oglethorpe presented Vanderveer with the battered pistol case. Vanderveer picked the weapon with only one notch. "It's time this one earned its pay."

Time passed in a cloud. Oglethorpe ran his hands lightly over Morgan's body, searching for objects which could deflect a ball: Morgan disdained to have Vanderveer searched too, and instructed Isaiah to forbear.

The reserve pistols were chosen, by another toss of the coin. Oglethorpe charged the flintlock for his man, capped his percussion in reserve. Morgan did the same for himself, before he gave both pistols to Isaiah. To his amazement, he found that his hand was not shaking in the least.

Vanderveer unclasped his coak. He was in full naval

uniform, wearing a sword and swordbelt. The brass buttons on his dark blue frock coat glinted in the rising sun, and his golden epaulets shone. He removed the swordbelt, leaning the blade in its scabbard against his carriage wheel. Then he took off his visored cap, and hung it on the hub.

He seemed absolutely calm. Morgan heard him say to Oglethorpe: "My father used this pistol, in 'nineteen. In defense of the *Chesapeake*'s good name, in the Boston Navy Yard."

His own father's voice came back: *"Distance favors the better shot.... Beware the hair-trigger, most of all. ... There are a dozen ways to win a duel, and a dozen ways to lose."*

"How did your father fare?" Oglethorpe asked the lieutenant, charging his own Derringer.

"Won, by thirty minutes," Vanderveer smiled. A shadow crossed his eyes. "And then he died."

Morgan did not want to kill. He had a flash of inspiration. *In not wanting to kill, his salvation might lie...*

"Have you chosen the distance?" asked Oglethorpe. "It's time."

Morgan met Vanderveer's eyes. They seemed to have lost their iciness.

"Three paces," Morgan said.

Isaiah gasped. A bluejay screamed.

"*Three* paces?" Oglethorpe glared at Morgan. "You're jesting, sir. Now what shall the distance be?"

"I said three paces," shrugged Morgan. Vanderveer was staring at him. "Otherwise... an apology to me and my wife, and I'm good for breakfast for everyone here, at the Nevada Hotel."

Vanderveer stared at him. "Three paces is suicidal, sir."

"But not without precedent, and not 'bizarre,'" Morgan smiled. "Major Biddle fought Congressman Pettis at only two, we're told."

Vanderveer frowned, turned away, thought for a moment. He turned back, and his eyes were hard. "Only one of us will breakfast today," he said. "I'll make no apology: it's your choice: three paces it shall be."

Thornberry made a mark on the dirt, and stepped three

paces off. He made another, wincing at the distance, and Oglethorpe placed Vanderveer on it. Morgan stepped to his mark. Isaiah followed him, carrying the flintlock and the reserve.

"Cock the flintlock," Morgan said. "Careful..."

Hand shaking, Isaiah cocked the gun.

Within spitting distance, Vanderveer stood, arm rigid at his side, pistol pointing downward. Morgan adjusted his position, holding his arms straight down. To move a muscle now, with Oglethorpe ready with his Derringer, could easily cost him his life.

"Why not each put a gun to the other's head?" hissed Isaiah frantically. "Morgan, in the name of God, get out of it! Kiss his boots, but live!"

Morgan shook his head to silence him. The pistol was heavy in his hand, the checkered stock warm with the sun. He had a scheme, perhaps his only chance, and he needed silence to clear his mind.

"Places, seconds!" commanded Thornberry. His voice was hoarse and tired. "Is Mr. Vanderveer ready, Mr. Oglethorpe?"

Morgan tried to concentrate. Vanderveer, three yards away, was smiling into his eyes.

"The lieutenant's weapon's charged," reported Oglethorpe. "He's positioned. His weapon's cocked. He's ready, sir."

Vanderveer will go for the kill, he thought, *my stomach, my chest, my head....*

"Are *you* ready, Mr. Oglethorpe?" Thornberry called, to Vanderveer's second.

"I'm positioned, and must warn Dr. Washburn that my weapon is on him."

Morgan chilled, but refused to look over. His eyes stayed on Vanderveer: he must not be distracted for a moment. *To hit my stomach, at this range, Vanderveer must swing a heavy pistol up through a four-foot arc....*

"Is Dr. Washburn ready, Mr. Hollister?"

Vanderveer wants to kill me. To aim to kill takes longer than to wound...

Dimly, he heard Isaiah reply: "Yes, he's ready." He sounded on the verge of tears.

"Are *you* ready, Mr. Hollister?"

But if I shoot low, a quick one-foot arc....

"I'm in position," he heard Isaiah answer, "but unarmed."

"That's your choice," said Thornberry. "Is Mr. Vanderveer's surgeon ready?"

Place a one-ounce ball in his leg or thigh, while his gun is coming up.... With a trigger so light, at the impact, perhaps he'll waste his shot....

"Here, and ready," called Dr. Marshall. "With instruments laid out."

"Dr. Cantrell, are you ready?"

"Of course, you goddamn fool!"

There came a moment of silence. Was it all silence, in the world beyond? *Was* there a world beyond, or nothing? He might know, soon enough.

His body soaked in the sunlight, warmer than any he'd known. A mountain canary warbled from a pine: he'd heard thousands, but this was Jenny Lind. An anvil clanged somewhere, more beautifully than a bell.

He brought his attention back to Vanderveer, who stared steadily into his eyes.

Ignore the sun, the bird, the anvil: wait for the call. Then shatter skin and muscle and bones....

"*Present!*" he heard, as in a dream. He felt his hand swooping up with his gun. "One..."

His gun fired, jolting him to his core. He heard the crack of a ball on flesh, and then another blast. A low, soft whistle sounded in his ear, and was gone. Smoke obscured all. He was unhurt, but he could not see, his eyes were smarting, he squeezed them shut.

When he opened them, the smoke was clearing. Vanderveer reappeared, erect before him, like a ghost in the mist, but the pain in his eyes was real. The trouser leg of his uniform was bloody from knee to boot.

He'd ruptured the femoral artery! He took a step to help Vanderveer down.

"Hold, Washburn!" Oglethorpe called from the side.

He froze, and glanced at Vanderveer's second. He found himself staring into the muzzle of a Derringer, under eyes that swore to shoot.

303

Vanderveer was screaming, but not in pain. "My reserve, Oglethorpe! Goddamn it, bring my reserve!"

Oglethorpe dropped his own gun and leaped to his principal's side, thrust the charged percussion pistol into his hand.

"Sir, let us stop!" called Morgan. "You're damn hard hit!"

"And you not at all, not yet!" grunted Vanderveer.

"Ready, gentlemen?" called Thornberry. "Are you ready now?"

"No!" yelled Isaiah. He rushed through the drifting smoke to Morgan's side, shoving the reserve pistol into his hand.

Morgan thrust it away. Vanderveer's face was turning ashen. "Lie down, sir!" demanded Morgan. "Marshall! Cantrell! He's losing all his blood!"

"The signal!" Vanderveer shouted. "The firing signal, once again!"

The pistol in Vanderveer's hand came up. For an instant Morgan stared down its barrel, three paces off, dead center on his head.

Mary, my darling, I'm sorry....

"*Signal*," Vanderveer begged, more weakly. "Give the goddamn signal, once again..." He moaned, suddenly threw the piece aside. It fired harmlessly in the dirt, and went spinning across the field. Vanderveer sagged to the ground.

In two steps, Morgan was on him, grappling for the artery. Vanderveer looked up into his face.

"I'll die, sir?"

"Just lie back."

Vanderveer smiled faintly. "If I die, I fear I'll haunt you. I've killed men, and I know."

Morgan looked into the clouded eyes, and knew that he was right.

"Will I lose the leg?" murmured Vanderveer.

"Your surgeon will decide."

"My 'surgeon's' a fraud, and yours is a quack." His eyelids sagged. He clung for a moment to consciousness, and Morgan had to lean down to catch the words. "I hate the goddamn air you breathe, but Washburn?"

"Yes?"

"If someone's got to take it, I want *you*."

In half an hour, Morgan was with Mary in his surgery, fighting for Vanderveer's life.

THE ADMIRAL
AND BUNKIE

THE ADMIRAL HOVERED BY THE MEDICINE CABINETS LINing the surgery's wall. Stalling, he had told Jeff that they must prepare the room before bringing Terry in; had told Kelly to tear up sheets for compresses. She was ripping them at the operating table, while Miguel lounged nervously nearby.

He could hear Howard moaning from the parlor, through the open surgery doors.

But all would be well. By this time, Bunkie was surely out and safely slithering down Isaiah Lane: perhaps already banging on the Hanifans' door: perhaps Hanifan was already on the telephone, and policemen already rushing to their cars.

All at once he heard a thumping from the toilet.

Madam's Door must be swollen from rain. It had happened before. He remembered having to force it, playing hide-and-seek with Bunkie on a rainy afternoon, when she was small.

If Jeff heard the thumping, or Miguel, and evaluated it properly, all of them were doomed.

Be careful, Bunkie. Careful . . .

The thumping stopped. His heart quit pounding. Perhaps *now* she was free. They must still survive to wait

305

for help. He tried to concentrate on setting the stage for his stage play here and now.

Three generations of Washburns—Morgan, and Morgan's son and grandson—had used the surgery, but since the restoration there was no trace of any practice but Morgan's. The admiral had donated his father's surgical instruments to the Miners' Hospital, so there was nothing in the room that had not been there for a century.

From Morgan's years, there was only an antique operating table—guttered for blood—that the Hanifans had found in the stable, a dental chair—for Morgan had practiced dentistry as well—a few walnut medicine cabinets, an examining table with obstetrical stirrups, and the treasured mahogany medical kit.

Morgan had written to Mary of the survival of his medical equipment, from his bed in Odd Fellows' Hospital after his arrival in Sacramento: *"You will remember on my departure from Rensselaerville how brightly my brown medical case shone in its throne by the driver of the stage? It rests at the foot of my cot now, scarred, like me, with the battles of the trail, and everywhere marked with contusions and blemishes. On it stands a daguerreotype of the most beautiful face on earth. You will wonder that my kit was not abandoned with the rest of my possessions at Laramie, or along the cursed Humboldt, or on the evil ascent to Carson Pass, though you are not to wonder at the survival of the portrait. I wonder too, but I found myself unable to leave the kit, perhaps because that certain portrait lay within.*

"Now I am grateful, for such instruments and remedies as it contains are unobtainable in this cursed town of Sacramento. I am told by the 'physician' who is treating me that he is charging his other patients four ounces of 'dust,' or sixty dollars the ounce, for quinine and one dollar a drop for laudanum. You are to tell your father that he offered me one hundred dollars *for the craw-beak forceps. My medicines and instruments I would not sell for a thousand!*

"Later this day: My 'doctor's' name is Van Ness; he has purged me roughly; he claims to have apprenticed under Rush of Philadelphia. I confess I doubt this, but

would like to think it true. If so, I may be in better hands than I thought, provided he does not do away with me for the tools of my trade.

"In all seriousness, I am on the way to recovery."

Now the medical kit sat by a rolltop desk near the hallway door, as if ready for a house call on the buckboard in the barn. The varnished tray of surgical instruments had been removed from it for display in a glass case. Knowing where the Hanifans left the key, the admiral felt behind the case and found it. He unlocked the case and took the instrument tray to the counter and set it under glass cabinets filled with antique bottles labeled in Spencerian script: calomel, Dover's Powder, soda, rhubarb, snakeroot, camphor, ether, sulphur pills, and opium. All the bottles had long ago been filled with substitute contents: talcum powder, salt, or colored water: harmless stand-ins for ancient medicines which had killed more than they cured.

He opened the box of instruments. He had inspected it as a child, in the attic, and again when the house was opened and supplied with antiques from the Washburn residence itself and with all of the ancient props Mrs. Hanifan had unearthed from other donors. The mysterious instruments glittered, after one hundred and thirty years, each in velvet splendor in its own little nest in the tray. The Hanifans had typed labels: "chain hook," "director & file," "probe," "Valentin knife," "lancet," "bullet forceps," "cross-legged forceps," "scalpel," and, presumably, the same "craw-beak forceps" Morgan had mentioned in the letter.

The admiral studied them. Tentatively, he picked out the scalpel. It was heavier than it looked. He touched the blade and found it razor-sharp.

His hands began to shake. A modern doctor would sterilize the instruments. Good, another ploy for time. His father's sterilizer had been removed by the Hanifans, as anachronistic: they had told the admiral that Morgan would never have heard of Lister or Pasteur until late in his practice; that before then, he would probably have considered it eccentric to do more than wash his hands.

He puttered long moments away, laying out the in-

struments on the counter top. Everything slow, slow . . .
He was listening for sounds from the bathroom, and each
long moment counted. Again he thought he could hear a
gentle pounding from within. Damn! Still there! If *he* could
hear it, certainly Jeff and Miguel would hear it, too.

Stop it, before they hear you! the admiral begged his
granddaughter. *Flush the toilet before you pound the door
again. Let the sound of water drown you out! Just flush
the john!*

Bunkie gave up beating on the secret door. Slowly she
closed the wooden toilet seat, sat on it, and began to cry.
She had been so *sure* she'd save them all. Pops had trusted
her, Mom had too, and now the door was jammed!

She sobbed uncontrollably. She was tired, and very
hungry. Her gums hurt. If she knew how to yank out her
braces, she would.

Weird thoughts jackknifed through her mind. She saw
her mother with Jeff, all naked, doing awful things, while
her daddy, hanging by his thumbs from a dungeon rack,
howled in anger and in pain.

She screamed into a microphone, and her voice came
out Hard Rock.

Miguel kicked Halsey, who turned and bit *her*.

Suddenly she was sick. She had barely time to whirl,
lift the toilet lid, and upchuck into the toilet bowl. She
reached up and pulled the wooden handle on the big brass
chain. From the varnished wooden reservoir near the ceiling the water roared down through old, enameled pipe,
swirling the toilet bowl almost over, then gurgling away.

She turned. In the flakey, gold-framed mirror on the
wall, she saw her face, dirty and streaked with tears.

She was starved. She wanted a chocolate-chip cookie.

She regarded herself with disgust.

"Pig!" she whispered fiercely. "Baby! *Goddamn* baby!"
She turned and pulled the chain again. The roar of water
started. She stepped back to Madam's Door.

You couldn't tell the secret knot of wood from the
others unless you knew just where it was. It was the one

second from the left, and three knots down from the almost invisible crack that meant the top of the door.

Maybe she remembered wrong, was pushing the wrong knot? She tried another, pressed it, and leaned against the door. It was as solid as if someone had nailed it shut.

So she'd had the right knot in the first place? And the door was just plain stuck?

She turned away, still sniffling.

Slowly, she turned back.

Pops wouldn't quit.

Her mother had been scared to death, but kept her cool.

Her throat tightened. And her dad! He might be tubby and look soft. But he never quit when they were jogging, no matter how pooped he got. And he had tried to get the gun when he didn't have a prayer. And cursed the man when he should have begged for him to stop!

She mustn't give up, *couldn't*.

She pressed one knot, and pushed. Nothing moved. She pounded, tried another knot. And another...

She flushed the toilet again. Under the sound of rushing water, sobbing, she began to beat on the door with all her strength.

The admiral heard the rattle of the ancient chain scraping on the wooden reservoir above the toilet. Beneath the sudden roar of water he heard the pounding again, more positively.

Jeff had gone to carry Terry in. He sneaked a glance at Kelly. He reminded her of Madam's Door in a whisper. She paled.

"They'll hear her!" she whispered hoarsely. "God knows what he'll do! I'm going to tell her to come out!"

"*I* know what he'll do. He's killed three men already— Halsey, too. And look at Howard! It's her only chance."

So now she knew they'd killed already. She closed her eyes, and rubbed them slowly. "Oh, my God..." She stared at him incredulously. "That man... He said you picked them *up*?"

He felt sick. "Kelly?"

"Yes?" she murmured.

"I'm a goddamned idiot, Kelly—"

He felt her clasp his hand and squeeze. "No!"

"And if she can't get out of there, I may have killed us all."

Jeff came in, carrying Terry in his arms, told Miguel to mount guard over Howard in the parlor.

Terry's head was lolling. Jeff laid her on the operating table. The gentle thumping from the bathroom rose in volume; the admiral heard the toilet flush again.

To divert Jeff, he picked up the box of instruments. "Boil these in the kitchen," he told him, in his flag-bridge voice. Anything to get him out while Bunkie worked at the goddamned door. "And have Miguel cook her up a Talwin. We got other things to do."

In Spanish, Jeff yelled to the parlor. He picked up the instruments. There was a healthy bump from the toilet: he saw Kelly stiffen but Jeff was preoccupied with Terry and didn't hear. Terry was conscious again. Jeff drew a finger across her forehead. "Back in a minute, Teresita," he murmured, taking the instruments. "How long I got to boil them?"

The admiral took a deep breath. "Half an hour."

Terry's eyelids flickered open. "No," she groaned. "Jeff? We cannot wait so long, I want it now!"

"You heard her." Jeff set down the box.

"I won't operate!" the admiral protested.

"Oh, yes, you will," Jeff said softly. "Look, I saw corpsmen cut on the Mekong, everything covered with Cong-shit. People lived. They got antibiotics in Mexico. Cut!" He glanced around the room. "Where's the kid?" He moved to the toilet and rattled the door. "Come out!"

"I can't," moaned Bunkie. "I'm being sick!"

Oh, God . . . still there. The admiral began to wash his hands in the surgical sink: there was no scrub brush.

"She's better off *in* there," the admiral said. His heart was pounding. His breath was short. He fought to control his trembling hands. He heard a creaking from the toilet and the reservoir flushed again. "If she's sick out *here*, she's just another problem."

Jeff thought for a moment, returned to the operating

310

table, began to rub Terry's temples. The admiral heard another thump from the toilet. Quickly he raised Terry's upper body, and with Jeff holding her, unwound the bloodstained bandage.

She was gasping weakly, cold as steel. Her eyelids were trembling and her pupils distended and darting. He took her pulse. It was as erratic as his own.

Jeff leaned over her. "Think of Ipala, Ter.... The garden above the ocean...flowers and surf...."

The admiral left the operating table, opened the glass medicine case, drew out a tray of ancient hemostats and clamps. He was flying on the gauges now, drawing on his memory of TV shows, forgotten table-talk between his dad and other surgeons, half-remembered scenes from movies.

"Going to need hemos...mosquito clamps..." he muttered to Kelly. He lifted a leather strap at the foot of the table. "You're going to have to strap her down."

He began to open drawers, as if looking for something. Then he ripped sections from the sheet which covered Terry, gave the pieces to Jeff to fold, found a suturing kit and ancient gut and needles—God knew how old—displayed in a case at the end of the counter. He carried them back, and left them within reach.

Time, time, time...

He heard the thumping again in the toilet, but then, thankfully, heard the drumming of the rain increase, until it drowned out the noise from within.

Jesus, Bunkie, *shove*! He couldn't stall much longer.

He began to clean the area around the bullet hole, with water from a bottle labeled alcohol, using a swab made from a sheet. There, the firm young skin was taut with fluid, black and swollen; the rest of her skin was white.

He opened the medicine cabinet, brought down the bottle labeled "ether." He lifted the cap and sniffed. No odor: water, just as he'd thought: another prop. He would have to depend on the injection to put her to sleep, if he had to cut.

"Where's that shot?" he demanded.

"Miguel!" shouted Jeff.

Miguel stepped away from the desk, where he had been

311

heating a Talwin in a spoon. In his hand was the needle. The admiral held up Terry's arm. Her brother glanced at the instruments and turned pale. He closed his massive hand around her bicep, inserted the needle into her forearm, and squeezed. In a moment her eyes fluttered shut.

Again the admiral heard faint thumping. *Crash through, Bunkie, and to hell with the noise.* He cursed the rain and the swelling wood: weekly, on dry days, Mrs. Hanifan, a frail lady of sixty, opened the door with a gentle shove, as the climax of her tour.

For a moment the thunder abated. The silence caught Bunkie unprepared. He heard her bump heavily against the door, and saw Jeff cock his head.

Miguel blurted in Spanish that he thought he might be sick. "Permiso," he demanded, turning from the table.

Christ, he wanted the john!

"Kid," yelled Jeff, "get out of there!"

"Tell him there's one upstairs," the admiral muttered. He heard another bump from the toilet as Miguel turned and ran from the surgery.

Good. He didn't want the Mexican watching while he murdered his sister.

For he could wait no longer. He must start, to give Bunkie time. He grabbed the scalpel and drew it from below the ivory breast across the rosy, dark-rimmed hole.

For a moment, there was nothing but a thin red scratch. Then the blood began to flow.

MORGAN

MORGAN WASHBURN STOOD READY, HAND ON THE SHUT-tered window of his surgery. It was time to gather himself for his—and Vanderveer's—ordeal but he hated to open the window until the last moment.

Mary would soon uncap her ether bottle. Though he still had little faith in anesthesia, he had let her use ether before, and had enough experience with it to know that if he did not ventilate the room she would put them all to sleep. He began to tug at the window.

He had deliberately kept it closed against the big blue-bottle flies that swarmed around the outhouse just outside, and would descend on the wound when they smelled blood. But the effect of the ether on him and the others, the fierce July temperature, and the coals in which his white-hot cauterizing irons were glowing would soon make the operating room a hell. Cantrell, sweating in the crowded surgery as they prepared for the procedure, had already complained.

He and Mary had begun to suspect—from a paper on puerperal fever by Dr. Oliver Wendell Holmes and the works of the German physicians Helmholtz and Henle—that dirt contributed to sepsis, and that flies alighting in the wound might cause infection. No matter. Something always did, and there was no alternative but to let in air.

The window resisted him: green wood, cut from the local pine, was always swelling in this house. Mary saw him struggling. She went quickly to the little apothecary.

She opened Madam's Door for ventilation, and returned with a polished whalebone corset-stay she kept for just this purpose. He worked it under the window jamb, slid it along the sill, and when it had loosened the frame, tugged at the window. It slammed up with a squawk.

He swung open the shutters outside to let in the morning light, and turned to face the room.

He found himself shivering despite the heat. He had amputated at the thigh three times, and never lost a patient: according to Cantrell, he would soon run out of luck. Mortality from the procedure in Eastern city hospitals was close to fifty percent: he tried to tell himself that Eastern air was foul, and that miasmatic vapors caused the deaths.

Besides, he had no choice, he must proceed. The knee was shattered, the femoral artery pierced. Vanderveer was doomed if the limb was not taken. The cards were dealt; the odds not good, but an improvement on the hands that both had held at dawn.

Surreptitiously, he spread his long slim fingers, and glanced down at his hands. They were trembling as if he had the ague.

Mary joined him at the window. She looked up into his face. "I woke up. You were gone. Something told me to look on your desk, and I read your ... note. Will you tell me what happened?" she asked softly.

"I ... Later, please, my love?"

She shrugged. "I'm ready with the ether...."

He glanced at his shaking hands. "I'm *not*. A dram of whiskey?"

She raised her eyebrows—he never drank before major procedures—but she nodded and swept off, her skirts trailing in the sawdust she had sprinkled on the floor.

He flexed his left hand, the important one for amputations. Liston, of London, who had a thousand limbs to his credit and of whom it had been said "the gleam of the knife was followed so instantaneously by the sound of sawing so as to make the two actions almost simultaneous," reportedly had hands like hams, the left one made strong by grabbing arteries and veins to ligate them; he was said to remove a leg in less than thirty seconds.

Did Liston's hands ever tremble? He doubted it.

But had Liston ever taken the leg of a man he'd shot himself?

He heard Vanderveer mumbling to Marshall. The lieutenant had been fortified with brandy on the field of honor, then dosed with half a grain of morphia, then made to swallow a half-scruple of laudanum that Morgan had compounded on his return. Now he lay stripped of his uniform, in a nightshirt, no longer in shock, strapped to the operating table—calmly enough, like the fool he was—waiting for the knife.

All was ready. Dr. Marshall had accepted his rejection by Vanderveer in good grace, having no wish to be cornered in so risky a procedure anyway. Marshall would retract the skin flaps and muscle when the slicing incisions were made. Cantrell would support the leg as Morgan sawed through, and assist in the extraction of the bullet from the stump.

Mary, having—he hoped—rendered the patient unconscious, would move to the Petit tourniquet placed on the upper thigh, and loosen its screw or tighten it as directed. Isaiah, white-faced and frightened, had refused to leave despite his squeamishness: he was stationed by the brazier to hand Morgan whatever smoking iron he needed to sear the offending artery or vein, if a ligature should fail.

Oglethorpe, green in color, had long ago fled the room. Reverend Thornberry had never even entered it.

Under the operating table was a long box filled with sand, to absorb blood dripping from the table's gutters, and to receive his blood-soaked rags and sponges.

Rags—lately, always freshly laundered at Mary's insistence—were stacked nearby on the floor, to swab blood from the wound. More rags for bandages were available, on the cabinet shelves. Now with the shutters open, the lighting on the operating area was good.

His instruments were ready on a table set by the side of the operating couch: a transfixion knife, a catling—shaped like a double-edged dagger, for dividing interosseous muscles and ligaments—bone-nipper pliers, and a stubby nine-inch amputating saw, with a roughened ebony handle that was easy to hold when everything else was slippery with blood.

On examination Morgan had found that his ball had traveled upward from the knee, a full twelve inches into the thigh. As Vanderveer chewed on a piece of buckskin to stifle his screams, he had gently followed its course, using a long, silver probe with a blunted brass end. He had finally felt the roughened surface of the missile between rectus and adductor magnus, under the sartorius.

He could not amputate above the ball, if the patient was to survive. He and Cantrell had agreed that Morgan should wait until after the amputation to extract the projectile, if Vanderveer survived. Done otherwise, felt Morgan, the tissues of the upper leg would strangulate and the lieutenant would die of gangrene.

So his bullet forceps, never used before, lay on the tray with his other tools, ready to use when the leg was gone.

His linen thread was freshly flaxed and his needles wiped clean by Mary. He stuck a half dozen into his shirtwaist pocket to tie off the descending genicular artery and the great saphenous vein.

In the brazier by the operating table, the irons were white-hot and throbbing with incandescence. He hoped not to have to use them, for they scarred tissues. He preferred to tie the vessels off, but if the patient awakened and began to thrash, one never knew what arteries would escape his grasp and thread.

Mary returned with his dram of whiskey. He lifted it to Vanderveer.

"Good luck, sir," said Morgan.

The lieutenant raised his head. His face was stubbled and shadowed with pain, but his hard gray eyes seemed fearless. "We've traveled a long road," he murmured hoarsely. "If I die, you are forgiven, but I'm sure we'll meet in hell." He worked his arm free of the strap and extended his hand. Morgan pressed it firmly. Vanderveer smiled: "May *I* choose the distance *there*?"

Morgan shook his head helplessly, downed his whiskey, and signaled to Mary.

She folded a rag from a pile nearby, and placed it over

Vanderveer's mouth and nose. She began to drip ether onto it, stroking his forehead all the while. He coughed, began to retch, and then relaxed.

Morgan donned his bloodstained butcher's apron, and took the ten-inch-long transfixion knife from the amputation kit he'd been given on graduation from Geneva.

He wiped his hands on his apron. He waited for the rasping breath that would mean that his patient had crossed the river of consciousness and reached oblivion.

He began to hone his blade on a leather strap hanging from his nearby dental chair.

The surgery was all at once silent, save for the buzzing of the flies. The slap of the blade on the leather seemed to hypnotize Isaiah: he was staring at the knife.

Slap, slap, slap, slap . . .

Once this blade met flesh, speed was all. Even in these modern days, his patient's survival depended on his speed with knife and saw. His rule was to operate as if the mysterious properties of ether had never been discovered.

Morgan felt the edge with his thumb. Sharp, but not sharp enough.

Slap, slap, slap, slap . . .

He listened to Vanderveer's breathing.

It was steady and deep.

If the lieutenant died on the table, he was a murderer.

In the eyes of the law, at least. And of Mary, perhaps. And, certainly, of himself.

THE ADMIRAL
AND BUNKIE

BUNKIE SAT CRUMPLED WITH HER BACK TO MADAM'S
Door, feeling like an abandoned rag doll. The door had
not budged. She stared at her hands. They were red and
chafed from pushing at it. Her right shoulder was bruised
from butting it. Her knees were scraped from kneeing it.
Her right foot hurt: scuff marks from her running shoes
ran all along its base.

She knew suddenly why it wouldn't open.

It was not the rain. She'd played hide-and-seek on a
rainy day with Pops and nudged it open when she was
only five.

It was not firewood stacked outside: she'd noticed,
when they'd arrived, that the firewood was all gone.

It was the latch. The secret knot worked a latch, somehow, from either side of the door. Something was broken,
and the knot didn't work anymore.

She was wasted. She was too tired to cry.

Help me, somebody help me! Pops? Momma? Daddy?

She could hear them murmuring in the surgery. The
rain rattled on the roof. There was a drip, drip, drip from
the big wooden thing near the ceiling, that flushed when
you pulled the chain. It was soaking her leg and she was
too tired to stir.

But she had to move. She had to get out of here. Jeff
or somebody had already rattled the doorknob long ago.
If she didn't come out, they'd break the door down.

She could hear Pops in the surgery, talking quietly,

now and then. She'd rather be out there with him than crying in here all alone.

She reached up to the rim of the old iron sink to pull herself up. Next to it was a locker, under a counter made of zinc. Pops had told her Morgan mixed his medicines on the counter, before the room was made into a john.

She stared at the closet beneath it. She was somehow fascinated by two little ivory knobs, which she'd never really noticed, which opened the closet doors. They looked like a dead fish's eyes.

She had a sudden wish to look inside the closet. She pulled the knobs. Inside was a stack of towels, some bars of Ivory soap, and a million medicine bottles, empty, with faded labels.

She suddenly began to pull them out. She had to get behind them, something she wanted was there.

Thunder boomed. She dropped a bottle. It crashed loudly. She flinched. Frantically, she shoved the others aside.

She was having another déjà vu. But this one stayed, and wouldn't leave.

She fingered something. She knew what it was before she drew it out.

It was long and flat and whippy, and made of some kind of bone. Whalebone, she remembered now. It was a corset-stay, like the ones in the bodice of the dress she'd worn in the attic.

But scarred and scratched from other uses.

And she knew exactly how it had been used.

She jumped to her feet.

She had a sudden memory: a hotel thief on television, slipping the latch on a room door with a plastic credit card. And then a stronger memory, of herself, at a window, sometime, she couldn't remember when, sliding this same piece of whalebone under the jamb to get it loose.

She slipped the corset-stay into the tiny slit of Madam's Door. She slid it upward, found nothing. She slid it down. It stopped. She took it out, leveled it, eased it in again. She felt resistance, slowly easing. She pushed gently on the door. It did not move.

319

She took a deep breath, pushed harder. Nothing. Suddenly it opened, with a mighty croaking squawk.

She was through it in an instant, into the pelting rain. Slipping, sliding, falling, she sprinted for the Hanifans' lighted window, at the end of the muddy lane.

The admiral stared, sickened at what he had done. A red tide of blood was seeping from the incision he had made; it guttered between the firm young breasts and began to soak the sheets.

Now, Bunkie, now or never.

He heard Kelly gasp at the flowing blood.

He was suddenly very tired, as tired as he had ever been. A giant, familiar hand grabbed him by the chest, squeezed him like a vise. The pain was monumental, shocking.

Another attack, and this the last, he was sure. His escape was easy: he had only to let it happen. But what of Bunkie, and Kelly and Howard?

And the girl whose skin he had slashed?

The room spun. He found himself hanging on to the edge of the table; the scalpel clattered to the floor.

Suddenly all changed.

The surgery was suffused with glowing light and a warming, gentle presence. He heard a deep, resonant tone, comforting beneath the thunder and the rain. The pain in his chest remained, but he was somewhere away from it all, and free.

"Jesus!" he heard Jeff yell. "Admiral?"

"Daddy!" called Kelly, from across a void. "Daddy, are you OK?"

OK? OK? A phrase he knew from long ago, but strange. All was strange. "Yes. 'OK.'"

He inspected the surroundings. Changed, and yet the same. The clothes they wore, he and the other man, and the woman by his side—Mary—were different from any clothes he'd seen.

He stooped, picked up the scalpel. The pain in his chest had gone, replaced with a warmth like none he had known, and yet had known forever. The room remained in golden light.

He was all at once above himself, and the others, towering over the girl on the table; above her, but a part of her, part of every living thing; knowing all and nothing.

He was suddenly free of his body and free of the bonds of time. He saw things he could not rightly see: the child working at Madam's Door with Mary's whalebone stay; Howard trussed in the parlor, struggling with his bindings; his piano resonating to the thunder in the hills; his buckboard in the stable, all quite foreign and familiar. He was part of it and none of it: the rain and hail and thunder clouds above the Sierra Buttes, each with a moonlit spire above, swooping on the town; Deer Creek, swollen and tugging at the highway bridge.

A clap of thunder shook the house. From Madam's Door came the creak of a rusty hinge: the blond man looked up, startled.

"That clamp on the counter," the surgeon said, diverting the other's attention. The blond man handed him the instrument.

From somewhere, and everywhere, he saw the child fly through the secret door, into the driving rain.

Now she too was free.

"Pulse?" asked the surgeon. The woman felt the patient's carotid, with a practiced touch, glancing at the ancient surgery clock. "One hundred twenty the minute. All right?"

The surgeon nodded, his fingers flying to instruments they had wielded long ago. Speed, speed, speed was all.

"Hemostat, my love? And a ligature?"

The woman, eyes distant and smiling, gave him a hemostat.

"Scalpel, please?"

Peering at the incision, he felt the scalpel slapped magically into his palm.

He clamped the supraclavicular artery, and then the axillary vein. Quickly he palpated the incision, and the patient hardly stirred.

The young woman on the table had fainted. Good.

Speed was the secret of his skill, for, as always, the patient's pain was his.

"Probe?"

He reached out his hand, and found the slender, flexible probe put suddenly between his fingers.

Working swiftly, surely, happily, he inserted it and began to track the ball.

MORGAN AND MARY

SLAP, SLAP, SLAP . . .

Morgan felt the blade. Now it was sharp.

A fly buzzed near Vanderveer's mouth. Mary brushed it away.

Vanderveer's breathing, stertorous until now, began to rasp.

Morgan loosened the strap on the lieutenant's good leg, lifted the leg, and let it drop. It fell flaccidly onto the table. He strapped it down again and glanced at Mary. She raised one of Vanderveer's eyelids.

"I believe he's quite unconscious now," she said.

"Lieutenant?" he called, into Vanderveer's ear. There was no answer.

He could only hope that he was anesthetized; there was no sure way to tell. Anesthesia, much-heralded since Morton's demonstration in Boston five years before, could trick the unwary surgeon. Give ether too liberally, and the patient would die in a coma. Give it too frugally, and he might awaken screaming, at the most inappropriate stage.

If a thrashing patient caused his surgeon to nick himself

322

with a scalpel, the surgeon's wound invariably became infected. Erysipelas would follow, and sometimes the loss of the surgeon's limb, as if the maddened body on the table had inflicted a curse. No one knew why this was so, but it was a clear and constant danger.

He had always liked this moment, when a man's life lay balanced on the skill of his flashing hand, but he did not like it today. He glanced at his assistants. Mary was ready at the Petit tourniquet, which was set loosely above the femoral artery. Marshall, still in his frock coat despite the heat, stood tensely at the side of the table, popeyes straining, ready to retract the skin flaps. Morgan lifted the shattered limb to drain what blood he could from it, nodded when it turned pale, and watched Mary screw the Petit down.

Hollister was standing near the brazier, sweating profusely. Morgan turned to Cantrell. The homeopath had removed his coat, but his face was florid and dripping with perspiration; the pockmarked skin was blotched; the coarse-grained, alcoholic nose was gleaming in shafting light. Between his lips were a half a dozen ligatures, handy to Morgan's grasp. "Ready, sir?" asked Morgan.

Cantrell nodded, snapping open his watch and placing it on the instrument tray. He had bound Vanderveer's right calf in adhesive plaster to give his fingers better purchase. Now he took the calf firmly and lifted the leg clear of the table.

Morgan had learned two methods of thigh amputation: the circular one at Geneva, and the flap procedure from Mary's father. He favored the latter, as neater; the muscles and tissues at the front of the leg were stabbed through by the amputating knife, from one side to the other, then separated in a single slash from the inside out, on a bias, to produce an oval flap of skin. The same would be done from the rear, the femoral artery and others clamped, the muscles and skin peeled back to reveal the femur, and the bone sawed through in an instant.

Morgan took a deep breath. He had marked the point of penetration with a dab of ink on Vanderveer's thigh, four inches above the kneecap.

He felt for the pulse in the femoral. None: good: the

tourniquet was doing its job. He grasped the patient's thigh from the back, pushing up the muscle in front.

"Time," he called to Cantrell, tensed himself, and stabbed, from the inside of the thigh to the outside. He felt the knife cut easily through the muscles, felt tendons snap, the rasp of the femur against the back edge, and felt the point emerge. He sliced toward himself, beveling the tissue, tightened his hold on the bloody haft of the transfixion knife, steadied himself, and stabbed again, this time behind the limb.

Marshall was grappling ineffectually with the front flap, blood squirting between his fingers. "Mary," grunted Morgan, "help him!"

She dashed her hands into the reddened mass, and peeled back the flesh he had cut, as Morgan sliced the back of the leg. Blood was spurting suddenly, splattering the tourniquet. Morgan grabbed for the femoral artery, felt it slide out of his slippery fingers, and decided not to risk a ligature.

"An iron," he called to Isaiah. "The rod with the flat face."

Isaiah found it, handed it to him, hot end first; Morgan shook his head, grabbed the handle instead, and jammed it down on the femoral artery.

There was sizzling and smoking and the smell of burning flesh. Isaiah crashed to the floor, unconscious. No one spared him a glance.

"The saw, my love," demanded Morgan; it was swiftly in his hand. The bare bone had disappeared.

"Retract, goddamn it, Doctor," Morgan grunted. "Retract the anterior flap!"

Marshall peeled the flesh back like a trouser cuff, and the pink thighbone appeared, as always surprisingly slim. Instantly, it disappeared in blood. Mary reached into the wound with a sponge, whisked a fly away, and swabbed the thighbone clear.

Delicately, with three fingers through the saw grip, and the thumb and forefinger guiding the blade, he began to saw the limb.

Suddenly all was in motion. "Goddamn it!" screamed

324

Vanderveer, his stocky body straining at the straps. "God-damn it, goddamn you..."

With Vanderveer's muscles straining and jerking, Morgan could hardly make the cut. If the thighbone broke at the saw cut, it would leave a jagged end, and the stump would never heal. He extracted the saw quickly, moved to Vanderveer's head.

While Mary grabbed another rag from the pile, Morgan placed his hand on the jerking forehead. Vanderveer's eyes, wild with pain, rolled back.

"You son of a bitch—"

"Steady, sir. Breathe deeply. Now, you must relax, *don't move that leg*. Relax, and soon you'll sleep..."

"I *felt* it, every saw stroke!" groaned Vanderveer, but his eyelids dropped. Mary slapped the folded rag over his mouth and nose. She dripped more ether from the bottle. Vanderveer coughed, strangled, and began to thrash again, but soon the jerking and pulling ceased and the patient slept once more.

Morgan moved back and carefully reinserted the saw blade. Then there was silence save for the rasping of Vanderveer's breath and the gentle grating of the saw teeth on the bone.

Carefully, he finished the cut as Cantrell, solid as a granite boulder, kept the limb from breaking off. When Morgan felt the saw come free, he nodded. Gently, Cantrell pulled the lower limb away. It twitched as it left the body forever; Cantrell dropped it into the sandbox beneath the table.

Morgan was halfway through. He wiped his bloody hands on his apron, ligated the arteries and veins, and left the wound to crust. Then he moved higher up the thigh, made an incision near where the probe had found the ball, and entered it with his closed bullet forceps. When he felt the grate of metal, he gently opened the jaws and seized the ball.

He drew it carefully from the flesh, revived Isaiah with ammonia, and brushed the flies away from Vanderveer's leg.

"Time?" he asked Marshall.

"Three minutes forty seconds, from first blood to separation," smiled Cantrell.

"And the bullet?"

"Four minutes, thirty-five."

"Not bad," he conceded, "considering..."

Morgan found that his hands were shaking. He needed another drink.

Mary stood up suddenly. Her eyes were full of tears. "Not bad at all, Morgan, I'm sure." She rose, felt the patient's forehead, and turned away.

"Mary—" he began.

"It probably took you even longer than that to put it there!"

She whirled and ran from the room.

"Dress it when it clots," he told Cantrell, and followed her out the door.

He found her in the orchard, in the mottled shade of their favorite oak. She was gazing west toward the green foothills hiding the Sacramento's golden valley. Her shoulders were shaking, and at first he thought that her cough, which had grown deeper in the last few weeks, had worsened even more.

But she was crying. He chilled. The last time he had seen her cry was in Rensselaerville, when he left for California.

"Mary," he murmured, taking her into his arms, "I'm sorry. I had no choice."

She would not look up. "You had a choice," she said. Her voice was muffled in his chest. "You had a choice, all right."

"I'd turned the other cheek too often, I was trapped."

"That isn't what I meant." She was trembling. "You chose not to tell me last night."

"I couldn't have been dissuaded," he said softly. "Even by you, my love."

"I know. But this morning... Well, if you'd chosen to tell me, I could have gone with you."

He drew her chin up, so that she was looking into his

326

eyes. "To a *duel*?" he asked, astonished. "Why would you want to be *there*?"

"Because *you* were." Under her steady amber gaze, he felt a flush of shame. "Because we must not *be* apart. Because your angers and your joys and faults—and all your fears—are mine!"

She grew silent. Deep in her eyes he saw despair, and knew. "All my *fears*?" He had but one: that she was too weak to bear the child. A gray mist of terror descended on him. "Mary, darling Mary—"

"Because you must never leave me, nor I you..." She smiled and dabbed at her tears. "Or who knows? One of us, or the other, might get lost...."

He fell suddenly to his knees, his face buried in her skirts. Racked with sobs, he fought his tears, but could not stop. He kneeled there, crying like a child, while her hand brushed through his hair, and the pine trees keened above.

"Never shall I leave you," he whispered. "Never again."

"Nor I you," she promised. "At least, not for very long."

She was dead of childbed fever two weeks after their son was born, before the snows had come.

He very nearly remarried twice, once to a minister's widow, once to a schoolteacher he met when he took the new railroad to New York. But he did not: he thought of the amber eyes, and the risk of their getting lost.

He was commissioned as a surgeon in the California Militia during the Civil War. He served his time guarding Catalina Island against Confederate troops, which were massed, as he liked to say, "just offshore, two thousand miles away."

He lived in the house in Nevada City for fifty years, and never lost his guilt over bringing her to it. By the time his son had taken over his surgery, Morgan's hand had begun to tremble from too much medicinal bourbon drunk too early in the day.

He delivered twenty-seven hundred babies, and saved untold miners' lives. He was the first in the county to sterilize instruments and the last to join the County Medical Society.

When his heart failed, during a Christmas party in Vanderveer's saloon, he was seventy-eight. He had read with great excitement, only a week before, that Orville Wright had flown at Kitty Hawk.

On December 23, 1903, he was laid beside his Mary in the Pioneer Cemetery, on the hill.

He had long outlived Cantrell, and Isaiah Hollister, too. His will rejected a service in church, so Vanderveer, in uniform, stumped to the graveside to speak the eulogy.

Morgan had delivered half the mourners at the grave. Three, besides his son, were named Morgan: one, Morgan Wong, gray-haired and arthritic, had never learned to pronounce his own first name correctly.

Vanderveer spoke of cradling Morgan's head as he died on the sawdust floor.

"I don't know what he meant," he said, "but he smiled, like he did, and said—"

His throat quivered with age, and he cleared it. A blackbird cawed above.

"He said," reported Vanderveer, "'See? Not for very long.'"

MARY

OVER THE LITTLE MINING TOWN IN WHICH SHE HAD LIVED
so short a time, Mary's presence hovered beneath the
towering rain clouds.

Their white-haired great-grandson had, for a moment,
joined them: for a while Morgan had guided his fingers and
thoughts. Now their descendent, surviving for earthly
things, was gone from them again, but still seemed very near.

The woman standing at the operating table was equally
their seed. So Mary had hummed a tune of unity, and the
woman heard it too. She had begun to work with the man
as one, and together they closed the wound.

But it was the child who heard the song most clearly.
She found the silly makeshift tool that Mary had used so
often, and bounded like a frightened deer from the secret
door, slithering and sliding down Isaiah Lane. At the care-
taker's home the child burst in. Over singing wires and
radios, the news she cried was told, and the forces of
Nevada County law drew very close.

A siren wailed on the highway which had ripped their
town in two. It was quickly stilled, but other machines
drew silently, like ants to a spilled jar of syrup, around
the house she'd loved.

Still, she sensed great danger. The twisted man who
had caused it all had a shattered and crumpled mind, and
in the father of the child, love bred reckless fear.

That the child had fled, and was safe at last, the father
could not know.

329

THE ADMIRAL

DAZEDLY, THE ADMIRAL EMERGED FROM HIS DREAM. HE stared at the sutured wound, at the instrument he had laid on the counter: a device which—dimly—he remembered naming a moment ago, and could not have named now to save his life.

Clamped in its tongs was a snubnosed bullet crushed to a mushroom shape, in a little pool of blood.

He had found the bullet, got it out, and sewed up— God knew how—the wound he had enlarged.

He was sagging with fatigue. He touched Terry's brow, expecting cold, finding warmth.

His eyes met Kelly's. In her hand was another clamp— he did not know its name either. She glanced down at it, dropped it on the counter, and looked up blankly. "What happened?"

Jeff was staring at him. For the first time in the thirty hours the admiral had known him, he saw confusion in his eyes. "You got it out?"

"Yes," said the admiral thoughtfully. He began to bandage the wound. "Blankets, get her blankets."

Kelly moved swiftly to the bedroom down the hall. He finished the bandage and stroked Terry's forehead. She seemed to be asleep. Kelly returned with blankets and began to cover her.

Jeff was rattling the door to the bathroom. "Come on, kid, we're leaving." Without waiting for an answer, he walked to the door and shouted for Miguel.

Kelly whispered: "Daddy? How'd we *do* it?"

"I don't know.... But Bunkie's gone," he murmured, certain of it.

"I know," she said softly, "but I don't know why I do."

A distant thunderclap told him that the storm was fleeing east. Bunkie would have crossed the lane to Hanifan's by now, and the word would be out, and soon the place would be surrounded. And then?

He could not cope with plans for that. Wearily, he collapsed on the chair at the rolltop desk. His heart had brought him very close to death, and might carry him there soon again. He glanced at the woman on the operating table. Jeff was looking down at the wound, wearing a puzzled frown.

"All right, son, I got it out," the admiral muttered. "You going to let us go?"

Jeff looked at him. "The minute we're in Tijuana, like I said."

"You can't move her yet!" protested the admiral. "You'll kill her!"

Jeff moved to the window, stared out for a moment, and turned back. His eyes were glittering coldly. "You want to cut the bullshit?"

The admiral chilled. Something had changed. "What do you mean?"

"If *you* couldn't kill her with that knife, moving her won't. Look, I saw your ID, and I got your Annapolis ring! They don't make doctors there! You never heard of Talwins! You should have briefed the professor, man: medics don't have flagships! You're no more a fucking surgeon than—"

Miguel returned to the surgery. The Mexican, seeing his sister lying quietly, stepped to the counter and picked up the mushroomed bullet. He stared at the admiral, held it up. The admiral nodded. Tears started into Miguel's eyes. He leaned over and kissed his sister's forehead. "¿Cómo está?" he asked Jeff.

"Está bien."

Miguel crossed himself. "¡Gracias a Dios!"

Jeff moved to the woman and lifted her into his arms: "Déténlos aquí. Voy por aquel tanque de gasolina..."

"Hold them here. I'm getting the gas tank...."

Gas tank? He caught the alarm in Kelly's eyes: her Spanish was as fluent as his own. He must think of something, and very soon.

Jeff carried Terry to the door and turned. In Spanish, he continued, with a tiny smile, "These two hombres and the kid are going to have a little campfire when we leave."

The admiral heard Kelly gasp.

The son of a bitch was going to kill them after all. And take Kelly for cover, and for God knew what else....

From far out on the distant freeway, the admiral heard a siren, quickly stilled.

He had a vision of Howard and himself lying crumpled on the surgery floor, their bodies flaming, while the gunmen dragged Kelly into a shoot-out outside.

Jeff carried Terry through the door, and was gone. In moments he would return. There was no time to think. The admiral took a deep breath, stumbled to the counter, held up the forceps and slug to show Miguel.

"I took this from your sister," he said in Spanish. "Can you then kill me?"

"¿Habla español?" gasped Miguel.

"Sí. No importa." The admiral continued in Spanish: "I saved her life. How *can* you kill me now?"

Miguel lowered his eyes. "I do what I must to be free. Jeff is my compadre, he is like my *brother*—"

Time, time, they needed time, and time was running out.

"Brother?" scoffed the admiral. "Hear me: there is something you should know."

He heard the screen door slam in the kitchen. The Winnebago was only ten feet from the kitchen door: in a moment Jeff would be back inside the house.

"Miguel, I am no doctor."

Outside the shuttered window, a frog began to croak. He heard the Winnebago's door open, and then shut.

"¿Cómo?" Miguel frowned. "What is that you say?"

"I'm no doctor," he repeated. "Just an admiral in the Navy, nothing more."

The Mexican sucked in his breath. "I cannot believe this."

"It is true."

"You are *not* a doctor?" Miguel's voice dropped in pitch. "And you play with my sister's life?"

"But I *saved* her, Miguel. She was dying."

The massive chest was heaving. "You lied?"

The admiral took a deep, long breath. He heard the screen door slam again, then Jeff's footsteps on the floor, passing through the waiting room, making the pine planks groan.

"I lied to save my grandchild. I *wanted* your sister in a hospital, for doctors to treat her wound. He *knew* I was no doctor, from the first!"

The giant's face twisted. "¡No!"

"He has *told* me that he knew, Miguel. ¡Verdad!"

Jeff's footsteps drew closer. From somewhere in the distance, the admiral heard the slosh of tires on Isaiah Lane. Police? The sheriff? He sensed movement in back of the house, and in front.

"¡No!" Miguel shouted. "He did not know! ¡No es verdad!" He drew the .45 from out of his belt, and swung it toward the admiral, holding it in both his hands, dead-center on the Admiral's chest.

Kelly screamed. The admiral could hear Jeff passing through the waiting room. His voice trembled, but he continued: "He needed me to keep you from the hospitals. He cared nothing whether she lived or died. Now he cares only to escape."

Jeff stood suddenly in the doorway, holding the gas tank. "What the hell—"

The admiral continued in Spanish, in a firm and steady voice: "Why did he pose for photographs—"

"You son of a bitch," growled Jeff, "that's enough!"

"—while she cried and screamed in pain?"

Jeff leaped, and slammed the gas tank across his jaw. The admiral reeled and crashed into the dental chair, slipped to one knee on the bloody floor.

"One can see that she needs rest," he mumbled to Miguel in Spanish. "Ask him why he moves her now?"

"Ay..." screamed Miguel. His eyes went wild. He

swung his gun at Jeff. "You lying Gringo bastards, you lie and lie again!"

Jeff's hand moved, and the admiral caught the gleam of gun metal behind the bright red can. Miguel saw it too. His .45 blasted the little surgery like a thunderclap.

The gas can went up in a mighty *whoof* of flame. All at once the surgery was alive with fire, racing across the rough pine floor.

"You fucking Greaser!" Jeff roared as fire engulfed him. Beating at his legs, he lurched toward the bathroom door. Flames licked suddenly at the operating table and danced to the dentist's chair between the admiral and Miguel.

Miguel swung his pistol to the admiral. Kelly, trying to tug him to his feet, cried out to the Mexican: "¡No! ¡Su hermana! He *saved* her!"

Miguel held fire for an instant. Then, from the flaming, writhing pyre which was Jeff, a shot rang out, and Miguel sagged. A spot of blood, dead-center on his chest, spread across his shirt. He dropped and lay shuddering on the fiery floor.

"Bunkie!" Howard's voice came from the surgery door. The admiral, struggling to his feet, gaped.

Howard stood in the surging light of the fire. His hands were dripping blood. A strand of wire hung from one, and another was wrapped around his ankle, raw and oozing.

The operating table, the dentist's chair, and the rolltop desk, all were engulfed in flame. Jeff, still on his feet by the bathroom door, was a blackened, struggling demon, beating at his shirt. A wall of flame hid the bathroom.

Howard peered into the flames. "Where is she!"

"She got out Madam's Door," the admiral shouted.

"I'll check around the back," cried Kelly, and was gone.

"Let's go, she's *out*!" The admiral grabbed Howard's arm.

"Look, you stupid bastard, *you've* been wrong before!"

Howard shook off his hand and lurched toward the flames. Jeff was a blur of flailing motion in front of the bathroom door. All at once he dropped to his knees. Face contorted, white teeth flashing across his blackened mouth, he raised his automatic in both hands, aiming at the figure rushing toward him.

"Howard!" screamed the admiral.

A shot blasted out from the fire. Howard clutched his leg, spun and fell at the edge of the flames. The admiral dove for him, dragged him by his belt to the surgery door. Another blast echoed from the fire and the admiral heard the *zing* of a ricochet from the doorjamb above his head.

As the admiral tugged Howard down the hallway, he began suddenly to struggle. "Let me loose! I'm OK. Get Bunkie!"

The admiral pulled him to his feet, got an armlock on him, and wrestled him out the front door.

"She's all *right*," the admiral growled. "Howard, she's *out*!"

Then, in glorious, spotlighted safety, they stood upon the porch. "Nevada County sheriff," a distant bullhorn blared. "Raise your hands above your heads! Walk down those steps!"

Halfway down, Howard's leg folded and they sat upon the steps. A sturdy little figure raced from a group of ruby lights flashing on the street beyond the boardwalk. The figure stumbled on the roots of the great oak tree, recovered, dashed up the shaggy lawn, and Bunkie ran into her father's arms.

The admiral turned. The gabled windows had turned orange behind them. There was warmth upon his cheeks.

He heard a single shot from deep within the house, muffled and distant.

He knew, somehow, that Jeff had got out too, the hard way.

He began to rise. Then the dreadful, familiar hand gripped his chest and squeezed. Pain crept to his shoulders and his jaw, and seared his arms and hands. He saw Bunkie's startled face, felt her arms around him.

He could hear sirens from the center of town, and the

335

ancient firebell clanging loudly. All went dark, but before he sagged back to the steps, he knew.

The house behind him, which had stood an eternity—or a lightning flash in time—was helpless under the roaring flames, and would burn to the ground tonight.

THE ADMIRAL

HE AWAKENED IN A HOSPITAL BED.

He had swum through layers of unconsciousness, surfaced in a narrow world of beeping oscilloscopes, tubes, dripping bottles, and hurried nurses. To escape, he had dived again into darkness, eased through an underwater tunnel with Ellen, lost her and surfaced again.

This time he had found himself in a two-bed room, which he recognized from his pacemaker operation. He was exhausted.

"Pops?" It was Ellen's voice.

"Ellen?" he murmured. And then: "Bunkie?"

She was sitting by the side of the bed, eyes level to his face, and now she arose and felt his cheek. She smiled, and her braces caught the afternoon sunlight.

Strangely, she looked different. Even more like Ellen than she had before, and more like Kelly too.

She was a woman, not a child. He struggled to sit up, and she smiled and pressed him down. "It's my watch, Pops, they'll kill me if you sit up!"

Watch? Deathwatch? "How long have I been out of it?"

336

She looked at the clock on his bedside table. "Since last night...maybe eighteen hours?"

His mind flashed back. Jesus! Howard was shot!

"How's your daddy?"

"Two broken ribs from that...that..." She flushed.

"That bastard?" he prompted her.

"That bastard! But the bullet in the leg didn't touch the bone. He can even *walk* already, Pops, with a cane. They didn't even keep him here." She grinned. "But he wants you to check out his leg."

"Funny, very funny, that's your dad."

She grew thoughtful. "He thinks you're fantastic, getting us through."

"*He* never would have got you into it in the first place."

She shrugged. She seemed bubbling with joy. "Oh, Pops, I'm so...you know...proud? Isn't he something *else*?"

He felt a twinge of jealousy, but took her hand and squeezed it. "Yes," he agreed. "And Bunkie, so are you. Where's your mom?"

"With Dad. The Hanifans were here.... Anyway, Pops, go back to sleep."

"It's gone? The house? I want to know!"

Her eyes filled with tears. "Pops, I'm sorry. You loved it so much!"

He touched her hand to his lips. "The only thing I cared about was you."

"Well, you saved me," she smiled, "so—"

"You saved yourself, it's a Washburn trait...."

She grinned. "Us *Zaleskis* don't do bad." She told him that Teresa had already been sent to a prison ward in Sacramento. "She said to tell you 'gracias.' But she says she wants to die."

She's not alone, the admiral thought. He felt as if he'd been slammed by a sledgehammer in the middle of the chest. His jaw ached from the blow Jeff had given him with the gas tank: he touched it with his finger and felt a bandage.

She smoothed his pillows. "Now, Pops, you aren't going to like this, but the sheriff will be in." She told him that the police had questioned her mother and father, herself, and Teresa, and still doubted that he had heard the whole story. "The doctors say we must have stopped at a hospital, somewhere along the road."

He felt his anger rising. *"What?"*

"They want to get the surgeon's name, the one who cut her bullet out!"

His anger at the sheriff fled: he laughed. He felt a sudden warmth, and a droning in his ears. He was all at once quite sleepy, and suffused with a gentle glow. The sunlight shafting into the room was touched with purest gold.

"And what do *you* think, Beautiful?" he murmured with a grin. "You know, you lost weight?"

She nodded and touched his forehead again. She smiled, like a woman, not a child.

"What do *I* think?" she mused. "I think something . . . *somebody* . . . helped me out Madam's Door. I was like somebody *else!* And I think when you had to cut that girl, the same thing happened to you!"

He felt a shiver, as he had on Independence Rock. What had transpired with the woman on the table, he couldn't explain. He didn't want to talk of it. If he turned it into words, then the truth would surely fade.

"Tingly?" he asked, drowsily.

"Yes," she nodded. "And you are too. *Did* it happen to you? Pops, I want to *know!*"

She always had to search his innermost thoughts. He sighed. "Yes, Lambchop. It did."

The shaft of sunlight haloed Bunkie, who would be Kelly and Ellen and Mary before too very long.

He drifted off to sleep.

ABOUT THE AUTHOR

Hank Searls, born in San Francisco, followed his own great-grandfather's Gold Rush journey from the wagon-train starting point in Independence, Missouri to Sacramento, California. Living in Newport Beach with his wife, Bunny, Searls is the only fourth generation Californian in town without a Spanish surname. Other novels he has written include SOUNDING, OVERBOARD, and JAWS 2.